One Love

by TAM

D1307111

DORRANCE
PUBLISHING CO
EST. 1920
PITTSBURGH, PENNSYLVANIA 15238

Dorrance Publishing Co
585 Alpha Drive
Suite 103
Pittsburgh, PA 15238
Visit our website at www.dorrancebookstore.com

ISBN: 978-1-4809-5510-3
eISBN: 978-1-4809-5487-8

Acknowledgments

I would like to thank my mother for encouraging me to write this story. Thank you, God, for guiding me through these years of writing at nights only. Thank you to my favorite Korean movie stars who, without knowing me, influenced me to create these storylines.

I am forever grateful to Norman, who has the patience of a saint.

To all the people who laughed at me when I told them that I wrote a Korean love story, I am happy that you thought that I was crazy because you only encouraged me more. To my relatives whom I have not spoken to since 2014, I love you all. Please forgive me.

To all the people who will give me a chance and read this book, I thank you for taking this journey with me. Blessings to you all.

Thank you, Chris, for taking this journey with me.

From the Author

I wrote this fictional novel based on things I saw in my world travels, functions I attended in my life, buildings viewed from the streets, night-clubs I visited, former bad boys I knew, my dreams, beautiful homes I saw when I traveled, and the beautiful cars and jets I saw while traveling around the world.

Any similarities to anything or anyone is purely coincidental.

TAM

Chapter One

The sun rose very early one autumn morning over the New York City skyline. The streets were not yet alive with pedestrians bumping into each other as they hurried back and forth down the sidewalks. The absence of loud car horns making excessive noise throughout the city made Lee Hyo feel very strange.

At the South Korean Embassy, darkness and silence filled the hallways. There were no signs of workers walking along the corridors or sitting at their computers. But the lights in the Ambassador's bedroom shined brightly. The South Korean Ambassador to the United States woke up at five o'clock that morning. He usually woke at seven o'clock and left the Embassy by nine o'clock to attend meetings.

Ambassador Shin had been a civil servant in the South Korean government for many years before being assigned to the Embassy in New York City. It was his dream to represent South Korea in the United States and at the United Nations.

The Ambassador was the oldest civil servant to be assigned to such a prestigious post. He had spent the last seven years working tirelessly to promote South Korea and its culture, until that autumn morning, when his cell phone rang at five A.M. and a man spoke to him.

The man's voice instructed the Ambassador to go to 2106 East 54th Street by seven o'clock A.M. The Ambassador knew that the instructions were genuine because he recognized the voice at the other end of the cell phone.

He had heard that voice every day for the past six months. The man usually spoke four words, "We are watching you," then he would hang up.

Ambassador Shin got dressed and called his chauffeur, Lee Hyo, to have the car ready by six o'clock A.M.

Lee Hyo, a fifty-year-old South Korean man, enjoyed chauffeuring the Ambassador to various destinations in New York City. He had been the personal chauffeur to the Shin family since he was twenty-five years old. He traveled with the Ambassador wherever he went. His loyalty to the Ambassador was unquestionable and he knew, or at least he thought he knew, everything about the Ambassador and his family.

Lee Hyo always received the travel schedule for the Ambassador the previous night. He had looked at the schedule and found it strange that the address of 2106 East 54th Street was handwritten onto the Ambassador's schedule for the day. He felt that something wasn't right.

Mr. Lee drove the Mercedes to the Embassy side entrance. He held the car door open and the Ambassador looked both ways before he entered the car. Mr. Lee greeted him, but he looked too preoccupied to respond. As the car exited the Embassy, the Ambassador noticed two men sitting in a parked car across the street. He remembered what the man on the cell phone told him. He felt a shiver in his body as he slumped down in his seat.

Ambassador Shin said nothing as he sat in the back of the Mercedes while it passed the designer shops on Madison Avenue. From his rearview mirror, Mr. Lee observed the Ambassador staring out the window. The Ambassador looked solemn and weary. His eyes were red and he looked apprehensive about what or whom he was going to meet at the unscheduled address. He did not have the usual smile that decorated his face each day. Mr. Lee noticed the look of sadness on his face.

Upon arrival at the building, Ambassador Shin's demeanor resembled that of a man who was about to receive a life sentence. His face looked pale and void of any emotion. Mr. Lee noticed that the Ambassador paused for five minutes before exiting the car. He said nothing as he slowly walked up the cracked concrete steps and into the building.

The building looked decayed and out of place as it stood amongst modern architectural structures. From afar, one would think that it was abandoned and waiting to be demolished. The windows were partially sealed with black curtains and there was no light in the entrance. The dark stones that covered the entire building made Mr. Lee anxious and afraid. He watched the Ambassador push hard on the revolving door as it slowly turned and he disappeared inside.

Mr. Lee woke up tired that morning. He had not slept the night before. He had stayed awake thinking about why he had sent away his only child to live in California with his sister. Lee Areum was the only child of Mr. and Mrs. Lee. At the age of fifteen, she won a scholarship to a private high school in Los Angeles. Mr. Lee and his wife were happy that their daughter would receive the education that they could not obtain. But he questioned whether he made the right decision by sending her to the other side of the United States.

The car radio played Chopin's piano concerto while Mr. Lee sat in the Mercedes Benz, with the window half open. The autumn breeze gently blew through the window onto Mr. Lee's face as he sat patiently waiting for Ambassador Shin to return. The sound of the soothing music caused him to close his eyes and think about Ambassador Shin. He recalled how kind the Shins were to his family. He remembered how they invited his family to every Embassy event. He was grateful to Ambassador Shin for treating his daughter like she was a family member. He never made them feel like employees. He felt honored to work for Ambassador Shin.

An hour had passed and Mr. Lee fell into a deep sleep. The voice of Ambassador Shin yelling his name startled Mr. Lee and he sat up at attention, still disoriented from the sudden shout.

Ambassador Shin had finished his meeting at the strange building and was walking hastily to the car. Still dazed from his sleep, Mr. Lee jumped out of the car and ran to open the passenger door. As the Ambassador bent his head to enter the car, two tall men, with dark glasses, black suits, and bulging waistbands, grabbed the Ambassador and pushed Mr. Lee to the ground. As he attempted to get up, he was knocked in the back of the head with a foreign object. He fell unconscious onto the sidewalk with blood gushing from his head.

It would be an hour later before Mr. Lee regained consciousness from the assault to his head. He slowly staggered to his feet while holding his bloodied head. He looked around and realized that the Ambassador and the car had disappeared. He staggered to a pay phone, located at the corner of East 54th Street and Madison Avenue. He searched for coins in his wallet, as his cell phone was in the missing car.

As he started to dial the police, a man suddenly appeared behind him and grabbed the phone from his hand. Mr. Lee recognized the man as Roger Goo, who was the head of the Ambassador's security team.

Roger Goo was tall, handsome, well built, and well dressed. He had piercing dark brown eyes and salt-and-pepper hair. He rarely spoke or smiled. He was known around the Embassy as the "One-handed Assassin" because he could kill a person with one hand. No one knew about his background except for the Ambassador. He was devoted to Ambassador Shin and he would die for him.

Mr. Lee began to fall and Roger Goo grabbed him with one hand as he nodded his head to a man in a parked car. Mr. Lee collapsed in Roger Goo's arms. He woke up in his apartment, which was located at the back of the Embassy compound. Mr. Lee, his wife, and his daughter Lee Areum had moved into the two-bedroom apartment a week after the Ambassador arrived in New York City. Ambassador Shin had brought them from South Korea and he provided them with the apartment free of charge. The apartment was furnished and beautifully decorated to their taste.

Late that evening Roger Goo and a short silver-haired man with lots of acne on his face appeared at Mr. Lee's door. He had a black bag filled with medical supplies, and he said nothing while breathing heavily as he removed the bandaged from Mr. Lee's bloodied head. Mr. Lee was unaware that while he was unconscious, the man had stitched his head wound and bandaged it.

After he had finished bandaging Mr. Lee's head, he noticed that the "so-called doctor" was staring at him strangely. Mr. Lee suddenly remembered that the Ambassador had disappeared and he jumped up and yelled out the Ambassador's name. Roger Goo informed him that the Ambassador was safe and was at his residence. Mr. Lee sighed and went to sleep. He rested at home for two days because the cut on his head gave him migraine headaches that caused his eyes to hurt.

Saturday night was cold and eerie at the Embassy compound in New York. A dark cloud had covered the stars and the moon was partially hidden. Feeling uneasy and unable to sleep, Mr. Lee slowly got out of bed, looked at his sleeping wife, walked to the window, and looked up at the mansion, which housed the Ambassador. Mr. Lee noticed that it was midnight and the lights were on throughout the Ambassador's living quarters. He knew that the Shin family always turned in early unless there was a function being held at the Embassy.

When Mr. Lee turned away from the window, he noticed the silhouette of two men walking toward his apartment. As they got closer to the apartment, he noticed that it was Ambassador Shin and Roger Goo. He found it strange that they would visit his apartment so late at night.

He thought to himself that maybe the Ambassador wanted to visit him to check on his health. But why so late, thought Mr. Lee, and what happened at East 54th Street? Maybe the Ambassador came to tell him what happened. Mr. Lee opened the door and invited the two men in. Ambassador Shin walked in, but Roger Goo remained at the open door with a blank stare in his eyes and two large items in his hand.

Ambassador Shin told Mr. Lee and his wife that they would have to leave the Embassy quickly and they could only pack personal items in a hurry. He told them that he would explain everything to them the next day. It was time for everyone to disappear.

Roger Goo stood outside the door with two empty suitcases in his hand. Ambassador Shin took the suitcases from Roger Goo and he handed them to Mr. and Mrs. Lee. The Ambassador stood in the doorway of the Lees' bedroom as the Lees packed their personal items as instructed.

The next day, Roger Goo, Mr. Lee, his wife, Ambassador Shin and his wife, and their nineteen-year-old son Shin Kang-de were on board a private plane that was headed to Seoul, Korea. Mr. Lee realized that something big had happened at East 54th Street and he became afraid.

Before he could ask about his daughter, Lee Areum, the Ambassador advised him that she was being looked after. He knew that the Ambassador was meticulous when it came to details. He felt at ease knowing that his daughter would be safe, but what would he tell her and anyone who asked why the sudden return to South Korea?

The flight was long, smooth, and solemn. Everyone except the Ambassador ate, slept, and stared out the window into the dark sky. After three hours in flight, Ambassador Shin walked over to Mr. Lee and told him not to worry. He said nothing else to him until the flight was finally approaching Incheon Airport.

Ambassador Shin handed Mr. Lee a bank book, a deed to a home in Busan, and a brown briefcase. He told him that if anything should happened to him, he should look after Shin Kang-de, read the documents inside the briefcase, then hand the ones that were marked "classified" to a certain man at the National Intelligence Service in South Korea.

Mr. Lee reluctantly accepted the briefcase and asked no questions. He sighed and stared out the airplane window with trepidation. Mrs.

Lee asked her husband what was happening, but he didn't respond because he himself did not know. He only knew that they should be afraid of the unknown.

As the plane descended, everyone looked at the city of Seoul with contentment on their faces. A sense of calm overpowered the faces of each passenger. When the plane landed, Mr. Lee and his wife were escorted into passport control. Roger Goo, Ambassador Shin, his wife, and Shin Kang-de had disappeared into the unknown.

Eleven months had passed without any contact from the Ambassador or Roger Goo. Then came Christmas and the television station played Christmas carols. Mr. Lee watched the programs with a distant thought of New York at Christmas. He thought about calling his daughter, Lee Areum, once the television program had ended.

Suddenly, a newscaster interrupted with breaking news that a train had derailed and several people had died. Among the dead were former Ambassador Shin and his wife. Stunned by the news, Mr. Lee quickly ran to his safe and got a private cell phone. He dialed the only number that was registered in the cell phone. The phone rang, and the voice on the other end of the phone told Mr. Lee that Ambassador Shin and his wife were murdered and that he should open the briefcase and follow the instructions inside. The voice also instructed him to contact a certain man at the National Intelligence Service (NIS).

Mr. Lee recognized the voice as that of Roger Goo, the Ambassador's personal bodyguard. He followed all the instructions that were given to him. He read the documents that were in the briefcase and the next day he handed a brown tattered envelope, marked "classified," to a man at the National Intelligence Service (NIS) office in Busan.

Mr. Lee found a USB drive hidden under the lining of the briefcase, labeled "East 54th Street." Mr. Lee inserted the drive into his laptop. It took one minute for Ambassador Shin's face to appear. Mr. Lee began to cry as he listened to Ambassador Shin speak. The message began:

"Greetings, Lee Hyo. If you are watching this, it means that I am no longer alive. Do you remember the morning you took me to East 54th Street? I went there to meet the head of a secret organization that my father once worked for. Do you remember the story that I told you many years ago? I won't talk about that right now, but I can tell you that when I entered the building, the elevator took me down to a dark basement. A man escorted me through a large door, which he shut and locked behind me. I was unable to see the man in charge, but I recognized his voice from cell phone calls that he made to me daily. There were at least ten people sitting at a large table and I could feel their eyes staring at me, but I couldn't recognize them, as the place was barely lit.

"The voice told me that my father was a traitor and that he stole files from the secret organization and hid them. He was killed for giving NIS names of its members. He said that I was not Korean. He told me that I was an illegal resident of South Korea and that I would be exposed and arrested for the fraud that I had committed by holding such a distinguished post as Ambassador. The voice said that I could remain as Ambassador, and undetected as an illegal, if I were to hand over the stolen files and gather secret information on the government of South Korea. I agreed immediately because I realized that if I said no, then I would have been killed immediately. The man from the cell phone told me that they would be watching me and my family.

"He told me never to tell anyone about the meeting. I agreed. Immediately, the door unlocked and I was escorted to the main entrance. As soon as I got to the main door, I heard the sound of many footsteps behind me. That's when I ran down the stairs and yelled out your name. Three men accosted me and tried to take me back inside. That's when you were hit in the head. I am sorry that they hurt you. I am truly sorry. Roger Goo was already at the building before we arrived and he saved my life and yours. As you know, instead of helping them commit espionage, I chose to resign my position and disappear.

"Unfortunately, they must have found me, because I am not alive. Mr. Lee, please be careful. These are dangerous people. Please go ahead and follow the instructions that I left for you in the briefcase.

"Did you take a picture of the documents in the brown envelope as I instructed? Please take care of my son, Kang-de. Roger Goo knows where he is. I want him to live with you temporarily. Roger will teach him to defend himself. Please see to it that he gets his daily instructions. And when the time comes for Kang-de to be informed about his true identity, please be gentle with your presentation. Thank you for your loyalty and your service to me and your country."

The USB drive went blank and Mr. Lee continued reading personal documents left in the Ambassador's briefcase. Later that week, he found Kang-de, who was living with Roger Goo in Seoul. Roger returned to New York and Mr. Lee took guardianship of Shin Kang-de until he finished his undergraduate degree in Business Administration.

On his twenty-first birthday, Shin Kang-de returned to New York City to obtain his Master's degrees in Finance and Business Administration. At age twenty-four, Shin Kang-de graduated with honors and became a smart, fearless, and very rich international businessman. He inherited his parents' multi-million-dollar estate after graduating.

Chapter Two

Shin Kang-de, Roger Goo, and Bob Goo

Nine years after the death of his parents, Shin Kang-de met a friend and former classmate, Eddie Wai, for a late dinner. After four hours of reminiscing of the past, he said goodnight to Eddie and he watched him drive south toward the Queensboro Bridge. Kang-de stood outside the restaurant looking at the East River, thinking about his time in the Embassy. He remembered the young Lee Areum who, before being sent to California, often told him that he was handsome, even though his right cheek was badly scarred from a campfire that accidently exploded in his face when he was a child.

He remembered how he would ask his father to invite her to all the functions at the Embassy. He recalled that she rarely attended the outdoor activities, but her parents brought her to most of the indoor events. Kang-de wondered what had become of her. He noticed that she never visited her parents while the Lees were his guardian, and he was afraid to ask Mr. Lee about her due to their diverse social status.

The phone rang as Kang-de took a puff from the cigarette that he had just lit. He pulled it from his lips and answered the call. The man

11

on the line spoke in Korean. Something was wrong. He hurried from the restaurant, got in his BMW, and drove across the bridge to his apartment on Park Avenue. His apartment was a three-bedroom split-level penthouse. A private elevator with a key stopped on his floor. When he exited the elevator, he walked past the chef kitchen and looked down to his right. The man sitting downstairs in his living room was familiar to him.

"Greetings, Master Kang-de," said the man.

"Hello, Uncle Roger. You are up very late."

It was Roger Goo, the personal bodyguard to Ambassador Shin.

"Uncle, did you rest well?"

"No, Master Shin. I was awaiting your arrival at home," he said.

"I am sorry that I am late. Uncle Roger, I got a phone call from Seoul. I have to go and look about my business. Your son will meet me when I arrive."

"Good," said Roger Goo. "I will take care of everything here until you get back," he said.

Roger Goo had been staying at the penthouse apartment, which was owned by Ambassador Shin. He had been acting as the martial arts instructor and bodyguard to Kang-de when necessary. Kang-de was grateful to have his company, but he felt uneasy using Roger Goo as his bodyguard. Roger Goo was now middle aged and not as healthy looking as when he protected Ambassador Shin. The years had taken a toll on his face and body. But he could still kill anyone who threatened Kang-de's safety.

Kang-de Arrives in Seoul

A black SUV pulled up in front of Incheon Airport as Kang-de walked out the door. The driver, Bob Goo, greeted him as "BOSS." He opened the door for Kang-de and he got into the back of the SUV and lay back in the seat with his eyes closed.

While Bob Goo sped onto the highway, Kang-de asked, "Bob, what the hell is going on with my store?"

Bob replied, "Boss, the accounting just doesn't look right."

Bob was the handsome assistant of Kang-de and the son of Roger Goo. He had dyed blond hair with a goatee and a thin mustache. He spoke softly and had the gentle mannerism of a monk. He resembled a model in a fashion magazine and he spoke four languages. He possessed a black belt in Taekwondo and he was a ruthless killer like his father. He was known to be very intelligent and very wicked when necessary.

As they traveled along the highway, Kang-de called his lawyer, Sun-hee. He got no answer. Sun-hee had been Kang-de's lawyer in Seoul for five years. She was a smart, slim, beautiful blonde-haired twenty-six-year-old female. Although she was very bright, she suffered from anxiety attacks, which began after working as a law intern for a very rich businessman who was also an attorney.

Bob drove Kang-de to one of the two hotels he owned in Seoul. As they exited the SUV, Bob uttered, "It's good to have you back in Seoul."

Kang-de smiled at him and entered the front door of his hotel. As he walked into the lobby, all the employees welcomed him with a smile and a bow. He entered the elevator with his black briefcase and he pressed the button to his suite. Within minutes, his six designer luggage cases were delivered to his suite. The housekeeping staff unpacked Kang-de's clothes and placed them in the walk-in closet. Meanwhile, he continued to look at all the documents that were provided to him by the store manager in Gangnam.

"What the hell is going on here?" he said to himself as he looked at the documents.

Kang-de had opened computer stores and repair factories throughout Seoul, Ansan, and Busan. He had recently opened one more in Gangnam and now he suspected that it was not doing well because of fraudulent accounting. Kang-de began to think about the employees at that branch. He suspected that one or more of them had been embezzling money from his store.

"Bob, don't tell any of the employees at that branch that I am in Seoul," said Kang-de. "I want to catch them off guard," he said as he flipped through paper documents and computer screens.

"Okay, Boss."

"Go home, Bob. It's late. I will call you tomorrow," Kang-de said.

Chapter Three

Lee Areum Arrives in Seoul, Korea; Woo Jin and Mi-hi

While Kang-de slept into the late morning, a flight from Los Angeles landed at Incheon Airport. Lee Areum, now twenty-five years old, had just arrived in Seoul to finish medical school. Unknown to her, the men who sat four rows behind her, in economy, were actually following her.

She walked to the taxi stand and took a taxi to University Medical School. A black sedan was waiting for the two men who had followed Areum to Seoul. They followed her along the highway and they pulled up behind the taxi as it arrived at the main gate of University Medical School. They made a phone call, while watching Areum struggle to retrieve her suitcase and handbag from the taxi.

"She is here," said one of the men who was in the sedan. He hung up the phone and they slowly drove past Areum as she pulled her suitcase along the cobblestone street.

Lee Areum was a short, slim, fairly attractive-looking young lady with beautiful brown eyes that mesmerized anyone who met her.

She had transferred from a California medical school to complete the last year of medical school in Seoul. Although school had not started, the Director of Medicine had given her pre-admittance to her dormitory.

Upon entering the main gate at the University, she saw that the campus was huge and she had no clue where Bern Dormitory was located. Areum walked down the lonely campus road and she saw a sign that said "Campus Café."

The front of the café had green pane glass with a long red awning. Tables and chairs were placed outside the café to relieve overcrowding inside. She noticed a tall, handsome twenty-six-year-old man with black hair and muscles outlining his tight grey T-shirt. He was sitting at one of the tables with a cup in his right hand and a book in the other hand.

Areum greeted him and said good afternoon, but he didn't hear her or maybe he pretended not to hear her. She asked in a loud tone, "Where can I find Bern Dormitory?"

He looked up at her slightly and said, "It is at the end of North Campus Road."

"Where is that?" she asked him as he continued reading.

The man whispered inaudibly, "Silly girl."

"Follow me. I will take you there." He closed his book and began to walk down the main campus road ahead of her.

Areum thanked him and told him that she was new at the school and the campus was huge.

"Didn't you see a map of the campus at the entrance gate?"

"Yes. I took one but it was confusing."

As they walked down the campus road, Areum looked at him intensely and she introduced herself. She asked him his name and he reluctantly told her his name was Kim Woo Jin. Areum noticed that he had a foreign accent and she inquired about his origin.

"Where are you from?" she asked.

Woo Jin replied impatiently, "I was born in London but I was raised in Seoul and Hong Kong. "Are there any more questions?" he asked.

Areum replied in an apologetic tone, "Oh, I am sorry. I did not mean to ask so many questions. "Please do not misunderstand," she said. "I was just trying to make conversation while we are walking."

"This is Bern Dormitory," he said while walking away from her.

"Thanks so much!" she yelled. "I really appreciate the help!"

Areum watched Woo Jin walk down the main road and disappear into a large building. After speaking with security, she entered into her dormitory room and saw her new roommate, twenty-five-year-old Mi-hi. She was a beautiful fair-skinned girl with long black hair, grey eyes, and a model figure. Areum greeted Mi-hi and she introduced herself.

"What's your name?" asked Areum.

She replied abruptly, "I am Mi-hi. I took the bedroom with the window and I am taking this reading desk, too."

"So what do I get?"

"What's left over. The person who is first in the room gets her first preference," said Mi-hi, walking away.

Areum replied, "It is okay. We will work it out."

Mi-hi went into her bedroom without speaking. Areum sensed that Mi-hi was going to be very difficult to deal with. She felt that the negative energy she was getting from Mi-hi would become a problem later.

Areum was unaware that Mi-hi was looking at her through the cracked door of her bedroom.

Areum slowly unpacked her suitcase with deep thoughts about the man she had just met. She remembered how handsome and well spoken he was. She recalled gazing at his muscular back and firm butt as he walked ahead of her on the uneven cobblestones that lined the campus street.

She returned to reality as Mi-hi walked out of her bedroom, looked at her, and slammed the front door while leaving the apartment. Areum shook her head in disbelief of Mi-hi's aggressive behavior toward her.

What a witch, she thought to herself.

Chapter Four

Woo Jin, Sun-hee, Bob, and Kang De

Kim Woo Jin left the University cafe and went home to his empty apartment. He lay on his bed and stared at the ceiling, while trying to decide if his decision to get a roommate was wise. His roommate would not arrive until school began. Feeling lonely, Woo Jin picked up his car keys from his kitchen table and he drove to a bar near his apartment.

When he arrived at the bar, he saw a beautiful young lady sitting at a table drinking alone. Woo Jin noticed that she was being harassed by a drunken man. He watched her and continued to drink. She told the man not to bother her but the drunken man insisted on having a drink with her. He tried to force himself on her and she told him to get lost, but he continued to move closer to her. Woo Jin saw that she was in distress and he yelled at the drunken man to leave her alone.

The man turned to Woo Jin and told him to mind his own business. Woo Jin walked over to the man, grabbed on to his throat, squeezed it and pushed him to the floor. "Leave now, before I make you wish that you were dead."

The drunken man staggered out of the bar and disappeared into the night. The beautiful lady began to cry as she thanked Woo Jin for helping her. "Thanks so much. I didn't know how to get rid of that man," she said with tears in her eyes.

"My pleasure," he said hesitantly as he looked at her face which had turned crimson red. Woo Jin thought about buying her a drink after looking at her shaking uncontrollably.

"Let me buy you a drink," he said, as he nodded to the bartender.

"Thanks for your help. I really appreciate what you did for me."

Woo Jin handed her the drink and asked her for her name.

"My name is Ahn Sun-hee, and yours?" she asked in a slurred tone.

"My name is Kim Woo Jin," he replied. He looked at her as if he were assessing what type of woman would be hanging out in a bar late at night.

As he smiled and placed the glass to his lips, Sun-hee said, "I have never seen you in this bar before." Surprised by her statement, Woo Jin asked her if she visited the bar regularly. She replied, "Only on Fridays. My colleagues and I gather here on Fridays after work."

Woo Jin called the bartender to pour another round of drinks for he and Sun-hee. They continued to drink until the bar closed. They left the bar together as the sun slowly began to rise.

The morning sun shined brightly through the blinds in Woo Jin's apartment. The strong rays on his face woke him up and when he rolled over, he saw a blonde-haired female in his bed. Stunned and dazed he tried to remember what happened last night. He took a shower, got dressed and made a cup of coffee. As he drank the coffee, he realized that Sun-hee was at the bar with him. He recalled that she had gotten into a taxi with him. And he remembered their sexual encounter last night.

Woo Jin woke her up with a cup of coffee and an apology for what happened last night. She told him not to apologize because she had fun. She vaguely remembered both of them taking a shower. Sun-hee recalled his naked firm body pressing against hers. She recalled him grabbing her and entering her as the shower water fell between them. She remembered her drunken moan as he grabbed her breast and squeezed them from behind. Sun-hee recalled sucking on Woo Jin's private parts when he led her to his bed. They climaxed and went to sleep. *Does he remember last night?* she asked herself as he handed her a towel to take a shower.

"I will take you home when you get dressed," said Woo Jin in an embarrassed tone.

Woo Jin went to the garage to get his car, when suddenly he remembered that his car was still at the bar. "Oh, I must have been real drunk last night, because I left my car at the bar and I had sex with a stranger."

Sun-hee heard him and replied, "It's okay. I will take a taxi home." He called a taxi to take her home. "Thanks again," she said, as he paid the taxi driver to take her home.

Sun-hee arrived at her home, took another shower, got dressed and listened to her messages. Her home was a three-bedroom townhouse filled with lots of antiques, books and wall paintings. Sun-hee took a pill to erase the headache from last night's drinking fiasco. She flipped through her texts while drinking a glass of water. Sun-hee stopped to read one from Shin Kang-de, which said: "Emergency, come to my office immediately." She realized that the next ten texts were from him. She wondered what could be so important that would cause him to leave so many messages. And why was he in Seoul?

It was ten o'clock when Sun-hee arrived at Kang-de's office. His office occupied the third floor of a ten-story glass building. There were two permanent secretaries and one temporary secretary that handled the daily operations of the office. Kang-de's right hand man, Bob Goo, occupied the first office by the elevator. On the right side of the office there were several cubicles with people answering phone calls as if they were a part of a telethon. On the left side there were two offices filled with men, who were dressed in black suits, walking back and forth from the main office.

Sun-hee walked into the main office and greeted Kang-de and Bob Goo, who was sitting at Kang-de's desk. "Where have you been? I have been trying to reach you all night," he said. "Your eyes look tired."

"I am sorry. Something came up with one of my clients and he kept me busy all night."

Kang-de pretended that he didn't hear what she had just said. He replied with the response, "We have a problem. One of my store managers has been stealing money from me."

"Are you sure?" she asked.

"Of course I am sure. I suspected this has been going on for a year now, but I had no proof until now."

While Sun-hee looked through the papers Kang-de gave her, he told Bob to bring the Chief Financial Officer to his office. The CFO 's office was located on the second floor of the building. His office was decorated with bookshelves along two walls. A single computer, a fax machine, a laptop, and several cell phones lay across CFO's desk.

Bob knocked on the door of CFO's office but no answer. He was not at his office. CFO's secretary had no idea where he had gone. She could only say that he had received a phone call and he exited his office in a hurry with a laptop in his hand. Bob ran to the elevator, but it was too late. CFO had already left in a second elevator. Bob called the front desk security to stop the CFO, but he had disappeared from the building without a trace. Bob ran down the stairs listening for footsteps ahead of him, and he heard nothing. He called Kang-de on his cell phone as he entered the elevator.

"Boss, CFO is gone."

"What?" said Kang-de as he yelled in the phone. "Take some of the boys and find him, right now," yelled Kang-de.

Sun-hee asked Kang-de, "What are you going to do to the CFO?"

Kang-de replied, "Don't concern yourself about that. You go and prepare two termination letters for me."

"Okay. I will do that," said Sun-hee. She walked out of his office and headed to the elevator.

Suddenly she heard Kang-de yelling, "Sun-hee, keep your phone on. I might call you later."

After an hour of searching for the CFO, Bob walked into Kang-de's office with a disappointing look on his face. "Boss, he is nowhere to be found."

"It looks like we have to go to the Gangnam store today," said Kang-de.

Bob nodded his head as they left his office. They headed down the busy highway to the store in Gangnam.

Bob drove along the highway in silence. He knew that Kang-de was in deep thought. Kang-de said nothing while thinking about how much he missed his parents and the Embassy. He wished that they were alive to watch him handle what he was about to face at the store in Gangnam. His thoughts about the fun times at the Embassy reminded him of Areum, but the cool breeze flowing through the car window, and the jet lag that was still ravaging his body quickly threw him into a deep sleep.

He had not been sleeping for very long when he felt a tap on his hand.

"Boss, we are at the store in Gangnam."

He sat up, wiped his face, and exited the car. He stood by the car and looked at the store window decorations. Kang-de had noticed that the advertisements that were posted on his store windows were past dated.

He became angry as he gazed at the organized signs that decorated the window of the store that was next to his. He buttoned his jacket, placed his designer sunglasses on his face, and he opened the door to his store, leaving Bob to wait by his SUV.

Chapter Five

Kang-de, Yejoon, and Areum

Areum needed a new laptop for medical school, and she walked into a computer store in Gangnam. A salesclerk greeted her at the door and said, "Good afternoon. Welcome to our store. How may I help you?"

"I need to see your laptops. Where can I find them?"

"Follow me, please," said the clerk.

While the clerk was assisting Areum, Kang-de walked in. Some of the clerks ran to greet him. He nodded and asked, "Where is Bak Yejoon? I don't see him."

"He is not here, Sir. He went out."

Kang-de removed his sunglasses, looked to the door, and asked, "Out where?"

The clerk replied, "Sir, I don't know. He has been gone all morning."

Kang-de sighed as he walked to the back of the store to search for Bak Yejoon. Before he could get to the back door, he noticed a clerk assisting a young lady who was looking at a laptop.

"Miss, did you see any laptop that you would like?" asked the clerk.

"No. Thanks," she said. Areum turned around to leave the store and she bumped into Kang-de. "I am sorry," said Areum.

Kang-de stared at her as if she looked familiar. "Do I know you?" he asked.

"No," she said, hurrying out of the store.

Kang-de followed her out the door and he watched her walk down the street. His view was obstructed by his employee, Bak Yejoon, who was walking toward him.

He immediately turned his focused onto Yejoon and he asked, "Yejoon, where have you been?"

"Hi, Boss. Welcome to Seoul. I went to the bank to make a deposit."

Kang-de looked at him and smiled, knowing that he was lying.

"Have you seen the Chief Financial Officer? Because I have been looking for him." Yejoon nervously replied, "No, Boss. I don't know where he is."

Suddenly, without any warning, Kang-de slapped Yejoon across the face. "LIAR!" he yelled. "You know where he is, because the both of you have been stealing my money. Which one of you hacked into my computer?"

"Not me, Boss," said Yejoon holding his jaw.

Kang-de stepped toward Yejoon and said, "If you stand here and lie to me one more time I am going to kill you right now."

Yejoon looked in Kang-de eyes and saw that he was serious with his threat. Fearful of being killed, he fell to the floor and said, "I am sorry, Boss, I needed the money. I lost my house on a gambling debt and my wife and kids left me. I was just trying to get my house back."

Kang-de sat in the chair behind the counter, stared at Yejoon, and said, "I want you at my office with all the financial records you have by tomorrow. Now get out of my sight."

Yejoon walked away from Kang-de, then he turned and said, "I don't have any records, Boss. The CFO has all the records."

Kang-de jumped out of the chair, looked at Yejoon, and screamed, "Find the CFO and both of you better be at my office in the morning.

Do you know who you are messing with? I will have both of you killed," said Kang-de with his eyes bulging as he stared at him. "And remove that outdated sign from the window."

Yejoon began to cry when Kang-de walked out of the store. He watched Kang-de's SUV drive away and he ran and hid himself, in fear for his life.

Chapter Six

Sun-hee, Woo Jin, and Mr. Park

It was morning and Sun-hee was at her office thinking about her sexual encounter with the handsome Kim Woo Jin. She recalled his beautiful eyes and sexy body that made her feel good. She wanted to see him again, but she didn't get his number. "What an idiot," she yelled out.

"Who is an idiot?" asked her client, Mr. Park, slowly walking into her office.

Mr. Park had degrees in pharmacy, business administration, chemical engineering and law, and he also owned the largest pharmaceutical company in Seoul. He was about five feet nine inches with grey hair and a receding hairline. He was a smart and competitive businessman, who loved women who were not his wife.

He wanted Sun-hee to file an injunction against a rival company (AZAXCO Pharmaceuticals) that was planning to open a business next to his company.

"Sun-hee, I want you to stop that company from building next to me. I don't care how much money it costs. Just stop them."

"I will do my best, Mr. Park."

He replied with a perverted smile, "I know that you will do your best. You've always done your best, as I recall."

She looked at him and remembered how Mr. Park forced her to have sex with him when she was an intern at his office. Tears came to her eyes as she remembered those traumatic times spent as an intern in his law office. Suddenly, Mr. Park held her hand and told her that he was having a party at his home on Saturday.

"Bring a guest," he said.

Reluctantly she agreed, while pulling her hands away from him.

Sun-hee walked him out of her office and she remembered that there was no grocery at home. She got into her car and drove to the supermarket. She waited in the back of the checkout line for a few minutes. Then she saw Woo Jin, who was ahead of her on the line. He had a shopping cart full of groceries.

"Hi there. How are you?" she yelled out to him.

He turned around and replied, "Good, and you?" slowing down to wait for her.

"Fine. I wanted to call you but I didn't have your number."

He hesitated for a moment and then he handed his number to her when she walked up to him. "What is yours?" he asked.

Sun-hee handed him her business card.

"Oh, you are a lawyer," he said.

"Yes. What do you do?"

"I am finishing my master's degree in Petroleum Engineering," he replied.

"Engineering. Oh, that is great," she said with a smile on her face.

"Well, I will see you soon," said Woo Jin as he pushed his shopping cart to his car.

"Woo Jin," she yelled, "would you like to attend a party with me this weekend?"

"I am not sure. I have to get prepared for school on Monday."

"Oh, please come. You don't have to stay very long."

He hesitated and then said, "Okay. Text me the address."

"Sure. I will see you on Saturday," said Sun-hee, smiling brightly as she watched Woo Jin drive away in his black BMW.

Chapter Seven

Kang-de, Bob, Chul-Moo, Yejoon, and CFO

The morning had passed and Kang-de and Bob were still waiting at his office for Yejoon and CFO. There was no word from CFO and Bak Yejoon. The office was filled with men in suits carrying documents for Kang-de to sign. Kang-de looked at the gold clock hanging on his office wall as it ticked the time away.

"Bob, it's twelve o'clock in the afternoon and I told Yejoon to be at my office by morning." Kang-de got up from his chair and began to pace back and forth in his office. He glanced at the clock on the wall one more time. Then he asked Bob, "Where are those two jerks? Do they think that I was not serious?"

"Boss, give them a few more minutes. If they don't show up then I will call Chul-Moo."

"They better not keep me waiting any longer," he said angrily.

Two more hours had passed and Kang-de got tired of waiting for Yejoon and CFO. He yelled for Bob to call Chul-Moo. "I am tired of waiting for those idiots," he said as he pushed his chair away from his desk.

Chul-Moo was a large man in stature and weight. He had the body of a wrestler and the face of a fearless warrior. Anyone who was unfortunate to meet him would eventually know what it was like to be scared. He feared no one except Kang-de. He respected Kang-de because he had seen Kang-de easily beat a man of larger stature in a fist fight. As the years passed, he grew to love Kang-de as a kind older brother and a mentor. He learned how to manage a business from Kang-de. With Kang-de's financial help, Chul opened a successful security firm in Seoul. He employed forty men who knew how to inflict serious bodily harm without exerting themselves. As Kang-de's enforcer he would torture and kill anyone who tried to harm Kang-de in any manner.

The phone rang at Chul's office. Chul answered the phone. It was Bob Goo calling. "Chul, the Boss wants you to find Bak Yejoon and the Chief Financial Officer."

"Okay, I will get my men on it right of way." Kang-de took the phone from Bob and yelled, "Take them to the warehouse when you find them."

Late in the evening Kang-de and Bob were at the office waiting for Chul-Moo to call them. The phone rang and it was Chul on the phone.

"Boss, I have the two of them here at the warehouse."

"I am on my way," said Kang-de hurrying from his office.

Bob drove Kang-de to his warehouse. He opened the car door and slammed it shut before Bob could turn off the engine. As he entered the warehouse, he saw the two men looking bloodied and crying. Chul and his men had beaten them. Blood was dripping from Bak Yejoon's lip and nose. His right eye was swollen shut. CFO had the imprint of a large hand on his right jaw. His bottom lip was swollen and he was crying.

"Where is my money, Yejoon?" asked Kang-de as he slowly lit a cigarette and exhale in Yejoon's face.

"I don't have it, Boss. I am sorry. I tried to get it but I could not," said Yejoon.

Kang-de punched him in the face and his neck snapped back as he fell to the floor. "You bastard. You have two days to bring my money to me. You got that?" said Kang-de.

"I am so sorry, Boss. I will get you the money. I promise," he said with a crackling voice.

"Don't promise me anything. I want my money."

Chul kicked him as he lay on the floor crying from the pain of the punch he received.

"Bring CFO to me," said Kang-de in an angry tone.

Two of Chul's men dragged CFO and threw him at Kang-de's feet. Kang-de slapped him as he kneeled in front of him. Then, he kicked him and he fell backward onto the ground and curled up in pain.

"You bastard. I trusted you with my parents' business and you betrayed me with your greed. I paid you a lot more money than most company CFO's make. Why did you do it? Why?"

CFO replied that Yejoon threatened him with violence, if he had not embezzled the money from the new Gangnam store.

"That's a lie," said Yejoon, whimpering in pain. "Boss, I was afraid. I am so sorry. Have mercy on me, please. I am sorry. Please don't kill me, Boss."

"Shut up. Do not beg. While Yejoon was threatening you, you were helping yourself to your share of my money." Kang-de thought about the damage the both of them did to his company. "I think there are more people involved than you two and I will find out." Kang-de walked between the two men, slapping them, as he thought about his mother and father's hard work being jeopardized by them. "It's my fault. I should have kept a closer watch on my business. I should have come home more often," he sighed.

Kang-de punched CFO in his head and he fell on his face. Chul stomped him in his back and his forehead bounce off the pavement. CFO tried to move and Kang-de turned, look at him, and told him not to get up or he would die immediately. Kang-de walked to his car, looked back at Yejoon and CFO, and told them that they were fired.

"Bob, I don't want to look at them anymore. Get me out of here."

Bob drove Kang-de to his hotel in Dongjak-gu. Bob pulled up into Kang-de's parking space at the hotel underground garage. As Kang-de exited the car, Bob reminded him that he was invited to a party at Mr. Park's home on Saturday.

"Oh, yeah. Let's check it out," he said. "Maybe we can get some information on that Mr. Park. I don't trust him. I'm suspicious of that guy. He's always trying to get something for free. Bob, go home and rest. It has been a very stressful day and I want to turn in early tonight."

"Okay, Boss. You restrained yourself well back at the warehouse. Those guys have no idea how easily you could have killed them."

Kang-de said nothing as he smiled at Bob, and entered the elevator.

The elevator took Kang-de to his penthouse suite on the twenty-third floor. He removed the clothes he had on, took a hot shower, and looked at his face in the gold rimmed mirror in his bathroom. He could vaguely see the scar that had once covered the right side of his face for many years. The surgeons had done a fantastic job on his face, he thought to himself.

Kang-de stepped into his pajama pants and laid across his bed, thinking about the girl he saw at the store. She looked so much like Areum. He told himself that it had to be Areum.

"How silly of me. I should have followed her down the street," he said to himself. "That idiot Bak Yejoon really interfered with my concentration," he spoke out loudly. "I am really going to make him and CFO pay for betraying me," he said quietly as he closed his eyes and fell asleep.

Chapter Eight

Areum, Bora, Woo Jin, and Sun-hee

It was late Friday night and school had not begun. The cafeteria was closed until Monday. The vending machines were the only source of food available to Areum. She walked to the machine and the rich and pretty Bora Park came behind her and said, "Don't eat that junk! Come with me."

"Oh, no. It's okay. I can eat what is in the machine," replied Areum.

Bora looked at her in amazement and said, "No, you cannot. I have a lot of good food here and I can't eat it all. Come with me."

Areum followed her to a small coffee room that had a table and chair. Bora's maid served them different foods and Bora introduced herself.

"I am Park Bora. What's your name?"

"My name is Lee Areum."

"Nice to meet you, Lee Areum. Well, now that we have gotten formally introduced, let's eat," said Bora.

Areum looked at Bora with hesitation. Then she slowly began to eat when she saw Bora eating the food that looked like it was prepared by a chef from a high-end restaurant. "My chef prepared the kimchi, truffles, salmon, rice, salad and cakes," she said as she ate the food.

"Are you sure you don't mind sharing?" asked Areum.

"Not at all. Enjoy the meal. Are you in the medical program?" asked Bora.

"Yes. Are you?"

"Yeah. I am specializing in Oncology, and you?"

Areum replied that she was specializing in Cardiology.

"That's great. I am living on the third floor. What floor are you on?"

"The second floor," said Areum.

"Listen, my dad is having a party at my house tomorrow. Do you want to come?" asked Bora.

"No, thanks. I am a transfer student and I have a lot of things to do before school starts Monday."

"Okay. Maybe next time."

Bora called to her maid, Maria, to come and clean up the leftover food. As Maria took the leftover food and threw it in the garbage, Areum looked mystified that someone could just throw away good food.

"I will see you at school on Monday," said Bora as she got into a black Mercedes sedan. Areum watched as Bora's driver slowly reverse out of the narrow parking lot at Bern Dormitory.

Bored and lonely, Areum took a walk to the campus library that was open. She walked in and saw the man who showed her how to get to Bern Dormitory. Areum tried to think of his name. She remembered. She walked up to him. "Woo Jin, right? Hi, how are you?" she asked.

"I am fine, and you? You are Areum, right?"

She smiled when Woo Jin called her name.

"Yes. That's right. Thanks again for the help in finding my dormitory. I really appreciated it."

"You don't have to thank me again. I will assume that you are in medical school?"

"Yes. I am a transfer student from California and I am finishing my last year at medical school here in Seoul."

"California. Do you live there?"

"Not now. I used to live there. I was born in Seoul but I was raised in New York. My dad worked for the Ambassador at the South Korean Embassy in New York. When the Ambassador retired he came back to Seoul and he took my mom and dad with him."

Areum was told that the Ambassador had retired. She had no idea that he had unwillingly left his post because of the danger he and her family faced from the secret organization.

"Wow. Your life sounds interesting. Anyway, I have to go now. I will see you when school starts," said Woo Jin.

"Okay. See you then."

Areum walked to the back of the library and he watched her as she sat down to read a book.

Suddenly his phone rang and it was Sun-hee calling to give him the address to Mr. Park's home. He walked to the front door of the library and he answered it.

"Hello. How are you?"

"Did you get the text that I sent to you? I left the address for to-morrow's party in it."

"I'm sorry. I didn't get a chance to look at my messages as yet."

"I am at the library. Can I call you later?"

"Sure."

Sun-hee hung up the phone.

Woo Jin went back into the library and sat down. He looked to the back of the library and Areum was still there. He smiled, picked up his books and walked down the steps of the library without speaking to her.

Chapter Nine

Sun-hee, Woo Jin, Mr. Park, Kang-de, Bora, Bob, and Mr. Moon

It was Saturday night and Sun-hee called Woo Jin to find out if he was ready for the party at Mr. Park's home. She was excited that Woo Jin, the handsome man, would be with her at Mr. Park's home. She told herself that she will be the envy of every female at the party.

Woo Jin answered the phone and told her that he was leaving in five minutes. "Do you want me to pick you up or should I meet you there?" he asked.

"No. I will meet you there.. Listen, wear a suit and tie, okay?"

"I think that I can find one."

"Funny. Ha, ha, ha. See you later," she said.

Woo Jin drove through the large iron gates that had guards posted on each side. He drove up a hill and saw a large yellow and brown two-story mansion that was decorated with beautiful lights. A valet ran to his car as he pulled up in the circular driveway and he handed his car keys to him. As he walked through the open door, which was held by two giant looking security guards, he looked through the massive crowd to find Sun-hee. She saw him first and walked over to greet him. She wore a dark blue mini dress with black pumps. Woo Jin wore a black tuxedo with black shirt and a dark grey bow tie. They both looked at each other and smiled.

"You look very handsome, Mr. Kim Woo Jin. Look at all the eyes watching you right now."

"So do you. You look beautiful."

"Thanks. Let me introduce you to our host, Mr. Park."

Bora and Mr. Park were standing next to each other in a greeting line. Bora looked at Sun-hee and rolled her eyes when she walked up to greet them.

"Mr. Park, this is Mr. Kim Woo Jin. He is a friend of mine."

"Good to meet you," said Mr. Park. "This is my daughter, Bora. Hello, Mr. Kim. You look familiar. Do you attend the University of Seoul?"

"Yes," replied Woo Jin.

"I am pleased to meet a fellow student," said Bora, smiling with him.

Meanwhile, Woo Jin's eyes steadily moved around the room and he saw someone he recognized. It was a man he had seen at his home in Hong Kong a few years ago.

"Please excuse me, Bora. I think I see someone that I might know."

He walked over to the man and held out his hand to greet him, but the stranger hurried toward the front door. He bumped into Kang-de and Bob while rushing through the crowd to get to the door. Kang-de turned to look at him and he continued to walk into the party. Woo Jin ran to the front door but the stranger had vanished into the hot night.

Mr. Park walked up to Sun-hee and asked, "Have you taken care of what we discussed?"

"Yes, Sir. I served them the papers the next day."

"Good. Now go and have fun."

Sun-hee saw Kang-de and Bob walking into the party.

"Excuse me, Woo Jin. I see a client over there. I will be back. Kang-de, what are you doing at this party? Bob, you too. Who invited you?"

"What do you want to know? That's my business. Who invited you?"

"Mr. Park is a client of mine. He invited me."

Kang-de and Bob looked at each other and nodded as if they agreed on something.

"If you must be nosy, then Mr. Park invited us. Satisfied? Now go back to that man that I saw you with," said Kang-de.

"You can be so rude, Kang-de."

"Well, go on."

After an hour into the party, Sun-hee and Woo Jin left the party together. Woo Jin drove Sun-hee to her home. She had taken a taxi to Mr. Park's home, hoping that Woo Jin would take her home and that he would spend the night with her.

It was two in the morning when he arrived at her home. Sun-hee invited him in for a cup of coffee. He hesitated, then he walked into her home and closed the door behind him. His eyes slowly observed her apartment before sitting down.

"Would you prefer coffee or a glass of wine?"

"Wine. Please."

Woo Jin looked at his watch while drinking the wine. When he got up to say goodnight, Sun-hee kissed him on his cheek. He looked at her and kissed her passionately. She lead him to her bedroom and she turned off the lights. Woo Jin tried to undress her but she pulled a zipper and her dress fell to the floor, exposing her naked body. He pulled out a condom from his pocket before removing his clothes.

"Do you always walk with that?" she asked.

"No, but isn't it great that I have two now?"

Sun-hee laughed.

Woo Jin let his fingers run between her legs and to his delight, her body was ready for him. He gently pulled her on top of him and she rode him until he turned her onto her stomach. He thusted his hard muscle into her and she moaned loudly. Woo Jin lifted her off the bed and he poured himself into her until they climaxed together.

Sun-hee was still asleep when Woo Jin left her early in the morning. She turned over to touch Woo Jin and he was not there. She got up and called out his name. "Woo Jin, where are you?" She called his cell phone and he answered.

"Hello there, Sleeping Beauty. How are you?"

"Fine, thanks. I had a great time last night. Why did you not wake me up before you left my home?"

"You looked so beautiful sleeping. I didn't want to wake you up."

"I hope to see you soon," she said.

"Sure. Let's have dinner and a movie tonight," he said, walking into a twenty-four-hour diner to get breakfast.

"That would be great. See you tonight."

Kang-de and Bob left the party shortly after Sun-hee and Woo Jin. Bob took Kang-de to his hotel (ITO Hotel). The ITO Hotel had twenty-three floors with three floors comprised of six deluxe suites each. Kang-de occupied all the suites on the twenty-third floor. He reconstructed all the suites into one gigantic apartment. Bob and Kang-de exited the elevator on the twenty-third floor and a security guard greeted them at the elevator. Kang-de and Bob entered the suite looking exhausted by the long drive from Mr. Park's home.

"Looks like I will have to think about Sun-hee working for me."

"Yeah, Boss. She is working for Mr. Park. And I know you don't trust him."

"He is a cunning fox. I have to keep my eyes on him. Go home, Bob. Get some sleep. Goodnight."

"Goodnight, or rather good morning, Boss. See you in a few hours."

"Sure. I will see you at the office in a few hours."

Kang-de, although exhausted, was unable to sleep. He took a pack of cigarette and went outside the hotel to smoke. As he sat down by the water fountain that was located in front of his hotel, he observed four men sitting in a Mercedes Benz SUV. He didn't recognize them and he thought that it was strange that four men would sit in an SUV so early in the morning.

Kang-de smoked two cigarettes, looked at the men and walked into the lobby. He saw chief security guard, Mr. Moon, and he told him to keep an eye on the black Mercedes Benz SUV that was parked in front of the hotel.

Mr. Moon replied, "Sir, we have been watching the SUV for twenty minutes now. I am giving them ten more minutes before I tell them to leave. Sir, they could be friends of a hotel guest."

Kang-de looked at him and then looked across the street and told him, "Okay. Goodnight, Mr. Moon."

"Goodnight, Mr. Shin."

Kang-de went to his suite and fell asleep on his couch.

Chapter Ten

Areum, Mi-hi, and Woo Jin

It had been a week since Areum arrived, and her roommate, Mi-hi, rarely spoke to her. Areum felt the hostility that Mi-hi had toward her. She tried to be nice to Mi-hi because they were roommates and she had no friends.

Mi-hi woke up and sat at her desk. Areum hesitated before greeting her.

"Good morning. You are awake early on a Sunday morning."

Mi-hi replied, "I have to fill out this form. They want to know what I plan to specialize in."

"What are you planning to specialize in?"

"I am not specializing in anything. I am going to practice Internal Medicine," said Mi-hi in a sarcastic tone.

"That's good."

The room became silent after Areum spoke. Mi-hi left Areum standing in their living room and she went to her room to finish filling out her form. Areum left the room and walked outside to avoid Mi-hi's hostile behavior.

Mi-hi heard the door closed and she dialed a number on her cell. She told the person on the other end that Areum was her roommate. "Yes, she just left. I will keep an eye on her. And I am waiting for the right time to eliminate her."

The person on the other end of the phone told her to wait for their directions.

"Okay, Sir. I will wait for your orders…. No, Sir, she has no idea who I am…. Goodbye, Sir," said Mi-hi in a robotic tone. Mi-hi went into Areum's room to search for anything that she could find.

Frustrated and hungry, Areum went searching for something to eat. She walked out the main campus gate and she saw a small breakfast diner. As she entered the diner, she saw Woo Jin eating breakfast. Areum's heart began to beat fast as she walked up to him.

"Good morning. You are awake very early," Areum said as she began to breathe heavily.

"No. In fact, I am awake very late," he said as he stared at her with a smile.

"Oh. Enjoy your breakfast."

"Areum. Please join me. Sit down."

"Okay. If you don't mind?" she said.

He looked at her and leaned his head to signal the waiter. The waiter came to the table and Areum ordered tea and toast with butter.

"I can't wait to start school tomorrow. I just want to finish my studies," he said.

"Me too."

"What do you want to specialize in?"

"Cardiology. However, I'm not sure that I can pass the classes."

"That's a great field. You will do well with your courses. I am sure."

"I am nervous because this is Seoul. The medical program here is much more demanding."

"You will be fine. Don't worry so much," he said.

Woo Jin stared at her as she ate her breakfast. Areum observed his eyes looking at her. Feeling uncomfortable, she asked him another question.

"So what do people do here on a Sunday morning?"

He replied, "They go to the park. They go for picnics. They go to the beach. They go shopping. There are a lot of things to do here on a Sunday."

"Oh, that's great. I must do a tour of this city. It has been a long time since I have seen Seoul."

"Maybe one day I will take you to see Seoul, but right now I need to go to sleep. Breakfast is on me this time. Take care."

"Thanks so much, Woo Jin. Bye."

Woo Jin went home to sleep and Areum walked around trying to familiarize herself with the campus. She walked into every building that was open and each time she circled the map. Areum slowly walked up to the medical school but the doors were locked. She circled the map and walked back to Bern Dormitory.

Chapter Eleven

Bora, Areum, Mr. Park, Mrs. Park, Minjae, Maria, and Mi-hi

Late in the afternoon Bora's driver drove her to Bern Dormitory. When he pulled up in front of the building, Bora saw Areum walking slowly into the dormitory.

"Areum, good afternoon. How are you?"

"Fine. How are you?"

"I left some things at my parents' house and I went to get them."

"Okay. I am going upstairs now."

"Wait. Let me put these things in my apartment and then we will go for a drive," said Bora.

"That's not necessary."

"I insist. I need to go shopping. Don't you want to come with me? Come on!"

"Okay," said Areum reluctantly.

Neither Bora nor Areum noticed the two men who were watching them when their car left the dormitory. A grey sedan pulled up behind Bora's car as Bora and Areum got out and walked into the mall.

Bora and Areum walked through the mall filled with high end stores, looking for items to buy. Bora bought handbags, shoes, dresses, jewelry and perfumes. Areum bought nothing.

"Areum, aren't you going to buy anything?"

"No. I don't need anything here. I just need a laptop and that's all I need."

"Okay then. You can carry some of my bags for me. Wait, I see a gold bracelet. I have to get this. Isn't it beautiful?"

"Yeah. It is beautiful. Now can we go?"

As they walked in and out of stores, Areum noticed three men following her and Bora at a distance.

"Bora, do you have bodyguards following us, because three men have been following us for the past twenty minutes? Don't turn around. Look in the store window on your right."

"How do you know that they are following us?"

"I lived in New York. I know when somebody is following me. They stopped when we stopped at every store."

"I am going to call my dad to see if he sent anyone to follow us."

Bora called her dad at his office, shaking as she touched the cell phone screen. His secretary answered and told her that Mr. Park left early. Bora became distraught and she began to tremble.

"Listen, don't panic. Don't let them know that we know they are following us. Stay calm. Okay?" Areum said holding her hands.

"Let's leave the mall now," said Bora.

"No, no, no. We can't leave now. There are a lot of people here. They won't do anything to us if we are in a crowd," said Areum.

"I am going to call my mom," Bora said anxiously. Her hands continued to tremble each time she touched a number on the cell phone. The phone rang at her home and the maid answered it.

"Maria, let me speak with my mother quickly."

"Yes. Miss Bora. Is everything okay?"

"Please put my mother on the phone now."

Maria handed the phone to Mrs. Park.

"Hello, Bora, what is the matter, dear? Are you alright?"

"Mom, did Dad send anyone to follow me at the mall?"

"No, I don't think so. Let me ask him. Here he is. Honey, did you tell any of your workers to follow Bora?"

"No. Why? She should have a driver waiting outside for her, but that is it. What's wrong? Give me the phone," said Mr. Park, grabbing it from his wife's hand. "Bora, what is wrong? Is everything alright?"

"No, Dad. Some guys are following me and Areum."

"How many men? Where are you? Who is Areum?"

"Dad, I am scared. I am at the mall. Please come and get me," said Bora. Areum reached over and touched Bora's hand to calm her.

"Stay where you are. Your mother just called Minjae (Mr. Park's enforcer) and he is parked a block away from the mall. I am sending some of the guards there right now. It will be okay, honey. Stay on the line with me."

"Okay, Dad. I see Minjae with another man," said Bora anxiously.

"Go with them. Everything will be fine."

"Okay, Dad. Let's go, Areum," said Bora. She looked back to see if the men who were following had caught up to her and Areum.

Areum looked back and saw the men hastily following them. Minjae held Bora's hand and they ran through the mall, pushing patrons to the side.

"Stay calm. No matter what you see. I am with you now," said Minjae as he pulled her through the mall.

The other man, a driver, ran ahead to get the car.

"Hurry. They are catching up to us," said Areum.

"Minjae. Where are the bodyguards?"

"Miss, they should be waiting around that corner over there. Hurry, Miss Bora." Minjae grabbed Areum's right hand and pulled her to his left side. Bora was already at his right side. He pushed them into the arms of two guards who were waiting for Bora and Areum. Minjae turned around and kicked one of the kidnappers which sent him falling backwards into the other two kidnappers.

The guards grabbed Bora and Areum and they ran out the door and into an awaiting car. The driver sped off into the street and onto the highway toward Bora's home.

Meanwhile, Minjae and two bodyguards had overpowered the three kidnappers, but a fourth man, with exceptional experience in martial arts, assisted them to escape in the mall. The fourth man was one of the persons who followed Areum from Los Angeles. He was not a part of the kidnapping team but he assisted the three men to escape.

"I am glad that you were with me, Areum. I was so scared."

"Thank you, driver," said Bora.

"Yes, thank you, Sir," said Areum.

"You are both welcome," he said, while speeding along the highway.

Thirty minutes later, Bora and Areum arrived at her home. Mr. and Mrs. Park ran outside to greet Bora. Mrs. Park hugged Bora and Mr. Park looked at Areum as he held onto his daughter.

"Are you okay, honey?"

"Yes, Dad. I was a bit scared but Areum kept me calm. Dad, this is Areum, my friend, from Medical School. She is studying to become a cardiologist."

"Good, come in. Let's talk about what happened today."

"Come in, Areum," said Bora.

"When did you notice that someone was following you?"

"Areum did. She used to live in New York. Tell my parents when you first noticed the kidnappers."

"I first noticed them when we left the handbag store, but I realized that they were following us when we went into the jewelry store. I had turned around to look at them and they pretended that they were window shopping." Minjae rushed into Mr. Park's home minutes after the two ladies had arrived.

"Minjae, we need to find out who they are working for. I will not tolerate anyone trying to harm my daughter."

Mr. Park called a meeting with all his bodyguards. They met Mr. Park in his library. He told them that he wanted Bora to be protected at all times and he wanted the kidnappers found. He yelled at the guards who lost the kidnappers in the mall.

"I want all of you to be on the alert. Find those bastards who tried to kidnap my child. Now," he said screaming.

Mr. Park was interrupted by Bora who had entered the meeting. She overheard her father telling the guards that she should be protected at all times.

"Dad, I have to go to school tomorrow. I don't want security guards following me all the time."

"Bora, you have nothing to say in this matter. Men, don't disappoint me. Minjae, I want to talk to you. Everybody get out. Minjae, I want you to find out how did those bastards know that Bora would be at the mall. We might have a mole in our organization. And take Miss Areum home."

"Okay, Boss, consider it done."

Minjae took Areum to Bern Dormitory and he escorted her to her room. While leaving the dormitory, unknown to Minjae, a black sedan, with two men and a woman inside, was parked between several cars. They waited until Minjae left, then Mi-hi exited the car. She turned to the driver and said, "That man is the bodyguard for the friend of Areum who lives on the third floor."

"Keep an eye on all the people who visit the subject, Areum. The Boss wants to know."

"Okay, Sir. Can we erase the subject soon? I will have exams soon and I could be exposed."

"Wait for our instructions. It will come soon."

They drove off and Mi-hi watched them disappear into the night.

Chapter Twelve

Woo Jin, Sun-hee, Areum, Mr. Park, Kang-de, and Bob

Woo Jin and Sun-hee were at the movies when Mr. Park called her to ask questions about the company who she filed an injunction against.

"Sun-hee, I want you to find out everything you can about the company (AZAXCO Pharmaceuticals). I want that information on my desk by morning. Dig deep. I want to know the name of the owner. Okay?"

"Yes, Sir."

"Don't discuss anything with anyone," he said firmly.

"I won't," said Sun-hee as she clicked the end button on her cell phone.

"What did he want? Does he not know that you are entitled to free time?" Woo Jin said whispering to her.

"It's okay, Woo Jin. It was an emergency. Let's have an early dinner and call it an early night. School starts tomorrow."

Two hours later he took her home, kissed her goodnight, and he went home to prepare for a new semester. Sun-hee sighed. She was disappointed that he couldn't spend the night with her. She thought about his sexy body lying next to her and how sweet he felt when he made love to her.

Woo Jin, Areum and Bora woke early Monday morning to start their respective programs. Areum took the tram to the clinic and she saw Woo Jin walking to the School of Engineering but she didn't say hello. When Areum arrived at the clinic, she saw Bora.

"Hi, Bora. How are you? Are you okay? Are you still nervous?"

"I am fine, but I am still nervous too."

"I am a transfer student. I am not used to people trying to kidnap me. I have no money."

"Don't be anxious. Look behind you. As you can see we have body-guards everywhere," said Bora.

"You have bodyguards. I don't," she replied.

"Oh, stop it, Areum. Let's go and report to our supervising doctors."

It took Bora and Areum two hours to complete their clinical programs. Bora left with Minjae and Areum got on the tram that would take her to her dormitory. When the tram stopped at the Engineering Building, she saw Woo Jin walking to the library. She got off the tram to speak to him.

"Hello. How are you? How was your first day?" he asked.

"It was great, and yours?"

"Fine," Woo Jin said.

"I was so nervous, but it went well. I am heading to the library now. Tomorrow is my cardiovascular class. I am not feeling great about it, so I am going to do some additional reading."

"Good. I am going to the library too. Let's go."

"So how was your weekend?" he asked.

"Very scary. My friend and I were at the mall. Three guys followed us and we had to run. Thank goodness her bodyguards came to help us. It was really a scary situation."

"As I said before, you live an interesting life. Be careful, Areum. Don't wander to places where you don't know anyone."

Areum shook her head in agreement with him.

They studied at separate desk in the library. After two hours Woo Jin got up to leave. He saw Areum studying and he went to speak with her.

"I am leaving now. Would you like me to drive you to your dormitory? It's getting dark."

"Ah, no. I want to read some more."

"Areum, close your books and let's go. It's getting dark and you said that men were following you."

She looked at her watch and replied, "Okay."

She waited at the library until Woo Jin went to get his car. He pulled up in his black BMW and Areum got in the car.

"Thanks for the ride. I am a bit scared. I don't know anyone in Seoul, so why would anyone want to harm me?"

"Maybe it's not you. It could be your friend," said Woo Jin.

It took eight minutes for Woo Jin to arrive at Bern Dormitory. As he parked the car, his phone rang and it was Sun-hee calling. He looked at the phone and turned off the ringer.

"Have you eaten already?" he asked.

"No. But I am not hungry."

"Well, I am, so I can either leave you here and go and eat, or you can eat with me. You choose."

"Where would you go to eat at this time of the evening?"

"Areum, don't ask so much questions. When we get there you will see."

Areum and Woo Jin went to the ITO Hotel for dinner. Woo Jin ordered for the both of them. The food arrived quickly and Areum looked at the large plates of foods. There were lots of meats and chicken stew and rice.

"Let's eat," he said.

"Okay," she said hesitantly.

While they were eating Kang-de walked into the restaurant. Several waiters ran to greet him. They said hello to him in unison. Areum looked up and noticed that it was the man who spoke to her at the computer store in Gangnam.

Kang-de was escorted to his seat and when he sat down, he saw Areum seated at the next table. He looked at her closely for a few minutes. Then he remembered where he had seen her before. It was at the South Korean Embassy in New York. That was Areum, the girl he had liked since he was a teenager. Kang-de walked over to their table.

"Excuse me, Miss. Did you live in New York? We met at the computer store and I have been trying to think of where we have seen each other before. It was at the Embassy, right? You are Mr. and Mrs. Lee's daughter, Areum, right?"

"Yeah. Who are you?"

"I am Kang-de, the Ambassador's son. Do you remember me?"

"Oh, my gosh! Yes, but you look very different. How are you? What are you doing here? I thought you were in New York," she asked excitedly. "Um, um," said Woo Jin in an annoyed voice.

"Oh, sorry, this is my friend Kim Woo Jin."

Before Kang-de could greet him, Woo Jin said, "Areum, we can't stay long."

Kang-de replied, "I am sorry to interrupt your meal. Waiter, their bill is on me."

Woo Jin replied, "It's okay. I can pay for my own food."

"Not a problem. Areum, I hope to see you again. Here's my card."

Kang-de slowly walked to his seat. While sitting down, he heard Woo Jin ask Areum what was the relationship between the two of them. Areum replied that he was the son of her dad's former employer and they had not seen each other since she was a teenager living in New York. Kang-de smiled and called a waiter.

Woo Jin called for the waiter to bring the check. He paid for the meal and they walked out to the lobby. Kang-de watched Areum as she followed behind Woo Jin, with her head turning to smile at Kang-de.

He smiled as he remembered that Woo Jin was the man who was at Mr. Park's party with Sun-hee.

Kang-de pulled out his phone and called Bob. "Hello, I need you to find out everything you can about a man name Kim Woo Jin. Also find out where a girl name Lee Areum's parents are now. I know that they used to live in Busan. Her dad's name is Lee Hyo."

Woo Jin took Areum home and he watched her as she went into the dormitory. Then he went home. After parking his car, he saw Sun-hee waiting at the gate to his apartment complex.

"Hi there. Where have you been? I have been calling you"

Woo Jin looked at his cell and noticed that the volume was lowered. He had lowered the volume while he was with Areum. "What are you doing here? School has started so I won't have time to socialize, I am sorry. You understand, don't you?"

"Can I spend the night? I promise that I won't make any noise. I just want to see you."

"Okay," he said reluctantly, "but please don't forget that I have work to do."

"Sure. I brought my work with me too."

"How did you know that I was going to say yes?" he asked.

Sun-hee laughed as she entered his apartment behind him.

Sun-hee spent the night at Woo Jin's house. He gave his room to her. He fell asleep on the couch with his engineering book resting on his stomach. About two hours later, Sun-hee removed her clothes and went to the couch. She unzipped Woo Jin's pants and began to suck on his private parts, which immediately woke him up. She opened his shirt to look at his gorgeous body and he noticed that she was already naked. He grabbed a condom from his bedroom drawer and he returned to the couch and entered her. She moaned from the sweet feeling of his hard muscle moving inside of her with force. He grabbed her hair as they climaxed together. She fell asleep on his back. As the sun rose, Sun-hee woke up, took a shower and got dressed. Woo Jin got up behind her, took a shower and got dressed.

"Sun-hee, I have to go to class. If you want to stay it's fine, but I won't be back for a while."

"It's okay, I will leave with you. I have a lot of work at the office today," she replied disappointedly.

"I promise to have an uninterrupted meal with you soon. Okay?"

"Okay. You promise?" she asked again.

Woo Jin smiled at her and they went in different directions.

Later that afternoon Woo Jin finished his classes and headed to the library. He saw Areum at the library and went over to greet her.

"Hi, Areum, study hard. How long are you planning to stay here?"

"About two hours. I went to the cardiovascular surgery class and everyone had to introduced themselves. I was the only one whose parent is not a doctor. I am in trouble. My classmates have help from their parents to pass cardiovascular surgery exams. I better study real hard."

"Don't worry. You will do well. Do you want to meet me here Monday through Friday so that we can study together?" he asked.

"That will be nice. Thank you. You're really very kind."

"It's okay. Now let's study."

Throughout the week Areum and Woo Jin spent many hours in the library together. They took turn quizzing each other for examinations.

Woo Jin's roommate arrived at the end of the week. He was tall, and handsome and his family owned many commercial real estate. His father was a member of the secret organization that killed Kang-de's family and he was told to live with Woo Jin until the repairs in his apartment was completed.

Chapter Thirteen

Bora, Dave, Areum, Mr. Park, and Mrs. Lee

Since the attempted kidnapping, Bora was driven to school daily and a guard remained with her as she did her rounds at the clinic. One day the guard accidentally bumped into her at the clinic and she yelled, "Stop following me around!"

The guard walked away without responding. When clinical rounds were finished, the guard took her home. She ran into her home yelling for her dad who was in his library. He was sitting at his desk reading the newspaper when Bora begged him to let her move back into the dormitory."

"Why do you want to move back there? You can travel from home to school every day," he said. "Until I find out who was trying to harm you, it's not possible for you to stay in the dormitory."

"Oh, Dad, I have friends there. I would like to be there. It is closer to classes."

"Bora, let me win this time, please. I promise that you will go back as soon as possible. Okay? How is medical school? Did you have fun? Did you notice anything that was strange?" asked Mr. Park.

"School was fine," she replied walking up the stairs to her room.

Bora's boyfriend, Dave Jong, just got the news about the strange men who were following Bora. He ran into her home, greeted her parents and called her to come downstairs. He went to hold Bora's hands tightly before she stepped off the last stairs.

"Are you okay? What happened? Did you recognize the men?" he asked excitedly.

"I am fine and no, I didn't recognize the men," she said in an annoyed tone. "Why are you here? I am still upset with you for having me beg someone to go shopping with me. Had you been with me, maybe nobody would have tried to kidnap me," she said angrily.

"Bora, you know that I have been busy with my dad's business. I am his right hand. I am sorry. I will spend time with you this weekend. Okay?"

"Okay. Excuse me. I have to call my friend Areum," she said. "Hello, Areum. How are you? How was class?"

"Not bad. I hope that I can pass the final test. Bora, I am at the library. I will speak with you later."

"Okay, study hard," replied Bora.

Areum's phone rang again and it was her mother, Mrs. Lee.

"Hi, Mom. How are you and Dad? Is everything okay?"

"Yes, we want to know how you are doing. Is everything fine with my only child?" asked Mrs. Lee as she continuously coughed into the phone.

"Yes, Mom. It's not like New York City. It's more quiet here. I like it."

"That is good, my child. When are you coming to see our new home? You have not been here since we left New York."

"Soon. I met the Ambassador 's son a few days ago. He remembered me from the Embassy," said Areum excitedly.

"Oh, that's great, Areum. I want to speak with him. Do you have his number? I misplaced it."

"Yeah. He gave me his card, but it's in my room and I am at the library."

"Okay. When you get a chance, give it to me. Get lots of rest and do well in school. I love you, honey."

"Thanks, Mom," replied Areum. "I promise to come and visit soon, and take something for your cough."

Unknown to Mrs. Lee and Areum, their conversation was being monitored. Somewhere in the Lees' home there were listening devices that only Mr. Lee was aware of, but he had not informed his wife because he feared that she might say something that could cause them to be killed.

Chapter Fourteen

Kang-de, Bob, Yejoon, and Chul-Moo

Kang-de and Bob had spent long hours at his office looking through computer logs from the Gangnam store. After waiting two days for Yejoon and CFO, who failed to show at his office, Kang-de called Chul-Moo (the Enforcer) to go and get his money from Yejoon and CFO.

"Chul, take some of your men and go and get my money from Yejoon and that Chief Financial Officer. If they don't have my money, then you know what to do. This will send a message to the other employees not to mess with me."

"Yes, Boss."

It took a few days for Chul to find where Yejoon was hiding. Chul called Kang-de at his suite to inform him that he found Yejoon hiding at a cheap motel. He told Kang-de how he had to kick the door down when Yejoon tried to escape through the window.

"I had to hit him in the back of his head and he fell back on the bed. I asked him for the money and he said that he needed more time so I slap him a few times. He was begging for mercy. Boss, I am sorry but I cut the tip of his index finger. It's still attached. He yelled in pain so I covered his mouth," said Chul.

"Well, he is still alive, right?" asked Kang-de.

"Yeah, Boss."

"Good. Take him to that quack doctor that we know. Let him bandage his finger. I don't want him bleeding to death until he gives me my money."

"Boss, he finally told us where he hid most of the money."

"Where is it?" asked Kang-de excitedly.

"He has a home in Ansan and we are heading there now."

"Good, call me when you get there. I will be at the office."

Yejoon sat in the car with a bloodied towel wrapped around his right hand. It took four hours to reached an old house in Ansan. The paint on the outside of the house was chipped and dull. It had the appearance of a haunted house with broken-down furniture and lots of roaches crawling throughout the rooms. One of Chul's men went with Yejoon to look for the money that was hidden inside the wall of a closet.

Chul came up behind them quietly and asked, "Where is it? If you lie, I will bury you in this house."

"It's over there in the closet," replied Yejoon.

Chul's men moved the tattered clothes that were hanging in the closet, and they broke the wall in the closet. They retrieved a grey duffle bag that was covered with dirt. Chul opened it and said, "This doesn't look like a lot of money. Where is the rest of it?" he asked while grabbing Yejoon in his chest and pulling him toward his face.

"I used the rest to gamble, but I will pay Boss back. I promise. Please, I promise," said Yejoon in a frightened voice.

Chul called Kang-de when he picked up the money from the closet. He told Kang-de that he found most of the money but Yejoon had spent some of it on gambling.

"What do you want me to do with him, Boss?"

"Hurt him. Then let him go so that we can follow him. Don't let him out of your sight. He might run away."

"Got it," replied Chul as he slapped Yejoon on the head. "Oh, Boss, we're still looking for the CFO. I still haven't found his location."

"Keep looking. Don't let him escape and bring the money to the hotel in the morning. Bob will be here and he will count it. I have to go out for a few hours."

"Okay, Boss," said Chul.

Kang-de hung up the phone and turned around to walk out of his office. Bob took a step back from the door and told Kang-de that he found the number for Mr. and Mrs. Lee.

"They live in the countryside, "said Bob as he tried to keep up with Kang-de brisk walk to the elevator.

"Great, I will call them later," replied Kang-de.

"Oh, Boss. The man Kim Woo Jin, he's good. His parents are wealthy business people. They live in Hong Kong. They own a lot of oil refineries world-wide. His mother is half English and half Korean. His dad is Korean. He is doing his graduate studies in Petroleum Engineering."

"And he is a ladies' man. I saw him with Sun-hee at Mr. Park's residence. Now he is trying to play with Areum. I won't stand for it."

"Boss, you like that girl, don't you?" asked Bob with curiosity.

"Yeah, I liked her for a long time. We used to talk with each other in secret because our position in the Embassy were different. My parents liked her parents, but I couldn't date her the way I wanted to. She was the child of an employee and we were young. I erased her from my mind because I thought that there was no hope for us."

"Well, she is here now. She is studying to be a doctor at the University Medical School," said Bob as they walked into the elevator and he pressed the button for the lobby. "A doctor. That is great. I want to see her again. One day I will see her," he said eagerly. "Bob, I want you to call my stock broker. Tell him to find out if Woo Jin's parents' company has public stocks that I can buy. I want to buy the maximum amount of the shares that I can possibly buy, "said Kang-de. "Tell him to let me know when it's done," he added.

"Okay, Boss. Consider it done," said Bob gliding his hands over the face of his cell phone to make the call.

"Bob, you said that Woo Jin guy is good, but there is something about him that doesn't feel right to me. My instinct tells me that he is bad news and I am worried because Areum is involved with him."

"I will check him out again, but my source in Hong Kong is pretty good."

"Nobody is that good. There must be a secret in his family and I want to know what it is."

"Okay, Boss, I will check him out again."

Chapter Fifteen

Areum, Woo Jin, Mi-hi, Bora, and Dave

Areum and Woo Jin spent a lot of time studying together at the library. And as a result, she had passed all her exams. Areum walked to the back of the library to get books on surgery. Woo Jin admired her while she searched through the bookshelves. When she turned around, he pretended to look in his book. Two hours had passed and Areum picked up her books, walked by Woo Jin and said goodnight.

"Goodnight to you," replied Woo Jin. "Are you leaving so soon?" he asked.

"Yes. I want to get home early tonight. I want to get something to eat."

"Why don't I buy you something to eat?" he said.

"No, thanks," she said placing a book under her arm.

Woo Jin closed his book and walked out of the library behind Areum. "Areum, I am taking you to get something to eat. I will not take no for an answer."

She slowly processed his statement. Then she agreed to go with him.

They walked to the campus café but it was closed. All the food stores were closed because it was a public holiday. Woo Jin suggested that they go to eat at his home.

"Areum, I have lots of food at my house. I went to the supermarket. I will cook something for you."

She was shocked that Woo Jin suggested to take her to his apartment. She hastily replied, "No. Ah, I cannot go to your house," she said. "It is not proper for a young lady to go to a man's home."

"Areum, do not be afraid. My roommate arrived two days ago. We won't be alone. I promise to be a gentleman," he said. "We are just going to eat," he muttered quietly.

"Okay, but can we stop at my dormitory first? I have to get something."

"Sure," he replied.

Areum ran into the building and she called Bora to let her know that if anything happened to her, she was with Woo Jin.

"Bora, I am scared. This student named Kim Woo Jin is taking me to his house for dinner. I am definitely carrying my pepper spray with me. If he tries anything then I will blind him."

"The name sounds familiar. Kim Woo Jin. I know the name. There was a Woo Jin at my dad's party. What's he studying?"

"Petroleum Engineering."

"My boyfriend Dave will know him. Let me call him."

She called Dave who was sleeping when she called.

"Goodnight, Dave, are you asleep?"

"Not anymore. What's wrong?"

"Do you know a student named Kim Woo Jin?"

"Yeah," replied Dave. "Why?" he asked.

"My classmate is going somewhere with him and we want to make sure that he is a good person. Is he dangerous?"

"Of course not. He is rich and mature and he is very honest. What's going on with you girls?"

"Never mind. See you tomorrow," said Bora as she hung up from him and called Areum on the phone. "He is a good man, Areum. Don't worry. He is very, very rich too. Did you know that?"

"No, we never discussed his life outside of school. Thanks, Bora."

Woo Jin was on the other line calling Areum. She answered his phone call.

"Where are you? What is taking you so long to come downstairs?"

"I am coming right now," she replied.

Woo Jin and Areum arrived at his home. His apartment had three bedrooms, a large living room, a chef kitchen and three and a half bathrooms. The rooms were neatly decorated with modern furniture. Areum was impressed with his large apartment and how neat he was.

"Woo Jin, your apartment is huge. It is not like my tiny dormitory."

"Have a seat. I will go and change and cook something for you real fast," he said smiling. "So, are you feeling more secure with your work?" he yelled from his bedroom.

"A bit secure. Thanks to you. I really appreciate your help," she yelled back, still glancing around his apartment.

"I didn't do anything. You did the studying," said Woo Jin as he entered his kitchen and began to cook.

"I was focused. Thanks to you," she said.

An hour later he said, "Okay, the food is ready. Come and sit at the table."

Suddenly, Woo Jin's roommate and his girlfriend ran out of their room and into the kitchen, almost running into Areum.

"Excuse me, but I have a guest," said Woo Jin in an angry tone.

"Sorry, we just want to get something from the refrigerator. Don't worry about us," said his roommate laughing. "Hello, Miss."

"Excuse me, Areum. I will be right back," he said angrily.

He went to speak to his roommate while Areum waited on him to eat. Ten minutes later he returned looking unhappy.

"My food must be cold. Shit! Sorry, Areum."

"It's fine. The food is still hot. It smells and looks great. Who taught you how to cook like this?" she said trying to taper his anger.

"I was raised with servants, but I told myself when I started university that I must help myself. I didn't want to hire anyone to cook for me. I think over the years I got better at it."

"You cook better than me. Wow. This food is really tasty. You should be a chef on the side," she said.

"Ha-ha…. I am going to take you home as soon as we finish eating. I have a long day at school tomorrow."

When they finished eating, Woo Jin's cell phone rang and it was Sun-hee calling. He excused himself from the table to answer the phone.

"Hello," he said in an annoying tone. "I can't speak to you right now. I will call you later,.okay?"

"Can I see you tonight? I need to see you," asked Sun-hee.

"I told you that I don't socialize when I am studying."

Areum looked at him perplexed about what he had just said. She thought to herself that he was socializing now. She got up to go and get her handbag. Woo Jin noticed that she was ready to leave.

"I will call you later," he said quickly hanging up so that he could catch up to Areum before she headed to the door.

"Is everything okay? I don't want to get between you and your girl-friend."

"I don't have a girlfriend, yet," he said staring at her.

Areum smiled, feeling flattered about what he said to her.

When they arrived at Bern Dormitory, Woo Jin paused for a moment then he said, "Areum, I would like to date you outside of school. After midterm, next week, I want to take you out. I hope you don't mind. Do you?"

Areum closed her eyes and responded that she didn't mind going out with him. Embarrassed by what she had just said to him, Areum hurried out of Woo Jin's car, said thanks and ran into the dormitory without saying goodbye. Woo Jin noticed that she was shy, and he smiled and drove away.

The men who were watching her were parked across the street from Bern Dormitory. When she entered the building they made a phone call. Mi-hi hung up her cell when Areum walked into the room. She pretended to be studying late when Areum walked past her.

"Goodnight," said Areum. "You are studying late."

"I have lots of work to do. Don't you?" said Mi-hi looking down at her book.

Areum looked at Mi-hi and slowly walked into her room and slammed the door, without responding. She sat on her bed and thought of ways to get out of the dormitory at the end of the semester.

Shortly thereafter, Mi-hi brought Areum a cup of coffee. Areum refused as she was upset with Mi-hi's rude behavior. Mi-hi handed the cup to Areum again, but Areum refused.

"Take it, please. It's my way of apologizing to you for my unfriendly behavior."

"I don't like coffee. I can't drink coffee. It keeps me awake, but thanks anyway."

Disappointed, Mi-hi turned around, walked to the bathroom and flushed the coffee.

Mi-hi waited until Areum fell asleep and then she called the men who were waiting outside in the black sedan.

"She fell asleep, and I couldn't give her the poison. You didn't tell me that she doesn't like coffee," said Mi-hi angrily. "I will get another opportunity," she said as she looked at Areum's closed door. Mi-hi waited for an hour to pass, then she tried to enter Areum's room.

She tried to open the door but it was locked. The noise from the door, alerted Areum. She yelled out, "What is it?"

Mi-hi ran to her room and closed her door. Areum went back to sleep without questioning Mi-hi.

Mi-hi stayed awake plotting what method to use to kill Areum, when she realized that Areum would not eat from her. She had to think quickly as to what would be the easiest way to kill her without being caught.

Chapter Sixteen

Sun-hee, Mr. Park, Kang-de, Areum, Bora, and Woo Jin

It was early morning and the clouds covered the blue sky. The day appear grey and gloomy. Sun-hee went to see Mr. Park at his office. He opened his office door and she walked inside. She looked back at him as he closed the door behind her. An uncomfortable feeling overcame her when he walked up behind her and stood close.

"What did you find out about AZAXCO Company," he said stepping away from her.

"Well, it is not good. They have been doing a lot of hostile mergers and acquisitions of other pharmaceutical companies. Their headquarters are in New York. They have subsidiaries across the globe. They look harmless, but they are not."

"Are you able to verify who the owners are?" he asked.

"I am not able to verify who owns it as yet. It's very difficult to access the private records of the owner' s name, but I am working on it," she replied. "I have a friend in the government office. I have already asked him to help me get the name or names of the owners."

"Thanks, Sun-hee. I know that what we did with filing an injunction against them was the best thing for my company. We will find out who owns the company. They don't know who they are dealing with," said Mr. Park. "That will be all, Sun-hee. Keep at it. I need information as quickly as possible."

As she turned and walked out the office door, Sun-hee's phone rang and it was Kang-de.

"Hi. Good morning, Kang-de, what's going on?"

"I am at your office very early. Where are you?" he yelled. "Why is it that each time I need to speak with you, you are never available to me?"

"Kang-de, I have other clients. You are not the only one who employs me. I will be right there," she snapped at him.

"You had better hurry. I have things to do today," he replied.

Kang-de and Sun-hee's offices were located three blocks from Mr. Park's office. Sun-hee walked briskly up the blocks and entered the glass building. As she entered the elevator, two strange men entered with her. They said nothing as they rode the elevator to her floor. She exited the elevator, but they stayed and watch her open the door to her office.

"What's so important that you have to make me rush to my office?" she asked breathing sharply as she sat at her desk.

"I want you to review the contracts of all my companies in Seoul. I want you to look at the contracts that the CFO had access. I want to make sure that he didn't change anything," he said anxiously.

"Kang-de, that will take time. I will need to get more attorneys on this case."

"You do what you have to. Just get it done for me quickly. By the way my business supersedes all other clients. Okay?"

"Okay, Boss," Sun-hee said jokingly.

"This is not a joke, Sun-hee. This is my parents' life work here."

"Oh, Kang-de, I was only joking with you. Don't be so serious, okay?" she replied apologetically.

"Goodbye, Sun-hee," said Kang-de as he walked out of her office and returned to his hotel.

Sun-hee was at her office doing research and she glanced at Woo Jin's number on her desk. She picked it up and laid it down on her desk again. She called Woo Jin but no answer. *Where is this man? He promised to call me. He must be at the library. I should take lunch for him,* she pondered to herself.

Within twenty minutes, she went to purchase lunch from the restaurant next door to her office and she headed to the library to see Woo Jin. When she entered the library with the bag of food, she saw Woo Jin and a woman studying together.

"Hi, Woo Jin, how are you?" she asked looking down at Areum. "I thought that you should be starving by now, so I brought you lunch."

"What are you doing here? I told you that I would call you."

"Sorry," she said while looking at Areum studying.

Areum kept looking at her book. She didn't want to make eye contact with an angry woman.

"Is she the reason why you are so busy these days?"

Woo Jin jumped up out of his chair and grabbed Sun-hee by the arm. "Come with me outside. We need to talk right now. Sun-hee, you are my friend. I am your friend. We are not boyfriend and girlfriend. Why do you think that you can just interrupt me without permission? I told you that I must finish this graduate Petroleum Engineering degree. My parents are waiting for me to take over their companies." Woo Jin thought about what his next words would be before he spoke. He looked at Sun-hee, apologized, and told her that they had good sex and that was it.

"How could you say that? I thought we meant more to each other than that. How could you do this to me? You are the one who invited me out again," she said crying.

"Sun-hee, stop crying. Do you not remember when you went to law school? Don't you remember the long hours you had to put into your study so that you could pass the bar?"

She nodded yes.

"But I wanted to do something nice for you. I thought about you not eating so I came here to bring food for you. How could you be so inconsiderate?" she said sobbing.

"That's nice of you, but you can't disturb me like this. Yes, I did invite you out and we will go out, but you can't disturb me when I am studying. I am sorry, Sun-hee, I have to go and study my books.

"Woo Jin, I have fallen in love with you."

"Sun-hee, stop saying that," he yelled.

"But it's true. I love you."

"Okay, I am done talking. I said that I will call you and I will. Go and take care of your clients. Okay?"

Sun-hee left Woo Jin at the library. He went and sat next to Areum and he was angry. Areum said nothing about what just happened as she glanced at him.

"Woo Jin, I am going to leave now. I will see you tomorrow."

"Areum, is there something you want to ask me?" he asked, staring at her.

"Oh, no, not at all. You have a good evening, okay?" she said.

"It's getting late. Let me drive you home," said Woo Jin with a sigh.

"No, thank you. I will walk home," she replied.

"As you wish. I have a test tomorrow anyway. Goodnight," he said looking at her in angry glance.

"Goodnight, Woo Jin."

Areum left first and Woo Jin watched her walk across the campus before he got into his car.

While Areum was walking across campus, her phone rang. It was Bora calling to invite her to a her parents' anniversary party that weekend.

"Hi, Bora. How are you doing?"

"I am fine. I wanted to invite you and your new friend to my parents' anniversary party this weekend. It's going to be nice. Do not say no because you said that you would come to my house the next time I had a party."

"Oh, Bora, I have to study, but I will come for a short while. Okay?"

"Don't forget to bring that friend of yours. What's his name again?" asked Bora.

"Kim Woo Jin," Areum replied. "Don't count on him being there."

"I will see you tomorrow in class."

While Bora called Areum to invite her to her parent's party, Mr. Park called Kang-de to invite him to the party.

"Good evening, Kang-de. How are you? I believe my secretary invited you to my party this weekend. I want you to come so that we can talk about our companies."

"I am not sure, but I will try to make it."

"It would be good for your business."

"Okay, I will come."

Kang-de hung up and called Bob.

"Bob, Mr. Park just invited me to another party at his house. He is up to something. I can feel it."

"Are you going to attend?"

"You bet that I will be going. I have to keep an eye on him and besides, I am curious to see who will be there. Get some sleep, Bob. We have things to do tomorrow."

"Goodnight, Boss," replied Bob.

Kang-de went to his suite at the hotel. He saw the telephone number of Mrs. Lee, Areum's mom, lying on the dining table and he decided to call her in the morning.

Chapter Seventeen

Sun-hee, Woo Jin, Areum, Kang-de, Mrs. Lee, CFO, and Chul

The rain came early in the morning and Sun-hee had stayed awake all night thinking about what Woo Jin said to her. She thought about calling him, but she was afraid that he might insult her like he did last night. She told herself that she had to exercise self-control. Sun-hee picked up her briefcase and pulled out the documents for Kang-de's store. She stared at his documents and made notes.

Meanwhile, Areum left the dormitory very early because she wanted to avoid obnoxious Mi-hi. While she waited for the tram that took her to the clinic, she saw Woo Jin walking on the other side of the road. She quickly turned and walked to the next stop.

When the tram pulled up, Woo Jin yelled out, "Good morning. How are you this rainy morning? I hope fine. About last night. I want to explain to you what happened."

Surprised by his statement, she stared at him and said, "There's no need to do that. That's your personal business." She stepped onto the tram and said, "I will see you later." Before the door to the tram closed, she turned to him and asked, "Would you like to go to a house party this weekend?"

Stunned by the sudden invitation, he replied with a loud "yes" while waving goodbye to Areum. He grinned and ran to his classes. She smiled and stared at him until he was out of her sight.

Meanwhile, Bob and Chul had counted the money from the duffle bag the previous morning and they left it with Kang-de.

The morning rain and thunder woke Kang-de from his sleep. He got up, took a shower and got dressed. He picked up the phone and called Mrs. Lee. She answered and he was filled with excitement.

"Good morning Mrs. Lee, how are you? It's Shin Kang-de. How are you and Mr. Lee?" he asked happily.

"We are doing fine. It has been a long time since we have seen you. When did you arrive in Seoul?" she asked in a jubilant tone.

"Not long ago. I left your number in New York. I am sorry for not calling you earlier. I have been busy trying to manage my companies."

Kang-de didn't notice that his voice was echoing back to him. Neither he nor Mrs. Lee were aware that someone else was listening to their conversation. He continued to speak to her.

"Mrs. Lee, I wanted to ask you a personal question, if you don't mind? Did my mom tell you anything about me and your daughter? I vaguely remember overhearing a conversation about me and Areum when I was about seventeen. Was it a joke?"

"You are right, but it was not a joke. Your mother and I spoke about you and Areum marrying each other in the future," she said in a surprised tone. "Do you have a reason for asking me now. Are you and Areum dating? She told me that she had seen you recently."

"No, no," he replied. "I just wanted to know how you and Mr. Lee felt about a relationship with Areum and me, if it ever happens."

"Oh, Kang-de. You have our blessing whenever that happens," replied Mrs. Lee laughing and coughing on the other end of the phone.

"When can I see you? I want you both to come to Seoul. Can you get to the airport? I will send my private jet for you and Mr. Lee."

"That would be lovely, but we can take the train to Seoul," said Mrs. Lee coughing in a low tone.

"Please think about using my jet when you are ready to come. As Areum is in Medical School, I think school recess would be the best time to come," said Kang-de. "It would be nice to have all of us together again. Besides, you are my family," he said as he silently waited for Mrs. Lee to reply to him.

"Yes, yes. It would be very nice for all of us to get together again. When are you going to see Areum, Kang-de?"

"Very soon," he replied. "Thanks again for being there for me when Mom and Dad passed."

"Kang-de, I am very sorry for the loss of your parents. My husband is still sad. It will be good to see you and we will take the train."

"Okay. I will call you to find out when your train will arrive."

Kang-de got an unidentifiable incoming call, while he was speaking with Mrs. Lee. Kang-de told her that he would call her again.

"Hello, who is this?" asked Kang-de.

The person on the other line replied that he was sorry and felt terrible about what he did. Kang-de recognized the voice of his Chief Financial Officer and he yelled out to him.

"What is it?"

"I know that there is nothing that I can say that will make you forgive me. I am so sorry, Boss. I am really sorry," said the CFO crying on the phone.

"Where are the rest of my files? I want them," said Kang-de in an angry tone.

"I destroyed some of them and the rest, Yejoon has them."

"Why did you destroy them? Why? You bastard!" asked Kang-de, as the phone disconnected. "Hello, hello, hello? This bastard," Kang-de said to himself. "I'm going to kill him." Kang-de called Chul to tell him about the phone call.

"Hello, Boss, is everything okay? I still have not found the CFO as yet."

"Well, he just called me and I think he might try to kill himself. He sounds ominous. Find him, Chul. Quickly."

"I am on it, Boss."

"Where the hell is Yejoon? He has more explaining to do. He lied to me. Why does he have my files and what is he planning to do with them? Chul, get those two bastards back in my office by morning."

Kang-de grabbed his phone and car keys and he headed to his office. He greeted the security guard at the entrance of his building and he rode the elevator to his office.

It was early and he was the only one at the office. He entered his office, sat in the chair at his desk and powered up his computer. He searched through his files on the computer and he made notes for Sunhee to address.

Twenty minutes later, the secretaries and Bob arrived with Kang-de's security team. They all greeted him and return to their duties.

The afternoon arrived quickly and Kang-de said nothing as he observed the beautiful mountain view from his office window. The rain had stopped and Bob handed him a cup of coffee as he waited at his office to hear from Chul. He waited and waited for news about his former employees, but the phone did not ring for a very long time.

Chapter Eighteen

Areum, Bora, Dave, Woo Jin, Sun-hee, Kang-de, Bob,
Mr. Park, Mrs. Park, Mr. Chin, Mr. Jong, and Minjae

It was late afternoon and Areum and Bora were at the medical center attending to patients. Bora saw her last cancer patient and Areum had completed examining a patient who recently had heart surgery. They met in the lobby of the clinic to discuss their next project. Bora saw Areum and she invited her to lunch.

"Are you almost done with your rounds? Let's go and eat. I am starving."

"Give me five minutes and I will be finished with my patient," said Areum.

"Okay. I will wait for you outside. Dave is going to take us out to eat."

Five minutes had passed and Areum went to meet Bora and her boyfriend, Dave Jong.

"Areum, meet Dave Jong, my boyfriend."

"Hello, how are you? I have heard a lot about you," said Areum shaking Dave's hands.

"You've heard good things, I hope?" asked Dave, as he turned to look at Bora and smile.

Areum nodded her head in agreement with Dave.

Dave took Bora and Areum to a building that had three restaurants on the first floor and twenty fast food outlets on the ground level. As they exited the car the valet took the keys from Dave and was very happy to park Dave's yellow Ferrari.

"What food should we eat? Italian, Chinese, Korean or Vietnamese?" asked Dave.

"Can we eat Korean food? I have not been in Seoul for a long time and I would love to taste some more of my native foods," asked Areum.

Dave turned to Bora and asked her what kind of food she would prefer. Glancing at Areum, she told Dave that she would like to eat Korean dishes.

Dave, Bora and Areum went into the Korean restaurant and they ate Japchae, crab in soy sauce, ginseng soup, spicy rice cakes, Korean BBQ and many other dishes. The meal lasted for two hour. Dave ordered two bottles of French wine for the table. He poured wine for Bora and then Areum. She stopped him at half a glass of wine.

"I am not a wine drinker," she said.

"That's okay, Areum, Dave and I will finish the bottles," said Bora as Dave poured another glass of wine for her. The wines were finished within an hour.

When they had concluded eating, Dave walked out of the restaurant without paying for the meal. Shocked by what she had just seen, and with her heart beating rapidly, Areum told Bora that Dave forgot to pay for the meal.

Bora replied, "Areum, his family owns all of what your eyes can see in this building."

Dave, noticing that she was feeling uncomfortable, told Areum that as the owner, he didn't pay for food.

Areum sighed and continued walking toward the valet stand.

The valet brought Dave's car and he drove Areum back to the dormitory. Bora and Dave went to the movies and spent the rest of the evening kissing and holding hands.

Areum quietly entered her room to study. The phone rang and it was Woo Jin calling. She turned down the volume and whispered, "Hello."

"Hi, how are you? I was looking for you in the library today. What happened?" he asked in a curious manner.

"I went out with my friends," she whispered.

"Which friend? Oh, I am sorry. It's none of my business," he said while waiting for Areum to answer.

"It was my friend Bora. We went out to have a late lunch, which turned into dinner."

"Okay. Have a good evening. Study a little," he said.

Areum hung up and began to read a book on cardiology.

Woo Jin's phone rang. He looked at it and sighed. Then he answered. "Hello, Sun-hee, how are you?"

"I am still feeling insulted from what you said to me at the library."

"Let's not talk about that now. I have to study for my exam," replied Woo Jin with an annoying voice. "So how was your day?"

"It was okay. Woo Jin, I have a party to go to tomorrow night. Do you want to come with me?"

"I cannot. I have a previous engagement but I will call you. I promise," he added.

"Okay. You promise?" said Sun-hee as she wondered what kind of engagement Woo Jin had to fulfill.

The Weekend Party Is Here

It was the night of the party and Sun-hee arrived at Mr. Park 's home looking very pretty wearing a silver and pink silk dress and a six-inch silver shoes. She rang the bell and Maria, the maid, answered the door. Maria greeted Sun-hee and she walked down the hallway into the circular atrium where some of the guests were standing and talking with each other. She saw Bora and Mrs. Park staring at her. She turned around to walk into the living room and Mrs. Park followed her.

"What are you doing here, Sun-hee? Who invited you?"

"I was invited by my boss, Mr. Park. We have business to discuss."

"What business do you have to discuss with my husband this late at night? We don't want you here," said Mrs. Park angrily.

As Sun-hee started to walk to the door, she heard Mr. Park's calling her.

"Mr. Park. Good evening," she said nervously.

"Yes. Good evening. Come into my office. Did you find out anything as yet?" he asked as they walked past Bora and her mother watching.

Sun-hee followed Mr. Park into the library and he closed the door.

The doorbell rang again and it was Kang-de and Bob. Kang-de was dressed in a black tuxedo, white shirt and black silk tie. Bob wore a dark grey suit with a silk grey shirt and a black tie. The butler greeted them and escorted them to the living room. All eyes turned to Kang-de while he walked in. He could hear the women who were in the atrium whispering, "He is so gorgeous and his bodyguard is gorgeous too. Wow!"

"Is he married?" asked one of them.

The other replied, "I will find out."

Kang-de avoided looking at the women. Instead, his eyes were glancing throughout the room. He wanted to see Mr. Park's friends. Meanwhile, Bob stood by his side firmly watching and smiling at everyone who walked closely to Kang-de.

"Where is Mr. Park.?" Bob asked the butler.

"He is in his office, Sir. This way, please."

Kang-de and Bob went to Mr. Park's office and the butler knocked then opened the door. As they entered, Kang-de saw Sun-hee sitting at Mr. Park's desk.

"Let me guess. Mr. Park you invited Kang-de and Bob, right?"

"Yes, yes, yes. Sun-hee, did you find out who owns the company?" asked Mr. Park while looking at Kang-de facial expression.

"Well, not yet. My friend has not gotten back to me as yet."

"Then go and enjoy the party. Keep me informed as soon as you find out something." Sun-hee nodded her head, walking past the two men. Kang-de and Bob showed no emotion when they looked at Sun-hee walking out the door. Mr. Park closed the door behind her.

"Mr. Park, what did you want to discuss with me?" asked Kang-de.

Before Mr. Park could respond, Minjae knocked on the door and entered the office.

"I'm sorry, Sir. My apology, Mr. Shin, but this is urgent," said Minjae.

"Kang-de, please excuse us, we will talk later. Please enjoy the party," said Mr. Park as he opened the door for Kang-de and Bob to exit.

Minjae waited until Kang-de and Bob left Mr. Park's office. He told Mr. Park that the men who were following Bora at the mall were dead except for one.

Shocked by the news Mr. Park yelled out, "What, how, where, when?"

Minjae informed him that they were found floating in the river with stab wounds.

"Minjae, somebody did not want them talking to us. We need to get to the bottom of this. We need to find the one survivor. I want all my men working on this. I am not going to stand for this. I want my daughter to continue to have twenty-four-hour security. Give my wife the same too. Post guards at all the gates around the house. Check all cars for explosives. When you travel, I want two cars to travel together at a time," yelled Mr. Park. "Minjae, we won't scare the women in this house. Let's keep this our secret. Don't let Bora see you following her."

"Okay, Sir," said Minjae calmly.

Sun-hee walked around the brightly lit pool, admiring its design. At the same time, Woo Jin and Areum walked up the driveway. Woo Jin looked handsome in a dark blue tuxedo trimmed with black satin edges and black shirt and black tie. Areum was dressed in a black satin dress with white and black chiffon overlay. Bora ran to greet them as they entered the foyer.

"Hi, Areum. Come in, come in. You look beautiful."

"This is my friend Kim Woo Jin."

"I have seen you before. Don't I know you?" asked Bora pretending not to remember that Sun-hee and Woo Jin were at her previous party.

"I believe you saw me here with a friend of mine," said Woo Jin smiling.

"Oh, yes," she said walking with them to the living room.

"Bora, your home is beautiful and huge."

"Come let me show you around. Woo Jin, would you like to come too?"

Woo Jin nodded no. "You both go ahead. I will wait here for you, Areum." He took a glass of champagne from a waiter and he went to sit down on a couch by the window.

Kang-de saw Mr. Park walking toward him and he asked him, "What did you want to speak to me about?"

"You supply computers to AZAXCO Pharmaceuticals, don't you?"

"Yeah. Why?"

"Do you know who owns that company?"

"I never asked. I get an order and I ship it. What's wrong?"

"I can't talk about it right now. But I will let you know that you must be careful of the owner. They are doing hostile takeover of many companies. I thought that you would know who the owner was."

"Now you have me curious. Hostile takeover, huh? I will find out. Bob, you have work to do," said Kang-de.

"Yes, Boss."

"Excuse me, Mr. Park. Bob, let us go and have some fun," said Kang-de looking at Bob with a smirk on his face.

Sun-hee saw Woo Jin as she entered the living room. She walked over to him and said, "I didn't know that you were also invited. Did Bora invite you?" she asked. "Is this the party that you were talking about? What a coincidence."

"How are you? You are looking very pretty," said Woo Jin avoiding her many questions.

"Thanks. You didn't answer me. Who invited you? It must be Bora, right?"

"Ah," he stuttered and then sighed as he saw Areum and Bora enter the living room. Bora saw Woo Jin and Sun-hee together and she walked over to them, leaving Areum to watch.

Turning her back to Sun-hee, Bora asked Woo Jin, "Would you like a drink. The waiters are coming around with drinks now."

"Thanks. I will have another glass of champagne," he said looking at Areum with a smile on his face.

Sun-hee, feeling disrespected, slowly walked toward the atrium. Areum glanced at her but she did not notice Areum watching her.

"Woo Jin, this house is huge and beautiful. Don't you want to see it?"

He whispered in her ear, "Not interested."

The waiter came back with a glass of champagne for Woo Jin. Bora and Areum took a glass and the three toasted to each other.

"Woo Jin, could you excuse us for a second?" asked Bora.

"Sure," he said as he sat down and crossed his legs on the couch.

Bora pulled Areum to introduce her to Dave's father, Mr. Jong. He had just arrived from California. Mr. Jong was a tall, well-dressed, muscular man with the appearance of arrogance and vindictiveness on his face. He had a commanding voice that made people fear him when he spoke. His pupil were always dark. No one knew whether he wore contact lenses or his real eyes were black.

Bora grabbed his attention and she introduced Areum. "Areum, this is Mr. Jong, Dave's father."

"Pleased to meet you, Mr. Jong. I have read many articles about you in American magazines."

"Oh, you have? I hope they said nice things about me," said Mr. Jong sarcastically. She had no idea that Mr. Jong could kill her at any time because of what her father knew.

"I have not read any bad things about you," Areum replied.

"Good. Good," said Mr. Jong looking skeptical of what she was saying.

Mr. Jong saw Dave pushing through the crowd and he excused himself, took Dave by the elbow and introduced him to his friend Mr. Chin. "Dave, this is Mr. Chin. He is a very important partner in our business. You will be working with him as soon as you graduate," said Mr. Jong proudly.

"Good evening, Sir. I am pleased to meet you and I hope to work hard so that you can be proud of me."

"Yes, yes. Very good to meet you. I am waiting to work with you very soon," said Mr. Chin, a contract killer hired by Mr. Jong to do anything and everything.

Mr. Park walked into the atrium filled with people and he greeted Mr. Jong with a pretentious smile on his face. "Welcome to my home. Make yourself comfortable. Enjoy yourself."

"Hello, Dave, how are you? Is my daughter keeping you busy?"

Before Dave could reply Mr. Jong introduced his friend Mr. Chin to Mr. Park.

"I hope you don't mind that I brought him with me," said Mr. Jong.

"Of course not, I believe he was at one of my previous party and besides, our children are dating. This is your home. You're both welcome."

"Thank you, Mr. Park," said Mr. Chin looking intrigued.

Earlier, Sun-hee had seen Woo Jin and the strange woman speaking. She watched Bora and Areum walk over to greet Mr. Jong and she slowly went to Woo Jin and asked, "Woo Jin, that girl looked familiar and she acts like she knows you. Do you know her?"

Feeling cornered, Woo Jin replied, "Sun-hee. You are not my mother. Why do you keep asking so many questions? You know that I don't like to answer such questions. Oh, I forget. You are a lawyer. Waiter, another drink, please. And yes, Sun-hee, I do know her. Okay? Please excuse me," he said walking away from Sun-hee.

Stunned that Woo Jin reacted so angrily, Sun-hee left the living room and went back to the pool. The pool was an infinity pool decorated with blue Moroccan tiles and reflective blue and white lights shining from the bottom of the pool.

Areum saw Sun-hee walking away from Woo Jin.

"Bora, who is that girl with Woo Jin? She looks familiar."

"A man stealer," replied Bora. "Her name is Sun hay or Sun-hee. Something like that. She worked for my father and I don't like her. That's all I will say for now."

Kang-de and Bob stood by the Grand piano in the living room observing Mr. Park, Mr. Jong and Mr. Chin speaking with each other. The room was crowded with influential people and heads of government agencies who were all trying to make deals with each other.

"Bob, all the dirty players are in this room. Mr. Park doesn't know who his enemies are. Mr. Jong doesn't know who is friends really are and we are going to watch them all fall on their faces. Bob, look at that jerk Woo Jin. Why is he staring at that man? Do you think that they know each other?" asked Kang-de.

"You never know," said Bob.

Suddenly Kang-de remembered that Woo Jin had bumped into him while chasing after a man who looked like Mr. Chin.

"Bob, I think that guy and Woo Jin know each other. We must find out his name before we leave this party. He looks like a very bad man."

"Boss, this is going to be an interesting game. I can't wait to find out how it all ends for them. Mr. Park does not know that you know Mr. Jong owns AZAXCO Pharmaceuticals and now this Woo Jin man is connected to bad men. Wow," said Bob excitedly.

While Kang-de laughed with Bob he saw Areum walking through the crowd. "Bob, I will be back. I see someone I need to speak with."

Kang-de called Areum by her full name. She turned around and saw Kang-de.

"Hi. How are you? What a coincidence that we are at the same party. Wow. How are you doing?" asked Areum.

"Fine. Let's take a walk," said Kang-de, turning her around.

She looked back to see if Woo Jin was nearby. She wanted to let him know that she would be back. But Woo Jin was not in the living room. He noticed Mr. Chin was staring at him and he followed Mr. Chin to the pool area. He sat at a bar that was located by the pool area. He didn't see Sun-hee standing at the end of the bar. There were too many people crowding the bar area.

Kang-de took Areum to a secluded area of Mr. Parks home. The area had a television, a pool table, a ping pong table and a machine with snacks in it. Kang-de concluded to himself that the area was Mr. Park's game room.

"Areum, I wanted to talk to you for a long time now, but I know that Medical School can be challenging. Wait. Why are you not studying your books tonight?"

"It's okay. I am doing well in school."

"Good. I spoke with your mom recently. It was good speaking with her and your dad. Your dad became a father to me, when I lost my parents. He knew that I had no close relatives so he and your mom were my rock."

Areum looked at him with pity.

"I am so sorry that I didn't attend the funeral. I remembered that your dad was very good to my family. I remember your family parties and I remember how your dad used to give my dad tickets to the various sports games," said Areum smiling.

"Yeah. I know. You only showed yourself at a few of them," he replied. "Do you recall the first day I met you in New York? My face was badly scarred from a campfire explosion at one of our retreats. You looked at me, smiled and said, 'You are very handsome.' You don't know how good I felt that day. The kids at school used to tease me about my looks," he said blinking back tears in his eyes.

"If they could see you now. You have changed a lot. You are still very handsome."

Kang-de smiled as he looked at her with passion in his eyes. "Areum, I would like to take you to dinner, whenever you are free."

"Uh. Yes. Why not?"

"Do you have free time at the end of next week?"

"Sure. I will call you. I still have your card," said Areum.

Woo Jin left the poolside and went searching for Areum. He searched the rooms on the main floor. He went down the stairs and into a closed room where he saw Kang-de and Areum speaking with each other.

Woo Jin interrupted them with an apology. "Excuse me, Areum. I am ready to go."

"Okay, I am coming," she said.

"Did he bring you here?" asked Kang-de in front of Woo Jin.

"Yes. I will call you," she said walking away from him.

Kang-de followed them upstairs and into the atrium. He watched Sun-hee looking at Woo Jin and Areum walk out the door together. Kang-de felt sad for Sun-hee. He could tell that she had feelings for him.

"Hey, Sun-hee, were you not here with that man last time? Did he bring you to this party?"

"No, Kang-de. He did not bring me to this party. And what is it to you?"

"Nothing. Nothing at all," Kang-de said staring at Woo Jin and Areum.

The valet brought Woo Jin's car and he and Areum drove down the long driveway and disappeared into the night. The drive to Bern Dormitory was silent on the way home. Areum turned on the car radio to listen to music. Woo Jin reached over and turned down the radio.

"Areum," said Woo Jin.

"Yeah?"

"What did that man want? Why were you in a game room talking alone with him?"

"Woo Jin, he is a family friend. We have known each other for many years. Don't you remember him from the ITO Hotel restaurant? He looked different than how he looked back in America. He has changed a lot," Areum said.

"I don't want you to see him anymore," he said in a demanding tone.

"Woo Jin, he is a family friend and I don't want you to dictate whom I can and cannot see. Okay?"

"Areum, I want you to be with me always. You know that I like you, right?"

"I don't know what to say. Thank you. You are very kind. I was not sure that you really like me. I thought that you pity me a poor girl amongst a group of happy rich, young, classmates."

"Oh, Areum, money doesn't always make rich people happy. Trust me on this one. More money equals more problems," replied Woo Jin.

"I understand," Areum said as Woo Jin pulled up to Bern Dormitory. "I have to say goodnight now. I need to get rest. I have three exams next week," she said while opening the car door quickly.

Woo Jin, noticing that she was uncomfortable, said goodnight. He watched her open the dormitory door and enter the elevator. He drove home thinking about Areum and Kang-de's encounter at the party.

An hour later at Mr. Park's home, Kang-de said goodnight and Bob drove him to the ITO Hotel. As they drove along the highway, Kang-de said, "Bob, that was an interesting party. Wasn't it?"

"Yeah, Boss. All your enemies were under one roof. It's too bad that you didn't let me and Chul take care of them with one hit."

"Patience, Bob. You know that I don't believe in rushing. I will get my opportunity to destroy each of them one at a time," said Kang-de as he lay back in the car seat.

Observing that Kang-de had left the party, Mr. Jong and Mr. Chin said goodnight to Mr. Park.

"It was a pleasure to see you both. Let's have lunch soon," said Mr. Park.

"We will have lunch as soon as I return from Hong Kong," replied Mr. Jong. He slowly walked out the front door and waited for the valet to bring his car.

"It was a pleasure to see you again, Mr. Park," said Mr. Chin.

"You too, Mr. Chin."

They all stood at the front door watching a long line of cars drive up to the front door.

"We will be back in a few days. Dave, take care of your mother until I return. Bye, Bora. You must come by the house soon," said Mr. Jong.

"Okay, Mr. Jong," Bora replied.

"I am leaving too. Mr. Park, goodnight. I will let you know when I get the information," Sun-hee added unaware that Mr. Jong was listening.

"Yes, you do that, and hurry. I have a feeling something bad is about to happen," Mr. Park said in a concerned tone.

Mr. Park walked into his front door and security closed it behind him. The last guest had left and he grabbed a bottle of champagne and he went into his office and sat down.

Chapter Nineteen

Chul, Kang-de, Bob, Yejoon, Areum, and Woo Jin

Chul called Kang-de early the next morning, while he was having breakfast.

"Hello, good morning."

"Morning, Boss. Last night we followed Yejoon to his hotel room. He had a black briefcase with him. We waited for about half an hour and we saw a man come out of his room with the briefcase. I had one of the men follow him and we stopped him and took the briefcase."

"Did he put up a fight?"

"Yeah, but he was no match for your men."

"Good. Bring the briefcase to me."

"I am downstairs at your hotel," Chul replied.

"Good job, Chul-Moo. Tell the men good job."

Kang-de opened the elevator for Chul to enter his penthouse suite.

Kang-de's penthouse was large with floor-to-ceiling windows, marble tiles, a chef kitchen, chandeliers in every room and four bedrooms with four and a half bathrooms. Each room had private balconies that were attached to each other.

He handed Kang-de the briefcase that he had already opened for security purposes. Kang-de read all the documents and called Sun-hee.

"Kang-de, good morning. How are you? I was just going to call you to let you know that I have good news," she said.

"Well, I am good if you have good news for me."

"It's always such a joy to speak with you, Kang-de," Sun-hee said sarcastically.

"Yeah, yeah. What do you have for me?"

"Yejoon opened two dummy corporations under his name. He used the Gangnam store as collateral. I didn't see anything else filed under his name, but you never know," said Sun-hee. "He received about five million won for his criminal act."

"And yet he stole money from me. I am going to kill that man with my bare hands. I will call you back. Thanks, Sun-hee." Kang-de hung up the phone in a rage. "Chul, have one of the men get Yejoon and take him to the warehouse. I will meet you there."

"Yes, Boss."

"Yejoon, Yejoon, I am going to kill you. You bastard," Kang-de said to himself while looking at the fake contracts in the briefcase.

It took ten minutes for Chul's security to find Yejoon and take him to the warehouse. They had been following Yejoon at Kang-de's instructions. Chul called Kang-de to come to the warehouse. He had Yejoon tied to a steel door.

"Chul, I am on my way. That bastard was about to illegally take my company. I want to know who he was in contact with. Call Bob to meet us over there."

Kang-de and a lot of muscular men arrived at his warehouse. The CFO was still missing. Kang-de saw Yejoon and he grabbed him by the collar and pushed him against the steel door. Yejoon felt the impact from being slammed against the door. He could feel the pain in his ribs.

"Yejoon, why do you want to see the bad side of me?" asked Kang-de. "Why are you forcing me to hurt you? The last time I saw you, I asked you to tell me everything, but you didn't. You kept my contracts. You opened up dummy corporations with my documents. You had better tell me everything now because I am going to use these hands to wrap around your throat in a few minutes," said Kang-de grabbing Yejoon's neck tightly.

"Wait, Boss. Let me do it," said Chul.

"Okay, okay, okay," said Yejoon as Chul grabbed him. "Last year a man came to see me. He said that I owed his boss a lot of gambling debts. I told him that I will pay him as soon as I can. He said that he didn't care. He wanted me to get access to your contracts and open a few corporations. I told him that I didn't have access to your contracts. I told him the CFO had access to everything. He made me take him to the Chief Financial Officer. I threatened the CFO with bodily harm because I was desperate. Boss, I am so sorry."

"Shut up. Keep talking."

"The CFO gave the man all the documents to the Gangnam store that I manage. That's all. Boss, I didn't know that the CFO was helping himself to your money. I did not know that someone hacked into your computer. I swear, Boss."

"Yejoon, do you know what is keeping you alive right now? I want to know who is the man and who is he working for. If you don't tell me, Yejoon, I swear, I will take your life this minute," Kang-de said tightening his hand around Yejoon's neck.

"The man works for Mr. Park. I swear, Boss, I don't know the man's name, but I know he works for Mr. Park. Please, Boss, please don't kill me," said Yejoon barely able to breathe.

"Chul, make him sorry that he stole from me," said Kang-de pushing him to the ground.

Yejoon grabbed his neck and coughed.

"My pleasure, Boss."

Chul pulled him up by his face and he beat Yejoon and threw him in the back of his car. Kang-de and Bob watched Chul and his men drive away with Yejoon, Kang-de asked Bob if he heard what Yejoon said.

"I knew it. I knew that Mr. Park was a snake. I am going to make him real sorry that he ever interfered with my business. I need a strong drink," said Kang-de. "Mr. Park is about to see how wicked I can become. He messed with my father's dream. I am going to make him so, so, so sorry."

Bob drove Kang-de to his nightclub for drinks. As Kang-de entered the door all the workers ran to greet him.

Angrily, Kang-de told them to get back to work. "Somebody bring me a vodka on the rocks. No, make it three glasses of vodka on the rocks. I need to cool my thoughts."

He took two gulps of each glass and swallowed. He wiped his mouth and ordered another glass of vodka. He sat at the bar and thought about how he was going to destroy Mr. Park.

Meanwhile, classes were finished for the day. Areum headed to the library and Woo Jin was already there. She saw Woo Jin and she waved to him.

"Hi, how were your classes today?" asked Areum.

"Great. I might finish school ahead of schedule."

"That's great. I am happy for you," she said in a disappointing voice.

"Areum, we need to talk seriously," said Woo Jin pulling his chair close to hers. "About what?"

"About us. I will be leaving school sooner than expected and I want us to get engaged."

"Engaged. Stop joking. You don't know me that well," she replied.

"I know you well enough to know your character is what I am looking for in a wife. I know that if you were my wife that you would be loyal to me and you would protect me if I needed protection. I know that you are capable of defending yourself and you are not after my money. Areum, I understand why that man likes you. He also sees the good in you."

"Your parents won't approve of me. And my parents, well, I don't know what they will say, " she said.

"Let's go and find out," he said.

"What? I can't leave right now. I have to wait until school recess next week."

"We will wait until then. I am taking you to Hong Kong to meet my parents."

"Hong Kong? Oh, no. I can't afford to go to Hong Kong. I am on scholarship. I want to move out of the dormitory as soon as school ends. I have to save my money," exclaimed Areum.

"I said that I was taking you. I didn't ask you to pay for anything. Did I?"

"Oh. I am sorry. I didn't think before speaking."

"Let's go. I want to take you out tonight. I think that we should celebrate our next step."

"I have not said yes as yet."

"You will," he said smiling.

Areum looked at him in amazement. Woo Jin got his car and took her to KG Nightclub, owned by Kang-de. The club had two levels. Upstairs had VIP private rooms and an office that Bob used for meetings.

The ground level had a dance floor surround by chairs and tables and the DJ was in an enclosed glass booth overlooking the dance floor. The bar was located in a corner opposite the entrance.

"A club. You brought me to a nightclub dressed like this?" she asked looking at her clothes.

"You look fine, Areum. This is not just a nightclub. It has a VIP area and the food here is excellent."

"Okay," she said looking around the nightclub.

A pretty waitress dressed in a black mini skirt and a white blouse, that looked smaller than her size, greeted them at the door. She escorted them to one of the VIP rooms upstairs. The room closest to the stairs was the only one available without reservation. Woo Jin and Areum sat on a circular lounge leather seat with a round table enclosed.

"Waitress, please bring a bottle of the best champagne that you have," said Woo Jin.

"Okay, Sir."

The waitress brought Krug Grande Cuvee. Woo Jin looked at it and nodded his head. The waitress poured the champagne for Areum and Woo Jin.

"I would like to make a toast to you, Areum. You have brought sunshine into my life. I am glad to have met you."

"That's a nice thing to say, Woo Jin. Thank you. I want to toast to you. You have helped me focus on my work and because of you I am prepared for the exams coming up. Thank you very much."

"My pleasure. Let's drink," said Woo Jin raising his glass to toast her.

Areum raised hers and took a sip of the champagne.

Kang-de felt a little buzz from drinking too much vodka and he slowly walked up the stairs to Bob's office to lay on Bob's couch. As he passed by the first room, he saw Areum and Woo Jin in the private room. He tried to turn back but Areum saw him.

"Kang-de, we meet again. How are you?"

"Not good, Areum," he said slowly slurring his speech. "How are you? Hello, Wijun."

"My name is Woo Jin and not Wijun, and you are interrupting my meal."

"Okay. I will let you enjoy your meal," said Kang-de attempting to walk away. Kang-de did not notice that the waiter had walked up behind him, while he was facing Areum.

"Boss, your vodka is ready, and Mr. Bob says that he has the receipts for you to look at in his office," said a waiter.

"Tell him that I am coming."

Surprised by what the waiter just said, Areum asked Kang-de, "Do you own this place?"

"Yes. I own this place," he replied. "Woo Jin, I see that you have an expensive champagne taste."

"Trust me. I can afford it and more," replied Woo Jin.

"I am sure you can. Areum, see you soon," Kang-de said while walking slowly to the office.

"Okay, Kang-de," said Areum.

"I really don't like that guy. I don't care if he is your friend. I don't like him. Does he know who I am? I want to punch the rudeness out of him."

"It's okay, Woo Jin. Don't let him make you angry. He is not a bad person," said Areum as she touched Woo Jin hands to calm him.

Kang-de sat in Bob's office. He looked at the receipts and told Bob that he didn't like Woo Jin.

"That Woo Jin guy is too rude. I could break up that dinner right now by calling Sun-hee, but I won't. The woman I like is eating with him. I want to wipe that arrogance off his face. One day I will. Bob, let's get out of here. I want to plan how I am going to make that Mr. Park pay."

"Where to?" asked Bob.

"Take me to my suite. I have a lot of things to do before bedtime."

Kang-de and Bob walked past Areum and Woo Jin's room. They had closed the door after Kang-de left the room.

Woo Jin and Areum left the nightclub an hour later. He took Areum home and went to his apartment. He thought of inviting her to his home but he decided that it was not a good night to ask her. Instead Woo Jin called his parents to let them know that he would be coming to Hong Kong with a friend.

"Good evening, it's Woo Jin. I want to speak with my mother, please."

"Good evening, Sir. Your parents are in London. They will be back tomorrow. Do you want to leave a message?" asked the butler.

"No, I will call them in London. Thank you."

Woo Jin called his London home and the maid answered the phone and gave it to his mother.

"Hello, my son, is everything okay?"

"Yes, Mama. I am fine. I wanted to let you and Dad know that I am bringing a friend to meet you and Dad."

"When?"

"During school recess."

"Woo Jin. You are not planning on getting … remember Yoo-mi?"

"Mama, I told you that I have no interest in that girl."

"Let's not talk about it right now. Your dad and I will be glad to see you. Bye, honey."

Chapter Twenty

Bora, Areum, Woo Jin, and Sun-hee

Later that evening Bora and Dave went to look for an apartment for the rest of the semester. She wanted to move off campus to a more secure apartment. Bora found an apartment in a gated community with twenty-four-hour security, a barbeque pit and a swimming pool. Dave liked it, but it was late and the rental office was closed. Bora planned to return the next morning to rent it.

Bora rose early to call Areum about the apartment.

"Good morning, Areum. How are you?"

"I am fine. I am a little busy. What's going on?"

"I have a proposal for you. I found an apartment and I want you to come and live with me off campus as soon as you finish school this semester. I am going to move out of the dormitory by this weekend. It has a lot of security and it's safer than the dormitory."

"It sounds good but I have to ask my mom and dad. Let me call you back."

Areum called her parents to get permission to move off campus. Her mother answered the phone.

"Hello?"

"Mom, how are you and Dad?"

"Fine. Are you too busy for your mom and dad?"

"No. I will see you soon. The reason I called you is because I want to move off campus. What do you think?"

"Wait until school is in recess then do it," she said coughing.

"Thanks, Mom. I love you and Dad."

Before hanging up from Areum, Mrs. Lee noticed an echo on the house phone and she told Mr. Lee to check it out. He pretended to examine the phone, but he was already aware that they were being monitored by the same people who hit him in the head in New York City.

Areum called Bora to tell her that she would move in with her as soon as school recessed next week.

"Great. It will be fun. And the maid, Maria, and some of the housekeeping staff will clean before we move in," said Bora.

"The maid? Okay, Bora. My professor changed the schedule. One of my exam is today. I've got to hang up now."

"Good luck. I am off until tomorrow. Dave and I are going to fly to Jeju Island for the day."

"Good for you. I keep forgetting that you rich people have private planes. Enjoy yourselves."

"Oh, stop it, Areum," replied Bora as she hung up on her.

Late that afternoon Areum took her exam and passed it. She called Woo Jin to tell him.

"Hi, Areum, what's going on?" he asked.

"I passed my test. I am so happy," Areum said screaming.

"Great. Congratulations, pretty lady. Uh, Areum, I got a text invitation to go to Brunei for the weekend. They want to interview me to see if I qualify to work on the Oil Rigs. It's only for the weekend. I will be back by Monday or Tuesday."

"That's great, but I will miss you."

"I want to see you later," Woo Jin said.

"I can't. I have something to do. I will call you later."

"Okay. Call me later," said Woo Jin. He gazed at the incoming call from Sun-hee. This time he was happy that she had called because he wanted to speak with her.

"Hello," said Woo Jin.

"I just wanted to hear your voice," said Sun-hee.

"I am glad you called. I want to come and see you. Is that okay?"

"When?" asked Sun-hee.

"In an hour, if it is okay with you?" Woo Jin replied.

"Let me clear my calendar. You can come after two hours. I will cancel my appointments and go home."

Excited that Woo Jin was coming to her home, Sun-hee rushed home, took a shower and got dressed. She prepared a meal and anxiously awaited Woo Jin's arrival. She dreamed of having another sexual encounter with him.

Woo Jin arrived at Sun-hee's home twenty-minutes late. He rang the bell and she opened the door for him. She hugged him and kissed him on the cheek.

"Nice to see you. Make yourself comfortable. Would you like something to drink?"

"No, thanks. I have something to say and I need to say it now. Sun-hee, I can't see you intimately anymore. I met someone that I like and I want to see where it will lead. We can be friends but not intimate friends."

"Woo Jin. How could you say something like this to me? We were having a great time. We satisfy each other well, so why are you being like this?" Sun-hee asked sadly.

"I told you why. We can't have three people in a relationship. It doesn't work. I am sorry, Sun-hee. I wish only good things for you."

Sun-hee began to cry. She grabbed Woo Jin's arm as he tried to leave. "Please, don't do this to me. Please."

"Sun-hee, I am sorry I have to go. Let me go."

Woo Jin pulled her hands off his arm and he walked out of her house and closed the door. Sun-hee fell to the floor sobbing. It took her twenty minutes to get up from the floor. The break-up didn't make any sense to her. They were having so much fun, she thought to herself.

"I can't give him up, not now, "said Sun-hee talking to herself. She thought about what she could do to get Woo Jin back. She wanted to have her friends at the police department run a background check on Areum. She wanted to speak with anyone who knew Areum.

She thought about getting pregnant so that he would have to stay with her. She thought about contacting Woo Jin's mother to have her break up the relationship between Woo Jin and Areum. She was desperate to keep him at any cost.

Chapter Twenty-one

Kang-de, Areum, Bora, and Woo Jin

Kang-de thought about Areum all day. He was looking forward to the moment when he could be with her privately. He picked up his cell phone several times during the day to call her, but he didn't want her to think that he was desperate. He waited until she arrived home from the clinic, then he called her. When she answered, he asked timidly, "Do we still have a date today?"

"Of course. When do you want to meet?"

"In about an hour. I will send the driver to pick you up," he said in a delighted tone.

"No. Give me two hours," Areum said hesitantly. She took a shower, changed her clothes, changed her hair style, applied on makeup and waited for the driver.

The driver had arrived twenty minutes earlier and he waited for the exact time to call her. Areum slowly walked out the door and into the waiting car. He drove Areum to a yacht by the bay. It was the prettiest yacht that was at the dock. She walked down the plank to a yacht with the name "Cool Breeze."

As she stopped to look at the name she heard Kang-de yell, "Areum. Up here!"

A crewmember held her hand as she walked up the stairs and onto the boat.

"Hi, Kang-de. Don't tell me that you hired a yacht to take me out to eat?"

"No. I am using my yacht to take you out to eat."

"Sorry. I keep forgetting that I am the poor one."

"Oh, come on, Areum. I inherited a lot of this from my parents. Now let's start over. Welcome, Miss Areum. I am honored to have you dining with me tonight."

"Thank you, Mr. Shin," she said, feeling embarrassed.

"May I show you around?"

"Sure," she said walking slowly behind him.

"This yacht can accommodate three couples and a crew. It has a mini green for golfing and it carries a small dingy. Now, let's go and eat. I don't want to bore you anymore."

"Kang-de, it is beautiful. I love the glass panels and the big rooms."

The crewmembers brought lobsters, shrimps, scallops, salmon, champagne, wine, vegetables, salads and rice for them to eat. They served Kang-de and Areum and then they placed the foods on the dining table.

"It's okay now. Thank you. I will call you if I need you," Kang-de said to the crew. "Areum, let's eat." He poured crystal champagne for Areum and himself. "I am so happy that you are here."

Kang-de felt his heart beat rapidly as he looked at Areum. They held up their champagne glasses and Kang-de made the first toast.

"To Areum, the young lady who stole my heart so long ago."

"To Kang-de, I am happy that you are here in Seoul. Cheers." While they ate, Areum asked, "Kang-de, is it okay if I ask you, how did your parents die? My dad refused to say anything about how they died."

"They were in a train derailment. The conductor fell asleep at the wheel. Their compartment turned over with a few others. They were thrown from the train. That's what I was told by the police."

"I am so sorry, Kang-de. You must feel so lonely. You have no siblings. What about your grandparents, are they still alive?" she asked curiously.

"My father's parents died many years ago. My mother's parents died recently of old age. They died three months apart from each other. I think they felt guilty for my parents' death because my mom and dad were on their way to see them."

"My heart goes out to you."

"Please don't pity me. I have learned to be strong because I am alone in this world."

"May I hug you? I really feel badly. Your parents were so nice. I am really sorry."

Areum hugged him and he had tears in his eyes. She felt the warmth of his body and his muscles rubbed on her chest. Her heart skipped a beat as she embraced him. Suddenly he released her from the hug.

"I am sorry, Areum. When I think about them it makes me very sad. They didn't get to enjoy their retirement."

"Cry if you want. It's okay for a man to cry. Let me keep hugging you on behalf of my parents. I feel your pain," she said.

Kang-de felt his heart skip a beat and he gently moved away from her arms. "Areum, I am sorry I did not bring you here to cry on your shoulders. I am sorry. Let's change the conversation."

"Stop it. I am sad too. I liked your parents a lot. Let me mourn with you. Again I am truly sorry that I was not here to attend the funeral."

"It's okay. Your mom and dad were by my side. Dignitaries from around the world came to pay their respects. There were some strange looking men there too. But, it was a good funeral," he sighed. "Areum, enough of the morbid times. How have you really been. I want to know what is happening in your life. Anything big as yet?"

"Not yet. But a few weeks ago some men tried to kidnap me and Bora from the mall, but we got away."

"What? And you are telling me at this late time?" his voice said in a loud tone.

"Bora's family took care of it. Mr. Park gave her twenty-four-hour protection."

"And you, what did you get? I am sure nothing," said Kang-de in a disgusted tone as he walked to the table to get his cell. "I will change that right now."

"It's okay, Kang-de, I don't need protection. No one is looking to kidnap me," she said calmly.

"Areum. You are always with Bora, right? That puts you in danger. Listen, Areum, I will do what I have to do to protect you. I am not asking you if you would like protection. I am giving you protection," he said with a stern look. "I promise that my men will not be obvious. And they won't interfere with your medical work. You will be okay. As for that rude man, why did he not provide security for you? Areum, are you serious about him?"

"Well, he wants me to meet his parents," said Areum.

"Oh. I see. Don't rush anything. Okay?"

"I won't."

While Kang-de's punched numbers into his phone, a call came in and it was Chul-Moo.

"Excuse me, Areum, I have to take this call. Hello, Chul. Did you find him?"

"No, Boss. He is still missing."

"Okay, keep looking. By the way, Chul, I am going to need a few of your men to guard a friend of mine. I will give you the details tomorrow."

Suddenly, Areum felt the boat moving.

"Excuse me, Kang-de, the boat is moving."

"Yes. We are going out to sea for a short time. Put on the life vest," he said as he handed it to her. "I want you to see the beauty of this place."

Kang-de escorted Areum on deck and he stood next to her shoulder to shoulder. A crewmember brought a blanket for Areum, and Kang-de wrapped her in it. Her heart tugged again when his hands touched her shoulders.

"It's okay, Kang-de, I can manage."

Areum's phone rang and it was Woo Jin calling. "Hello, Woo Jin."

"Where are you?" he said in a rough tone.

"I am with a friend."

Kang-de looked at her and smiled.

"I want to see you later. Don't forget that I am leaving tomorrow."

"No. I will see you tomorrow. I have something to do tonight."

"Okay. Whatever you say. Goodnight."

"Goodnight, Woo Jin."

"Looks like we have all night to ourselves. Let 's go see Seoul. That is, if you don't mind?" said Kang-de.

"No. I don't mind. I have not seen this city in a long time."

"Okay, let's go."

They sailed away from the harbor for two hours.

When the boat returned to the dock, Kang-de's driver stood by the car door, waiting for them. The driver took them to the airport where a private plane took them to Jeju Island. Areum felt excited. It was her first time on a private jet..

"Is this plane yours too?" asked Areum.

"If I say no, will you feel better?"

"Wow. You have a plane too?" she said looking with disbelief.

"Areum, I have something to tell you. Your parents are coming to Seoul during your school recess. Your mom wanted it to be a surprise. I don't want you to think that I deceived you, so I am telling you now."

"Kang-de, thank you for telling me. Where are they staying? I have no place to put them."

"Oh, Areum, they are staying at my hotel. Nothing is too good for your mom and dad."

"Thank you, Kang-de. I really appreciate everything that you have done for my parents."

Kang-de and Areum arrived in Jeju Island and he checked in at the hotel. They had adjoining rooms overlooking the beach. Kang-de decided not to tell her that he owned an apartment on the island.

"We can't stay very long. I have to get back in the morning and so do you. Let's go for tea and coffee."

As they drank tea and coffee, Areum asked Kang-de about his personal life.

"Do you have a girlfriend? You are a gorgeous man with beautiful eyes and a pretty smile and you are rich. I am sure that you have had many ladies chasing after you."

He turned his head away from her and smiled. "Do I have to answer that question?" he asked looking at her.

She nodded.

"Okay, yes. I have had several ladies trying to marry me, but my heart belongs to one person and that will never change."

Areum pretended that she did not hear Kang-de's statement.

He noticed that she looked embarrassed and he told her to finish her tea so that they could take a walk along the beach. Areum finished her tea and followed him out of the hotel lobby. He gently took her hand and held it, as they stroll along the walkway. Areum looked down at her hand as Kang-de held it tightly.

"You don't mind me holding your hand, do you?" he asked.

"No. It's okay."

Kang-de squeezed her hand and smiled as he walked with Areum.

"Kang-de, this place is really beautiful. I didn't know that this place existed in South Korea. The water is so nice. I am happy that I came."

"You don't know how happy I am to hear you say that. We could do a lot more trips like this. It's up to you. Wow, look at the time. Let's get some rest."

Kang-de wanted to be intimate with Areum but he told himself that it was not the right time or place and it would be disrespectful to her.

The morning came quickly and Kang-de knocked on Areum's hotel room. She opened the door and he waited for her to come out. Within minutes, they left for the airport and the jet took off for Seoul. Upon arrival, Kang-de's driver took them to ITO Hotel.

"I had a wonderful time. I hope that you did too," he said.

"I had a beautiful time with you. I would love to do it again. If you don't mind?" said Areum.

"I am so happy to hear that you enjoy being with me, Areum. Driver, please take Ms. Lee to Bern Dormitory. Wait for her and then take her to the clinic."

"Thanks, Kang-de. See you soon."

The driver took Areum to Bern Dormitory and then to the clinic. Bora was already at the clinic when Areum arrived.

"Hey, where have you been all night? I wanted to fill you in on the apartment. I spent the night there last night against my dad's wishes. Dave was there with me and of course a few bodyguards. They were outside of the apartment. I had to agree for them to stay. My dad would not have allowed me to stay there without security."

"Great. Does Dave like the apartment?" asked Areum.

"Yeah. He loves it. Areum, we are going to have lots of fun there."

"Okay, Bora." Areum's phone rang and it was Woo Jin. He was at the airport and he was leaving for Brunei.

"Hello. I called you early this morning. Where were you?" he said quickly as he walked to the boarding gate.

Areum answered, "I was out with my friends in Gangnam. I am sorry that I didn't hear the phone ring."

"I am not going to ask who your friends are because I don't want to get upset. I am leaving for Brunei and I will call you when I get there. I may be back Monday or Tuesday. I want you to go and stay at my apartment until I get back."

"What about your roommate?"

"He is no longer there and I had the locks changed and the door-man is aware that you will be there."

"Okay, and I am sorry that I am not there to see you off," Areum added.

"Well, it's best that I don't see you because if I do, I am going to think about you all the time. I miss you already," he said sadly.

"Focus on the interview. Have a safe journey. I will look after your apartment while you are gone."

"Okay. I love you, Areum."

"Safe travel to you."

Chapter Twenty-two

Areum, Sun-hee, Woo Jin, Bora, and Kang-de

Areum went to stay at Woo Jin's apartment. She attempted to clean his apartment, but she looked around and realized that Woo Jin kept a very clean and organized home. While she cooked a meal, the bell rang at Woo Jin's home and Areum opened the door without looking at the door camera to see who it was. When she opened the door a stranger asked for Woo Jin. Areum told herself that it was not a stranger. It was that pretty girl that was at Bora's party Sun-hee. She was talking to Woo Jin at Bora's home.

"May I speak with Woo Jin, please?"

"He is not home. May I take a message?"

"What are you doing here?" asked Sun-hee.

"Are you questioning me?" Areum asked. "I should ask you what you are doing here."

"I am Woo Jin's girlfriend. Didn't he tell you? We have been dating for a long time."

Areum looked stunned after hearing Sun-hee's words. She was speechless. Unable to respond to Sun-hee, she closed the door. Sun-hee yelled through the door that she would return when Woo Jin got home. Areum stood at Woo Jin's door for several minutes before slowly walking to the living room. Lots of questions for Woo Jin rushed in her head. She picked up the phone to call him. Confused about what to say, to him, she threw the phone on the table. It took her several minutes before she could process what Sun-hee said. She called Bora.

"Bora, I have a big problem. Can you come over? I am staying at Woo Jin's house for the weekend. I will text you the address."

Bora went to see Areum immediately. "Areum, what's so important that you could not tell me on the phone?"

"The girl that was at your party, she came here. Do you remember her? You said that her name was Sun-hee or something like that?"

"What did she want?" asked Bora.

"She said that she was looking for Woo Jin and that she was his girlfriend. I am so upset with Woo Jin right now, but I don't think that I will say anything to him. We are heading to Hong Kong so I don't want to start any trouble."

"Areum, you have to tell him what happened. Do not leave him in the dark. That Sun-hee is a crazy girl. She had an affair with my dad. My mother found out and threatened to take away all his money and his businesses around the world. And that is what stopped him. My dad still works with her because she a very good lawyer. I don't know how true it is, but I heard that, years ago, she tried to kill herself while she was an intern at my dad's legal department. Oh, Areum. I don't speak to her unless I have to. She is a man stealer in every sense of the word. Be careful of her, Areum."

"Thanks, Bora, but I am not afraid of her. She can do whatever she wants so long as she doesn't bother me. Bora, I will tell Woo Jin that she stopped by to see him."

"Yeah, do that. And look at his face when you tell him. You will know if he is still seeing her by the expression of guilt on his face," Bora added.

"I have never had a real boyfriend before. I am not sure what to do about this. If I were to think about it, he is not my boyfriend. He told me that he wanted me to meet his parents, but I am not sure what that really means. Yes, I know that they have to approve of me, but I am not sure what will become of us."

"You have been living in the U.S.A. too long. Our parents approve everything here. Dave had to be approved by my parents and I got approved by Dave's parents."

"Yes. You both match each other in finance and in status. I don't match Woo Jin. I can't match him. He is rich and my parents are barely middle class. In fact they are more on the poor side. We have no status. This is why I have to become a doctor. Bora, you know that I liked Woo Jin even before I found out that he had money. I don't care about other people's money. I was taught to work and make my own way. I am not depending on any man to validate me. I would love to be with a man who loves me for myself. I am not the prettiest girl but I think that I know how to make a man feel like a king."

"Well, good luck to you. After you have finished talking to Woo Jin call me."

Bora called Minjae to tell him that she was ready to go home. Minjae parked in front of Woo Jin's apartment and Bora got in the back seat. They drove off without noticing the two men in the black car parked across the street.

It's Tuesday and Woo Jin Is Home

Woo Jin arrived home late in the afternoon with flowers in his hands and a box of chocolate. "Areum, I missed you. How are you?" he said while hugging and kissing her on the cheek.

"I am fine. How was your trip?"

"Great, they liked me and I have the job if I want it. Are you okay? You look unhappy."

"A woman came to ask for you."

"Did she give her name?"

"No, and I didn't ask. She did say that she was your girlfriend."

"What?" asked Woo Jin.

"Woo Jin, what's going on with you? I don't want to be with a man who has another woman."

"Areum, I will find out what's happening and then we will talk. Stay here. I will be back."

Woo Jin went to see Sun-hee at her office. He parked his car, slammed the door and stormed into the elevator. Woo Jin walked past her secretary who tried to tell him that Sun-hee was with a client. Woo Jin stormed into Sun-hee's office while the secretary ran behind him, yelling for him to stop.

"What the hell do you think you are doing coming to my home and harassing my girlfriend?" he said pushing the door wide open.

"Woo Jin, what are you talking about? I went to return an item that you left at my home."

"An item, huh. When did I leave an item at your home?" he asked as he looked around and noticed Kang-de in the corner listening to them. "Hey, you may want to leave. I need to speak with this lady in private."

"No. You leave. I am paying her to look about my business and we are talking here. You get out and wait until I am finished with her," Kang-de said in an irritating tone.

"I am not leaving. I need to talk with Sun-hee now."

"Listen very carefully, Go and wait outside until I am done with her. And you better not be cheating on my Areum. I am not going to allow that. You got that?" he said pointing his fingers at Woo Jin. "Who the hell do you think you are talking to? Do you know who I am?"

"Who the hell are you to talk to me like this?" asked Woo Jin.

"I am Shin Kang-de, and I am telling you that I don't care who the hell you are. Sun-hee, take your boyfriend outside and talk because I am not leaving this office. You have exactly five minutes to sort out your mess."

"Please come with me, Woo Jin. He doesn't need to hear what we are talking about." Sun-hee slowly pushed Woo Jin out of the office. Woo Jin looked at Kang-de and smiled as he left her office.

"Our friendship was a mistake. And I am sorry if I encouraged you, but you need to move on with your life. Let's not see each other anymore," Woo Jin said looking at Sun-hee.

"Woo Jin, stop saying that. I love you and I think that you love me. Let's try to work things out. I promise that I will never go to your home without your permission. I am sorry. I had no idea that she was there," she replied.

"Sun-hee, listen to me. I don't want a relationship with you ever again. Do you understand?"

Woo Jin walked away from Sun-hee who was crying. Kang-de looked at his watch and opened the office door. He saw Sun-hee crying and he held her in his arms and consoled her.

"WHAT IS IT WITH YOU WOMEN AND THAT GUY? Stop crying. We have work to do. He is not worth your tears, Sun-hee."

She wiped her eyes and went back into the office with Kang-de. "I am sorry, Kang-de. That should never have happened in front of you. I am sorry."

"It's okay, Sun-hee. That guy irritates me whenever I see him. One day he and I are going to have a good talk. Let's continue. Have you found out anything else about my company?"

"All the documents that were found show that your company is still in your name. We check and re-checked and everything show that an attempt was made to infiltrate your company but it was not successful. Yejoon and his friends were not successful in using the Gangnam store as collateral."

"Were CFO, Mr. Park and Yejoon the only culprits?" Kang-de asked.

"I can only say to you hypothetically, what if a CFO was living at one of my clients' apartments? I cannot say anymore because it might become a legal issue later. I don't want that. You have your men do the research."

"Okay, you have told me enough. I will take this information and work on it. Sun-hee, you will have to leave one of us eventually. It's either going to be Me or Mr. Park. You can't have both of us as your client after today. Your life may be in danger after today," said Kang-de.

"I know. I have to do one thing for Mr. Park then I'm going to quit."

"Okay, be careful. I am leaving now. Are you going to be okay after what happened earlier with that jerk Woo Jin?"

"Yes, I will be okay. Thank you, Kang-de, for your support."

"Bob, the CFO is hiding at one of Mr. Park's apartment. No wonder Chul couldn't find him. Tell Chul to check Mr. Park's hidden apartments and find that bastard."

"Okay, Boss. We will find him."

Kang-de thought about what happened at Sun-hee's office. He thought about Woo Jin and Areum's relationship. He picked up his cell and called her.

"Hi, Areum, are you alright? Is everything okay with you? You would tell me if you were unhappy. Right?"

"Sure, Kang-de. I am fine. I am studying for exams coming up this week."

"Okay. Study hard. Your security has started. Bye."

Woo Jin walked into his home and overheard the conversation with Areum and someone who he guessed to be Kang-de. He waited until she closed her cell phone and he took her by the hand. He looked her in the eyes and apologized to her for any misunderstanding that occurred.

She accepted his apology and he took her to a rooftop restaurant. The view was beautiful and they could see as far as one mile away. They spent the time talking, eating, drinking non-alcohol beverages and holding hands.

Chapter Twenty-three

Bora, Dave, Mr. Jong, Chin, and Mr. Park

Bora was doing patient visitation at the clinic when she saw one of the men that tried to kidnap her. She hesitated and then walked past him to take a better look at him. He did not notice that she was watching him and she ran outside to call one of her bodyguards.

The man was holding his side while blood seeped through his fingers. Suddenly he saw the bodyguard and ran outside. Dave was at the clinic to pick up Bora when the man ran in front of Dave's car. Dave noticed the man as one of his father's driver.

"Hey, hey, stop. It's me, Dave Jong. What is the matter with you?"

The man looked at Dave and he continued to run. Bora and her bodyguard ran behind the man. Dave saw Bora running and he ran with her.

"Bora, what's happening?"

"That is one of the guys who tried to kidnap me. Get him."

Dave stopped running and told himself that Bora was mistaken because that was one of his father's driver. She had to be mistaken. Bora returned to Dave exhausted from chasing the kidnapper.

"We lost him. He got into a car and it took off down the road. Did you recognize him?" she asked Dave.

"No," said Dave pretending that he didn't know the man who tried to kidnap Bora. "Bora, who did you say he was?"

"I told you. He was one of the men who tried to kidnap me. I am going to call my dad."

"Oh, okay. I will see you later. I have something to do," he said while running to his car with his cell phone in his hand. Dave called his dad, Mr. Jong.

"Hi, Dad, what's going on? I just saw one of your driver at Bora's job. She said that he was one of the persons who tried to kidnap her? What's happening, Dad? How is that possible?"

"That's absurd, but I will find out and tell you what's happening as soon as I get home tomorrow. Do not panic."

The line went dead.

"Dad, Dad. Talk to me now," said Dave.

There was silence at the other end of the phone. Mr. Jong had hung up. Dave thoughts turned to Bora and what she saw today. He had to find out what was happening before speaking with Bora again.

Bora called her father to tell him that she saw one of the men who tried to kidnap her at the clinic. "Dad, I saw one of the men who tried to grab me at the mall. Send some people to look for him," said Bora in an anxious tone.

"It's okay, Bora. I have my men on it. One of the guards already told me what happened."

"Dave helped me chase the man, but we lost him," she said breathing rapidly.

"Don't worry. It won't be long until we find him. Come home, Bora."

"Not yet, Dad. I am going to stay at my place. Dave is coming over and the guards are there."

"Bora, I do not want you staying there. I can keep you safe at the house. You are so stubborn. I insist that you come home until this is over. It is not a good thing to have Dave spend the night."

"Do you know what is happening? I want to know why someone was trying to kidnap me. That man was injured. I don't think he was there to kidnap me this time. Dad, can you answer any of my questions?"

"No, Bora. I cannot answer any of your questions at this time. As soon as I find out what is happening, I will tell you. Right now, I want you to spend the night at home with your mother and me. I am not asking you. I am telling you. Have Dave come here to see you if necessary."

"Okay, okay. I will call Dave. I will see you later."

Bora told Dave that she was going to stay at her parents' home and he was welcome to visit her there. Dave was still trying to process what happened at the clinic. He felt upset with his Dad. He could not understand why his Dad's driver would want to kidnap Bora. He went to see Bora at Mr. Park's home.

"Bora, are you really okay? I am in shock. Why would someone try to kidnap you?" asked Dave.

"I don't know," replied Bora.

Mr. Park overheard the conversation between Bora and Dave as he walked into his library. He blurted out that somebody was trying to kidnap his daughter to get to him.

"I will find out who is trying to harm my child and I will be merciless to them."

Dave looked at Mr. Park and walked away before Mr. Park noticed the look of guilt on his face.

"I hope that you find out soon, Mr. Park. I will ask my father for help."

"No. No. No, Dave. I will handle this on my own. Thank you. You two continue talking. I am going out for a while." Mr. Park paused then said, "Bora, do not leave this house."

Dave remained with Bora for several hours until he went home to confront his father.

Mr. Jong Is Home

Dave walked into his father's office and saw Mr. Jong talking on the phone. He signaled to Dave to have a seat at his desk while he finished his conversation. He hung up the phone, got up and walked over to the chair where Dave sat.

"Good evening, my son. Tell me what happened. Who did you say you saw and where?"

"Someone tried to kidnap Bora a few days ago and they were not successful. She was at the clinic yesterday and one of the men was at the clinic getting attended to for a stab wound. She said that she can identify him. Dad, I saw one of your driver and he is the man Bora said tried to kidnap her. What is going on, Dad? I need to know."

"I am not sure. I did not approve any kidnapping. I would never have my future daughter-in-law kidnapped."

"Stop lying to me. I don't believe you."

"Dave, watch your mouth. I have no reason to lie to you. Everything that I have done in my life has been for your benefit. I want you to believe that."

"Dad please do not bring family into whatever you are doing. Family can get hurt. Remember that. I am leaving now," said Dave.

The office door closed and Mr. Jong called Mr. Chin to ask who let the driver escape.

"He was not supposed to survive. How did he get away?" asked Mr. Jong. "It's a mess now. I have to call Mr. K. and tell him what's happening. My son's girlfriend can identify him. Take care of him. I don't want him being traced back to me or the organization. Do you understand?"

"Yes, Sir. I will take care of it," said Chin.

Chapter Twenty-four

Sun-hee, Mr. Park, Minjae, Kang-de, Areum, CFO, and Mrs. Lee

Sun-hee went to see Mr. Park to tell him that the Chief Executive Officer of AZAXCO Pharmaceuticals was Mr. Jong. He was very angry.

"So that bastard really owns AZAXCO Pharmaceuticals?"

"Yes, his company consists of seven Board of Directors and his son Dave owns a lot of stocks in the company. Even though they are a vast conglomerate, it was very difficult to obtain information on them."

"Good job, Sun-hee. Thank you," said Mr. Park.

"If I didn't have an inside friend, I would never know this information. It is like a secret society," Sun-hee said intrigued by the complexity of Mr. Jong's company.

"Thank you again, Sun-hee. You just verified what I suspected for a long time. I will handle it now."

"Ah, Mr. Park, now that you have all the information that you need, I will not be representing you any longer. I thank you for your support."

"What? What is the meaning of this? I did not tell you that you can cancel our agreement."

"I have the right to decline representation if I choose to. I do thank you for your help with starting my law firm. Let's just say that we both paid our debts to each other. Goodbye, Mr. Park."

"Sun-hee, come back here. Sun-hee, Sun-hee," yelled Mr. Park.

Mr. Park called Minjae immediately after Sun-hee left his office. He informed him that Mr. Jong was the owner of AZAXCO Pharmaceuticals.

"Wow, Boss, it is as you suspected. You knew who the owner of AZAXCO company was."

"Let's not discuss it over the phone. Meet me at the apartment. You know which one I am talking about."

"Okay, Boss."

The apartment was located on a third-floor walk-up. It had a bed, a television and a small kitchen. The building was abandoned, except for one occupant. Kang-de's CFO had been hiding there for several weeks undetected. Mr. Park and Minjae arrived behind each other.

Unknown to Mr. Park, Kang-de's men followed him to the building and they watched Mr. Park and Minjae walk up to the third floor. CFO jumped up from the old broken down chair that he was sitting in.

"How are you?" said Mr. Park. Before CFO could respond, Mr. Park said, "I have work for you today."

"Whose work, Mr. Shin?" asked CFO.

"No, no. That rat Mr. Jong. He has been trying to take over my company. Let's see what we can do to take his companies away from him. Here are some documents that you can start working on."

"Okay, Boss. What about Mr. Shin? He is still looking for me?"

"Don't worry. He won't find you. No one knows about this place. I will be in touch. You have everything that you need here," said Mr. Park while walking to the door.

"Boss," said Minjae. "Mr. Jong really owns AZAXCO Pharmaceuticals? That is real interesting. What should we do about him?"

"Nothing. CFO is going to find out if he has any outstanding credits and I am going to buy all of his debts. Also, CFO knows the Chief

Financial Officer of AZAXCO and he will get all the information we need to acquire as much shares in his company," replied Mr. Park. "If I can't destroy him, then I will make his life terrible. He will know that I tried to take his company."

"Your plan sounds great," said Minjae with excitement.

They walked downstairs to Mr. Park's car and they drove away without noticing Kang-de's men watching their movements.

One of Kang-de's men was sitting in a car a few meters away from where the CFO was hiding. He watched Mr. Park and Minjae leave the apartment building. He called Kang-de immediately after their car drove away.

"Hello, did you find him?" asked Kang-de.

"Yes, Boss. He is staying in an old apartment building. There are guards everywhere and Mr. Park just left."

"Keep your eyes on the building. Don't do anything until I tell you. Call Chul and let him know what's going on. Thank you," said Kang-de.

Moments later Kang-de's phone rang. It was Areum's mother.

"Hello, Mrs. Lee. How are you? Is everything okay?"

She replied, "If you do not mind, I would like to come see Areum now."

"I don't mind, Mrs. Lee. It is fine. You said that you will take the train. But, I will send the jet for you tomorrow. You will stay at my hotel. I cannot wait to see you," said Kang-de with anticipation.

Kang-de called Areum to tell her the good news.

"Areum. Your mom says that she is coming alone tomorrow because your dad is not feeling well."

"So why is she coming? She should stay with my father."

"I didn't suggest that to her. It is not my place. Come on, Areum. Be happy you have a mother who wants to see you. I wished that I had my mother and father right now."

"I am sorry, Kang-de. I was being insensitive. I was not thinking. Sorry. I will call her."

"She will be here at 4 P.M. tomorrow. I will send the driver to pick you up and take you to meet her."

"Can I bring Woo Jin with me to the airport?"

"No. You go with my driver to meet your mother. Maybe this weekend you can bring WIJUN to see your mom."

"Okay, I will bring Wooooooo Jin to greet my mom this weekend. Don't call him Wijun. That's childish."

"Okay, Miss Areum," he replied sarcastically.

The night turned into day quickly and Mrs. Lee arrived at the local airport. The driver and Areum saw her. Areum ran to greet her mother.

"Mama. How are you? I have missed you so much. How is Dad?"

"If you miss me so much, then you need to come and see me and Dad."

"Sorry, Mama. I have been busy with medical school," said Areum as she entered the car.

They held hands as the driver took them to Kang-de's hotel.

The driver glanced in the rearview mirror and noticed a silver SUV had been following him since he left the airport parking lot. On cue, Mrs. Lee and the driver nodded at each other and he quickly sped down the exit ramp. The SUV continued along the highway. Areum who was busy telling her Mother about medical school was unaware of what just occurred.

The car pulled up in front of the hotel at six o'clock and Mrs. Lee slowly got out and walked into the hotel lobby. She looked around in awe of the beautiful lobby. She noticed the tall columns covered in glass, the grand staircase on the right. She raised her head to look up at the balcony that overlooked the lobby and she saw the beautiful marble tiles that expanded throughout the lobby.

"This is a beautiful hotel. Where is Kang-de?" she asked.

"I don't know. Clerk, what room is Mrs. Lee in? I believe that she has already checked in," asked Areum.

"Miss, I believe that the room had been changed. One minute, please. Oh, yes. She has a suite," replied the hotel desk clerk.

"Wow! Mom, a suite," exclaimed Areum. "Thank you, Miss."

Mrs. Lee and Areum went up to the twentieth floor. They opened the door and saw Kang-de sitting in the living room with a bottle of champagne.

"Welcome, Mrs. Lee. Make yourself comfortable. How are you? How is Mr. Lee? I hope feeling better. Did you have a good flight?"

Mrs. Lee gave Kang-de a hug and she began to cry.

"I wished that your parents were here to see how wonderful and successful you have become. Thanks, Kang-de."

"Mrs. Lee, we are having dinner in here tonight. I know that you must be tired. Areum, I had the maid prepare the other room for you to stay the night. I already checked, you do not have classes tomorrow."

"Mr. Shin Kang-de, are you checking up on me?" she asked smiling.

The doorbell rang and the chef was standing at the door with lots of waiters. They brought lots of different foods for Mrs. Lee to eat.

"Bring it in. guys. Thank you. Mrs. Lee, Areum, come and eat."

It took them one hour to finish eating. Kang-de noticed that Mrs. Lee didn't eat a lot. Kang-de looked at her with concern in his eyes because she had a terrible cough.

After dinner was finished, Kang-de toasted to Mr. and Mrs. Lee's health. Mrs. Lee walked to the window, looked out at the view, then she turned around and looked at Kang-de and Areum.

"Areum, I came early because I wanted to speak to you and Kang-de together. First thing, Kang-de, I want you to call me Mom. Areum, your dad and I have discussed this for a few years now. We spoke with Kang-de's parents who had given their blessing as well. We want you and Kang-de to get married sometime in the future. Kang-de, do you like my daughter?"

"Mom! What are you saying?" asked Areum in an embarrassed tone.

"Yes or no, Kang-de," asked Mrs. Lee insisting that she get an answer immediately.

"Ah. Yes, Mom, I do like her very much, but I think this a conversation for the two of you only. I am going to say bye now. If you need me I will be upstairs." Kang-de began to walk slowly to the door feeling embarrassed that he had just confessed his feelings for Areum in front of her mother.

"Kang-de, stay," Mrs. Lee said firmly.

"Kang-de, it's fine, go. I will see you later," Areum said embarrassed.

He walked out the door and closed it behind him and stood at the door for a while.

"Mom, why do you want me and Kang-de to get together? I have someone else that I like very much."

"What? I have known Kang-de since he was a baby. He grew into a wonderful man. Areum, he is handsome, loving, very loyal and rich. How could you not want a man like him?" asked Mrs. Lee snapping at Areum.

"I never said that I didn't like him. I like him a lot, but Woo Jin has my heart. Mom, I am sure that you will like Woo Jin when you meet him."

"No. He is not your match. Kang-de is your match. Listen to me, Areum. When a man loves you, you had better hold on to him tightly. Do you know for certain that this Woo Jin man loves you? Tell me," she asked abruptly.

"Mom, I know that I love Woo Jin. Please let's not discuss this anymore."

"Tell me about this Woo Jin man. What does his parents do? Where is he from? What do you really know about him or them?"

"I will let you ask him. He will be here this weekend."

"Areum, it has been decided. We are your parents we know who is best for you."

"Mom, let's not argue. I am happy that you are here with me. Let's not fight, please."

Areum's phone rang and Woo Jin was calling to determine her location.

"Areum, where are you?"

"I am with my mother. She wants to see you this weekend."

"Good. I want to meet her too."

"I will speak with you later," said Areum while looking at her mother's expression. "Mom please don't come to any conclusion until you meet Woo Jin."

"Okay," said Mrs. Lee secretly clenching her stomach as she cough.

Chapter Twenty-five

Kang-de, Bob, Chul, Woo Jin, Mrs. Kim, Areum,
Mrs. Lee, Mr. Kim, Dave, Mr. Jong, and Chin

Kang-de went upstairs to his suite and he saw Bob waiting at the door. They entered his suite and he walked to the cabinet that had several bottles of alcohol. The drinks were decorated in alphabetical order. He grabbed a bottle of whiskey and two glasses. Kang-de and Bob sat on the bar stool and they slowly drank the whiskey. He asked Bob to call Chul-Moo. Bob dialed the cell phone and handed it to him.

"Chul, have the men keep an eye on Mr. Park and the CFO. Mr. Park will have to move him to a better location soon. I want one of your men to inform Mr. Park's guys that we know where CFO is hiding. Mr. Park will panic and when he tries to move CFO we will grab him," Kang-de said quietly.

"Right away, Boss. It's a great idea. We will get him, Boss."

"Good. I am a patient man. I can wait to get CFO. Bob, I have to go downstairs. Ms. Areum's mother is here and we have a lot to talk about. I am leaving now. Let yourself out."

"Goodnight, Boss," said Bob Goo as he continued to drink the whiskey.

The phone rang while Kang-de walked into the elevator. It was the driver who picked up Mrs. Lee from the airport.

"Hello?"

"Boss, this is Jin, the driver. I wanted to let you know that a silver SUV followed us when we left the airport. I lost them when I got off the exit."

"What?" said Kang-de in an astonished tone. "Thanks for telling me." Kang-de called Bob who was still upstairs drinking. "Bob, someone followed Areum's car from the airport. Please contact your security connections at the airport. Have them check for the car and the license plate. It was a silver SUV and it was behind our car. Quickly, Bob."

"I am on it," said Bob as he walked away from the whiskey glass that was almost empty.

Kang-de continued downstairs to see Areum's mother. He paused for a minute, then rang the bell to the suite. Areum answered the door with a disappointing look on her face.

"Kang-de, what have you been telling my mother?"

"Nothing. I have not spoken to your mother about your personal relationship. If that is what you are referring to? Why are you accusing me so fast? You are accusing the wrong man. Don't you think?" said Kang-de whispering in her ear.

"Sorry. I am sorry, Kang-de. I wasn't sure what my mother knows."

"Do you have something to tell me, Areum? Kang-de, do you know something that I and my husband should know?"

"Nothing at all, Mother," he said remembering the conversation between Sun-hee and Woo Jin at her office. Kang-de said nothing.

"Areum, I want you and Kang-de to go out on a date."

"We did already," said Areum.

"Yes, Mother, we already went on a date. It was a wonderful date. I believe that we had a great time. Did we have a good time, Areum?" asked Kang-de.

"Yes, Kang-de. It was very good."

"I want you to go on another date while I am here."

"Not right now, Mom. I have clinic this week. I will bring Woo Jin to meet you this weekend," said Areum. "I am going to bed now. I have an early start tomorrow. Goodnight, Mom. Goodnight, Kang-de."

"Goodnight, Miss Areum. You don't have classes tomorrow, do you?"

"No, but I have a meeting with my clinical supervisor."

"Goodnight, my daughter."

Areum smiled as she closed the bedroom door and went to sleep.

"I will leave too, Mother. You must be tired," Kang-de said walking to the door.

"Kang-de, wait. I want to tell you something and then I want to ask you for a favor. I am not well and neither is Areum's dad. I will have to go to the hospital soon. If anything happens to me or her dad, I want you to take Areum back to New York. I don't want her living here by herself."

"Mother, what is wrong? Please don't get sick. Your daughter needs you very much. Please, Mother, can I help in anyway?" asked Kang-de with concern in his voice.

"No, Kang-de. You are such a good person. We will continue our conversation after I speak to this Woo Jin character."

"Mother, please rest well. I will see you tomorrow at breakfast downstairs. Make yourself very comfortable."

"Thanks so much, Kang-de. I wish that your parents were here to see what a fine young man you have turned out to be," she said with a tone of sadness in her voice.

"Thank you, Mother. Goodnight."

"Oh, Kang-de, I think someone was following us today. But your driver lost him."

"Is that so?" said Kang-de pretending not to know what she was saying. "Don't worry, Mom. I will check into it. You go and rest well."

The next day, Areum left early in the morning to meet her clinic supervisor. Bora arrived one hour late to clinic. They passed each other at the X-ray room.

"Hey, Areum, I have not been able to talk to you about what happened here recently. One of the kidnappers was here at the clinic a few days ago and we chased him, but he got away. He had a stab wound, which he tried to get attended to. I hope that they find him before he bleeds to death."

"Why didn't you call me so that I could come and stay with you? I am so sorry, Bora. Yes, I do hope that they catch him. So how are you? Are you still scared?" asked Areum. "No. I have been staying at my dad's house."

"Oh. Okay. Bora, my mom is in Seoul. She is staying at the ITO Hotel in a suite."

"Wow. I thought you said that you were from a lower-middle-class family?" Bora said sarcastically.

"My friend owns the hotel and he is taking care of everything. Yes, Bora, I am poor."

"Sorry, I didn't mean to disrespect you. Which friend is this? I want to meet him. Is he very rich?"

"You already know him. It's Shin Kang-de," she replied.

"Oh, yes. He is Dad's associate. He is very handsome and very rich. I like him. He has been very nice to me. Have you noticed his beautiful eyes?"

"Okay, Bora. You have a boyfriend who is very rich too and he is handsome too."

"Areum, you never know what the future holds."

"Bora, you will be engaged soon. Stop talking like that."

"Oh, Areum. I forgot that you have never had a boyfriend before. Right?"

"I am not going to talk about it again. Let's go. We have work to do."

Areum spent an hour in clinic when Woo Jin called her.

"Hi, Areum, how are you? How is your mother? Where is she staying?"

"At the ITO Hotel," she replied.

"Why is she staying there? Could she not stay at some other hotel? That hotel belongs to that rude guy Kang-de. Wait a minute. Did he make arrangement for your mother to stay there? Tell me," he said curiously.

"Woo Jin, why are you making a big deal about this? Mom has known him for many years. He likes her and she has helped him through a bad time. Don't be jealous, Woo Jin," Areum said in an annoyed tone.

"Jealous. Why would I be jealous? That guy is a jerk. I don't like him. He has ulterior motives. I know it."

"Listen, Woo Jin, I have to go now. I have work to do."

"I want to see you. I will come and pick you up."

"I am sorry, I cannot. I am staying with my mother until she leaves."

"Okay. I will see you in a few days," he said in a disappointing tone.

Shortly after speaking with Areum, two black sedans pulled up in front of ITO Hotel. Four men stepped out from the first car. Another two exited the second. Woo Jin's father exited the back seat of the second car followed by Mrs. Kim. The men surrounded the Kims as they entered ITO Hotel.

They took the elevator to a twenty-first-floor suite. The floor had no occupants because the Kim's rented the entire floor for themselves and their security.

As soon as Mrs. Kim entered her suite, she called Woo Jin to let him know that she and his father were in Seoul on business. "Hello, son, we are at the ITO Hotel. Your dad has a meeting here at the Seoul office and I decided to join him. Come and see us."

"Okay, Mom I am happy that you are here. I am coming over."

"Okay, see you soon."

Woo Jin arrived at the ITO Hotel within thirty minutes. Mrs. Kim went downstairs to see him. He ran to see his mother, hugged and kissed her on the cheek, disregarding the hotel patrons who were staring at him.

"Mother. It is so good to see you. Where is Dad?"

"He went directly to the office as soon as we checked into the hotel. I heard that the restaurant here is very good. Let's go and eat."

"Give me a minute, Mother. There is someone in this hotel that I want you to meet."

Woo Jin called Areum to tell her that his mother was staying at the hotel and he wanted them to meet each other.

"Woo Jin, why did you not give me advanced notice? I don't have any nice clothes here in the hotel. And my hair is not done. Oh, Woo Jin...."

"It is okay. She won't care what you look like. It's your personality that is important."

"I am not happy about this. It is too sudden," said Areum in a nervous tone.

"Areum, come downstairs. We will be in the restaurant."

"Give me a few minutes," Areum said unenthusiastically.

Thirty minutes had passed since Woo Jin called her. She walked into the restaurant and saw Mrs. Kim and Woo Jin laughing. She walked slowly toward their table and bowed to Mrs. Kim.

Areum greeted Mrs. Kim dressed in a white blouse and black pencil skirt. She had her hair in a ponytail. She had no makeup except for a red lipstick that looked like it was placed on in a hurry.

"Mother, this is Lee Areum. She is a medical internist and my girlfriend."

"Good afternoon, Mrs. Kim. I am pleased to meet you. Welcome to Seoul."

"Good afternoon. Please, sit down. So you are a medical student. Where do you go to school?"

"I attend the same school as Woo Jin."

"Oh. Woo Jin never mentioned you before. When did you two start dating?"

Woo Jin interrupted and said, "Not very long. But I liked her. She is a very nice young lady. Mother, when is Dad coming? I want him to meet Areum too."

"In a few hours. He had to meet an associate. Woo Jin, I want to speak with Areum alone. You don't mind, do you, my son?"

"Mom, I will leave for a brief moment. Be nice," said Woo Jin whispering in his mother's ears.

Woo Jin left Mrs. Kim and Areum at the table. He went to the bar and sat down on a corner stool so that he could see his mother and Areum.

Kang-de walked to the entrance of the restaurant and saw Areum and a lady in his restaurant. Then he looked to his left and he saw Woo Jin. He walked away without being noticed.

Mrs. Kim observed Areum for a few seconds. Then she said, "I am sorry to tell you this, but we have someone for Woo Jin already. Her parents have already agreed that she will be engaged to Woo Jin as soon as he graduates. He knows who she is. He doesn't want to admit it but she is a perfect match for him. She lives in Hong Kong near us. She already has a master's in Business Administration and her parents own the drilling rights to several oil rigs in Brunei. They don't need our money. Do you understand why it's not possible for me and my husband to accept you as Woo Jin fiancé or girlfriend?"

"Mrs. Kim, you have said what is on your mind. I love Woo Jin for who he is as a man. I am not trying to marry him at this time. I have medical school to finish as well. I can take care of myself. I don't need anyone's money. Your son says he loves me and I believe him. If Woo Jin has someone else, then when I hear it from him I will walk away. It was very nice meeting you. Now, If you will excuse me I must go and attend to my mother."

"Please don't misunderstand. As a Korean, you know that the culture has to be respected. My son's legacy must be a perfect one. There can be no outside interference," she said staring at Areum. "By the way, you are Korean, right?" she asked in a sarcastic tone.

"Yes," said Areum in a quiet voice.

"Then you should be aware that my son's future has been planned since he was born. We his parents cannot divert from his destiny. Please understand."

Areum got up, bowed and walked away from the table. Woo Jin walked over when he saw Areum get up quickly.

"Areum, where are you going? Why are you leaving so soon? Did my mother say something to offend you?"

Areum replied, "I have to go and attend to my mother. She has been by herself for a while now. I will call you later. Please excuse me."

"Alright. I will call you first," said Woo Jin looking at his mother. "Mother, what did you say to Areum? She looks upset. You didn't mention that girl in Hong Kong, did you? I have already told you and Dad that she is not my type. When will you and Dad accept and respect my decision? I am not interested in her," Woo Jin said in an angry tone.

Mrs. Kim looked at him and replied, "That girl's name is Yoo-mi. She is the most suitable person for you. Why Areum? What is so great about her? She is just a plain, simple girl. How did you meet someone like her?" She stretched across to him, held his hand and said, "Areum is not in your social arena. You are supposed to be studying hard so that you can assume your role as CEO of the company. Woo Jin, what's going on with you?"

Woo Jin pulled away from his mother and sighed. "Stop it, Mom. Areum is the most beautiful person that you could ever know. She is not pretentious, superficial, fake or malicious. It is difficult to find genuine people in our social circle. Mother, why don't you want me to be happy?" he sighed.

"Don't be insulting, Woo Jin. Where are your manners? Your dad is on his way. You can speak with him," she demanded.

"I don't want to discuss anything anymore. I just lost my appetite. I will wait with you until Dad arrives," Woo Jin said in a rough tone.

Nothing more was said between them. They sat quietly while waiting for Mr. Kim to arrive.

Kang-de was at the reception desk watching Areum go into the elevator. He felt sad that she did not like him as much as he liked her. He had no doubt that Woo Jin would hurt her. He walked out the front door, lit a cigarette and took a long puff while looking at the guests who were arriving at the hotel.

Areum returned to her room upset after thinking about the conversation she had with Mrs. Kim.

"Where have you been, Areum? Where is Kang-de?" asked Mrs. Lee questioning Areum.

"I went downstairs to see Woo Jin and his mother."

"Why did you not tell me? I could have met them both."

"Mom, you were not going to be nice. Please be nice tomorrow when you meet Woo Jin," Areum said begging Mrs. Lee.

"I will not be rude and you know it."

Meanwhile in the lobby, Woo Jin's dad and his bodyguards walked passed Kang-de who had his back turned to the street. He entered the hotel restaurant and sat down with Woo Jin and his mother while his security team waited in the lobby.

Woo Jin extended his hand to greet his dad. "Dad! Welcome to Seoul. How are you?"

"Fine, son. How are you? Your mother and I expect that you will be finished with your studies very soon. You have work to do," said Mr. Kim in an urgent tone. "The associates in Brunei are awaiting your arrival. I heard that you have the job if you want it. Congratulations."

"Thanks, Dad, but Mom just offended my friend. I wanted you to meet her but I don't think she is up to it for the day."

Mr. Kim replied, "What did your mother say that was so bad? She told me that you wanted us to meet a friend. Why are you leading this young girl on when you know that there is someone in Hong Kong waiting for you?"

Woo Jin immediately sat up in his chair. "Dad, I told you already. I am not interested in her. She is not my type. Do you really want me to be unhappy with someone that I do not love?"

"Woo Jin. Look at the greater picture, my son. Your union with Yoo-mi will allow our company to be a larger conglomerate," said Mr. Kim.

"You just met this girl. You don't really know her. What is your problem?" Mrs. Kim asked.

Noticing that the conversation was getting heated, Mr. Kim interrupted Woo Jin's response. "Okay, let's not argue here. We will continue this conversation in Hong Kong."

Woo Jin replied, "Yes, why don't we do that? Times have changed and my generation is seeking true love and not economic or political mergers," he said trying to respond to his mother's statements.

Mr. Kim angrily reacted. "Okay, Woo Jin, that's enough. I am hungry. Let's eat." Woo Jin ate with his parents and then he said goodbye.

The next morning, Dave, who had not slept well since the incident at the clinic, went to see Mr. Jong to speak with him about his driver. Mr. Jong was sitting at his desk drinking his coffee and reading the newspaper.

"Good Morning, Dad. That incident with Bora at the clinic is still bothering me. Why would one of your drivers try to abduct Bora? I don't understand. Make me understand, please?"

"Dave, I don't know why one of my driver would do something like that. I can't find him to ask him why he would do such a horrible thing. Dave, when I find him, I will let you know what is happening. He must be working for someone. I will find out. How is Bora, is she okay?"

He poured a cup of coffee, looked at his father and said, "She is still upset about the incident. She pretends to be brave but I know she is very upset. I feel real embarrassed to know that I know someone who could have possibly harm Bora."

"Don't be embarrassed. You don't know if my driver did something so horrible. It could be a mistake and if he did, there are so many explanations as to why someone does bad things. Are you going to accept responsibility for all of them? " Mr. Jong asked looking nervously.

"Dad, I want you to find him. I also want to hire a private investigator to help find this man. This is real important. It is for everyone's safety."

"Dave, I said that I would find him and I will. Be patient."

"Dad, you don't seem to be very upset that you could have such a person in your employ," said Dave, observing the tone of his father's voice.

Mr. Jong sighed with frustration. "Dave, I am very upset that someone could betray me. I expect loyalty from my employees. It is embarrassing. But we cannot comment to anyone, including Bora, until we find out what really happened. Do you understand?"

"Yes, Dad. I do understand. I am leaving now."

Mr. Jong could not wait for Dave to drive away. He grabbed his phone and called Mr. Chin.

"Good morning, Chin. Is there any word about the driver?"

"Yes, Mr. Jong. We found him and he is hidden away. We took him to the country side. No one will find him. I made him disappear permanently."

"Just make sure that my son never finds his body. Got it?"

"I will make sure of that," said Chin.

Chapter Twenty-six

Mrs. Lee, Woo Jin, Areum, Mr. Kim, Kang-de, and Bob

The morning sun shined bright and the restaurant was filled with patrons gathered to have breakfast. Woo Jin arrived very early at the hotel. He saw his parents first and then he called Areum and her mother to have breakfast with him. Mrs. Lee and Areum walked into the restaurant searching for Woo Jin amongst the crowd.

The waiter escorted them to Woo Jin's table. "Hello, Mrs. Lee. It is very nice to meet you at last. Hi, Areum. Good morning. Did you both rest well?" he asked.

"Yes, we did," she said looking at her mother.

Mrs. Lee replied, "I didn't get much sleep because I have a lot on my mind. But first, let's eat breakfast."

Woo Jin stood up until Mrs. Lee and Areum sat down. Woo Jin, Areum and Mrs. Lee ordered a full course breakfast meal. Woo Jin and Areum ate until they were filled. Mrs. Lee did not eat a lot. She began to cough during breakfast.

Feeling uncomfortable from the stares that Mrs. Lee was giving him, Woo Jin tried to make insignificant conversation, but Mrs. Lee interrupted him. She asked Areum to leave the table so that she could speak with Woo Jin privately.

"Mom, please."

"It's okay, Areum. Please give us a few minutes," said Woo Jin.

Areum walked to the bar and sat down watching her mother and Woo Jin talk.

"Woo Jin, may I ask you, what are your intentions with my daughter? We are not rich like you. She is busy with Medical School. What do you want from Areum?"

"I just want her love and I want to love her. I don't want anything from her. I am financially sound. I have seen the world. I am about to run a multinational corporation in a few months. I just want her love, Mrs. Lee."

"Woo Jin, I am certain that your parents have chosen a girl for you already. Am I right?"

"That's not relevant," he replied.

"Well, it's relevant to me because we have chosen someone for Areum. He loves her with his whole heart. He is financially sound. He has travelled the world and he already runs his own companies," she said proudly. "I don't think that you and Areum would make a good match. Besides, you just met her. You both don't know each other well enough."

Woo Jin remained silent for a minute. He drank his coffee, then he turned and look at Areum briefly.

"I beg to differ with you, Mrs. Lee. Areum and I have something special going on. I can't let her go. Your daughter is the lady for me."

"Her dad and I have discussed her future with Shin Kang-de's parents before they passed," Mrs. Lee replied.

"Shin Kang-de? Did you say Kang-de? He is not a good choice for any woman, Mrs. Lee."

"Young man, do not be disrespectful. You don't know him. He has a good heart, a great business mind and he loves my daughter more than you could. I am sorry but she cannot be with you."

"Mrs. Lee, I am sorry that you feel this way. Please excuse me."

Woo Jin got up from the table and walked out of the restaurant. Areum saw him and ran over to her mother's table.

"Mom, what did you say to Woo Jin? He looks upset. I asked you to be nice."

"I was. I just showed him reality."

Mrs. Lee and Areum walked out of the restaurant and headed to the elevator, which opened up with Woo Jin's parents and guards inside. Woo Jin, who was waiting for them at the reception desk, hurried to greet them.

"Mom and Dad, this is Mrs. Lee, Areum's mother."

Mr. Kim looked surprised to see Mrs. Lee, but he quickly said,"Nice to meet you, Mrs. Lee. You too, Miss Lee."

Unimpressed by his words, Mrs. Lee replied,"You have a very nice son. You must be proud of him."

"Yes, we are very proud of him. Woo Jin, are you taking us to the airport?" asked Mrs. Kim.

"Yes, Mother. Areum, would you like to go with me to the airport?"

"Sure," she said.

"Areum, would you rather not stay with your mother?" asked Mrs. Kim.

"Yes. Areum, please stay with me. Where is Kang-de? I have not seen him this morning." Woo Jin stared at Mrs. Lee then turned and touched Areum's hand and kissed her on the cheek.

Meanwhile, Kang-de stood on the balcony looking at the awkward encounter between the families. He saw Woo Jin kiss Areum and he smiled.

"I will see you later, Areum. Okay?" said Woo Jin.

"Okay," said Areum smiling sadly as she watched Woo Jin leave with his parents and their bodyguards.

As Mr. Kim entered his car, he texted someone. The text read: "I saw only two of the people we spoke about today. Did you give her the medicine as yet? I want all of them taken care of. Do we understand each other?"

The cars slowly left the ITO Hotel and made a right onto the main road. Then they sped away.

Mrs. Lee and Areum rode the elevator to their suite in silence. As Mrs. Lee exited the elevator she said, "Areum, be honest with me. That woman doesn't think that you are a good match for her son. Am I right?" asked her mother.

"Oh, Mother."

"Listen to me, my daughter. You are too good for them. I don't want to get upset. I hope to meet them again."

Although he had observed everything while standing on the balcony, Kang-de walked toward Mrs. Lee and Areum and greeted them.

"Good morning, beautiful ladies. Did you have breakfast as yet? I have not."

"Yes, we ate already. Where were you?" asked Areum.

"Mom, come and have tea with me. Areum, you too," he said without responding to Areum's question.

They went downstairs to the restaurant with Kang-de. The waiters ran to Kang-de as he sat down.

"I would like an omelet with whole-wheat toast and a large cup of coffee. Mom, would you like tea, coffee or hot chocolate? You used to like tea. Do you still like tea, Mom?"

She shook her head indicating yes.

"Areum, tea for you, right?"

"Yes, Kang-de," Areum said looking at her mother.

"I am so happy to see familiar faces here with me. I miss that. You two are my family. I am truly grateful that you are here, Mom. I must admit that I feel lonely sometimes."

"Areum, you are here. Please be there for him. Promise me that you will be there for Kang-de and I also want you to promise to listen to him if something important is about to impact your life. Okay, my daughter?"

"Yes, Mother. Kang-de is very important to me too."

Kang-de looked at Areum and smiled with a pitiful expression on his face. Mrs. Lee stared at Kang-de and Areum. She thought about telling Areum that she was very sick, but she could not bring herself to do it.

"I am going to get some rest. You two stay here. I will go upstairs alone," she said.

"Mother, are you feeling okay? Look, you have a doctor here and I will call additional ones if you don't feel well," said Kang-de. "Mom, are you alright? You will tell me if you are not feeling well?"

"I am fine. Enjoy each other's company," Mrs. Lee said while walking slowly to the elevator.

"I will keep her busy. Areum, would you like to go for a drive?"

"Yes, I think that I should go for a drive."

The drive to the park was short. Areum opened the car door before Kang-de could get to the passenger side. As they entered the park, he stopped, looked at Areum and asked, "What happened yesterday? I didn't mean to be nosy, but I was watching Woo Jin's mother speak with you and I could tell that she wasn't being nice to you. Areum, you didn't expect that she was going to be nice to you, did you? A few rich people in this country are unique. They won't let you into their circle without you being able to match them socially, economically and politically. You will have to accept that eventually. You have forgotten the culture here. You lived in America too long. I want you to remember that you are going to be a doctor. A cardiologist is a profession to be respected. Hold your head up and know that you are marketable. You are beautiful and you are going to be rich, Areum."

"Thank you, Kang-de. I appreciate you more than you know."

"And I love you more than you know. I am sorry but I have to say it," said Kang-de.

Areum nodded as she accepted his apology without saying anything. Kang-de escorted Areum to a park bench and he hesitated for a minute before taking Areum right hand into his.

"I am not supposed to tell you this but I don't want to deceive you ever. Your mother has cancer. She doesn't want you to know but I think that as a physician and her daughter you should know."

"What? What did you just say?" Shocked from the news, Areum fell to her knees.

Kang-de quickly pulled her back to the bench.

"When did she tell you and how long ago did you find out?"

"She doesn't know that I know she has cancer. When I spoke with your father, he said that she had seen a doctor and she wasn't feeling well after seeing him; so I had her see a doctor who gave me the result because he thought that I was her son. We have to get her to America in a hurry. You have recess this week and I want you to come with us. I have made arrangements for her to fly to the M Clinic in America. They have some of the best oncologists in the world. Will you come with me?" he asked.

Areum nodded without processing what Kang-de just said to her.

"Sure, I am going with you. Does my dad know?"

"No, he does not. At least, I don't think he knows. His blood pressure is too high right now."

Areum began to cry. "These are my parents and I have no idea what is going on with them. I thank you, Kang-de, for the interest that you have shown me and my parents. I feel so ashamed right now. It's my fault that my mom is sick. I should have insisted that she frequented a doctor," she said sobbing uncontrollably.

Kang-de embraced her tightly as she sat motionless in his arms. "Please don't cry. You have to be strong now. I will be with you every step of the way. I am going to finalize some things here and then we will leave right after your last final. You will have to tell Woo Jin."

"I know, but right now I am not thinking about him. Let's go back. I want to be with my mother. I am going to confront her about her illness."

"Yes. Go ahead and confront her. I want her to live. Not only for you but for me too."

Kang-de held her hand tightly as he drove back to the ITO Hotel. The drive was quick and silent, but to Areum it felt like forever.

Minutes later, they pulled up to the ITO Hotel and he handed the car keys to the attendant. Areum walked in behind Kang-de and her phone rang. It was Woo Jin calling Areum.

"Hi, Woo Jin, can I call you back?"

"Okay. But where are you? I am in the hotel restaurant," said Woo Jin.

"I am walking through the lobby," she said.

Woo Jin walked out of the restaurant and saw her walking behind Kang-de in the lobby.

"What are you doing with him? Why didn't you stay with your mother?" he asked while walking toward her.

"We went for a drive. Woo Jin, I really don't want to argue with you right now."

"What is there to argue about? I asked you a question. Why were you out with him?" he said pointing at Kang-de.

"Woo Jin, now is not the time to harass Areum," said Kang-de.

"What did you just say to me? I was not speaking to you. Stay out of our business."

"Woo Jin, you have been looking for a fight. And I am not going to give it to you today. But one day I am going to beat the shit out of you. I promise you that."

"Let's step outside now. I have had enough of you."

"Stop it, Woo Jin. I can't handle any problems right now."

"You should listen to her. Now is not the time for you and me to address our issues," said Kang-de walking into the elevator.

Woo Jin took Areum outside the hotel to speak with her. They sat on the bench that face the waterfall which was located across the driveway. The mist from the water fountain blew on them as Areum sat down with Woo Jin.

"Woo Jin, I just found out that my mom is very ill and I am going to take her to America to an oncologist next week."

"You mean you and Kang-de are going to take her to America. Have you ever thought to ask me for help? I would have made all the arrangements for you. I am sorry but, I feel left out of your life."

"This is between my mother and Kang-de. She likes him so I am not going to change anything right now. I really need your cooperation. Please don't place any additional stress on me."

"Okay. I am sorry, honey."

Kang-de returned downstairs to speak with Areum and he saw her sitting at the water fountain with Woo Jin. Kang-de decided to call her instead of having a confrontation with Woo Jin.

"Hi, Areum. There are a few transactions that I have to take care of before I can travel. I will talk with you later."

"Okay, Kang-de," she said looking at Woo Jin's face.

"Woo Jin, please, please don't make it difficult for me. My mom is very sick," she said while covering her face with her hands.

"I promise not to make it difficult for you. I am sorry," he said as he hugged her tightly.

Bob had just pulled up in front of the hotel when Kang-de called him to meet him at the hotel. As he threw the car keys to the attendant, he noticed Woo Jin embracing Areum at the water fountain. Bob stood watching them, for a few minutes, before going inside the hotel to see Kang-de.

He walked into Kang-de's suite and sat on the couch. Kang-de handed him a glass of water and he walked to the window and said, "Bob, I am going to America for about two weeks. If I have to fly back and forth then I will. I need to speak with Mr. Jong. Also, was Mr. Park's inside man informed that we know where CFO is?"

"Yeah, Boss."

"I need you to get some of Chul's men to grab CFO as soon as Mr. Park leaves. I also need you to get three men to protect Sun-hee. She doesn't need to know."

"Okay, Boss, consider everything done."

"Bob, I definitely want to see Mr. Jong as soon as possible," he said, unaware that Mr. Jong was his biggest enemy.

Bob called Mr. Jong's secretary and made an appointment for the next day. He hesitated before telling Kang-de about Areum and Woo Jin embracing at the fountain

"Ah, Boss, have you seen Miss Areum today?" he asked slowly.

"Yes, Bob. She is outside with Woo Jin. Is he still hugging her?"

"You know?"

"Yes. I saw them. It's okay. That relationship won't last for long because that guy is a jerk."

Chapter Twenty-seven

Mr. Jong, Kang-de, Woo Jin, Bob, and Areum

As planned by Kang-de, Minjae heard that CFO whereabouts had been compromised. He informed Mr. Park, who told Minjae, to move CFO to another location.

In the meantime, Kang-de and Mr. Jong met at his office to discuss Mr. Park's attempted acquisition of Mr. Jong's company.

"Mr. Jong, it has been a long time since we spoke. How have you been?"

"I have been well. And you? I heard that you are experiencing some problems with your company. How is that working out?"

Kang-de replied, "News gets around fast. But I have everything under control. Let me get to the point. Mr. Park is making an attempt to acquire your company. I just wanted to warn you that he is a dangerous man and you need to be on the alert."

"I find that interesting. I thought that he was trying to acquire your company. I didn't know that he had an eye on mine as well," said Mr. Jong in a sarcastic tone.

"He was trying to acquire my company, but I put a stop to it. I am only giving you prior notice because you and I do a lot of business together.

And it is in my company's interest to let you know what's happening," Kang-de replied. I do find it interesting that you knew that he was trying to acquire my company yet you said nothing. Why is that? Where is your honor, Mr. Jong?"

"Mr. Shin, I always look out for number one first. I can only tell you that I would never let him hurt your company."

Kang-de muttered to himself, "Yeah, right. Mr. Jong, I have warned you. Now you have a good day. Good luck to you. My secretary will see you out."

"Oh, I don't need luck. I make my own luck. Good day to you too," said Mr. Jong. He slowed down and smiled at Kang-de's temporary secretary before walking to the elevator.

Bob walked into Kang-de's office from another door. "Bob, were you listening to that arrogant bastard?"

"Yeah, Boss. That Mr. Jong is a snake too. He is worse than Mr. Park."

"Hopefully, this information will let him move faster in acquiring Park's company."

"Boss, he does not know that you know that he is trying to do a hostile takeover of Mr. Park's pharmaceuticals. Director number five in Mr. Jong's company has been an asset to us," laughed Bob.

"That's my mother's cousin. Only you and I know about him. After that snake Mr. Jong is finished taking away Mr. Park's company, I am going to take Mr. Jong's company away from him one piece at a time."

"Boss, they should never have messed with you. Do they know how clever you really are?"

"I hope not. Keep your ears open about CFO movements. Are we ready to grab him?" Kang-de asked.

"Yes, Boss. I also have security looking out for Miss Sun-hee."

"Good."

Kang-de poured Bob a cup of coffee and they stood at the window looking down at Mr. Jong getting into a black sedan. Kang-de noticed that the man who held the car door open for Mr. Jong looked like Mr. Chin.

A minute later, Kang-de's cell phone rang with an unidentifiable number on the screen. "Hello. How did you get my phone number? What do you want?"

"You think that you have won my girlfriend, don't you, but you have not. You don't know who you are interfering with. Take a look at my company and then tell me if I should be scared of you."

"I will crush you, Shin Kang-de. Areum is my woman and you will not have her. Do you understand?"

"Woo Jin, my hands have a very far reach. I know every Hong Kong dollar that your parents' company make. I know every holding that your parents have. I know when they wake up and when they go to sleep. And you think that you can crush me?"

"Young master, think again. I am not somebody you should be threatening at all. You cannot even handle your women. Does Areum know that you have been sleeping with Sun-hee?" Kang-de asked.

"Woo Jin, you don't want to threaten me. Finish school and then let's talk again," said Kang-de hanging up on him.

Startled by Kang-de's words, Woo Jin called Areum immediately.

"Areum, I want you to be very careful of that guy Shin Kang-de. He is not what he seems. He is a dangerous man."

"Woo Jin, did you two have an argument again? I don't want to discuss Kang-de with you. He might be a dangerous man to you but he is a lifesaver to my family. However, thanks for the warning. I have to go now. I want to see about my mother. I will call you."

"When are you leaving? I want to be at the airport with you."

"As soon as Mom and Kang-de tell me, I will let you know. I have to go and study. Will you be going to the library today?"

"Yes. I will see you there," Woo Jin said in a sad tone.

Within two hours later, Woo Jin and Areum met at the library. He felt badly that he was acting like a jerk.

"Hi. I am sorry for the confrontation with Kang-de. He brings out the worst in me. I just cannot stand the guy. Anyway, how are you doing? How is your mother feeling?"

"She is not well. I won't be away long. I believe that Kang-de hired a team of caretakers for my mother."

"Wow, he thinks of everything," said Woo Jin. "Anyway, let's study."

They studied for several hours without interrupting each other. Areum pretended to study but her mind was on her mother's illness and the long flight to New York City.

Chapter Twenty-eight

CFO, Mr. Park, Minjae, Kang-de, Bob, Mrs. Lee, Areum, Bora, Chul, and Woo Jin

The news of the exposed whereabouts of CFO made Mr. Park go to see him urgently. He went with several bodyguards to the abandoned building which was infested by several rodents and animals. Mr. Park dusted his suit as he entered CFO's small apartment.

"Hi, how are you? Have you spoken to the CFO of AZAXCO company as yet?"

"Yes, Boss. He sent me information of all the stocks listings and the names of directors of AZAXCO Pharmaceuticals. He told me who can be bribed to vote against Mr. Jong. I think we have some good news here. There's only one obstacle that may be a problem and that is Dave Jong. He owns a third of the shares in the company," said CFO.

"Give me all the papers. I want to put them in my safe. Don't worry about Dave Jong. He is going to be my son-in–law sooner than he thinks."

"Here you are, Mr. Park," said the short bald-headed man whose glasses were larger than his face. He had lost weight after his last encounter with Kang-de and Chul. Fear of being caught by them, and the surroundings that he currently resided in made him lose his appetite.

Shortly after receiving the papers, one of Mr. Park's men came into the apartment and whispered to Mr. Park that there were strange men outside the building.

Mr. Park looked at CFO and told him to pack his belongings. "You are going to another location," said Mr. Park.

"Sir, did they find me?" he asked nervously.

"Oh, no, no, no. Don't worry so much. We are just moving you to a better place. I am leaving first. My men will look after you. Don't worry, you will be safe," said Mr. Park walking out the door with one of his guards. "Don't put up any fight to save him. Save yourself first," whispered Mr. Park to one of his men. "Okay, guys, see you all later."

Mr. Park, Minjae and four cars drove away from the building leaving two cars with men in it to move the CFO.

Meanwhile, Chul and his men watched as Mr. Park and his men drove away. They got out of their car and entered the building. As they arrived on the third floor, they were accosted by Mr. Park's men. Chul's men knocked out Mr. Park's men. They entered the apartment and grabbed CFO before he escaped.

"You bastard, I have been looking for you for a long time. Boss wants to talk to you," said Chul grabbing him by his collar.

Chul pulled CFO down the stairs and threw him in the car trunk. He called Kang-de as they drove away from the building.

"Boss, we got him. I am taking him to the warehouse. See you there," said Chul.

"Good job, Chul. Remind me to give you and your boys a nice bonus. Bob, let's go."

It took Bob forty-five minutes to arrive at the warehouse. Kang-de jumped out of the car with a baseball bat and hurried into the empty warehouse that was once used for storage of computer parts. Kang-de had moved to a larger warehouse as the demand for his computers increased. The warehouse was cold and sound proof. Nothing that occurred there could be heard outside.

Kang-de walked over to CFO, looked at him for a second, then slammed the bat on CFO's right hand with force. CFO screamed loudly while holding his mangled hand.

"Shut up, you bastard, you have been hiding from me. I want you to tell me where are all my papers. What did you do with them? I want the truth or you will not be leaving here alive."

Crying from excruciating pain that had been inflicted upon him, CFO told Kang-de that he had given Mr. Park fake contracts that he had created. He said they had no value.

In a whimpering voice he told Kang-de that he had destroyed the fictitious contracts so that they would not be traced back to him.

"Where is my money that you took from me? I want it all," said Kang-de looking at him in a sadistic manner.

"I have the bank account numbers in my briefcase."

Kang-de got the account numbers and he had Bob verified the accounts.

"Chul, take CFO to the bank and have him transfer the money to one of my New York bank accounts. I don't trust his computer."

Chul went to the bank with CFO and completed the transfer.

"Boss, it is all done. What should I do with the CFO? Kill him?" asked Chul.

"No. I want you to hurt him, but don't kill him. I want him to remember what he has done. His mangled right hand will be a reminder to him. As for Yejoon he still owes me and I want every penny."

Bob watched as Chul and his men punched and slapped CFO. Bob kicked him as he walked with Kang-de to the car. Kang-de sighed as he sat in the front seat of the car with Bob and they entered the ramp to the highway. The ride from the warehouse to the hotel took longer than expected because of the massive highway traffic.

Bob noticed the distress look on Kang-de's face throughout the ride to the hotel and he said, "Boss. we are almost done with most of our distractions. I hope that now you can focus on the woman that you love so much," said Bob.

"Oh, Bob, I have to be very careful not to alienate her. I have patience. I can wait. After all, I have waited so long for her," said Kang-de sitting up in the passenger seat.

Bob parked the car in front of the hotel. The valet ran to open Kang-de's door. He walked into the hotel lobby, picked up the guest phone and called Mrs. Lee's room to tell her that he was on his way to see her.

Within minutes, he was stepping off the elevator and into the brightly lit hallway. He rang the bell at Mrs. Lee's suite. It took her what seemed like a long time to open the door. The door opened and Kang-de walked in with a solemn look on his face.

"Mom Lee, let's sit at the table. I know that you have cancer. Please don't ask how I know. I have made arrangements for you to travel to New York to get care," said Kang-de while holding her hands.

"I am sorry, my son. I didn't want you and Areum to know what was happening to me. Sorry, but why New York? I can be treated here. Does Areum know everything?" asked Mrs. Lee with tears in her eyes.

"Yes, Mom, she knows everything. In New York you have access to varied treatments. Don't worry about money, Mom. Everything has been arranged already. Do you want Mr. Lee to come with you?"

"I am not sure. His health is not good. What do you think?"

"Let's not have him travel so far. After you have seen the doctors then we will determine if he should come."

Mrs. Lee's tears began to flow after feeling overwhelmed. "Kang-de, I cannot thank you enough for all the kindness you have shown me and my family. What would we do without you?"

"Oh, Mom, please do not cry. I want you to save your energy. I need you to be strong for Areum and me too. I have no family. Please be healthy," said Kang-de hugging Mrs. Lee tightly. "I will take care of everything. The plane is ready. We will leave this weekend. Areum is coming with us. Do you want to call Mr. Lee now?"

"No. I will speak with him tonight."

The night came quickly and the clouds hid the moon briefly. Mrs. Lee went to bed after Areum spoke with her about her cancer and their trip to New York. Areum thought that once the treatment had taken effect, she would take her mother to Central Park to watch the geese swim around in the pond. When Areum was small, it was their favorite place to have mother and daughter conversations until sundown.

Moments later, Mrs. Lee yelled for Areum in a faint voice. Areum ran to her mother's room and saw blood on her mother's pajamas and on her bed sheet.

Areum called for an ambulance. Then she called Kang-de in a frantic voice. "Kang-de, sorry to wake you up, but Mom is vomiting blood," she said in a frightened tone.

"I am on my way. Did you call for an ambulance?"

"Yes. Mom, it's going to be alright. The ambulance is on their way," she said as she dropped the phone on the floor and kneeled at her mother's feet.

Kang-de rang the bell and Areum opened the door. He walked briskly to Mrs. Lee's room. She was alert but vomiting uncontrollably.

"Mrs. Lee, hang in there. The ambulance is on its way."

"Mom, are you okay? Where is the ambulance?" she said pacing back and forth to the window.

Meanwhile, Kang-de called housekeeping to clean the room as there was blood all over the floor. It took twenty minutes for the ambulance to arrive. The attendants began to check Mrs. Lee vitals. They called the hospital oncologist on duty to consult with him. He told them to bring her to the hospital immediately.

"We have to go right now," said the ambulance attendant as they strapped Mrs. Lee onto the gurney. "Mom, we have to take you to the hospital, but don't worry. Okay?" said Areum looking at Kang-de with a sad face as they entered the ambulance with Mrs. Lee.

The ambulance arrived at the hospital within ten minutes. A team of doctors were waiting for her at the emergency door. Mrs. Lee was rushed to emergency room. Areum held her hand until the doctor stopped her at the emergency door. She turned around and looked at Kang-de who was busy speaking with Dr. Sung, the managing director of the hospital.

Overwhelmed by the reality of what had just happened, Areum fainted in a chair in the waiting area. Kang-de, who was busy speaking with the administrator, was unaware that Areum had fainted.

"Sir, a patient named Mrs. Lee just arrived in your hospital. I want her to get the best doctors that this hospital has. Money is not a factor. I want them now, please," he said in a firm tone.

"Yes, Sir. We will do everything possible to get her the best doctors."

"Thank you, Doctor. Thank you."

Kang-de and Dr. Sung walked toward the waiting area where they saw Areum slowly trying to regain consciousness. Kang-de ran to her and held her. She slowly regained full consciousness as he grabbed her face and rubbed it in a circular manner.

"Areum, are you okay?" he asked frantically squeezing her hands. She pulled her hands away from him indicating that she was fine. She stood up slowly and walked to the emergency door to look through the glass window. The door was closed and the lights to the surgery room was still bright but she could not see her mother.

It had been more than ten hours since Mrs. Lee was brought into the emergency room. Areum was getting anxious because there were no news about her mother. As the clock moved quickly into the afternoon, Kang-de noticed that they had not been informed about Mrs. Lee's condition. Moments later, a doctor appeared from the emergency room.

Kang-de asked the doctor, "Is Mrs. Lee stabilized? Doctor, when can we take her to America?"

"You cannot. Her cancer has advanced into her brain and her lungs. Mr. Shin, her kidneys are failing."

"What?" said Kang-de and Areum simultaneously.

"Doctor, what if I fly her on a private plane to America, can she make it?" asked Kang-de.

"No. She will not make it. We have a good oncologist facility here. We will take very good care of her," said the surgeon.

"Areum, what do you want to do?"

"Kang-de, we have to keep her here and work on her here. She is not stable to travel such a long distance. Let's keep her here," Areum said in a solemn tone. She knew what it meant when the surgeon said that her organs were failing.

"Okay, Areum. I will do whatever you want me to do."

"Thank you so much, Kang-de. What would we do without you?"

"Areum, I NEED YOU and Mom Lee more than you know."

Kang-de hugged Areum for a long time. Areum and Kang-de went to Mrs. Lee private hospital suite that Kang-de ordered for her. The suite had two hospital beds with private bath, a living room with furniture, a coffee table and a small kitchen.

The guest bed was hidden in the couch. Areum rested on the couch and Kang-de laid in the reclining chair that could substitute for a bed. They fell asleep without waking throughout the night. Their lack of sleep for twenty-four hours placed them into unconsciousness. They were unaware that Mrs. Lee had been brought into the room.

Throughout the night, doctors and nurses entered Mrs. Lee's room to monitor her vitals. Areum and Kang-de were woken by the loud ringtone from Areum's cell phone. Woo Jin had been trying to contact her throughout the night. Areum answered her cell and Woo Jin eagerly yelled in the phone.

"Good morning! How are you? How was your night?"

"It was not good, Woo Jin. I am at the hospital with my mother. We had to take her in an ambulance to the hospital yesterday."

"Which hospital is she in? I am on my way." Areum gave him the name of the hospital. Then she called Bora who was studying to be an oncologist.

"Bora, I need you to come to the hospital. My mother was diagnosed with cancer. It's advancing," said Areum nervously clenching her left hand.

"I am on my way. Should I call Woo Jin?"

"No, he is on his way. Thank you."

Woo Jin arrived at the hospital and ran to the front desk. He asked for Mrs. Lee's room. He hurried to the room. He saw Kang-de holding Mrs. Lee's hand but he did not see Areum. He walked up behind Kang-de and greeted Mrs. Lee who was conscious.

"Good morning, Mrs. Lee. How are you feeling today? I hope better than last night? I am so sorry to hear that you are not feeling well. I am sure that you will recover fully."

"Thank you, Woo Jin," she said softly. Woo Jin turned to Kang-de and said good morning to him.

"Kang-de, thank you for your help. Where is Areum?" asked Woo Jin.

Kang-de shook his shoulders and replied, "I don't know. She said that she would be right back."

"I will wait for her. Mrs. Lee, if you need anything please do not hesitate to ask. I will get you the best doctor to fly in to take care of you. Just let me know," Woo Jin said looking at Kang-de.

Softly she said, "Thank you, Woo Jin, that is very kind of you. I think that Kang-de has taken care of everything already. Thanks anyway."

Woo Jin looked frustrated and helpless as he sat down on the chair in her room awaiting Areum's arrival. He gave a half smile to Kang-de as he noticed Kang-de holding Mrs. Lee's hand. Areum walked into the room and she observed that the two men look annoyed with each other.

"Hi, Woo Jin. Thanks for coming. Let's go outside to talk."

They walked out together and Kang-de turned his head to look at them.

"Why didn't you call me last night? I could have been here with you all night. I feel so left out, Areum. Why am I the last person to find out that your mother is in the hospital?" Woo Jin asked in a disappointing voice.

"I am sorry but I told you before, Kang-de and my mother have a special bond. I have no control over what they do. Please don't let Kang-de's presence be a factor. My mother's health is what's important and I want to focus on getting her the best care."

Woo Jin held Areum's hand and stroke it several times. "I am sorry. I just feel so bad that I cannot help her."

"No, Woo Jin. I am sorry for leaving you out this horrible situation. Why don't you call your people and get her the best oncologist? That will be our secret. Okay?" said Areum, unaware that her mother's cancer was a result of an attempted murder plot by someone Woo Jin knew.

"I will be happy to do that Areum. I am on it."

Areum and Woo Jin walked back into the room with Kang-de looking at both of them.

"Areum, I have to go and take care of something for your mom. I will be right back. Mom, I love you."

"I love you too. Thanks, Kang-de," said Mrs. Lee.

Areum turned and looked at Woo Jin's concerned face. "Woo Jin, why don't you make your call too?"

"Consider it taken care of," he said.

Bora entered the room with her hands saddled with flowers for Mrs. Lee. "Good morning, Mrs. Lee. Hi, Areum. I spoke with the attending oncologists. They want to discuss the various methods of treatment for your mother."

"Thanks, Bora. Kang-de and Woo Jin are getting the best oncologist for her also."

"That's great. Mrs. Lee, you are going to be fine. I will ask my dad about the best drug that is available to you," Bora said smiling at Mrs. Lee.

"Mom, you are in good hands. You will feel better soon," Areum said with a happy tone.

Kang-de overheard Woo Jin calling an oncologist. Kang-de smiled and walked back to Mrs. Lee's room, greeting Bora and Mrs. Lee. He looked at Areum and said, "May I speak with you for a minute, please?"

"What is it Kang-de?" she asked

"I wasn't being nosy but I overheard Woo Jin calling an oncologist. Did you tell him to do that?" he asked.

"Yes. He feels ignored, so I asked him for help. Kang-de, I will solicit anyone who can help my mother," she said in serious tone.

"Oh, I agree. If he has a better doctor than the ones I know, let him get them here immediately."

"Kang-de, you are a very nice person. I can never repay you for all that you have done for my family. Thanks, Kang-de, for understanding."

Areum hugged Kang-de. He could feel his heart beating rapidly and Areum felt her heart skip a beat. They held each other for a while. Woo Jin watched Areum and Kang-de hug through the window. He slowly walked into the room with the phone at his ear and he pretended that he did not notice them. Areum quickly stepped away from Kang-de as he walked in.

"Areum, I called the doctor. He will be here in two days. He has to get permission to consult at this hospital."

"Thank you, Woo Jin."

Woo Jin pulled Areum to him and hugged her in front of Kang-de. Kang-de smiled, turned and walk out of the room. Bora had already left the room to call her father.

"Dad, I need your help. Areum's mom has advance cancer and I need you to recommend a drug that can help her."

"Bora, I don't have time for that now. I need you, Dave and Mr. and Mrs. Jong to come and have dinner tomorrow. Can you do that?"

"Yes, I can. Can you recommend a drug for Areum's mother?" she asked again. "Dad, she has an incurable cancer."

"Okay. Okay. I will call the office."

"Thanks, Dad."

Chapter Twenty-nine

Mr. Park, Mr. Jong, Bora, Dave, Kang-de, Areum, and Woo Jin

Minjae pulled up in Mr. Park's driveway early in the morning and one of the guards opened the door for him. He walked into the house and went into Mr. Park's office.

Mr. Park called one of the guards that was with CFO. He got no answer. He had suspected that Kang-de's men had overpowered them and took CFO away.

"No answer?" asked Minjae.

"No, but it's okay. I got what I needed from him," Mr. Park said looking at the black briefcase on his desk.

Mr. Park sat at his desk with the black briefcase and he and Minjae examined the documents inside. He noticed Bora walking by his office and he yelled out in a loud voice, "Bora, I want to talk with you and Dave. When are you two kids getting married? Your mother and I want to set a date."

"Dad, what is the rush? You were not in any hurry for me to marry Dave before. Why now?"

"Bora, please call Dave. I want to speak with him."

Confused by her father's statement, Bora called Dave and immediately he drove to the house. Dave was greeted by Mr. and Mrs. Park and Bora in their family room.

"Good day, Mr. and Mrs. Park. Hi, Bora, what's going on? Did you get any news about the man at the clinic?" Dave asked nervously.

Mr. Park replied, "No, Dave. I called you here because I want to know when we should set your wedding date. You still want to marry my Bora, right?"

"Oh, yes, Sir. Have you spoken with my mom and dad as yet?" asked Dave.

"We spoke about your union two years ago," said Mr. Park.

"I would like to have their input on this," said Dave.

"Why, certainly. I am sure that your parents feel the same as we do. Let's call them," said Mr. Park.

Dave called his home and his mother answered. "Oh, hi, Mom, where is Dad?"

"He is not home. Why?"

"Mr. and Mrs. Park want to speak with the both of you regarding something."

"Okay. I will tell your dad to call you when he comes home."

The night passed quickly and it was mid-afternoon when the Jong family arrived at the Parks' residence. Mr. Jong had reluctantly agreed to have dinner with the Park family. Mr. Park ushered them to the dining room. They ate a five-course meal and drank champagne. Mr. Park rose from the dining table and began to speak to Dave and his family.

"Mr. Jong, the reason for our gathering today is to talk about our children's engagement and wedding. When can we set a date?"

"Mr. Park, you seem to be in a rush to get our kids married. Dave, what do think?"

"I want us to get married soon. I think it's a great idea," he said. Dave asked Bora, "What do you think, Bora?"

"I want us to get married too, but I want to finish my residency first," she said smiling.

"I want grandchildren soon," said Mr. Park.

"Dad, I will work on that as soon as I finish my residency. I agree with Bora. Let's both finish school and then we will get married."

"Mr. Jong, can you and I agree that they should at least be engaged?" asked Mr. Park. Mr. Jong replied, "I agree with that."

"Okay then, Dave, when do you want to get engaged? I will throw the biggest party that no one can top it," said Mr. Park.

"Bora, what do you say? We spoke about our engagement already. So when do you want to make it official?" asked Dave.

"How about next week? You get the ring and we will have the party next week."

"I already have the ring," he said.

Shocked by Dave's statement, Bora asked him. "When did you get it? Why didn't you take me with you?"

"There was no need to. I took one of your rings from the apartment and I just had the jeweler size it to match what I wanted for you."

"Oh, Dave. You are too clever and so sweet."

"Okay, then it's official. We will make the announcement at the party next week," said Mr. Park.

Mr. Jong thought to himself that Mr. Park was up to something devious, and he decided to play along. "Well, Mr. Park, I insist that my wife and I contribute to this mega-party."

"Sure, Mr. Jong. It will be my pleasure. Let's get our guest list together. We need a venue. What about the ITO Hotel ballroom? I will call the owner.

"Sure, you do that. We will have about two hundred of our friends. How many do you think that you will invite?" asked Mr. Jong.

"About the same," said Mr. Park.

Mr. Park called Kang-de to inquire about renting his ballroom for the engagement. He could have gone to another hotel, but ITO

Hotel had the largest ballroom in town and Mr. Park wanted to have the envy of his associates. Kang-de's cell phone rang and he saw that it was Mr. Park. He struggled to put a smile on his face and a friendliness in his voice.

"Hello, Shin Kang-de. How are you? I am calling because I want to rent your ballroom next week for the engagement of my daughter Bora to Dave Jong. Is it available?"

"I don't know. Why don't you call the business office?"

Disappointed with what Kang-de just said to him, he said, "Kang-de, I am asking as a friend. Could you work on it for me?"

"I will have the manager who handles those affairs call you. Will that be okay?" Kang-de asked in an annoyed tone.

"That will be fine," said Mr. Park.

Mr. Park hung up. Kang-de called his catering manager who immediately called Mr. Park.

"Hello, Mr. Park. How are you? Mr. Shin Kang-de ask me to call you to discuss the use of the ballroom next week. What date do you need next week, Mr. Park?"

"Saturday. We will have about four hundred-plus guests. Do you think your ballroom can hold that many people?"

"Yes, Sir. It holds six hundred fifty seated. Saturday will be fine. Will your family be coming down to choose the menu, the colors, the lighting and the theme?"

"My wife and Mrs. Jong will take care of all those things. Just send me the bill."

"Okay, Sir. Can you have them let me know when they will be arriving?"

"Honey, could you come and speak with this woman?"

"Hello. Yes. We will be there tomorrow at 12 noon," said Mrs. Park.

"Thank you, madam. Goodbye."

Mrs. Park, Mrs. Jong and the managing director of ITO Hotel social affairs met the next day and they chose the itinerary for the party. Bora called Woo Jin and Areum to invite them to the engagement party.

"Hi, Areum, I know that your mom is sick and you need to be by her side, but I still want to invite you to my engagement party next weekend. It will be at the ITO Hotel. I will call Woo Jin because its short notice."

"I will come for a short while. I have to go back to the hospital to see my mother." Areum thought about the party being held at the ITO Hotel and she called Kang-de to find out if he were invited to the party.

"Kang-de. Bora just told me that she is having her engagement party at your hotel. Will you be there?"

"Only if you are attending. Are you going?"

"Yes, for a short while."

"Then I will see you there."

Kang-de had decided that he would not ask her to be his date at Bora's engagement party.

Bora called Woo Jin to invite him to the party. "Hi, Woo Jin. I would like to invite you to my engagement party next Saturday. Can you make it?"

"Sure. Did you invite Areum? I won't attend without her."

"Yes, Woo Jin. She will be there."

"Okay. I will see you there."

Woo Jin was excited that he and Areum would get the opportunity to enjoy themselves, so he called his tailor in Seoul to have him design evening wears for he and Areum to wear at the engagement party.

When the clothes were ready, he called Areum to come to his home. Areum arrived late Friday night to see Woo Jin. She entered his home and she noticed that a beautiful dress was hanging on a mannequin.

"Areum, that dress is yours," said Woo Jin pointing at the mannequin.

"Oh, Woo Jin, it is beautiful. How did you know my size?" she asked.

"I know what I need to know," he replied. "Try it on. Please."

Areum's tried on the off the shoulder black and white brocade dress with a V cut in the back that accentuated her curvaceous body.

"Areum, you look stunning. I want you to wear this dress to the party."

She nodded and smile as she turned to look at herself in the mirror. "Thanks, Woo Jin, it's beautiful and I feel beautiful in it."

"Great," he said looking at Areum with lust in his eyes.

Chapter Thirty

The Engagement Party and the Altercation
Bob, Kang-de, Areum, Woo Jin, Dave, Bora,
Sun-hee, and Mr. and Mrs. Park

The engagement party caused a large traffic jam at the ITO Hotel. Valets were overwhelmed by the vast crowd and their expensive cars that drove up behind each other. Four hundred guests had walked through the ITO Hotel lobby within three hours. Bora and Dave were the last to arrive.

There were applauds and laughter in the ballroom as they walked in. Bora wore a white chiffon and gold mini dress. Her earrings and necklace were decorated with diamond and sapphire oval stones.

The room was decorated in white and gold satin drapes adorned with crystals. The chairs were covered with white satin and gold ribbons. The tablecloths were white with gold embroidery.

The centerpieces were tall crystal vases with gold balls inside. A variety of flowers were placed on top of the vase and small white and gold candles surround the main centerpieces. The menus were in white with gold plated letters. All utensils were gold plated. The Chinas were white with solid gold trimmings.

There were ten large gold and crystal chandeliers. Each one was surrounded by four small chandeliers. There were four liquor bars. One at each corner of the hall. There were eight hors d'oeuvre stations located outside the hall. Four had international foods for international guests. The dance floor was lit with Bora and Dave's name in filigree design.

A twenty-five-piece orchestra played Bach, Beethoven, Chopin and Modern music.

At Areum's table were Woo Jin, Bob, Sun-hee, Kang-de and four of Bora's classmates from Medical School.

Minjae, Mr. Chin and several of Mr. Park's and Mr. Jong's closest bodyguards sat at tables near the door.

After dinner had finished being served, the guests lined up to greet Bora and Dave. The line took two hours for all the guests to greet Dave and Bora. At the end of the line, Bora noticed Sun-hee, Areum and Woo Jin waiting to greet her.

"Who invited her?" asked Bora loudly so that Sun-hee could hear.

"Bora, be nice. I am sure that your dad invited her," said Dave.

"Congratulations to the both of you. Actually I am Shin Kang-de's date." Areum looked surprised. Woo Jin looked surprised and so did Bora.

Kang-de quickly walked up to Bora and said, "Ms. Park, Dave, congratulations and I wish you a happy life. I hope that you liked the decorations because my staff tried their best to comply with your requests. I love it. It's so opulent. Very rich, very beautiful. I am sure our mothers came up with the color schemes."

"You did a great job, Kang-de."

"Thanks to my staff. Please enjoy yourself."

Kang-de noticed the men at the table next to the door. He told himself that there were too many men in black suits sitting at that table. A disc jockey began to play R&B and electric music and Dave and Bora danced together. Then the master of ceremonies invited everyone to the dance floor.

Kang-de walked over to Sun-hee who was sitting opposite Woo Jin and Areum. He asks Sun-hee to dance with him. The DJ played a romantic song and Kang-de looked at Areum as he danced with Sun-hee. Woo Jin noticed that Kang-de was staring at Areum and he took Areum's hand and lead her to the dance floor.

"Thank you, Kang-de, for not giving me away, when I said that you were my date. I felt so uncomfortable," said Sun-hee.

"No problem. I owe you a lot."

Bob walked up to Kang-de and Sun-hee and said, "Boss, may I finish this dance with Miss Sun-hee?"

"Yeah, I have to make sure everything is working smoothly. Excuse me, lovely lady."

"Sure, Kang-de."

After he had spoken with the master of ceremonies, Kang-de walked past the men in black, glanced at them and he took the elevator down to the garden that was near the lobby.

"Woo Jin, I have to go to the bathroom. Please excuse me."

Areum had seen Kang-de leaving the ballroom and she followed Kang-de downstairs to the garden. Areum stood at the garden entrance and watched Kang-de lighting a cigarette. He took a long puff and blew it in the air.

"Kang-de, why did you bring that girl here? She is Woo Jin's ex-girlfriend. Did you know that?"

"Yes, Areum. The actual word is ex-girlfriend. Are you jealous?"

"Jealous? Oh, please," she said walking into the garden.

Kang-de noticed how beautiful she looked and he grabbed her and kissed her tenderly for at least ten seconds. Areum kissed him back and they embraced tightly.

"Areum, my body aches for you. I want you so badly. I am sorry. I know that I should not speak like this to you but I need you."

"We can't. I can't. I will be honest to say that I have thought about it, but I can't."

"We are both adults now. Are you worried about Woo Jin?" asked Kang-de. "Because I can handle him."

"Well, yes. But I also don't want to do anything to interfere with our friendship. I respect you a lot."

"And I respect you. That's why I have not pursued you. I am leaving," said Kang-de walking out of the garden.

Meanwhile, Woo Jin went searching for Areum. He saw Kang-de leave the garden and walk to the elevator. Then a few minutes later, he saw Areum coming through the stained glass door that divided the garden and the lobby.

Woo Jin waited until Kang-de entered the elevator before entering the garden. He grabbed Areum's arm and pushed her into the garden.

"Lee Areum, what do you think that you are doing out here with him. You said that you were going to the bathroom? Are you toying with me?" asked Woo Jin while shaking her. "No, I am not," she replied.

While in the elevator, Kang-de felt his pocket for his lighter. He realized that he must have dropped it in the garden. He returned to the lobby and walked toward the garden. He heard loud noises. He and a security guard ran to the garden to investigate the noise. They entered the garden and saw Woo Jin squeezing Areum's arm as she yelled in pain.

"Let go of her right now," Kang-de shouted.

"If you come one step further I am going to make you sorry," Woo Jin said threatening Kang-de.

"I have been waiting for this moment. Now I am going to beat the SHIT out of you," Kang-de said taking off his jacket.

Woo Jin dropped Areum's arm and she lost her balance and fell. Kang-de looked at Areum on the ground and he punched Woo Jin in the face. Woo Jin's neck snapped and he fell backward.

Woo Jin used his right leg to kick at Kang-de while he was on the ground. Kang-de jumped over his leg, turned around and kicked Woo Jin in the chest with his right leg.

Woo Jin rolled on the ground. Then he jumped up and he used his head to hit Kang-de in the stomach. Kang-de used his right elbow to hit Woo Jin's in his back. Then he placed Woo Jin's head into a frontal head lock. Woo Jin pushed Kang-de forward and he used his head to head butt Kang-de as he turned around. Kang-de held his head and staggered backward.

Kang-de kicked Woo Jin with a dropkick. Woo Jin fell to the ground. Kang-de jumped on him and punched him over and over until blood flowed from Woo Jin's mouth and nostrils.

His left eye began to swell. In the meantime Areum ran upstairs to the ballroom and got Bob.

"Bob, come quickly. Kang-de and Woo Jin are fighting in the garden."

"Don't make a scene. We'll walk out slowly," said Bob.

He hurried from the elevator and entered the garden. He grabbed Kang-de away from Woo Jin. Woo Jin tried to get up and Bob told him to stay down.

"Mr. Woo Jin. If you get up Kang-de is going to hit you again."

"Kang-de, stop it. Woo Jin, stop it. You are grown men. Please stop. This is Bora's engagement party. Please stop," she said crying.

Kang-de pulled himself from Bob's grasp. He stepped passed Areum and went upstairs to his penthouse.

Bob pulled up Woo Jin who pulled his arm away from Bob.

"Bob, take him to my suite so that he can clean up," said Areum.

"No, get me my car. I am going home. I don't need any help."

"Woo Jin, stop it. At least let me come with you."

"No. I am fine," he said walking to the valet parking area with a bloody nose and a swollen eye.

After watching Woo Jin drive away, Areum went to Kang-de's penthouse suite. She rang the bell, but the door was not locked. Areum knocked and walked in.

She saw Kang-de buttoning a new shirt. His face was not scratch. His knuckles were badly bruised.

"Areum, I don't want a scolding right now. That guy has been looking for a fight and I gave him one. Why do you let a man grab you like
that? What are you a punching bag? I am disappointed with you. You
seem to let that guy abuse you. When are you going to wake up?" asked
Kang-de.

"I could have handled the situation. I can defend myself, Kang-de.
We both grew up in New York. I know how to fight. You know that,"
she said.

"I am sorry for the embarrassment to you, but I had enough of that
guy. Let's face it. We don't like each other and it's because of you. Woo
Jin is no fool. He knows that I like you. He could feel it from the first
day he and I met. He is insecure and I have not disrespected him in
front of you. Have I?"

"No. I am sorry, Kang-de. I am going to try to talk to Woo Jin."

Kang-de looked at her while buttoning his sleeves. "If I were you,
I would leave him alone for the night. His PRIDE is hurt. Listen to
what I am telling you. Do not go to his home."

"Okay. I will call him."

"Listen, Areum. I am not going to watch him abuse you in front of
me. Behind your close door, I can't see anything, but if he ever disrespects
you in front of me again, then I will beat him up again. And I won't hold
back next time. Now I am going back to the party. Are you coming?"

"After I call Woo Jin," she said.

Kang-de looked at her without speaking and he walked to the elevator. He turned to look at her as she dialed Woo Jin.

"Hello, Woo Jin. I want to come over. I am sorry you got into a
fight How are you?"

"I don't feel like talking. Give Bora and Dave my apology. I will
talk to you tomorrow," said Woo Jin and he hung up on Areum.

Kang-de walked in to the ballroom while people were slowly leaving. He sat down next to Sun-hee who noticed that his right hand was
bandaged.

"What happen to your hand, Kang-de?" she asked.

"Your ex-boyfriend and I got into a little disagreement and his face met my hand.

"Kang-de, why? Where is he now?" asked Sun-hee.

"At home," Kang-de said murmuring.

Sun-hee saw Areum walking into the ballroom and she went to Bora, Dave and Mr. and Mrs. Park and said goodnight. Sun-hee told Kang-de that she had an early court case in the morning and she headed to Woo Jin's home. She rang his bell and knocked on his door several times.

"Woo Jin, open the door. It's me," said Sun-hee.

He could see her on his security monitor and he opened the door.

"What are you doing here? Why are you not with your date at the party?"

"He was never my date. I heard that you had an encounter with Kang-de. Are you okay? Why were you fighting? Your face is swollen."

"I don't like the guy. Never did. Go home, Sun-hee. I am fine."

"Let me get you a cold pack for your eyes. Please let me help you."

"I am fine, Sun-hee."

"Woo Jin, I am not leaving you like this. I will get a cold pack from your fridge." Sun-hee cleaned off the blood from Woo Jin's face. She rubbed his legs with ointment. She massaged his neck with ointment and she placed a cold slice of cucumber on his eyes. He fell asleep on the couch.

Sun-hee kissed his bruised lips as he slept on the couch. The pain from her kiss made him groan. Suddenly he woke up and saw her naked body sitting on top of him. She opened his robe, which exposes his showered nude body. She used her tongue to lick his chest and he moaned from the sensation of her tongue circling his nipple. He sat up on the couch and sucked on her breast.

Then her mouth navigated between his legs and he moaned in ecstasy as her mouth engulfed his private part. She licked his inner thigh and he grabbed her and turned her over. Woo Jin slowly, parted her legs and he entered her without a condom. She cried out in ecstasy as he slowly thrust himself in and out of her body. He grabbed her breasts and he lay on her chest as they climaxed together.

"Thank you for that. Now let me sleep. You can stay if you want to," said Woo Jin.

Minutes later Woo Jin's phone rang and it was Areum calling. Sun-hee looked at it and she ignored it. She went to sleep on Woo Jin's bed.

The party finished at four in the morning. All the guests had left, except for the Jongs and the Parks. The cleaning crew had begun to dismantle the tables and decorations. Kang-de and Areum were sitting at the table. He was staring at her as she focused on her cell phone that was not ringing. The Parks, the Jongs, Bora and Dave came over to speak with Kang-de before leaving.

"Goodnight, Mr. and Mrs. Park. I hope you had a great time. Mr. and Mrs. Jong, it was a great party. Did you all have a good time?" asked Kang-de sarcastically.

"We had a great time," Bora interjected.

"Yes, it was awesome," said Dave.

"Thanks, Bora and Dave. I had a great time in spite of my mom's illness," said Areum looking at Kang-de.

The hall was empty. Everyone except Kang-de and Areum had left the ballroom. The guards, including Bob, had left for the night.

"I am going upstairs. Are you coming?" asked Kang-de.

"Yeah. Woo Jin refuses to answer the phone," Areum said sadly.

"Okay. Areum, goodnight," he said with an annoying tone.

As he began to walk to the elevator Areum ran to him.

"Kang-de, let's talk. Can I buy you tea?"

"It's late. You have tea in your suite, don't you?"

"Okay, then I will make you tea."

"Areum, I am not in the mood to talk tonight."

"Then just listen."

Areum gave him a glass of wine instead of tea. Kang-de lay on the couch in Mrs. Lee suite and sets his head facing the chair where Areum was seated. Areum slowly gathered her thoughts and she began to speak.

"Kang-de, I am sorry about what happened tonight. I know that you like me and I like you more than I admit to myself. I was even tempted to sleep with you because my body yearned for you too. However, my heart keeps taking me back to Woo Jin. I know that he is a very jealous person but I love him, Kang-de. I like you a lot. I really do, but I would like to see where my relationship with Woo Jin goes. Do you understand?" she asked him.

She got no response.

"Say something, Kang-de."

Kang-de rolled over on the couch and snored. He was fast asleep. She brought a blanket and she covered him. Areum felt disappointed that he didn't hear what she said. Areum went into her room and slept leaving Kang-de stretched out on the couch.

Sunday morning Areum woke up at 7 A.M. She got dressed and headed to Woo Jin's apartment. Kang-de was still asleep on the couch when Areum left the hotel without informing anyone.

Woo Jin woke up early and made coffee. He thought about last night and what he did with Sun-hee. He felt regret that he slept with her. He went to his bedroom and saw Sun-hee fast asleep.

"Sun-hee, wake up. You need to go home now."

"What time is it? Is it Sunday morning?" she asked rolling over in Woo Jin's bed.

"I want you to go home and get some rest. Thanks so much for your help last night."

"Can I wash my face?"

"Of course. I made you a cup of coffee."

The doorman had let Areum in the building because he knew her. She rang the bell to Woo Jin's home. Woo Jin forgot to look at the monitor. He opened the door because he thought it was the doorman bringing his morning newspapers. Areum looked over Woo Jin's shoulder and saw Sun-hee at the table drinking something. Areum walked in while using her hand to push Woo Jin aside.

"Good morning. How are you both?" Areum asked in a sarcastic tone.

"I am doing fine. I told you not to come over. Why did you?" he asked.

"I am glad I did. I wouldn't have known that you had overnight guest."

"Woo Jin, I am leaving," said Sun-hee.

"No, please stay. How many men are you sleeping with?"

"Lee Areum. Watch your mouth," said Woo Jin.

"Listen, Areum. Don't act like you are Miss Innocent. I know that you have a thing for Kang-de."

Woo Jin turned and stared at Areum.

"I am not sleeping with him. I can't say the same for you and Woo Jin. Can I?"

"This bitch," said Sun-hee murmuring.

"Who are you calling a bitch, whore?"

Sun-hee jumped up and slapped Areum across the face. Areum slapped Sun-hee with the back of her right hand. Sun-hee grabbed at Areum and Areum twisted Sun-hee's hand and she screamed.

"If you want a fight, then I will give you one. But, you will end up in the hospital."

"Come on, bitch. Let's go," said Sun-hee.

"Areum, stop it. Sun-hee, let's go. Areum, you stay here until I get back."

Woo Jin walked Sun-hee to her car and they sat in her car for ten minutes. Then he watched her leave. Woo Jin returned to his apartment and grabbed Areum 's arm.

"Let go of my arm," said Areum in a harsh tone.

Woo Jin dropped his hand to his side and sat at his dining table.

"Areum, you could have handled this as an adult. Why did you have to act so common?"

"What? What did you call me? Woo Jin, I have overlooked your sleeping with this woman. I never said anything. She started it."

"No. You started it. You should have acted like a lady. You acted like a street fighter."

"I am leaving now. I have nothing more to say to you. If I say what I am thinking then I am NOT going to act like a lady." Areum slammed the door and went to see her mother at the hospital.

"Good morning, Mom. How are you, my sweet? I hope that you are feeling better."

"I am feeling a little better. How are you?"

"Great, Mom. When is Dad coming?" Areum asked.

"We must ask Kang-de."

"Kang-de has done enough. Let me call Dad and ask him when he is coming, okay? You both are my responsibility. Let me take care of things."

Areum called her father who answered the phone on the last ring.

"Good morning, Dad. Mom wants to know when you are coming."

"I don't know. I am not feeling physically able to make the trip. Let me talk to your mother."

"Hi, honey. How are you feeling?" asked Mrs. Lee.

"Oh, not that great. How are you, my dear? How is your treatment coming along?" he asked in a sad tone.

"Fine, honey. I feel much better. You know what happened to me, don't you, honey?

"We cannot speak on the phone ever. You know that. I will come to see you soon," said Mr. Lee.

"Excuse me, Mom, I am not staying today. Will you be okay? Tell Dad that I will speak with him later."

"Yes, go ahead, honey."

Areum went to the penthouse to gather her things. She had decided to return to the dorm. Kang-de was downstairs having a meal when he saw Areum with a suitcase and he ran after her.

"Areum, where are you going?"

"I am going back to the dorm. Mom won't be back for another two months. I want you to rent your hotel room. I thank you for your hospitality. I appreciate everything that you have done for us."

"Areum, I am about to lose my temper. Why are you insulting me? Do you want to see me lose my cool? Please go back to the suite. I am only going to say it once. Then I am going to drag you upstairs."

"Kang-de. Let's not fight. I never want to fight with you. I just feel embarrassed that we have accepted too much from you already."

"Areum, how big is your dorm room? Let's not do this now. I want to keep my mind clear. I will see you upstairs," he said hoping that she would change her mind and stay with him.

Kang-de went out to smoke. He took three long puffs of his cigarette, looked around and walked to the elevator. He slowly exited the elevator, walked over to Mrs. Lee suite and rang the bell. No one answered. He stood by the door and sighed. As he began to walk away, he saw Areum's head sticking out of the door. He smiled and turned toward her.

"Come in, Kang-de."

"I am so glad that you changed your mind. Areum, you know that I will do anything for you. Please don't leave me right now."

Areum walked to Kang-de and hugged him. He hugged her tightly.

They stayed embraced for several minutes. He lowered his head to kiss her. Areum raised her head and their lips met each other. Kang-de felt his body tremble. As she tasted his soft lips, she felt her heart beat faster. They continued to kiss for one minute. Then Kang-de released her from his embrace.

"If I don't let you go now, I will never let you go again. I want you, Areum, but on your terms. Let me get out of here."

"Wait, Kang-de, I am going to confess something to you. I am so embarrassed to say it, but... I am a virgin. I have always wanted to wait until I got married to have sex."

"Are you saying that you have not slept with Woo Jin?"

"Yes. And I don't intend to right now. In fact I have hugged and kissed you more than I have with Woo Jin."

"Wow, you just made me so happy!"

Embarrassed by Kang-de's outburst, Areum asked, "Is that what you were so upset with Woo Jin about?"

"No. Not at all. I don't like the way he is abusive to you and to…."

"Sun-hee. Is that what you were going to say? Oh, I know that he was sleeping with her.

I have nothing to say. I don't want to talk about Woo Jin anymore. Let's just relax for a while. Let me call the kitchen. What do you want to eat?"

"Whatever you choose to eat, I will eat as well."

Kang-de called the kitchen to have them send the best foods and drinks to Mrs. Lee's suite.

"Hi. I want lobster, crabs, kimchi stew, salads and a bottle of crystal champagne. Oh, and bring a plate of barbeque beef for me. Got it?"

"Yes, Sir."

"I feel free right now. I have never made a confession about my private life before."

"Well, I am honored that you chose me to confess. I love you even more. Let's have fun tonight."

As she walked to the dining table Woo Jin called Areum. "Hi. I am sorry about our misunderstanding. Will you forgive me?"

"I don't want to talk about it right now. I am still not in a lady mood right now."

Woo Jin heard Kang-de's voice asking Areum where the additional champagne glasses are.

"Who the hell is that? Areum, is Kang-de in your room right now?"

"Woo Jin. I have a lot of stress right now. Please don't make it worse."

"I am coming over there."

"Please don't. I am not doing anything wrong. Okay? I am hanging up now. Kang-de, I think we should move our meal to your place."

"No. We are not. If Woo Jin wants to come here and start anything, I will finish it for him. In fact, I will call security to let them know not to let him upstairs. Would you rather I do that?"

"That might make him more mad. Just work with me on this one, please."

Kang-de became furious. "Damn it, Areum, this is my hotel. I own it. Nobody is going to dictate how I run my hotel. Why should we have to hide from a mad man? Come on, Areum. We are staying right here. I don't like the fact that you are so afraid of Woo Jin. You are going to make me get mad and I will go to his house and beat him up right now. Stop being afraid. You cannot live like this. Is this the kind of life you want? Come on! Come on! You are going to make me lose my appetite."

"Okay, Kang-de. You are right. If he comes, we will deal with him. Call security."

"Now you are thinking properly. Come on, lady. Get your life in order. You are an adult. You are not a child."

The doorbell rang and Kang-de went to the door and opened it in a rage. Room service had brought two carts filled with food. Areum saw them and she made a silent sigh. Kang-de noticed that she was uncomfortable and he called the head of security to tell them not to let Woo Jin upstairs.

"Let's eat and drink and go back to an hour ago," Kang-de said.

Areum thought about how good Kang-de had been to her and her family and she said, "You deserve a good life, Kang-de."

"So why don't you give me a good life?" he asked.

"I have nothing to offer you. I am not working as yet. I can barely take care of myself. You deserve a pretty woman who you can show off. I am not a pretty woman. I don't know why you even like me?"

Kang-de replied, "Because you are beautiful inside and out. You are kind, loving, sexy and those eyes of yours can disarm anyone. I have loved you for a long time, but let's continue this conversation another time. I want to toast to love. To LOVE. ONE LOVE," he said raising his glass.

Areum raised her glass and replied, "My toast is to you. I am very happy that I got to see you again."

Chapter Thirty-one

Kang-de, Areum, Woo Jin, Mr. Jong, Bob,
Mr. Park, Sun-hee, Minjae, and Mr. Chin

Laughter filled the air as Kang-de and Areum enjoyed the evening together. They reminisced about the past and what the future held for
Areum as a cardiologist.

Kang-de got a phone call in the middle of toasting each other. It was
the bodyguard Kang-de assigned to Sun-hee. "Hello, what's wrong?"

"Boss, a group of men surprised us and they grabbed Sun-hee."

Kang-de put down his glass of wine and shouted at the bodyguard.
"Damn it. How could you let that happen?! Did you get the license plate?"

"Yes, Boss."

"Okay, that's good. Meet me at my office in about an hour. I will
call Bob. Areum, you will have to finish your meal by yourself. Something came up and I have to take care of it."

"I could not help listening to your phone call. Please be careful.
You know that this could be a setup. Don't trust anyone."

Kang-de smiled and touched Areum's shoulder and said, "Now
that's my girl. My brain is at work, Areum. Trust me."

Kang-de called Bob and Chul. They all met at the office simultaneously.

"Tell me exactly what happened. Step by step," Kang-de said.

"Well, Boss, we were sitting outside her home. About six men surrounded our car. We couldn't get out. We had to watch Ms. Sun-hee being dragged. She was yelling and trying to fight but there were too many of them."

"Did you recognize any of the men? Think carefully."

"Yes, one of the men belonged to Mr. Park's gang."

"Good job, guys. Bob, looks like we need to have a word with Mr. Jong. I need to have him destroy Mr. Park for me as quickly as possible."

Kang-de called Mr. Jong without knowing how dangerous he really was.

"Hello, Mr. Jong, we need to talk. Please meet me at my office in about an hour."

"Boss, are you going to use your information to force his hand?"

"You got it, Bob. I'm about to get real dirty with these people," said Kang-de, "and I won't allow my enemies to succeed."

Mr. Jong arrived earlier than scheduled. He sat facing Kang-de, trying to intimidate him.

"Okay, Mr. Jong, let me get to the point. I need you to squeeze Mr. Park tonight. He has something that I want back."

"Why do you need my help? You're a man of many talents and resources," said Mr. Jong.

"Yeah, but this job is for a man like you," Kang-de replied.

"And what's in it for me?" asked Mr. Jong.

Kang-de put a cigarette in his mouth without lighting it. He pulled it out of his mouth, waited for a second then replied, "Your freedom."

"Shin Kang-de, what do you mean by that?" yelled Mr. Jong.

"You know exactly what I mean. I have enough information on you to send you to prison for a long time. What would Dave think about that? In fact one of my men is waiting at the police station right now."

"He has something to hand to the police. Oh, by the way I also got one at a television station too. See, I know how you think. You have friends in high places, but I have friends everywhere."

Mr. Jong smiled, walked up to Kang-de and asked, "Are you trying to blackmail me? What do you think that you have on me, Shin Kang-de?"

Kang-de looked him in the eyes and said, "The survivor of your failed kidnapping came to see me before your men took him away. He confessed your part in the attempted kidnapping of Bora Park on video. He filled me in on some other things that you have been busy doing. It's all on tape and I made lots of copies."

"Mr. Jong, you should be careful who you stab in the back. Your driver/kidnapper is the brother-in-law of one of my most trusted employee."

Kang-de looked at Bob and smiled. Bob put his right hand in between Mr. Jong and Kang-de suggesting to Mr. Jong to step away from Kang-de. Mr. Jong stepped back and sat in a chair near the door to Kang-de' s office.

"Now Mr. Jong, I want you to move forward with your plan to destroy Mr. Park. I also want you to find out where Mr. Park is holding the woman he kidnapped. You will inform me and we will have the police arrest everyone, Except you and Mr. Chin, of course."

Mr. Jong looked surprised that Kang-de knew about Mr. Chin.

"Shin Kang-de, I underestimated you. I will not make that mistake again. You don't know what you have just done."

"Get going, Mr. Jong. Time is of essence for the kidnapped victim."

Mr. Jong stormed out of Kang-de's office murmuring to himself in a low voice. "Soon you will die like your parents did, but first you will beg for mercy."

"What was that, Mr. Jong? I didn't hear you."

He turned, looked at Kang-de, smiled and walked to the elevator.

"Boss, they should never have messed with you. They are all going to pay for their transgressions. Ha, ha, ha."

"Increase the security for Areum. Call that idiot Woo Jin. I am willing to work with him when it comes to Areum's security."

Bob called Woo Jin and put Kang-de on the phone. Woo Jin didn't answer immediately. He didn't recognized the phone number.

"Hello. Who are you?" he asked.

"Woo Jin, before you hang up on me, I want to tell you something. Areum is going to need extra security. The men who kidnapped Bora are not finished as yet. They might try to grab Areum. Woo Jin, they kidnapped Sun-hee."

"What? They kidnapped Sun-hee? Who, when, what happened?"

"That's not important right now. You and I need to get two teams of guards for Areum. Do we agree on that?"

"Yes, yes, consider it done," said Woo Jin.

"Okay. I will be in touch with you," Kang-de said.

Kang-de returned to the hotel to speak with Areum. He rang the bell to Mrs. Lee suite. Areum opened the door Kang-de walked in and had Areum sit on the couch with him. He began to speak with her.

"Areum, one of the things I love about you is that you can see trouble before it comes upon you. That's your New York upbringing. I don't want to scare you, but Sun-hee got kidnapped. You might be in danger too. The same people who tried to kidnap Bora may be involved, but I am not sure how they are connected. I spoke with Woo Jin and we agree that you will need more protection."

Areum looked at Kang-de and told him that she didn't need protection.

"We are not asking you. We are giving it to you. It won't be for long. I want you to move out of the dorm and into this suite. A driver will take you wherever you want to go. I have also sent men to the hospital to keep an eye on Mom."

"Okay, Kang-de. I won't argue with you. I trust you. Can I go and get the rest of my things from the dormitory?"

"Yeah. Bob and the men will go with you. Consider this a new beginning for me and Woo Jin. Isn't that what you want?"

"Real funny, Kang-de. But it is nice that the two of you are getting along in a crisis."

"Oh, Areum, it will not be long until he goes crazy. Once this crisis is over, he will go back to being stupid."

"Stop it, Kang-de."

"Okay. Let's stop talking about him. Go and get all of your things from the dormitory. I will go to the hospital to see your mother. The driver will bring you to the hospital and we will meet there."

"That sounds great. See you later," she said.

Kang-de arrived at the hospital to see Mrs. Lee. He walked in with flowers in his hands and a bag filled with change of clothes.

"Hi, Mom. How are you feeling today? I hope the medication is working."

"Oh, Kang-de, I am so happy to see you. I feel a little better than when I first arrived here. Thank you for all your help. I can never repay you."

"Mom, you are my family. Don't ever forget that. Areum is on her way here and we want to talk to you about something."

"Did you ask her to marry you and did she say yes to you?"

"No, Mom, it's not like that. That's not what we want to talk to you about."

Areum walked in with Bob and four men in suits before Kang-de could explain.

"Hi, Mama, how are you? Hey, Kang-de."

"Did you move everything out?" asked Kang-de.

"Yes."

"Areum, I told Mom that we have something to discuss with her."

"You tell her," said Areum.

Kang-de thought about what he should say to Mrs. Lee since she was not in good health. "Mom, I am placing security at your door. They will be there twenty-four hours a day. The reason for the security is because one of my employee got kidnapped and I don't want anything to happen to any of you because of my affiliations with you. Therefore, I have taken steps to avert any crisis that might arise. You, Areum and Mr. Lee mean a lot to me. I would be devastated if something happened to any of you. I hope that you don't mind. It will only be until I sort out a few things with some people."

"Kang-de, I trust you. We trust you and we don't want anything to happen to you either. I want you to be very careful. I hope that you have security to protect you too, Kang-de?"

"Yes, Mom. I am fine."

"I will see to it that he is protected, Mom."

Kang-de looked at Areum and smiled. His cell phone rang. It was Mr. Jong calling.

"Excuse me, I have to take this phone call outside."

Bob followed Kang-de down the hallway.

"Mr. Jong, I did not expect to hear from you so quickly. What do you want to tell me?"

"I have taken steps to do a hostile takeover of Mr. Park's company. Right now he is panicking and my associate (Mr. Jong avoided calling Mr. Chin's name in his conversation with Kang-de) found out where Ms. Sun-hee is being held."

"Great. Where is she being held and how many men are with her?" Kang-de asked anxiously.

"We will rescue her. We don't need the police," said Mr. Jong.

"Listen, Mr. Jong, don't even think about exchanging her for the tapes. Let's just say that if she is not at my hotel by tonight, the tapes go live on the television and at the police station. Do you understand me?"

"Oh, Mr. Shin Kang-de, don't try to use those tapes against me or you will be sorry. Okay?"

"Mr. Jong, did I just hear a threat coming out of your mouth?"

"It's not a threat. It's a promise."

"Well, since you are promising me something, let me promise you something. Your precious son Dave will be the first person to hear the tapes, should anything happen to me or my loved ones. Mr. Jong, you know that I don't joke with my words. Whatever I say, I will do. And don't ever threaten me again. By the way you are not the only company that I supply computers. Read between the lines."

"Just make sure that Sun-hee is at my hotel tonight. Okay?" Kang-de hung up the phone, thought about Mr. Jong's statement and spoke to Bob.

"Bob, I think that we have something very wrong. I am thinking that Mr. Jong might have kidnapped Sun-hee and he wanted it to look like Mr. Park was involved. He wanted us to see one of Mr. Park's men so that we would go after Mr. Park instead. But when I told him that he had to do the dirty work, it messed up his plans."

"That's why he said that he underestimated you when he was at your office," Bob replied.

"Oh, Bob, it's always good to talk to your enemies. They tend to let things slip out of their mouths. You have just got to analyze those things. If he really did a hostile takeover of Mr. Park's company, then he did me a great favor. We will find out tomorrow."

"Are you going to call your cousin who sits on the board at Mr. Jong's company?" Bob asked Kang-de.

"No, not yet. He will let me know if something is happening. Bob, let's go back to Mrs. Lee's room. I want to take Areum back to the hotel and then we will wait for Mr. Jong's call. I feel that there is more to this story that I don't know. I just feel it."

"Okay, Boss," said Bob signaling the driver to get the car.

While in the car Bob whispered to Kang-de that he thought that someone had followed them from Areum's dorm to the hospital. He didn't want to tell Kang-de that he thought that Areum might be in danger because she was in the car with them.

"Bob, I want Areum to be well guarded," he said looking at Bob and nodding that he understood what he was trying to tell him.

Meanwhile, Mr. Park got a call about an attempted hostile takeover of his company. He immediately called his directors and shareholders to have a meeting.

"Someone has just attempted to take over a few of my pharmaceutical companies. I think I know who it is and I will deal with that person. I don't want you to panic. This is only an attempt. I am in the process of performing a hostile acquisition of my competitor's company as we speak," he said while adjusting the glasses on his face.

Getting up from his chair, one of the directors asked Mr. Park who was the person that was trying to destroy his company. "How can we help?" asked the director.

Mr. Park replied, "I will not call his name right now. I need to verify some information first. I just wanted you to know that we are going to be fine as a company. This meeting is adjourned. I will contact all of you very soon."

Everyone who attended the meeting shook Mr. Park's hand as they walked out of the boardroom. As soon as the last person left the room, Mr. Park called Mr. Jong for a meeting at his office. Mr. Jong was already in the building and when he arrived at the office, he was escorted by one of Mr. Park's secretary into a boardroom. Mr. Park greeted him and told him that someone just tried to acquire a few of his pharmaceutical companies.

"Do you know anything about it?" asked Mr. Park.

Mr. Jong began to tremble. His heart began to beat rapidly. He was surprised that the news of the attempted acquisition got out so quickly. He was not sure how much Mr. Park knew about his involvement in the attempted acquisition.

He told himself that it's best not to acknowledge anything. "No. Why are you asking me about acquisitions? You are looking at the wrong person. Have you thought about that gangster Shin Kang-de? He is very cunning. You and I are about to be in-laws why would I want to take anything from you."

Minjae walked into Mr. Park's office, stood next to Mr. Park and he stared into Mr. Jong eyes.

"Hey, Minjae, Mr. Jong is telling me that Shin Kang-de had performed a hostile takeover of some of my companies. That is interesting, right?"

Minjae looked at Mr. Park and at Mr. Jong and he smiled. "Yes, Boss. It is very interesting."

"Mr. Jong, what if I told you that I have proof that you tried to acquire my company on several occasions? Now you are here in my face telling me a lie. Shin Kang-de might be cunning, but he lets you know what he is going to do. He is not devious like you. I want my company back. I am not taking this as a personal attack. I am going to consider this as just business. My company is not for sale and not available for hostile acquisitions. Mr. Park, let's not try to trick each other any longer. You filed an injunction against my company and I heard that you are attempting to do the same thing to me too. I even know that you tried to steal Shin Kang-de's computer business. So who is fooling whom? Let's stop playing games," said Mr. Jong.

"Mr. Jong, family is off-limits. My Bora must never be placed in danger again and your Dave is safe with me. He is going to be my son-in-law. I take the attempted kidnapping of my child very personal and I will retaliate against anyone who tries to harm my Bora. Do we understand each other? You have made yourself very clear. Now I am not admitting to any illegal actions against your company but I am sure that your company will be just fine. Can I say the same for mine?"

"We don't trust each other, but I have no desire to destroy your company. Let's leave it at that."

Both Mr. Park and Mr. Jong stood up and shook hands.

"Oh, by the way, Mr. Park, you have underestimated Shin Kang-de. If I were you I would not trust him. I know him very well. "

Mr. Jong held his hand out to Mr. Park who looked at him, hesitated, then shook his hand. Minjae escorted him to the elevator. Mr. Chin sat in the car waiting for Mr. Jong to exit the building. Mr. Jong entered the car and sighed.

"Boss, how did it go?" asked Mr. Chin.

"Not good. He knows that we tried to infiltrate his company. He knows that I tried to use Bora as leverage. He doesn't believe that Shin

Kang-de is involved. He doesn't know about our other business and we won't tell him right now. We may need his help in the future."

"So what are we going to do about, Shin Kang-de?"

"First we let the girl go. We only took her to get information on Mr. Park anyway."

"Boss, she can identify the men," said Mr. Chin.

"Tell her that she will keep her mouth shut or we will make her disappear."

"Okay. And what about Shin Kang-de? Do you want me to erase him permanently?"

Mr. Jong nodded "I want to get him and those tapes. Call Mr. Kim in Hong Kong. He will let us know what to do about Shin Kang-de. As for Mr. Park, once the kids are married I will have our friends get him on tax fraud. I am not done with him as yet."

Mr. Jong and Mr. Chin smiled with each other. Mr. Chin made a phone call to his men.

"Hello, take the girl to ITO Hotel and drop her off there. Make sure that she is still blindfolded. And get a truck with a fake license's plate.

Mr. Chin hung up and he made another call to Mr. Kim in Hong Kong. Mr. Kim was a grey haired handsome looking man. He had the physique of an old military soldier who kept his body in great shape. He was fearless and cold-hearted and he would kill anything or anyone who he thought should be killed. Mr. Kim was capable of killing members of his family if he felt that it was for a greater cause. No one in his family knew that he was a killer because his demeanor was one of a quiet docile man who spoke only when necessary.

Mr. Kim lay on his lounge chair reading a book when his cell phone rang.

"Good afternoon, Mr. Kim. Mr. Jong wants Shin Kang-de eliminated. He said it should be untraceable like the death of his parents."

"Okay," he said without thought. "Do it and let me know when it's done. If you need assistance call me. He should have been eliminated long ago."

"Thank you, Sir."

Several hours later at the ITO Hotel. A black SUV pulled up and Sun-hee, who was blindfolded, was pushed out of the car and the car sped off. The ITO Hotel doorman and security guards ran to assist Sun-hee. They removed her blindfold and helped her to her feet.

Shivering and crying, she asked, "Where is Mr. Shin Kang-de? Please take me to him."

"He is coming, Miss Sun-hee," the security guard replied.

Kang-de hurried to the front door of the hotel. He saw her trembling. He lifted her and took her to one of the hotel boardroom.

"How are you, Sun-hee? Are you okay? I was so worried about you. Do you want to go to the hospital?"

"No, just give me something strong to drink. Do you have any vodka?"

"Yeah, but I will get you a glass of sherry instead." He nodded to his security to get the drink. "Did they abuse you? Tell me the truth."

"No. They hit me once because I bit one of them. But I will be okay. Does Woo Jin know that I was in trouble?" she asked trembling.

"Must you bring him into this? Okay. Go ahead and call him. I know you will call him anyway," said Kang-de handing her his cell.

Her hands shook as she punched in Woo Jin's number in Kang-de's phone.

"Hello, Woo Jin?"

"Sun-hee. Are you alright? I heard what happened. Did they hurt you? Why do you have Kang-de's phone? Where are you now?"

"At the ITO Hotel."

"Okay, I am coming over right now."

Within minutes, Woo Jin arrived at ITO Hotel. He pulled up in front of the hotel and walked into the hotel, leaving the car door open and running.

"Where is Mr. Shin-Kang-de? Tell him Mr. Kim Woo Jin is here to see him."

The front desk called Kang-de and he told them to send Woo Jin to the boardroom. A guard opened the door for Woo Jin. He saw Sun-hee wrapped in a blanket that Kang-de brought to her.

"Sun-hee, how are you? Are you okay? How did this happen? Tell me everything," he said staring at Kang-de.

"Hello, Woo Jin," said Kang-de.

"Hello to you too. Why did Sun-hee get kidnapped? Is it because she knows you? Is this what the people around you should expect? Why should anyone be placed in danger because they know you?"

Kang-de looked at him, but he didn't respond to him.

"Sun-hee, I will leave you to talk with your friend. Let me know when you are finished. I am not in the mood for a confrontation. I am happy that you are back."

Sun-hee ran to Kang-de and whispered to him that she knew that he was the person who got her back safely. "Thank you so much, Kang-de. I really appreciate your help."

"Consider us even. My debt to you is paid in full. Call me when you are done." Kang-de walked out of the room and closed the door.

"That guy is an ice man. He has no heart. I don't understand why you women like him," said Woo Jin.

"You don't understand him Woo Jin. He has a big heart and he is truly a good friend," she said.

Woo Jin hugged Sun-hee while she cried. "Don't cry, Sun-hee. You are safe now. I will not let anything happen to you again. I am going to take control of your security as of now."

Sun-hee replied, "Woo Jin, thanks a lot but I don't think they will try again."

Woo Jin told her that he was not convinced. "Your security team just got bigger until I find the kidnappers and let them pay. Now talk to me. What do you remember about the entire situation?"

Woo Jin called someone and he gave the phone to Sun-hee. She told the person over the phone everything that she remembered.

"Let's get out of here. You must be hungry. Let me buy you something to eat," said Woo Jin.

"I think Kang-de called for food already," Sun-hee said.

"I don't care. I am going to take you out to eat. I do not want anything to do with this hotel right now."

"Okay, Woo Jin. Let me tell Kang-de that we are leaving."

"Here, call him. Let him know that I am taking you away from this place. Sun-hee, let me tell him."

As instructed, she called Kang-de and handed the phone to Woo Jin.

"Kang-de, I am taking Sun-hee out to eat. She will be staying with me tonight and tomorrow I will take her to the hospital. I have my men following us and they will be with her all night."

Kang-de smiled and said, "No problem. Make sure that she is healthy and safe. By the way does your current girlfriend know that your ex-girlfriend will be spending the night with you?"

"Don't concern yourself about that. Let me handle my business and my women," he replied.

Kang-de warned him in a threatening tone. "If you hurt Areum, then it becomes my business. Do we understand each other?"

Ignoring the threat, Woo Jin hung up the phone on Kang-de.

"This guy is really going to let me have to hurt him one day soon."

Kang-de called Areum's room to check on her.

"Areum, are you awake? I am in the lobby. Can I come up?"

"Sure. I will make tea for you."

Kang-de passed the guards that were posted at Areum's door and he went into her room. He sat down on the couch and used the remote to turn on the television. As he surfed the channels he looked at Areum and he became sad. He agonized over whether he should tell her that Woo Jin left the hotel with Sun-hee.

"Areum, I need a drink from your minibar," said Kang-de as he took out a bottle of cognac. "Would you like a drink too?"

"No, Kang-de, I am having tea. Did you find Sun-hee?"

"Yes, she was just here," said Kang-de in a low voice.

"How is she? Is she hurt? Where is she?"

Kang-de paused for a minute before answering. He thought that telling her would devastate her. He decided not to volunteer too much information to her. "She is fine. She went to dinner with friends," he replied.

"She went out so soon. She should go to the hospital and get a doctor to examine her?"

"Oh, Areum, you are too sweet and so naïve. I suppose that's why I love you."

"Well, I feel sorry for her because she did get kidnapped. She is not my friend. I don't even like her, but I do feel sorry for her."

"I know. Are you going to sleep now?"

"I was going to call Woo Jin to see if he wants to go out tonight."

Areum's remarks made Kang-de's face turned pale. He had to think quickly. He had to prevent her from calling Woo Jin. He could only think of telling her that it was late and they both needed to rest.

"Why don't you call him tomorrow? He's probably resting. Areum, don't forget that you have a big entourage who will be traveling with you. Let them rest tonight," he said.

"Okay, Boss. I understand.

"Goodnight, Areum."

"Goodnight, Kang-de."

Kang-de stayed awake thinking about how he had just prevented Areum from getting hurt by Woo Jin.

Kang-de told himself that he was going to have to hurt Woo Jin because he was playing with Areum's feelings. He slowly fell asleep after thinking about her and Woo Jin.

Meanwhile, at a restaurant across town, Woo Jin and Sun-hee sat at a table talking about her kidnapping ordeal.

"I am very happy that you did not get hurt. Are you sure that you are okay?"

"I am sure. This restaurant is nice and the food taste great," she said changing the topic of the conversation.

Woo Jin replied, "I think it is better than that ITO Hotel restaurant."

"Well…they are equally good."

Woo Jin thoughts turned to pity for Sun-hee. "Let's go back to my place. I want you to stay the night. I have the other room ready for you," he said hesitantly.

She quickly agreed to the invitation.

Three cars filled with men in suits followed Woo Jin and Sun-hee back to his home. Woo Jin held his door open for her to walk in. She slowly entered into his apartment and looked around carefully.

Woo Jin pretended not to notice her behavior. "Okay, Sun-hee, the room is ready for you. Go and take a shower and I will give you one of my new pajamas to wear."

"Okay, thank you."

Sun-hee took a shower, walked into Woo Jin's room and asked to sleep in his bed because she was scared to sleep alone.

"Sun-hee, you have five men who knows martial arts standing outside my door. What are you afraid of?"

"I want the company. I promise to behave myself. I won't touch you."

"Okay. I will go along with your wish. But I am not in the mood for any foreplay tonight. Okay?" said Woo Jin in a stern tone.

Sun-hee went to sleep in Woo Jin's bed. She lay under his armpit and he hugged her until she fell asleep. Three hours later she jumped up and screamed. Woo Jin woke up and hugged her.

"Sun-hee, you are fine. Were you having a nightmare? You are safe now. I won't let anything happen to you. Try to sleep."

She snuggled her head on Woo Jin's chest and she fell asleep.

The morning came quickly for Woo Jin who was unable to sleep throughout the night. He spent the night looking at the ceiling and thinking about Areum. He got up and made coffee for himself and Sun-hee.

He looked at her as she slept. Suddenly she sat up in the bed, looked around and stood up.

"Good morning, young lady. How do you feel?"

"Good. Did you sleep well? Your eyes are red," she asked.

"No, I did not sleep. I want to fix breakfast for you then I am going to take you to the hospital," he said.

"Oh, no. I will fix breakfast for the both of us. You have been very kind to me."

"Okay. Are you sure that you are feeling well?" he asked.

Sun-hee prepared Woo Jin's favorite breakfast foods. They talked and ate as if they were a real couple.

"I am going to sit on the couch for a while. Maybe I can fall asleep for a few minutes. We will go to the doctor as soon as I get up. Okay?"

"Yes. You do that. I will wash the dishes and clean up for you. I owe you that."

Woo Jin was hesitant to allow her to clean up for him because he didn't want her to misinterpret their relationship. Woo Jin's phone rang and he pulled it out of his pocket. He noticed that it was Areum on the phone and he went into his room to speak with her.

"Good morning, how are you? What are you doing today? We have to get back to the library. You need to start studying again."

"I know. I just can't think about school right now. Did you hear that Sun-hee is okay?"

"Yeah. I heard. Let me call you back later."

"Okay. Bye."

Areum thought to herself that something was not right with him, but she was not going to question him. Areum called Kang-de to invite him to have breakfast with her.

"Good morning, Areum. You are awake early. How are you?"

"Good morning to you. Would you like to have breakfast with me?"

"Sure. I will come down, or do you want to come up?"

"I will come up. I will make you tea. I like making you tea," said Areum, walking to the elevator.

"That's nice. See you in half an hour. I want to take a shower," said Kang-de smiling.

Areum got dressed up to go upstairs. She was followed by two of Kang-de's guards. She rang Kang-de's bell and he answered the door with no shirt on. Areum eyes widened and her mouth fell open as she looked at the sight of his half-naked body. She finally saw the six pack chest she had been feeling when he hugged her. She turned her back and looked down. Kang-de hid behind the door, when he realized that Areum was staring at his body.

"I am sorry. Wait a minute, let me put on my shirt."

"No. I am sorry that I came too early. Forgive me."

"Nothing to forgive. It's my fault. I should have been dressed before I opened the door. Please come in," he said while buttoning his shirt. "What are we going to eat? You decide," he said.

"I just want scrambled eggs with sausage and toast," she replied.

"I will have the same but no sausage. Let me call room service. I don't feel like eating downstairs. I just want the two of us to eat together. Is it okay with you?"

"Of course. I like eating with you," she said. "Did your mother call? Is she feeling better?"

"Yes, she is doing better. Thanks to you."

Kang-de hesitated then asked, "Did you call Woo Jin this morning?"

"Why do you ask? You have never asked before. Yes, I did. He said that he will call me back," Areum replied suspiciously.

"Okay. Should I expect to be disturbed during my breakfast?"

"No, Kang-de. I turned off my phone before I left my room."

"Good thinking."

The doorbell rang. Room service arrived with breakfast. They ate breakfast and told each other jokes. Kang-de looked at Areum with sadness in his eyes. He thought about telling her that Sun-hee was with Woo Jin, but he did not want her to be unhappy.

"Areum, I wanted to go to the office this morning, but I think that I am going to work at home today. Do you want to keep me company? You can bring your medical books and read while I am checking my store receipts."

"I think that is a great idea, Mr. Shin Kang-de. Next week I am going to be too busy to see you every day. Medical School starts again."

"Oh, that won't be any fun. The good thing is that you will be safe in the hotel. I feel good about that. Go and get your books. I will wait for you," said Kang-de with a firm tone.

"Okay, Boss," she said sarcastically.

Areum walked to the elevator and she turned on her phone to call Woo Jin. The guards opened the door for her as Woo Jin answered the phone. She heard someone called Woo Jin and she thought it sounded like Sun-hee's voice.

"Woo Jin, do you have company? I hear Sun-hee's voice."

Surprised by what Areum asked, Woo Jin snapped at her and said, "Are you checking up on me? Yes, she is here. I told you that I will call you later."

Areum yelled, "No. I will call you later."

Areum hung up and began to cry.

It had been thirty-five minutes since she left Kang-de's suite. Kang-de became concerned and called to check if she was okay.

"Areum, where are you? I am waiting on you. Are you okay?"

With a crack in her voice, she told him that she was coming.

Kang-de heard her voice cracking and he knew that she had been crying. "Did I do something wrong? What happened? You sound like you are crying. I am coming down," he said.

"No. No. I will come up."

"Okay. I am waiting for you."

Thirty minutes more had passed and Areum laid on her bed depressed. Kang-de went to her suite and rang the bell. She didn't answer. He knocked hard on the door and Areum answered the door.

He questioned her, "You left my place very happy. What could have happened since then? Oh, don't tell me. It's Woo Jin. What did he do?"

"He did nothing. I am fine."

"Tell that to someone who does not know you. What did he do? I want to know. If you don't tell me, then I will go over there and ask him."

"No, Kang-de. Please don't. I will tell you. I heard Sun-hee's voice when I called him and we had an argument."

"Why did you call him? You told me that you turned off your phone. Why did you call him?" he said angrily.

"Wait a minute. Did you know that Woo Jin was the friend that Sun-hee went out with?"

Kang-de thought about her question then he answered her. "Let me say to you again, I am not going to see you get hurt by anyone. Not Woo Jin. Not anybody. If Woo Jin is cheating on you, I don't want to be the one to tell you because later you will blame me."

"I don't want that. I didn't lie to you. I just didn't call Woo Jin's name."

"I knew that Sun-hee was going to spend the night with him. Areum, you have to decide what you want to do. I cannot get in the middle of your affairs with Woo Jin. As I told you before. If he hurts you in front of me, then I will deal with him. Your life behind closed door, I cannot control that. You are an adult. It is time for you take a stand with Woo Jin. I am done talking about him." Kang-de turned and walk to the door. He glanced at her and told her, "I refuse to make him important in my life. Come and join me when you are finished crying. I am leaving."

Kang-de shut her door and he went upstairs. Minutes later, Areum went upstairs. She could tell Kang-de was feeling hurt. She knocked on his door and he didn't answer. She knocked again and he did not answer. She yelled out, "Kang-de, open the door, please. I am going to stay at this door until you open it."

Kang-de opened the door and walked back to his dining table.

"I am sorry, Kang-de. I have not been considering your feelings. Can I get a hug?"

"No. I am not in a hugging mood."

"Okay, but I am going to hug you anyway."

Areum tried to put her arms around his neck. He walked away from her. She follow behind him and grabbed him around the waist. He tried to break her clasp, but she held on to him tightly.

"I am so, so, so sorry. I know that I hurt your feelings. Please forgive me. Kang-de, I don't mean to be a burden to you. I feel so badly. Tell me you forgive me. If you don't tell me that you forgive me, then I am going to stay in this suite and nag you until you give in."

"Okay. Okay. Areum, can't you to see what is in front of you? Why are you so blind?"

"I am slowly getting my life in order. I promise you. Can I hug you now. Please?"

Kang-de allowed Areum to hug him. She kissed him on the cheek and then on his neck. He felt aroused from the kiss on his neck and he pulled away from her.

"Don't do that unless you plan to go further."

"Okay. I will behave myself. May I stay and read my book. Please?"

"Yes, you may, but don't talk to me."

"Fine."

An hour later, Woo Jin called Areum.

"Woo Jin, we need to talk tomorrow. I have a few things that I want to say to you."

Kang-de looked up at her and then back to his papers.

Woo Jin insisted that he wanted to talk with Areum that evening because he needed to explain a few things to her. "I don't care to hear any explanations tonight. I said tomorrow."

She hung up her cell phone and she turned it off.

Chapter Thirty-two

Woo Jin, Areum, Mr. and Mrs. Kim,
Mr. and Mrs. Hwang, Yoomi, Sun-hee, and Kang-de

Woo Jin realized that Areum was upset and therefore he needed to remove Sun-hee from his life. He looked at Sun-hee who was sitting on his couch and he walked up to her and told her to gather her belongings.

"Sun-hee, it's time for me to take you to the hospital. The guards are going to be with you twenty-four hours a day. Don't be scared. I have my people looking for the kidnappers."

She looked at him with doubt on her face.

"Trust me, I will have my men deal with them. Just because my base is in Hong Kong, it doesn't mean that I don't have connections here. I have a lot of connections here. You will see. Let's go."

Woo Jin was unaware that his security was connected to Sun-hee's kidnappers and they were not searching for anyone.

Woo Jin and his driver took Sun-hee to the hospital. She got examined by a doctor who told her that she should return for a thorough physical the next day. Sun-hee agreed to go to the hospital next day.

While driving home he told himself that he no longer wanted her as a friend. The driver pulled up in front of her apartment and Woo Jin opened the car door for her. He escorted her to her door so that she could feel safe. Woo Jin and two security guards opened her door, searched her home and then they handed her new keys.

"Sun-hee, your apartment is cleared. They've changed the locks and two of the men will be staying outside your apartment."

"Thank you, Woo Jin. Are you going to stay with me tonight?"

"No, Sun-hee. Actually this is goodbye. I won't be seeing you anymore. You can let the security know whatever you need and they will contact me. It's is best this way. Take care." Woo Jin hurried to the car and the driver sped away before Sun-hee could respond to him.

Her phone rang and she grabbed it quickly and answered. Kang-de called her to see how she was doing.

"Hello. How are you? Are you okay?" he asked.

"Yes, I feel very secure," she uttered in a disappointing tone. She had hope that Woo Jin was at the other end of the phone.

"My men will be going to work with you. Okay?"

"Okay. Thanks again, Kang-de. You can be so sweet when you want to be."

"Don't ruin my reputation," he said smiling.

"Okay, silly. I won't. Thanks so much, Kang-de. Bye."

The next day the meeting between Areum and Woo Jin began early. Areum arrived at Woo Jin's apartment dressed in a blue pants and a pink T-shirt. She knocked on the door and he opened it.

"We need to talk," she said staring at his eyes.

"Good morning to you. What do you want to talk about?" he asked.

"I do not like how you treat me. I feel that you are being very disrespectful and I will not tolerate it. You should not grab me ever again. I don't like it. I don't like being humiliated. If you want to cheat on me, then let's call it quits. I don't need a man who feels that he can do whatever he wants without considering my feelings. I am not desperate for a man. I like you a lot. You have been very helpful with my studies, but I will go it alone if I have to. I have had enough of the disrespect."

Woo Jin, clearing his throat, asked, "Are you finished talking? I brought Sun-hee here so that she could feel safe. We didn't do anything. She needed my help and I gave it to her. I am sorry that I have not considered your feelings. I thought that you would understand me. I am loyal to you, Areum. I get jealous easily. I know that you like Kang-de and he likes you a lot. I am afraid of losing you to him and that's why I get so crazy. Areum, I want you in my life. I am sorry for my bad behavior. Sun-hee is not my girlfriend. She was just a sleeping partner before I met you. I apologize for my actions. Will you forgive me?"

"I am still hurt about the name you called me. You called me common. Is that how you think of me?" she asked.

"No. No. I am really sorry that I spoke to you like that. I did not want you to have a confrontation with her. It won't happen again. I am really sorry."

"I accept your apology, but it will take me a while to get over the words 'street fighter' and common.'"

Woo Jin walked up to her, took her hands and asked her out. "Let's go somewhere, just the two of us. Where do you want to go?"

"I have no preference."

"Let's go to Jeju Island," he said.

"I don't want to go there. Let's go someplace local," said Areum thinking about the time she spent with Kang-de on Jeju Island.

Woo Jin took her to Mt. Namsan.

"Areum, do you like this cable car ride? It's nice, right?"

"Yes, it's very nice and it's not too high."

Woo Jin and Areum held hands and enjoyed the view. Five hours later they returned to his home and he prepared a gourmet meal for Areum.

"This is the second time that you have cooked for me. I am really impressed that you can cook so well. How many servants do you have at your house in Hong Kong?"

"That's not important, but I will say that we have several. You know that I like doing things by myself."

Areum thought about what he just said to her. "Woo Jin, you know why I like you? You are really a normal guy. You are not pretentious. And you have never flaunted your money to me. Of course, you know that I am not impressed with rich guys who like to show off."

"What about Kang-de? He looks like a showoff," asked Woo Jin in a sarcastic tone.

"Woo Jin, let me tell you a little about Shin Kang-de. He has a lot of money. Yet he is the most humble person that you will ever meet. He speaks his mind. He tells you when he is going to do something and you can bet your life that he will do it. He doesn't tolerate nonsense from anyone. If you steal from him, he is going to hurt you. He would rather you ask him for money and he will give it to you," said Areum. "Woo Jin, he has no family, yet everyone who meets him, besides you, treats him like family. He is a very nice person, but don't mess with him. He can be like a lion who just woke up and is hungry for food. That is all I am going to say about Shin Kang-de."

"What you say is interesting. I suppose that if you were not in our lives, then he and I would have become friends. But, that will never happen. I still think that he is a jerk," said Woo Jin.

Areum looked at him with disbelief. She could not imagine that Woo Jin was filled with so much hatred for Kang-de.

"Please change the subject," she said.

Before he could respond to her, his cell phone rang. His mother was on the phone.

"Hello, Mom? How are you? Is everything okay?"

"Your dad needs you to come to Hong Kong for a few days. He has some people that you need to meet urgently."

"When do I have to come?" asked Woo Jin.

"Tomorrow. Your dad wants you to meet these people IMMEDI-ATELY. You are almost finished with your master's, right?" asked Mrs. Kim.

"Yes, Mother."

"Okay. See you tomorrow. Do you want your dad to send the plane, or do you want to travel on a commercial flight?"

Embarrassed by what his mother just asked him, he told her that he would travel commercially.

"Okay, safe journey, my son."

"Bye, Mother. Areum, I have to go to Hong Kong tomorrow."

"Is everything okay?"

"Yes. I think so." Woo Jin thought about how he was going to tell Areum about the job in Brunei. "Areum, I have to take the job in Brunei. And when you are done with medical school, I want you to come live with me."

Shocked by what she just heard, she showed no emotion. "Oh. It sounds exciting. Let's talk about it when I am finished with medical school. Okay?" she exclaimed. "Do you want me to come to the airport with you tomorrow?" asked Areum.

"Yes, but you will have a big following. Your security team. Areum, don't try to lose them. They are necessary until either my men or Kang-de's sort this mess out."

Areum helped Woo Jin pack his overnight bag.

"I will miss you," said Woo Jin.

"Me too."

"Areum," he said. "Do not let him touch you."

She glanced at him and smiled. "Oh, Woo Jin. I will be fine. You travel safely."

A few hours after leaving Areum in Seoul, he arrived at Hong Kong Airport. A chauffeured car was waiting to take him to his home in the mountains. When he arrived, the servants came out to greet him. He smiled and walked into the library where he saw several grey haired men, with stoic look on their faces, standing in a circular form. Woo Jin did not recognize the men and neither could he see his father because the men were blocking his father's view. Woo Jin greeted them and quickly ran upstairs to look for his mother and father.

The Kims' home had six bedrooms, seven bathrooms, a theatre room, an indoor basketball court, an indoor pool and sauna, a tennis court, a library, a family room and a chef's kitchen. Unknown to Woo Jin it also had an underground walkway that connected the house to the streets. The entrance was hidden behind the fireplace. No one knew about its existence except for his father and the members of the secret organization. Unable to find his father, Woo Jin anxiously went back to the library where the strange men were still standing in a circle.

Woo Jin yelled out, "Mom, Dad, I am here. Where is everyone?"

"Son, I am here," the voice said, as the men simultaneously parted the circle so that Mr. Kim could see Woo Jin. "Woo Jin, let me introduce you to these men who you will be working with when you take over the company. They started out on the oil rigs in Brunei, like you will be doing. They have shares in our company."

Woo Jin greeted each of them. He could sense that they were not oil workers. They were never on a rig, much less worked on one, he told himself. Who were these men and why was Mr. Hwang with them. He thought to himself that something didn't seem right. He glanced at all of them as they gave him several documents to sign. The papers looked legitimate Woo Jin thought, but why were there so many of them at his home to greet him. He looked at his father and his father's attorney and he signed the documents, while staring at the strange men.

"Well, Woo Jin, you are officially the president of our oil refineries, the rigs and all our financial holdings. Congratulations."

"Dad, why now?"

"Son, you don't have much time left with your master's. You already know how the oil business works. You grew up in it. I will still be the chairman and I will handle everything until you come home," said Mr. Kim, who was gazing at Mr. Hwang as he spoke.

"Thanks, Dad."

Woo Jin greeted everyone and the butler escorted them to the dining room where they had dinner. Woo Jin sat between his father and

Mr. Hwang during dinner. When the dinner ended Woo Jin excused himself from the room. Mr. Kim watched him as he exited the dining room and closed the door behind him. Mr. Kim locked the door behind Woo Jin and he began to speak to the men from the secret organization.

"Gentlemen, now that my son has taken his rightful place in our company, we have another problem. Mr. Jong needs our help to eliminate the son of our enemy."

One of the members of the secret organization, stood up and spoke to the men. "Gentlemen, I know all about the son, Shin Kang-de. He has many powerful friends here in Hong Kong and abroad. We must not make any mistakes. We have remained anonymous throughout the years and we need to remain that way because NIS is suspicious about whether we exists or not."

"I will let Mr. Jong know who we are dealing with," said Mr. Kim.

As they talked amongst themselves, the doorbell rang and the butler opened the door. Yoomi and her mother, Mrs. Hwang, were escorted to the entertainment room to wait for Mr. and Mrs. Kim. Woo Jin walked down the stairs saw the Hwangs and he tried to turn away, but his father yelled out to him.

"Welcome to our home once again. Woo Jin, look who is here."

"Hi, Yoomi and Mrs. Hwang. Please be seated. Woo Jin, come and greet your guests," said Mrs. Kim.

Woo Jin realized that he had been set up. He had underestimated his parents persistence in getting he and Yoomi together.

"Hello, Mrs. Hwang. Hello, Yoomi. How are you?"

"I am fine, Woo Jin. It has been a long time since we have seen each other."

"Yeah. What have you been doing?" asked Woo Jin.

"I have been working with my parents, "she replied. "Woo Jin, why don't you take Yoomi to our garden? Mr. Hwang is meeting with your dad and his guests and Mrs. Hwang will remain with me."

Woo Jin took Yoomi to the garden that was located on the rooftop. It had a bar, lounge chairs, several plants and a hammock. From the garden, one could see the ocean and the gushing waves rolling on to the beach. The rooftop was a place for family gatherings and entertainment. The maids brought refreshments and snacks for Woo Jin and Yoomi. Woo Jin and Yoomi reminisced about old days in Hong Kong.

Yoomi hesitated for a minute then she looked at Woo Jin and said, "Woo Jin, our parents have approved our marriage. I don't know how you feel about that."

"I think that you are a beautiful young lady. Any man would love to have you as a wife."

"But?" asked Yoomi.

"Right now I have a big responsibility to our company. I can't think of marriage right now."

"When do you think that you will be ready for marriage?"

"I don't know. I cannot say right now. Shall we go downstairs?"

Disappointed by what Woo Jin said, Yoomi walked behind him with thought of how handsome and sexy he was. She wanted to be his wife now, but she knew that he wasn't interested in her.

"You are back so soon?" asked Mrs. Kim in a disappointing tone.

"Yes, Mother. I have a few things to do while I am in Hong Kong. I am going back tomorrow."

Mrs. Kim noticed the disappointment on Mrs. Hwang's face when Woo Jin returned from the garden with Yoomi.

Suddenly, she said, "Woo Jin, why don't you take out Yoomi tonight?"

He agreed without any objections. "Yoomi, I will come and get you tonight. But I must go out now," he said looking at his mother's face. He walked into the room where the secret organization had gathered. He looked at all the men dressed in black suits and said, "Gentlemen, please excuse me. I have to go out now, I will see you in Brunei. Dad, please excuse me."

Woo Jin hurried out of the house and into the back seat of his family's Mercedes Benz that was chauffeured by Mr. Zhang

"Mr. Zang, please take me to the mall in Kowloon. The one by the harbor."

"Okay, Sir."

Woo Jin went to the jewelry store in the mall and he purchased a diamond neckless with the initial A for Areum. He went to the handbag store and bought Areum a navy blue Hermes handbag. He handed the items to the driver. Then he bought Areum three cashmere sweaters and an Italian leather jacket. Woo Jin also bought Areum a Fendi carryon bag. He walked out of the store and said to his driver, "Okay, let's go. I have to get flowers for Yoomi. My mother will kill me if I don't take that girl out tonight."

The dreaded night arrived for Woo Jin. He reluctantly went to pick up Yoomi at her home. He rang the bell and the maid escorted him in. He walked through a foyer and into an atrium. The atrium walls were filled with paintings of Van Gogh and Picasso. The spiral staircase was made of brown marble and the flooring was made of yellow and brown marble. The ceiling resembled the Sistine Chapel at Vatican City. Yoomi came down the stairs dressed in a yellow silk dress. Her long hair bounced as she walked toward Woo Jin.

Woo Jin smiled when she saw her. "Yoomi, you look very pretty."

"Thanks, Woo Jin. Shall we go? Did you drive or should we have the driver take us?"

"I drove," said Woo Jin.

He took her to dinner in his two-door McLaren car. He always used the yellow-colored car whenever he was in Hong Kong. They ate dinner at a prestigious hotel in Kowloon, while a violinist played classical music at their table. Yoomi looked very happy, even though Woo Jin was anxious to get back to Seoul.

"Woo Jin, I would like to go to a club after we leave here."

He said slowly, "I don't think I can. I have to go back to Seoul tomorrow."

"Oh, Woo Jin, please, let's go. I have not gone to a club in a long time," she said murmuring.

"Okay. If it will make you happy, then we will go. But I can't stay long."

Woo Jin drove to a club located on the mainland. There were several clubs opened on the busy street. He took Yoomi's hand and pulled her into the crowded club.

The music was loud and the beat heavy. Yoomi danced a lot and Woo Jin tried to keep up with her. His thoughts were about Areum, as he danced with Yoomi. Two hours later, he looked at the time on his cell phone and he said, "Yoomi, it's time for us to go home."

Reluctantly Yoomi left the club with Woo Jin and he drove her home. He walked her to her door and he said goodbye, hoping not to see her again.

Chapter Thirty-three

Sun-hee, Kang-de, and Areum
Meanwhile, at a Hospital in Seoul

Sun-hee went alone to the doctor's office to get the physical he had suggested. She sat amongst several women who were waiting to be called for their physical. After waiting for forty-five minutes, Sun-hee was given a physical and a pregnancy test. The doctor came out smiling at Sun-hee which caused her to become anxious.

"Miss, you are pregnant. You will need to take very good care of yourself. Based on your test results, you might not be able to carry this baby to a full term. You will need lots of bed rest," said the doctor.

Sun-hee was in shock from what the doctor blurted out to her. She didn't hear what the doctor said about bed rest. "Doctor, I can't be pregnant. Oh, my God, Oh, my God. What am I going to do?" she cried.

"If you need to speak with someone I will get you a counselor."

"No, Doctor, I will be fine," she said looking puzzled.

Sun-hee ran out of the hospital, sat on a bench and cried uncontrollably.

"Oh, what am I going to do? I can't tell Woo Jin. He will be so mad," she told herself.

After an hour she thought the perfect person to approach would be Kang-de. She knew that he would keep her secret and tell her what to do. Immediately, she called Kang-de.

"Kang-de, I need your advice. Please help me. Please help me."

"Sun-hee, what is wrong? Are you okay? Where are you? Meet me at the hotel later," he said.

"No. No, it's okay. I will see you tomorrow. I need time to think."

"Okay. As you wish," he said.

Sun-hee walked for an hour and a half, not realizing that she had left her car at the hospital parking lot. She was still in shock when she arrived at her office building without identification. As she bumped into the locked door, the security guard asked her for her identification. She turned and looked at him, then look at her hand and she realized that she had left her purse and cell phone on the hospital bench. She snapped back to reality immediately. "Guard, could you please call a driver for me? I have to get to the hospital."

A driver came quickly and he took her to the hospital.

Upon arrival at the hospital, Sun-hee ran to the bench where she sat, but her handbag was not there. She ran to the hospital reception desk looking for her handbag. A nurse opened a draw and took out a handbag. "Oh, thank you. That's my bag," she said.

The nurse replied, "A security guard found it and brought it to us."

Sun-hee searched the bag to make sure that nothing was missing and she got into her car and drove home.

Meanwhile, in Seoul

Kang-de called Areum to find out if she wanted to go to his club. He was anxious to take her out as often as he could. He wanted to cheer her up. "Areum, do you have plans for tonight?"

"No. I was just going to stay in and watch your lovely flat-screen television tonight."

"Don't do that. I have to go to the club later. Do you want to come with me?" Kang-de asked.

"Well...."

"Don't let me go out by myself. The girls may surround me and I don't have you to protect me. You told your mom that you would protect me."

"Okay, okay, if you are going to use my words against me then I better go with you."

"Great. Dress up. You never know where we are going after that. Buy something new in the boutique downstairs. Charge it to me. I don't want to hear the word no. When it comes to you I have no limit on my charge card. You got that?" he said laughing.

"Oh, Kang-de, you are too kind. What am I going to do with you?"

"Love me."

Areum hung up the phone and went shopping. She bought a beautiful red silk dress, with a beautiful red and black high heel sandal. Three hours later Kang-de went to pick her up at her mom's suite. He rang the bell. Areum opened the door.

"Wow, you look stunning. Oh, my, you are beautiful. Let me look at you for a while."

"Come on, Kang-de, let's go. I am not a beauty queen. It's just a dress."

"Areum, go and look in the mirror. You look beautiful."

Areum looked in the mirror, smiled and then they left for the club.

Three cars filled with bodyguards arrived at the club with Kang-de and Areum. Four men waited with the cars and the others entered the club behind Kang-de and Areum. He sat her at a table nearest the dance floor. Kang-de went to ask the DJ to play a romantic song so that he could dance with Areum. The DJ took a while to find a song. When Kang-de heard the music start, he stretched out his hand and asked her to dance.

"My lady, may I dance with you?"

She nodded yes. Kang-de took her hand, drew her close to him and began to whisper parts of the song that was playing. He rested his head against hers and he pulled her close to him. As he held her tightly, he noticed that there were men looking at her whenever he turned her around on the dance floor.

"Areum, look around you. All the men in this club are staring at you. If I leave you at the table, then they will come and ask you to dance. I am not letting you out of my sight tonight. You belong to me."

The song finished moments later and Kang-de took Areum and sat her at the table where she could be viewed by everyone in the club.

Unknown to Kang-de and Areum, two of the men that were watching them were employees of Mr. Jong. They were notified that Areum and Kang-de were heading to his club and they entered as club attendees. None of the security team noticed them because they were dressed in white T-shirts and black pants.

Areum noticed them staring at her and she asked Kang-de to move her to one of his private rooms upstairs. "I am feeling embarrassed. Too many people are staring at me," she said.

Kang-de looked at the crowd and said, "Yes, Areum. Let them stare. I want them to see that you are my woman tonight. And none of them can talk to you. You are all mine. Smile and bear it because you are not moving from this table unless it's with me."

"Kang-de! This is embarrassing to me," she said in an annoyed tone.

The waiter brought Kang-de and Areum various alcoholic and non-alcoholic beverages. Kang-de looked at the beverages on the table and he told the waiter to bring a bottle of Krug and some orange juice.

"Areum, have you ever mixed champagne with orange juice? I love it. I want you to try it tonight."

"You know that I don't drink a lot."

"Tonight you will drink a little," he said looking at her with an intimidating smile.

"Kang-de, you look devious. Oh, well, okay. But don't take advantage of me. And don't let me take advantage of you."

Kang-de replied, "I am all yours. You can do as you wish."

Areum held her face in embarrassment. Her laughter was intoxicating to Kang-de. They continued to eat and drink for a long time. Areum got drunk and Kang-de smiled at her for several minutes. He stared at her for several minutes, admiring how beautiful she looked even when drunk.

"Kang-de, you looked sexy without your shirt. I am glad that I saw your body. I've been dreaming about you without clothes. Ha, ha, ha," she laughed loudly.

Kang-de looked around the club and said, "Let's go, Areum. I had no idea that you would get so drunk."

Areum leaned on him and he held her at her waist. The bodyguards followed in synchronized formation as they left the club. Mr. Jong's men waited until Kang-de and his security left the club before calling Mr. Jong.

"The items are travelling with many bodyguards. Should we intercept the items now?" asked one of the strange men.

"No, we have BIGGER plans for him," said Mr. Jong on the phone.

Twenty minutes later, Kang-de arrived at ITO Hotel with his security. Kang-de escorted Areum to her suite. "Areum, I will make coffee for you."

"Um, um," she replied as the right side of her head hit the couch.

Kang-de rushed over, grabbed her and sat her up in the couch. He held Areum and gave her the coffee. She took a sip, wiped her mouth then grabbed Kang-de's mouth and attempted to kiss him. Kang-de moved his head quickly and the kiss landed on his ear.

"Hey, you. I want you. Let me kiss you," she said in a drunken state.

"Not until you are sober. When you kiss me, I want you to remember the taste of my lips."

"Oh, I remember the taste of your lips. They are soft and sweet. I remember. The taste of your lips sent chills up my body," she said murmuring.

Areum grabbed Kang-de and successfully kissed him on the lips. He returned the kiss with passion. She sucked on his tongue and he reciprocated. He lifted her and carried her to the bed. He removed her shoes and he covered her with a blanket. She grabbed his jacket and pulled him toward her. He grabbed her hands and placed them beside her.

"Areum, I am so tempted to let you take advantage of me, but you won't remember tomorrow and that will be sad. When I make love to you, I want you to remember every detail. Goodnight, Areum. Sleep well, my lady."

Kang-de closed her door and he went to his suite. He took a long and slow cold shower. The taste of Areum's tongue mingled with his, aroused every muscle in his body and he needed to calm himself.

"Areum, Areum, Areum, one day, my sweet," he said out loud.

After his shower, he called Bob to let him know that there were two men at the club who appeared to be foreigners. "Bob, tomorrow, I want you to take a look at the video tape at the club and ask Chul to check them out and get back to me."

The next morning, the tapes from the club and the airport were delivered to Bob within minutes of each other. They were analyzed through facial recognition and licensed plates. The results were interesting. He called Kang-de to let him know that the two men's names were undetermined and the airport cameras were unable to access the licensed plate of the car that followed Mrs. Lee from the airport.

"Bob, are you saying that we have no information about the men at the club or at the airport? What's going on here? Who are those guys and who are they working for? They were probably the same guys who were at both places," he said.

"Boss, I will have my guys in the intelligence business find out who they are."

"Bob, this is not good."

"I will have to make a few phone calls as well. Who were they following, me or someone at the club? I think that it was me," said Kang-de unaware that the men were following Areum as well.

Three days later a phone call came in from Hong Kong. Kang-de answered the phone. The voice on the phone said that the two men were killers and they worked for a big man in Hong Kong. The voice told him that they were following he and Areum. The phone disconnected before Kang-de could ask any questions.

"Bob, I just got a phone call from a friend who told me that those guys who were at the club work for a big man, in Hong Kong, like Mr. Kim or Mr. Hwang. But why would they want to follow Areum? Bob, step up the security for Areum until I find out what's really going on here."

Chapter Thirty-four

Woo Jin, Yoomi, Mrs. Kim, Mrs. Hwang, Areum,
Kang-de, Sun-hee, Mr. Park, and Minjae

After Woo Jin left Yoomi at her home, she opened her door looking disappointed. It was not the kind of date that she had anticipated having with the man she was destined to marry.

"How was your date?"

"It was okay. We went to dinner and then to a club."

"That's great. When he comes home, you can go on more dates."

"I hope so. He will spend a lot of time in Brunei."

"Your dad and Mr. Kim are great friends. They have arranged his schedule. He will be home often. You will see."

"Mom, I really like him, but I am not sure that he likes me," she said in a disappointing tone.

"Oh, Yoomi, you worry too much. Why don't you go to Seoul for a few days? When is he leaving?" Mrs. Hwang asked.

"Tomorrow," Yoomi said in a sad tone.

"I will speak with Mrs. Kim. She will arrange a meeting with you and Woo Jin. You will have business to discuss. I will see to it."

A smile came upon Yoomi's face and she hugged her mother.

"Mom, you are so smart."

"Of course I am."

"Goodnight, Mom."

Woo Jin woke early to get the first flight to Seoul. His mother was awake and sitting at the breakfast table waiting for him. The servants made breakfast for Woo Jin and his mother.

"Mom, I have to leave soon. In about two months' time I am heading to Brunei. I will stop here first."

"I am very happy for you, President Kim Woo Jin."

"Thanks, Mom."

"Okay, go and say goodbye to your father. The traffic can be a challenge in the mornings."

Woo Jin kissed his mother, said goodbye to his father, and he went to the airport with his packages.

Woo Jin arrived in Seoul five hours and fifteen minutes later. He called Areum from the airport and got no answer.

Upon arrival at his home, he called her again and she answered.

"Good day, Areum. I am home. Please come to my home later. I have some things that I want to show you."

"Okay. Did you have a good trip?"

"Yes, I did. I will see you later."

Areum waited a few hours, then she went to see Woo Jin. Areum rang his bell. He opened the door. They hugged each other. Woo Jin held her tightly and kissed her on the cheek.

"Areum, I missed you."

"I missed you too. What do you want me to see?"

Woo Jin brought out the packages and told Areum to open them. She hesitated then opened them one at a time.

"Woo Jin, who are these things for? They are beautiful.Are they not very costly?"

"Yes, they are costly and they are for my best girl."

"Oh, no, Woo Jin. I cannot accept such expensive gifts. These things cost a fortune."

"Areum. I bought them for you. I want to show you how much I care about you. Don't worry about the cost. You deserve more than these cost."

"Woo Jin. I don't know…. Why did you buy so many things? I can't carry a Hermes bag around. People will think that I am rich or that I am a kept woman. Woo Jin, why did you do this?"

"Okay, you are getting me upset. I want you to have them. They are yours. I can't take them back to the store. You are stuck with them."

Areum folded the sweaters and the jacket and placed them in her Fendi carryon bag. She placed the neckless in her Hermes bag.

"Thank you, Woo Jin. I am very grateful for your gifts. I appreciate them and you."

"That's what I want to hear you say. Are you going back to the hotel now?"

"Yes. I am going to put these things in my suite and then I want to go and see my mother."

"I will meet you at the hospital later. Is that okay?"

"Sure. Okay. I am leaving. Thanks again, Woo Jin. They are very lovely."

Areum kissed Woo Jin and he returned her kiss. He hugged her and then watched her leave with her security guards.

Areum arrived at ITO Hotel with the driver provided by Kang-de. Areum saw Kang-de walking through the lobby. She tried to hide from him, but her driver called out her name and Kang-de turned around and said, "Good day to you. How are you? Wow, you went shopping. That's great. I am glad you are feeling comfortable to use my charge card."

"Uh. Kang-de. I did not use your card. Woo Jin brought these in Hong Kong for me."

"Oh. That's nice. Is that a Hermes bag on your arm?"

"Yeah," she said quietly.

"That's nice, Areum. You deserve nice things," said Kang-de, disappointed that it was Woo Jin who bought them. He told himself that the bag alone cost over forty-two thousand Hong Kong dollars. The Fendi carry-on cost at least twenty-eight thousand Hong Kong dollars. He told himself that Woo Jin was either buying Areum's affection or he really loved her.

He glanced at Areum and told her that she deserved the best things life had to offer. "I was hoping that I would be the one to buy these nice things for you."

"Kang-de. The things you have done for my family outweighs all of these. These are material things, Kang-de. You have given my family love. That surpasses these things."

"I'm very happy to hear that, Areum."

"Kang-de, wait until you see how much that red dress cost. You will want to stop me from using your charge card. Ha-ha."

"Areum, what is mine is yours. Please don't ever forget that."

Kang-de drove to his office which was a few blocks away from ITO Hotel. As he walked into his office, the phone rang. Sun-hee was anxious to speak with Kang-de.

"Hello. Sun-hee, you don't sound happy. Why did you want to speak with me?"

"I have a big problem. What do I do?"

"Come and see me. We will figure it out together."

Minutes later Sun-hee arrived at Kang-de's office. Her hair looked disheveled and her dress looked like something she had taken from a washing machine without ironing it. She knocked on the door and he opened it.

"Come in. How are you. You look terrible. Are you sick?"

"I am and I don't know who to talk to. I can't tell my family."

"Tell me, what's wrong, Sun-hee? Get to the point."

"Ah. I am pregnant."

"What? Pregnant? You're pregnant! Okay, so what do you want to do? It's Woo Jin's. Isn't it? Tell me the truth."

"Yeah, " she said sitting down at Kang-de's desk.

"Oh, Sun-hee. I am sorry. It's too late to ask you why you didn't take precaution."

Kang-de walked over to her and touched her shoulders. She got up and hugged Kang-de tightly. Surprised by her actions, Kang-de slowly put his arms around her and she wept.

"I am sorry, Sun-hee. You came for advice so hear it is. You have to tell him. A man needs to know if he has a child somewhere. Even if he gets mad, you should tell him. I am sorry. I am here for you anytime. Let me know if you need anything and stop crying. You have a lot of thinking to do."

Sun-hee released his shoulder, walked to the door and said, "Thanks, Kang-de. You are such a good friend. Areum is a lucky girl. I have to go to my office. I will think about what you have said."

Sun-hee walked to her office with two of Kang-de's bodyguard who were waiting for her as she exited the building. Her cell phone rang and Mr. Park called to quiz her about her kidnapping.

"Hi, Sun-hee. I heard that something awful happened to you. How are you?"

"I am fine, now. I don't know why anyone would want to kidnap me. I have nothing to offer."

"Obviously, they thought that you knew something. Did you recognize them?" he asked.

"No. I was blindfolded most of the time. The people who I did see, I don't think they are from Seoul," she said, knowing that Mr. Park might have knowledge of who kidnapped her.

"I am sure that the police will find them. You be careful. Okay?"

"Bye, Mr. Park."

Immediately Mr. Park called Minjae to let him know that he had spoken to Sun-hee and she didn't know who kidnapped her, but he thought it was Mr. Jong.

"Yes. But we have no proof."

"Not yet. Minjae, I think Shin Kang-de knows a lot."

"He won't tell you. He knows that you tried to steal his company."

"Yes. You are right. Let's not talk to him right now. I am sure that he is planning his revenge on me."

"At least we know to watch our backs."

Chapter Thirty-five

Kang-de, Bob, Police, Chul, Mrs. Hwang,
Yoomi, Directors, Doctor, and Elderly Man

The plot to kill Kang-de began when Director 5, Kang-de's cousin and only living relative, called him at his office. Kang-de's temporary secretary took the call and passed it to Kang-de who was sitting at his desk. Director 5 was a tall, well-dressed man with black hair and brown eyes. He was born in South Korea, but earned a Master's in Business Administration in New York. He spoke fluent English, French and Korean. He was able to obtain a position on the Board of Directors of Mr. Jong's pharmaceutical company with Kang-de's help.

His temporary secretary listened to his conversation while he spoke with Director 5 in codes.

"Kang-de, how are you?"

"I am fine. Why didn't you call me on the cell?" asked Kang-de.

"Sorry. I have more information about the tenth hole on the golf course."

The tenth letter in the alphabet was J. Kang-de was aware that Director 5 was speaking about Mr. Jong. "Great, I am heading to Gangnam. Do you want to meet me at my new store?"

TAM

"Yeah. I don't want to be seen at your office."

Kang-de called Bob to let him know that he was on his way to the new store in Gangnam.

"Boss, let me drive you?"

"No. I will drive myself because you won't be here in time. I will meet you there."

"Boss, why don't you have one of the guards go with you?"

"It's okay, Bob. I don't want anyone identifying Director 5. I will have them meet me there later," he said as he walked past all the secretaries and smiled.

Kang-de's temporary secretary watched him walk into the elevator. She looked at her watch, got up from her desk, walked to the bathroom and made a phone call to someone.

"The item is traveling solo, please verify," she said to the person on the other side of the phone.

She replied, "Yes, Sir," to the voice on the other side of the phone and she left the building in a hurry.

Kang-de drove his BMW along the main street and onto the highway to his Gangnam store. Rush hour had not begun and Kang-de turned on the car radio to entertain himself while he cruised down the highway.

About fifteen minutes had passed when a red motorbike with a man dressed in black leather, cuts in front of his car. Kang-de swerve to avoid hitting the motorbike.

The motorbike sped ahead and switched in and out of lanes. Kang-de thought the rider was crazy because he was doing stunts on his bike. He had no idea that the rider was a distraction for what was about to happen.

Minutes later, two black sedans came alongside Kang-de's car and boxed him in. He accelerated on the gas and drove away from the sedans. Within seconds, they were alongside him again. A man in one of the sedan pointed a gun at Kang-de. He recognized him from the club and he was one of the two men who had no name.

242

Kang-de stepped on his brakes, put the gear in reverse and drove backwards toward the exit he had just passed. Before he could reach the exit, a white truck that was at a distance from Kang-de accelerated behind him and hits his car pushing it into a ditch.

Kang-de's car rolled three times and landed upside down. The truck driver slowed down, looked at the wrecked car lying upside down, and drove off when he realized that a man was watching him. An elderly man who drove behind the truck, saw the incident and called the police.

Bob, whose documents were found in Kang-de's wallet, was notified by the police three hours after the incident. When he answered the phone, the police asked, "Do you know a Mr. Shin Kang-de?"

"Yes. Why?" he asked calmly.

"He was in an accident. He is in the hospital in Gangnam."

Bob received the details from the police and he called Chul-Moo and Kang-de's security team. They headed to Gangnam Hospital with four cars filled with men who were his private security guards. They sped down the highway in silence. No one knew in what condition they would find Kang-de. They drove without noticing that they were being followed. Everyone's mind were on their beloved Boss. Chul and Bob drove in the same car.

"Bob, if Kang-de dies, I will kill Mr. Jong's and Mr. Park," said Chul.

Bob replied, "We will kill their entire family. No one will survive. Let the men know that if Kang-de dies, all his enemies must die with him."

Chul nodded his head in agreement with Bob. He called a team of assassins to wait for news on Kang-de's condition.

Gangnam Hospital

The cars pulled up in front of Gangnam Hospital. All the men except for the drivers got out and ran into the hospital. The drivers waited with the cars in the hospital parking lot. The car that followed them arrived a few minutes later. It drove away when two police cars pulled up behind them. One of Kang-de's driver noticed that he had seen the same license plate on a car that had exited on the highway with him.

"Nurse, where is Mr. Shin Kang-de?" asked Bob running to the nurses' station with Chul.

"He's in the emergency room. Please have a seat."

Chul slammed his hands on the nurse's desk and told her to get a doctor to come and speak with them now. The power of his hands shook the desk and it frightened the nurses. A nurse ran to find a doctor. Within five minutes, a doctor came to speak with Chul and Bob. "Doctor, can you tell me about a Mr. Shin Kang-de's condition?"

"Are you his relative?" asked the doctor.

"Yes, Sir," replied Bob.

"Well, he is still in surgery. We will be able to tell you more in a few hours."

"Doctor, please save him," said Bob.

"Sir, he has the best doctors operating on him."

Chul divided the men into four teams. "I want one team at the trauma door. The rest of you please stand by until the surgery is finished."

Bob asks the nurse which officer had the accident report. The nurse pointed to the policeman. "Officer, can you tell me if there were any eyewitnesses to Mr. Shin's accident?"

"Yes. That elderly man over there," said the officer pointing to the elderly man who was sitting on a chair.

Bob and Chul walked over to the elderly gentleman who looked shaken by what he had witnessed.

"Hello, Sir. Can you tell me what happened?" asked Bob.

"Two cars tried to crush the black BMW. The man in the BMW tried to reverse, but a truck accelerated and pushed it into a ditch. The car flipped over several times."

"Did you recognize the man in the truck?"

"No. But I got the license's plate number."

"Great. Thank you. Can you write it down for me?"

The elderly man wrote down the license's plate number.

"Here is my card. If you remember anything more, please call me," said Bob looking at the emergency room door. He was hoping that the door would open and Kang-de would walk out the door.

As Bob walked to a chair in the waiting area, a doctor came out of surgery with his mask and scrubs on. He removed the mask to speak with Bob and Chul.

"How is the patient, Doctor?" asked Bob.

"The surgery was successful. He should make a full recovery. He is a strong man with a strong will to live. You won't be able to see him for several hours."

"Thank you, Doctor. When will he be moved to a room?" asked Chul.

"Don't rush him. He has to be monitored for the next twenty-four hours. We have induced him into a temporary coma."

"A coma? Why?" asked Bob.

"Because of the unusual swelling on the brain. An induced coma is necessary," answered the doctor.

"Okay. Thank you, Doctor," said Bob in a disappointing tone.

Bob, Chul and the bodyguards kept watch at the hospital front door as well as the ICU. The police guarded the ICU door because they concluded that the incident was a crime.

Police told the elderly man, who was wandering through the hospital hallway, to go home. He walked slowly through the front door and made a left to the hospital parking lot.

He had only reached a few blocks from the hospital, when two SUVs blocked him in. One in front of him and the other behind him. Within seconds a third SUV pulled up next to him. Three men jumped out, pulled him from his car, and threw him into their SUV. They disappeared into the traffic jam within minutes.

Kang-de slept for seventy-two hours. Nurses and doctors monitored his vitals on intervals. On the fourth day, the doctors gave him medicine to wake him.

"Mr. Shin Kang-de, please wake up now."

He slowly opened his eyes and went back to sleep.

"Mr. Shin, please wake up. I am moving you to a private room," said a doctor who was checking his vitals.

Kang-de opened his eyes slowly and mumbled, "Where am I?"

"You are at a hospital in Gangnam," said the doctor.

"Please call someone for me," said Kang-de in a slow tone.

"They are already here, Sir."

A nurse called Bob. He signaled to Chul and they ran into the room.

"Boss, you are awake. We are here. All your main security team are here."

"What happened?" asked Kang-de.

"Don't talk, Boss. You need to rest. We are not leaving your side."

Kang-de went back to sleep. Bob, Chul and four of his most trusted bodyguards stayed in the room with him.

Bob called Sun-hee's and Areum's bodyguards to advised them to let everyone know, including Areum and Sun-hee, that Kang-de went away on business and he could not be contacted. Bob told Areum's bodyguard to be on the alert, as an attempt to kill Areum might occur at any time. The ITO Hotel increased security throughout the hotel and at Areum's clinic. Hotel guests were screened before registering and every car entering the parking garage were searched and their license's plate logged.

Meanwhile, at the airport, a private jet landed at a remote area. Yoomi and her mother walked off the plane and into an awaiting Mercedes Benz. They checked into the ITO Hotel accompanied by two security guards. Areum was walking through the lobby when she bumped into Yoomi by accident.

"I am sorry," she said.

"Watch where you are going," said Yoomi.

Areum looked at Yoomi and kept walking. "Mom, we need to call Woo Jin."

"We will, but I need to see our client first."

"Who are we here to see?"

"His name is Mr. Shin Kang-de. Let's check in and rest for a while."

Mrs. Hwang and Yoomi were escorted to their suite. The suite was the smallest in the hotel. It had one king sized bed with tables and chairs in each room. A flat-screen TV hung on the wall that was decorated with silver and chocolate brown wall paper. The living room had an open floor plan. One could see the small kitchen from the two chocolate Italian leather couches that were brightly reflected from the sun.

Mrs. Hwang called Kang-de's office and the receptionist accidentally transferred her to the temporary secretary's line. The voicemail of the temporary secretary, who had not returned to work since she made the phone call that caused Kang-de to be injured, came on.

Mrs. Hwang left her message: "Hello, Mr. Shin. Please call me. You have my number."

Chapter Thirty-six

Kang-de, Director 5, Bob, Chul, Areum, and Sun-hee

Eight days had passed and Areum had been calling Kang-de's phone and the voicemail advised her to leave a message. Although her bodyguard had advised her that Kang-de had traveled, Areum continued to leave messages on his cell. She called Bob several times and got no answer. No one answered the door at Kang-de's suite and the guards were not at his door. Areum's concern grew greater because it was unlike Kang-de to disappear without contacting her. She went to his office, but no one had any information about Kang-de and Bob.

On the ninth day, Bob called Areum and she answered quickly.

"Bob, where is Kang-de? I have been calling him for several days now."

"Miss. Areum, where are your guards?" asked Bob.

"One is in the room with me. Why? What's wrong? Let me speak with him, please. Bob, what is wrong? I want to speak with Kang-de."

"Miss Areum, put your bodyguard on the phone. Please."

Reluctantly, Areum handed the phone to the bodyguard. She heard the guard say, "Yes, Boss, I understand. I will bring her," as he hung up.

"Guard, what is wrong? Tell me, please?"

"Director Bob asked me to take you to Boss Shin Kang-de."

Areum noticed that the guard was driving in the direction to Gangnam. "Guard, is Kang-de in Gangnam? He must be at one of his stores."

The guard remained silent. He said nothing until he arrived at the hospital.

"Miss Areum, Director Bob and Boss Shin Kang-de are waiting for you inside."

He opened the car door and Areum stepped out. She noticed the emergency sign on the door.

"Why are they at a hospital? What's going on? Where is Kang-de?" she asked again.

Areum walked into the hospital lobby and saw Bob standing at the nurses' station. She ran to Bob and suddenly she saw a police officer walking over to him.

"Bob, where is Kang-de? Tell me now, please?" she said while looking at the police officer's face.

"He was in an accident. He is conscious, but he is asleep. He is in there," said Bob pointing to the room.

Areum ran to Kang-de's room. She suddenly stopped after looking at the bandage on his head. She slowly walked over to the bed and began to cry. She touched his fingers and she gently lifted his hand and cried loudly.

"Kang-de, wake up. Please wake up and talk to me."

Bob walked in behind her.

"What happened to him and how long has he been here?"

"Ms. Areum, he was hit by a truck and he has been here for eleven days now."

"What? A truck hit his car? Where is the truck driver? Is he hurt?"

"No, Miss. It was a deliberate hit."

Her eyes opened wide when she heard the shocking news. "Are you saying that someone tried to kill Kang-de? Where were you and his security team? Why didn't you call me?"

"I will explain later, Miss Areum."

"Bob, you better hope that he lives," she said staring at Bob angrily.

Doctors entered Kang-de's room while Areum sat motionless and holding Kang-de's hand to her face. She looked at the doctor who had walked over to the left side of Kang-de's bed.

"Doctor, how is he doing?"

"Who are you?"

"I am a medical intern specializing in cardiology and I am also his girlfriend," she replied.

Bob looked at Areum and smiled.

"He's progressing rapidly. He is a healthy man and he will recover from his head injury."

"Head injury?"

"Yes, Miss, he hit his head very hard which caused him to have a slight swelling on his brain. We had medicated him to decrease the swelling and we are still monitoring his vital status."

"Will he be fine?"

"Yes, yes," said the doctor as he opened Kang-de's eyes to look at his pupils. "Mr. Shin Kang-de, wake up, please. I need to examine you."

"Kang-de, wake up, please. I am here. Wake up, honey."

Kang-de opened his eye, looked at Areum and partially smiled and went to sleep.

"Bob, I want guards in this room twenty-four hours a day. Take the security team that he provided me and assign them to him."

"Miss. Areum, Kang-de would not approve of your decision."

"Bob, Kang-de cannot speak for himself right now. I want him protected. Please do as I ask. As soon as the doctor gives his approval, I want him moved to a hospital outside of Seoul. But, for this moment, I will register him under an anonymous name."

"Miss Areum, I have already done all those things," said Bob.

"And please make sure that you find out who tried to kill Mr. Shin Kang-de."

"Yes, Miss," said Bob in a calm tone. He had patience with her because he knew that she was worried. "I called his lawyer, Sun-hee."

"Why? I don't want her here. I don't want anybody here until you find out who tried to hurt Kang-de. Please call her back and tell her not to come. Have you thought that she could be followed? She was kidnapped before. Please tell her not to come."

Bob looked at her in a confused manner. Areum realized that she was making demands on Kang-de's right hand man.

"I am sorry, Bob, I mean no disrespect to you, but we cannot trust anyone until we find out who is trying to kill your boss."

"I understand but there are a lot of things that you don't know and Ms. Sun-hee, his lawyer, is privy to some of them."

"I still don't want her here."

"It's too late. I am here," said Sun-hee walking into Kang-de's room.

"Why are you here? What do you know about Kang-de's affairs? Do you know who tried to kill him?"

Sun-hee said nothing.

Areum walked up to her and looked in her face as if she wanted to hit Sun-hee. "I just asked you a question."

"I can't answer you. I don't know what happened. Bob, let's talk outside."

Sun-hee and Bob left the room to talk about Kang-de's enemies. They mentioned Mr. Park, Mr. Jong, Yejoon and CFO. Bob believed it was Mr. Jong.

"Kang-de recently threatened Mr. Jong. He is mean- spirited and vindictive," said Bob.

"Bob, you need to move Kang-de out of this hospital immediately."

"Soon. We can't right now, but we have this hospital locked down. Anyone who comes in or goes out of this hospital has to pass our men."

"I will have my investigators check out Mr. Jong and his friends."

"Thanks," Bob replied.

Suddenly, Areum ran to the door and yelled out, "Bob, come. He is awake."

Bob and Sun-hee ran into the room.

"Kang-de, you are awake. I'm so happy," said Areum.

"Bob, where am I?"

"You are in the hospital."

"Kang-de, you look terrible. How do you feel?" asked Sun-hee.

"Get me a mirror, Sun-hee," said Kang-de with a slight grin on his face.

"Oh, Kang-de, how do you really feel?" asked Areum.

"My head hurts and my body aches, but I will be fine."

"Good to hear that. Kang-de, you are strong. Get well soon. I am leaving now. I have thought about what you said."

"Thanks for coming, Sun-hee. Take care of yourself," Kang-de said slurring his speech.

Sun-hee walked out of the hospital disguised in a black wig and white hospital jacket. A car pulled up and she got in and drove off.

"How are you feeling right now?" asked Areum.

"I have a migraine headache. Why all the guards?"

"Precaution."

"Thanks for coming, Areum," Kang-de said slowly.

"I would do anything for you. Don't ever forget that. Okay?"

Kang-de smiled and squeezed Areum's hand.

"Miss Areum, can you excuse us for a moment? Guards, please step outside for a moment," said Bob.

"Kang-de!"

"It's okay, Areum."

She gazed at the two of them and left the room slowly.

"Boss, someone tried to kill you eleven days ago. They tried to run you off the road. What do you want me to do?"

"Who was I supposed to meet? I am trying to remember."

"Director 5."

"My cousin? Bob, please call Director 5, I want to speak with him."

Director 5 arrived at the hospital three hours later, disguised as a doctor. "Kang-de, what happened to you? I waited for you for several hours but you never came. I feel sorry to know that you were in an accident."

"Did you tell anyone that you were going to meet me?"

"No, no. I have always been discreet. You know that."

"I believe you," said Kang-de. "Bob, I remember that someone was following me. But, how did they know that I was going alone? Bob, check the office for bugs. We are not alone."

Chul walked in and greeted Kang-de. "Boss, I am so happy to know that you are awake. I was really worried about you. Do you want me to eliminate your enemies tonight? I feel that it's time to eliminate them all."

"Not yet, my friend. We have work to do. I must congratulate the person who tried to kill me. He or they won't get another chance."

"Kang-de, will you be fine?" asked Director 5 as he walked to the door.

Kang-de nodded his head.

"Chul, please make sure that Director 5 is escorted home and make sure that he is not being followed," said Kang-de.

"Sure, Boss."

"Boss, what do you want to do next?" asked Bob.

"I'm going to retaliate with everything that I've got. "

"Good," said Bob. "Now rest, Boss. We will all be here when you wake up."

Kang-de slept throughout the night and into the early morning. They checked his vitals throughout the night.

He woke up at noon and the doctors checked his vitals. They made him rest one more day.

On the thirteenth day, Kang-de sat up in the bed. Bob and Areum were by his bedside when he woke up.

"Miss Areum, can you get me some coffee, please?" asked Bob.

Areum looked at him and then at Kang-de. "Okay, you want me to leave the room again. I get it," she said walking away.

"Boss, the police have been waiting to speak with you."

"Send them in. I have nothing concrete to tell them right now."

Three police men walked into the room with paper and pen in their hands. Bob recognized one of the policeman as a guest at one of Mr. Park's party. He was busy guarding a closed door at Mr. Park's home.

"Mr. Shin," said the lead policeman. "I am happy that you are awake. What do you remember about the accident?"

Kang-de looked at Bob who stood behind them in his room and he noticed that Bob slightly turned his head to the left then to the right. He knew that Bob was trying to tell him not to speak with them.

"Officers, I can't remember what happened. My mind is at a blank. The doctors said that I hit my head very hard and I won't be able to remember anything for a while. I am sorry. Thank you for coming. If I remember anything, then I will have my assistant contact you. I am sorry."

The officers left without a report from Kang-de.

"Boss, one of those cops is working for Mr. Park or Mr. Jong."

"I thought so. Good job, Bob. We have no information for them. I have a war to prepare for. Get me out of this hospital."

Chapter Thirty-seven

Kang-de, Areum, Bob, Chul, and Roger Goo

The war was set in motion when Shin Kang-de called Chul to his hospital bed. He told Bob to send a copy of the disc that showed Mr. Jong planning to kidnapping Bora to Mr. Park.

"Chul, keep your men on standby. I might have to do some bad things to some bad people. They started it and I will finish it."

"Bob. Areum needs to go home. I don't want her in the middle of this."

"Boss, I think that lady loves you more than she is telling you. She stayed by your side while you were unconscious and she threatened to harm me if you died. I believed she would have harmed me, Boss."

"I am truly happy to know that she cares so much for me. Send her in."

Areum walked into the room slowly, with a cup of coffee in her hand, and she sat by Kang-de's beside. Bob took the coffee and walked out of the room.

"Areum, thanks for staying with me. I heard that you were in charge of my security."

"Well, Bob should never have let you travel alone. I am very upset with you both. Why didn't Bob call me immediately? I am upset."

"Sorry. This is my fault. I love you, Areum. You are a true friend."

"You have been a great friend to me too."

Kang-de slowly pulled her to him and he hugged her.

"Be careful of your head."

"I am feeling fine. I am checking out of this hospital in a few hours. I want you to go to your classes."

"No. I am not going to classes until you leave this hospital."

"Areum. Please don't be stubborn."

"Foolish man, who is the stubborn one?"

"Hey, watch it," Kang-de said as Bob entered the room.

"Boss, I have checked you out of the hospital, but you will need treatment. Shall we go to your home in Ansan?"

"No. Take me to the hotel and get a medical team to treat me there."

"Okay, Boss."

Kang-de, Chul, Bob and Areum left the hospital with a dozen security guards at his side. Each car drove in different directions, in order to confuse anyone who might try to follow them.

The next day, men with fake police identifications went to the hospital to find Kang-de. The nurse told them that there was no one by that name at the hospital. They showed her Kang-de's picture and she told them that he left the day before. The men made several phone calls to find out Kang-de's whereabouts. Someone told them that they saw a group of men walk into the ITO Hotel, but they didn't see Shin Kang-de with them.

The men in suits continued to search for Kang-de at different hospitals in Hongdae, Gangnam and Itaewon. The order had been given to eliminate Kang-de. No one knew the name of the man who gave the order to kill him.

Bob called his father in New York. He told him about the attempted murder on Kang-de's life. Roger Goo who was now retired, knew that the organization that killed Kang-de's father was now after him. He called his contacts in Hong Kong and Korea to find out the location of the secret organization. Roger Goo knew that he would have to help Kang-de destroy the enemy who had no name.

Roger Goo called Kang-de and told him to come to New York when he got better. Roger Goo felt that it was time for Kang-de to know everything about what happened to his parents and why.

Roger Goo was unable to travel to Seoul due to the so-called accident that occurred when he returned to New York after the Ambassador's death. He had been instructed by Ambassador Shin, prior to his death, to reside in the penthouse apartment until Kang-de finished his university education.

Two days after he had arrived, he was walking to his car in the underground parking lot when a bullet shattered his right thigh. He fell to the ground and crawled behind a parked car. Roger Goo laid on the ground so that he could see where the shooter or shooters were. He wanted to see how close they were to where he was hiding. He could see that there were three men walking toward where he was and he took out his gun and fired at their feet. A bullet hit one of the men in the ankle and he fell to the ground. He fired another shot and another man fell to the ground holding his leg. Roger fired two more shots at each men as they laid on the ground. The bullets passed through the men's clothes and they died instantly.

The third man ran to see where Roger Goo was located. Roger Goo watched him run to his car, turned to his left and fired at him. The bullet missed Roger by an inch and he returned fire killing the last shooter. He removed his tie and wrapped it around his leg to stop the bleeding. As he did so he made his eyes scan the area to make sure that there were no more shooters.

The noise from the gun shots alerted the parking attendant and he called the police. Hearing the siren in the far background, Roger used the two parked cars to prop himself up and drag himself to the penthouse. The young Shin-Kang-de was in the apartment when Roger Goo entered bleeding profusely.

Kang-de called the silver haired stranger who had treated Mr. Lee in the past. The man extracted the bullet from his leg and closed his wounds.

Shin Kang-de remained with Roger Goo while he recovered from his wounds. The doctors told Kang-de not to let Roger Goo travel long distances because he was susceptible to blood clots. Roger Goo was aware that an attempt would be made on his life, but he did not know when or where.

Roger Goo told Kang-de that he was robbed at gun point and that he was shot because he fought back. He felt that Kang-de was too young to handle the reality of what his grandfather and father were involved in.

Chapter Thirty-eight

Bob, Chul, Kang-de, Woo Jin, Yoomi, and Mrs. Hwang

A month had passed since the attempted murder of Kang-de and he had been resting at ITO Hotel. No outsiders were allowed to visit his suite. Bob and Chul controlled all movements on Kang-de's floor. Housekeeping was done by the most senior housekeepers. No new employees were allowed to have contact with Kang-de. The medical team were hired by Bob and Chul, and his men stood guard whenever they attended to Kang-de. Security was extraordinarily tight. Strangers in the lobby were monitored by Chul from Kang-de's room.

Chul viewed several strange men walking in and out of the lobby. He knew that they were looking for information about Kang-de. He had his men observe them from afar. When they left the hotel, Chul had them followed.

About 4 o'clock in the evening Chul's cell phone rang and one of his men advised him that Mr. Jong had met with three of the men. Chul immediately told Kang-de about what he had just heard.

"Boss, we need to kill Mr. Jong and Mr. Park now.

"Patience, Chul. I want to destroy them financially first and then you can kill them if I am not successful. Trust me, Chul, eventually Mr. Jong will be taken care of because he tried to kill me."

While Kang-de recuperated in his suite, Mrs. Hwang and her daughter went to see his office.

"Good morning. We have an appointment to see Mr. Shin Kang-de. Can you call him, please?"

"I am sorry but he had to cancel his meeting today. He had an emergency," said Kang-de's permanent secretary.

"What do you mean he cancelled? We came from Hong Kong to see him and he cancelled? No one contacted us to cancel our meeting. What kind of businessman is he?"

"Madam, if you don't mind, you can speak with his lawyer. She would have been at the meeting anyway."

"We don't speak to lawyers unless our lawyers are present," said Mrs. Hwang. "This is very regrettable. Tell him we will not be doing any business with him now or in the future," she said angrily.

"Please accept his apology, Madam. It cannot be helped."

Yoomi and her mother stormed out of the office and returned to the hotel. Mrs. Hwang called Woo Jin upon arrival at the ITO Hotel.

"Hello," said Woo Jin.

"Hello, Woo Jin, how are you? This is Mrs. Hwang. Yoomi and I are in Seoul on business and we would like to meet with you."

"Welcome to Seoul. I won't be able to meet you until tomorrow. May I meet you for breakfast?"

"Sure."

"Where are you staying?"

"ITO Hotel."

Woo Jin paused and said, "Oh, I see. Okay, I will meet you in the lobby tomorrow."

"Okay. Would you like to speak with Yoomi?"

"Yes, please."

"Hello, Woo Jin. How are you?"

"Fine, thank you. When did you arrive?"

"A few days ago. How is school?" Yoomi asked.

"Great. I will be finishing by the end of the month."

"Congratulations. That is fantastic," she said.

"Thanks. Please excuse me, but I must hang up now. I will see you at breakfast in the morning."

"Okay. Goodbye," said Yoomi in a sad tone.

Mrs. Hwang looked at Yoomi and saw that she was disappointed. She thought of something quick to say to Yoomi. "You both need to spend time with each other. I will go shopping tomorrow after breakfast. Yoomi, you will need to ask Woo Jin for his schedule."

"Yes, Mother."

Woo Jin looked at the cell phone and threw it on his bed. He took a shower, got dressed and called Areum. He wanted to make sure that Areum would not be eating breakfast at the ITO Hotel in the morning. He felt anxious, not knowing what Yoomi and her mother were really doing in Seoul. Areum answered the phone after several rings.

"Hello. Where are you? I have been trying to reach you for a long time now."

Areum replied, "I was at the hospital. Kang-de was in an accident."

"Is he alive? You know that school has begun," asked Woo Jin.

"Yes, he is alive and I am not thinking about school right now."

"Okay, sorry. You are now Kang-de's doctor?"

"Woo Jin, I am not in the mood for your sarcasm. I am hanging up now."

"Hello? Hello? I don't believe that she hung up on me. I didn't get a chance to ask her where she was having breakfast tomorrow," he said out loud.

Breakfast at the ITO Hotel

The next morning Woo Jin arrived at ITO Hotel. Mrs. Hwang and Yoomi walked out of the elevator and waved to Woo Jin.

"Good morning, lovely ladies."

With excitement on her face, Yoomi replied, "Good morning to you."

"Shall we go in?"

They followed Woo Jin in and they sat at a table in the rear of the restaurant. Mrs. Hwang thought it was strange for him to sit in the rear of the restaurant, when they passed empty tables in the front.

"Woo Jin, are you going to school today?" asked Yoomi.

"No. I am taping my classes today. Do you ladies want to see Seoul?"

"Sure," said Yoomi.

"Woo Jin, thank you but I have business to take care of before I leave. You two go and have fun."

"Okay, we will," said Yoomi.

Woo Jin and Yoomi went sightseeing in Seoul, while Mrs. Hwang called Kang-de's office.

"Good morning. Is Mr. Shin Kang-de available to speak with me today?" she asked.

"No. But his assistant is available to speak with you. Would you like to speak with him?"

"Yes, please."

"Hello, good morning. This is Bob Goo."

"This is Mrs. Hwang from Hong Kong. I had a meeting scheduled with Mr. Shin and he cancelled unexpectedly."

"I am sorry, Madam. He was in an accident. He is unable to see anyone at this time. May I help you?"

"No. Please give him my regards and tell him to call me when he is able."

"Okay, Madam. Good day."

Seconds later, Bob's phone rang.

"Bob, come and see me. I remember something."

Bob drove to the ITO Hotel and entered the hotel from a private elevator. He hurried to Kang-de's suite, passing several security checks.

"Boss, what did you remember?"

"When the two cars came alongside me, I stopped and started to reverse because I saw a gun pointed at me. I recognized the gunman from the club. As I looked in the rearview mirror, I saw Mr. Chin in a white truck."

"Are you sure that you saw Mr. Chin?"

"I am very sure. He was driving the truck. Have you delivered that tape as yet?"

"Yeah. Mr. Park should have listened to it by now. What do you want to do about Mr. Chin?"

"I am personally going to take care of him," said Kang-de. "Did Areum go to school?"

"Yeah. Boss, there was a bug in the office, but it was one of the temporary secretary who placed it there. We found her and she confessed that she was working for Mr. Jong. She told him about Sun-hee. She told him about your travel details."

"What else did she say?"

"She was a new temporary secretary, so she didn't get to see anything in detail. She did tell Mr. Jong about your meeting with Director 5. But she doesn't know what Director 5 looks like or that he is a members of Mr. Jong's board."

"Good. Where is she now?"

"I fired her and Chul took her to find out what else she knows."

"I can't wait to see what Mr. Park is going to do to Mr. Jong," said Kang-de smiling.

"Oh, Boss. I have two things to tell you about. First, the elderly man who could testify about the truck hitting you was found dead at his home. He was sitting in his chair with a single stab wound to his lungs. Poor man must have suffered," said Bob.

"Why am I not surprised? They are covering their murderous trail. What's the second news?" he asked.

"A Mrs. Hwang came to see you from Hong Kong."

"Oh, yes, I had a meeting with her. Where is she now?"

"She is staying at this hotel," Bob replied.

"Please get her room number."

Kang-de called Mrs. Hwang who was getting dressed.

"Good afternoon, Mrs. Hwang. I am so sorry that I did not keep our appointment. I was in a car accident."

"I am sorry, Mr. Shin. How are you feeling now?"

"Sore. But I am okay. Could we meet in my boardroom on the fifth floor in an hour?"

"Yes, please. I would like that," she said An hour had passed and Kang-de headed to the boardroom in a wheelchair pushed by his body-guard. Mrs.. Hwang was already waiting in the boardroom.

"Mrs. Hwang, it is very nice to meet you. I am sorry about my appearance. Please excuse me."

"You look fine, Mr. Shin."

"Please be seated, Mrs. Hwang. How can I help you?"

"You know that our stock price has recently taken a loss. And I was told that you have bought several of the shares. I am asking you to let us buy them back from you."

"Why should I do that, Mrs. Hwang? I am looking to invest in your company and many others. Does your husband know that you are speaking with me?"

"Mr. Shin, our company has been in my family for three generations. My husband's pride will not let him speak with you. When it comes to my legacy, I have no pride. I am asking you again to please reconsider selling the shares back to us."

"Out of respect for your family, I am willing to consider selling you some of the shares, but I have to resolve a few things first. Please give me a little time to think about it."

Disappointed she replied, "Well, it's not what I want to hear, but I am willing to accept it. Can you have your lawyer speak with my lawyer when you have decided?"

"Sure. Thank you for having the boldness to come and speak with me. I respect you, Mrs. Hwang."

"Thank you, Mr. Shin. Get well soon. I will see myself out. Good-bye."

Kang-de and his guards returned to his suite and he called Chul.

"Chul, I need to see you."

He was in the lobby and he hurried to Kang-de's suite.

"Chul, I want you to have one of your men follow Mrs. Hwang while she is here. I want to know where she goes and who she meets. I don't trust her, even though she seems sincere."

"Consider it done."

Chapter Thirty-nine

Mr. Park, Minjae, Dave, Mr. Jong, Chin, Bora,
Woo Jin, Yoomi, Sun-hee, Areum, and Kang-de

Mr. Park received the disc by messenger, but he didn't watched it imme-diately. Several days later, Mr. Park sat in his library and he watched the disc. His face turned red. He placed it on pause and he called Minjae.

Minjae was a block away from Mr. Park's home when his cell rang.

"Minjae, come to my home quickly."

Minjae arrived and hurried to Mr. Park's library.

"What is it, Boss?"

"I received an anonymous delivery a few days ago. Look at this."

They watch the disc and Mr. Park became enraged from what he was hearing.

"He was planning to kill Bora, his daughter-in-law-to-be. Wow," said Minjae.

"Minjae, call Dave Jong. I want him to see this. I will let him decide his father's fate."

He got Dave Jong's number from Mr. Park and he called him.

"Hello, Mr. Dave, Mr. Park wants to see you at his home. It's urgent."

"I will be right there."

A half-hour later, Dave arrived at the Park's mansion.

"Hello Mr. Park how are you today?"

"I got a disc that I want you to see and I want you to tell me what to do with it."

"Sure."

Dave watched it with horror on his face. He was in shock.

"Oh, my Gosh. Where did you get this? Who gave it to you?"

"It was delivered to my home a few days ago and it had no return address."

"May I have it? I want my father to see it."

"Yes. Please take it."

"Mr. Park, I am so embarrassed, horrified and sorry. I love Bora. I thought my dad did too. I am so ashamed. I am very sorry."

Dave dropped to his knees and apologized to Mr. Park. He took the disc and went home to see his father. He stepped past the maid and walked to his father's office. "Dad, I have something I want you to see," he said putting the disc into the television.

"What is it?"

"Look and then you tell me," said Dave.

Mr. Jong watched the video without showing any emotion. He turned it off when it reached the part where he gave the okay to kidnap Bora.

"Dad, how could you try to harm your own daughter-in-law? You stood on the podium at our engagement party and you told over four hundred people that you loved Bora like a daughter. All that time you were the one who tried to kidnap and even thought about killing her. How could you? I am so angry and ashamed to call you my father."

"I can explain."

"You can never give me an acceptable explanation. From today, you mean nothing to me. I don't want to see you ever again. I am moving out. We are not family anymore. I wanted to believe that you didn't know anything about your driver, but this disc solidifies my assumption that you did hire those men to kidnap Bora," said Dave sadly. "She is going to be my wife, Dad. Did you try to kill him too? What else have you done that I don't know about? No, I don't want to know. You and I are now strangers."

"Dave Jong, I am still your father and you will show me respect. Do you understand?"

"I will come back for my things. Goodbye."

"Dave, Dave, come back here. Right now. Dave, please don't leave. Let's talk about this."

Mr. Jong's eyes became teary. He threw the disc against the wall. Mrs. Jong heard the noise and she entered his office.

"Honey, what's going on? Why is Dave crying? What happened? Tell me."

"I just lost my son," said Mr. Jong dropping in his chair.

"What? What do you mean by that? What did you do?" she asked.

"I have to go after him."

Mr. Jong ran outside but Dave had already left. He fell to his knees and held his head. Mrs. Jong screamed at him loudly.

"What did you do? What did you do to my son?" she yelled.

Dave drove up and down the highway before arriving at a bar. He ordered several glasses of vodka which he gulped down quickly. Sun-hee and her friends left the law firm early, walked into the bar and she ordered club soda and mineral water. As she glanced around the bar she saw Dave sitting at the end of the bar. She walked over to Dave to greet, noticing that he looked unhappy.

"Hi, Mr. Jong. What are you doing here? Where is Bora?"

"I really don't want to talk to anyone right now. I am sorry."

"Okay. Please take a taxi when you leave here," she said walking away.

Sun-hee called Mr. Park to let him know where Dave was.

"Mr. Park, hello. I don't have Mr. Jong's number to let him know that his son is here at the bar and he looks drunk."

"I will be right there. Tell me where he is," said Mr. Park.

Mr. Park and Minjae arrived at the bar and Sun-hee pointed them to where Dave was sitting.

Mr. Park said, "Dave, you have had enough to drink. I am taking you home."

"No, no. I am not going home. I have no home."

"Okay, I will take you to my home. You can stay at the guest house."

"Thank you. But I am too ashamed to stay at your home. I cannot face your family. Please take me to the ITO Hotel. I will stay there."

"I insist that you should stay at our home. You are my son. No argument."

Dave was too drunk to argue. Minjae lifted Dave to his car and he drove to the Park's mansion. Dave woke up early and he went to ITO Hotel.

As he entered his hotel room, his cell phone rang. He noticed that Bora was calling. He hesitated and then answered.

"Good morning. Don't forget that we have a date tonight."

"I am sorry, Bora. Something came up and I can't take you out tonight."

"You sound sad. What's wrong, Dave?"

"Bora. Nothing is wrong. I have something to do. Okay?"

"Okay. I will call you later," she said.

Dave hung up and began to cry. He called his mother to assure her that he was feeling well.

"Mom, I just wanted you to know that I am doing fine. I don't want you to worry. I will stay in touch with you. I'm at the ITO Hotel but do not tell Dad where I am."

"A hotel? Dave, what happened between you and your dad? Please talk to me."

"Ask your husband. He is no longer my father. I will call you later," he said as he hung up his cell.

Mr. Jong overheard his wife talking to Dave and he called his security team.

"I want you to find my son. He is staying in a hotel. Go now. Search every hotel in Seoul."

Mr. Jong called Mr. Chin at his home.

"Chin, I want you to find out who gave the disc to my son. It is urgent. They might have copies and I want them."

"Mr. Jong. It has to be Shin Kang-de's team."

"I don't think so. It has to be someone close to Dave."

"Where is Dave? Maybe he will tell us who gave him the disc?"

"I don't know where he is right now. Did anyone see you driving the truck that day?" he asked.

"No, Sir," said Chin lying to Mr. Jong. He was afraid to tell him that the elderly man had seen him pushing Kang-de's car off the road. "By the way, Boss, we are still trying to find Shin Kang-de. We can't find him. We suspect that he is hiding in his hotel, but we have not been able to verify that as yet."

"Find that bastard. We need to shut him up permanently."

"Okay, Boss," said Chin.

Meanwhile, at the clinic, rounds were finished for the day and Bora and Areum met at the bench located outside the clinic. Areum looked down at her cell phone and then up at Bora.

"Bora, you look upset. What's is the matter?"

"Something is wrong with Dave. I can feel it, but he is not telling me anything."

"Why don't you go and see him?"

"I will. Later. My driver is here. Bye."

"Good luck," said Areum while tapping at her cell phone screen to call Woo Jin. "Where are you? Do you want to meet at the library?"

"No. I am not at school today. I took the day off."

"Is everything okay with you?" she asked as she heard a female voice in the background.

"Everything is fine. I am with a friend."

"I can hear your friend in the background. Bye."

Woo Jin could tell by the sound of Areum's voice that she was upset. But, he had to take out Yoomi. Her family's investments were essential to keeping Kim Industries afloat.

"Yoomi, let's go. Are you hungry?"

"Let's have dinner with my mom."

"Great. But let's eat out. I don't like hotel food."

"Let's ask my mom."

Woo Jin and Yoomi arrived at the ITO Hotel and Mrs. Hwang met them for dinner.

"Mom, Woo Jin wants to take us out to eat. What do you say?"

"No. Let's stay here and eat tonight. I am tired. Perhaps next time we can go out to eat at one of those nice restaurants in Gangnam."

"Sure. As you wish."

As Woo Jin entered the restaurant with the ladies, Areum saw him. She briefly hesitated, then she slowly walked over to him.

"Hi. How are you?"

"Good. Could we talk later?" he said nervously.

Areum looked at Yoomi and remembered bumping into her in the lobby. She turned around and walked to the elevator.

"Can we sit down and order?" said Yoomi.

Woo Jin glanced at Areum and nodded to Yoomi's suggestion.

"Sure. Let's go to the table," he said.

Areum felt humiliated that Woo Jin didn't introduce his friends. She got off the elevator and her guard was waiting to open the door for her. Suddenly her cell phone buzzed in her hand. She looked at it and it was Kang-de calling.

"Hello. Hi, Kang-de, how do you feel?"

"I am not feeling well today. Can you come up to see me?"

"Sure. Let me change my clothes."

Areum changed her clothes and went to see Kang-de. The guard opened Kang-de's door for Areum.

"Hello, Mr. Shin Kang-de, how are you? What's wrong?"

"I missed you and I wanted to know if you were okay."

"Of course. Why would I not be okay?"

Kang-de escorted her to a room in his suite with television monitors of the hotel. The monitors had pictures of the elevators, the exits, the restaurants, the banquet halls, the boardrooms, the hallways, the garage and the lobby. Areum looked at the screens with fascination.

"I just saw you get humiliated. Now you tell me that you're really okay?"

"I am fine. I do not want to discuss it with you."

"Okay. Don't discuss it. Are you hungry?"

"No, thank you."

"I am hungry. If you change your mind, I have more than I can eat."

"I will stay with you for a few minutes. Where are your nurses?"

"I sent them home for the next two days. But, don't stay if you are unhappy. I don't want any negativity in my suite."

"I said that I was fine. How is your head?"

"I have a headache thinking about how you let yourself be humiliated by that jerk. I am sorry but I have to say something. How much longer are you going to accept being treated like a nobody?"

"I am leaving this room now," said Areum embarrassed by his statement.

"Yes, go. Go and cry in your room as you usually do. When you grow up call me."

Areum ran out of Kang-de's room crying. Kang-de threw down his chopsticks on the table. He had lost his appetite. He thought about what he just said to Areum.

"Guard, take me to Miss Areum's suite, please."

Kang-de and his guards went to Areum's room. He knocked on the door and she didn't answer. His Security rang the bell and knocked on the door. One of Areum's security opened the door.

Kang-de wheeled himself in. "What took you so long to answer the door?"

"Kang-de, I am not in the mood for a lecture. Go back and get your rest, please."

"All of you, please leave us alone," said Kang-de.

Everyone left the room and closed the door. Kang-de got up from his wheelchair and sat on the couch.

"Areum, come here and sit next to me. Don't make me ask you twice."

"What do you want, Kang-de? I am tired right now," she said walking over to the couch.

"I know that you are embarrassed. I am very sorry for yelling at you. It hurts me to see you in pain. I just want you to be happy and I know that you are not. I love you and I don't ever want to raise my voice at you again. Do you forgive me?"

"I don't want to fight with you. I've told you that. You are forgiven. Kang-de, let me handle my life. I will be okay. I promise. Come let me take you to your room."

"Just hug me a bit. Let me stay with you for a while," he said.

Areum hugged him and he held her hands for a short time. He looked at her face and saw that she was still embarrassed by what he said to her earlier.

"Have you eaten as yet? Come, let's go back to my suite."

"I have something to tell you but I want to wait until the right time," said Kang-de.

"What is it that you want to tell me?" she asked curiously.

"It can wait," he said, staring at her beautiful eyes.

Woo Jin ended dinner early with Yoomi. He felt uncomfortable having dinner at the ITO Hotel, knowing that Areum was upstairs. He thought about her throughout the dinner. He felt guilty that he had to be rude to her when they met earlier. But, his family business would have been in jeopardy if Yoomi found out that he had a girlfriend.

"Woo Jin, thanks for treating us to dinner. It wasn't bad, was it?"

"No, it wasn't bad," he replied.

"I am glad that you both liked it. I am not a fan of the owner."

"What is the name of the owner?" asked Mrs. Hwang.

"Shin Kang-de. He owns several properties in Seoul."

Yoomi and Mrs. Hwang looked at each other, with surprise on their faces.

"Do you mean Mr. Shin Kang-de from the States?"

"Yes. Do you know him?" asked Woo Jin.

"He is an acquaintance of my parents," said Yoomi.

"Oh, yeah! Well, ladies, I must say goodnight. I have an early start tomorrow. It was very nice seeing you both. How long will you be staying here?"

"Mom has to go home tomorrow, but I will be here for a while. I have business to attend to."

"Okay, I will see you again. Goodnight, ladies."

Woo Jin ran to his car and he called Areum. Her voice recording came on. He looked at the phone and threw it on the passenger seat while he navigated out of the hotel parking lot.

The next morning, Areum saw Woo Jin in school. He was waiting at the clinic for her to come out.

"Areum, why have you not answered my calls? I called you all night."

"Did you really want to speak with me? When you were with your friends, you totally pretended that I wasn't important. You didn't have the respect to introduce me because you were ashamed of me, so why do you want to talk with me now?"

"I am sorry. There are a lot of things that I cannot explain and I need you to be patient with me until I can explain them."

"Humiliating me should not be an acceptable alternative. But if you want me to leave you alone, then I will."

"Oh, Areum, that is not what I meant. Please understand that I am in a dilemma and I am trying to get out of it. I just can't explain it to you right now. I am late for class but I want you to know that I love you. I love you a lot."

"If you say so then I will accept your word for now," she whispered so that he couldn't hear.

"Hey, keep the security around you. That Kang-de guy is bad news."

"Woo Jin. Stop it."

After Woo Jin had finished his second class, Sun-hee called his cell. He looked at the phone and turned the ringer down. She called him a second time and he answered in a whisper.

"Hello, I am in class."

"I know that you are in class, but I want you to come to my office today. I need to speak with you."

"About what? Why can't you tell me over the phone?"

"Because I can't. Please come. It's important."

After classes were finished, he went to Sun-hee's office. He walked in and spoke in an annoyed tone. "Sun-hee, this better be good. I have a lot to do. What did you want to speak with me about?"

"I don't know how to say this. Ah, ah, I am pregnant."

"What did you just say? Pregnant? You are pregnant? Who is the father?"

"Woo Jin, don't be rude. You know that you are the only man that I have been with for a long time."

"No, Sun-hee, I don't know that. I met you at a bar."

"And what does that mean?" she asked looking at him in embarrassment.

"Never mind. You know that we are not ready to be parents. I thought that you were taking precaution. I used a condom."

"Yes, I was, but I have been busy with a heavy legal load and I missed a few pills. And the night you got into the fight with Kang-de, you didn't use a condom."

"Sun-hee, we can't have this baby. I can't have this baby. I have a company to run in a few months," said Woo Jin. "I am not ready to be a dad. I wouldn't be able to give a baby my full attention," he said agitated and shocked by what she just said.

"Okay, Woo Jin. You have told me how you feel. I am not getting rid of this baby. I will take care of it by myself. You don't need to help me take care of this baby. I can do it by myself. Now get out."

Woo Jin sighed and said, "Sun-hee, we are not finished with this discussion. We have more to talk about. I am very sorry, Sun-hee. It's just bad timing for the both of us. You know that too. I am sorry."

"Don't be sorry. I am glad that we had this conversation. At least I know how you feel about me and our baby."

"Sun-hee, please think about what I have said."

"Woo Jin, please leave," she said slamming the door behind him while he slowly walked out of her office.

Chapter Forty

Bora, Dave, Mrs. Jong, Mr. Jong, Mr. Chin, and Kang-de

Bora called Dave's cell phone and got no answer. She found out from her father that he had taken him to the ITO Hotel. She had her driver take her to the hotel. Moments later, Dave walked out of the elevator at the ITO Hotel and walked to the reception desk.

"Miss, if anyone comes looking for me, please do not give them any information. I do not want to speak with anyone. Thank you."

Dave's phone rang while he was speaking with the receptionist. He glanced at the phone and saw that his mother was calling. He answered with hesitation.

"My son, what has happened? Why have you left home?" she asked.

Ignoring her question, he replied, "Mother, please don't worry about me, okay? I just want to be by myself to think. Ask your husband the questions. Maybe he won't lie to you."

"Dave, please don't speak about your dad like that."

"Sorry, Mother. Anyway, I have another call on the line."

"Dave, Dave, Dave, Dave, how rude."

Dave answered the call from Bora. "Hello, Bora. I am sorry I have not contacted you sooner. I need to speak with you later. Meet me at the ITO Hotel at 6 P.M. for dinner."

"I am on my way there right now. We need to talk."

"Bora, I won't be able to see you until 6 o'clock, so please don't come here now," said Dave.

Bora returned home to take out the clothes that she would wear for dinner.

Five hours later Bora arrived dressed in a two-piece Chanel outfit with the back half open. Dave saw her and yelled out, "Bora, over here."

"Dave, you have been acting strange for several weeks."

"I am sorry, Bora. Let's eat and then we will talk."

Dave and Bora dined on steak and salad. Dave ordered French wine and Bora's favorite flavors of macaroons.

"What is really bothering you, Dave? You can tell me."

"I don't know how to tell you this but we have to postpone our wedding. We cannot get married now or in the near future."

"What are you saying, Dave? Why can't we get married?"

"I am sorry, Bora, but we just cannot. I can't explain it right now. Once I rent a place and settle my mind, then I will explain everything to you."

"Explain now. You owe me that much. You can't just tell me that we won't be getting married without an explanation."

"Okay. I just don't want to get married to you or anyone right now. I'm sorry."

"Why the sudden decision? Why did you let us have such a big party? My mother started planning the guest list already. Is there another woman?"

"No, Bora. It's nothing like that. I love you. But, please tell your mom to cancel all wedding plans. I am sorry, Bora."

Bora began to cry and she ran out of the restaurant. Dave watched her run out into the lobby. He left the restaurant and went upstairs to his room. He entered his room, lay across his bed and wept.

Later that night one of Mr. Chin's surveillance team members told him that he had seen Dave entering the ITO Hotel elevator. Mr. Chin had men watching the ITO Hotel for information on Kang-de. He called Mr. Jong immediately to advise him that Dave was staying at the ITO Hotel.

"Thanks, Chin. I will go and see him myself. By the way did your men see Shin Kang-de while they were there?"

"No, Sir. But, he will surface soon."

An hour later, Mr. Jong entered ITO Hotel. He used the house phone to call Dave's room. Dave answered the phone with hesitation.

"Dave, my son. We need to talk. How do you feel?"

"I am sorry, but I don't want to speak with you right now. I am having difficulty trying to understand how you could be so evil. I am sorry but I have to go now." He hung up on his dad.

Desperate to speak with Dave, Mr. Jong tried to go upstairs, but Kang-de's hotel security stopped him.

Kang-de had seen Mr. Jong on his security camera and he contacted security to stop him from entering the elevators. Kang-de allowed two security guards to approach Mr. Jong. Kang-de knew Mr. Jong was smart and if he saw too many security guards, then he would know that Kang-de was in the hotel.

Mr. Jong left the hotel without causing any disturbance in the lobby.

Chapter Forty-one

Bora, Dave, and Areum

Bora arrived at her apartment exhausted from crying. She had spent the entire trip, from the hotel, thinking about what Dave had said to her. She felt sickened by the broken engagement and she hoped that he would change his mind. She picked up her phone and she pressed Areum's number on her cell phone.

"Hello, Bora. How was your dinner with Dave?"

"Areum, Dave called off the wedding."

"What? Why? How could he? Is he getting cold feet?"

"No, something bad happened and he is not telling me. Do you think that Shin Kang-de can help him? Dave likes him a lot."

"I can ask Kang-de. I am so sorry, Bora. Maybe he will change his mind. He loves you very much. He probably has wedding jitters."

"Thanks, Areum. I love him so much."

Areum was already at the ITO Hotel elevator when she ran into Dave as he was exiting the elevator.

"Hey, Dave, how are you? I just heard from Bora. She's unhappy but she is not saying why. Do you know why?"

"I can't talk about it. It's too painful."

"Why don't you talk to someone?"

"I will think about it. Please excuse me."

Dave checked out of the ITO Hotel and disappeared into an awaiting taxi.

Chapter Forty-two

Woo Jin, Areum, Kang-de, Dave,
Bob, Chul, Mrs. Park, and Sun-hee

Two months had passed and Woo Jin completed his graduate degree and he decided to leave for Hong Kong immediately. He called Areum to let her know that he had to go to Hong Kong, but he would be back for his graduation. She answered the call.

"Areum, could you please come to my apartment today?" he asked.

"What do you want to tell me? Tell me over the phone."

"Areum, please, I need to see you now."

Areum went to his apartment and as she entered his home, she asked, "What do you want to see me about?"

Woo Jin handed Areum a glass of champagne and he poured one for himself. "I want to toast to the completion of my graduate studies."

"Oh, wow. You are finished. Congratulations. Well done."

"Thank you. You are almost finished with medical school too."

"Yeah."

Woo Jin paused for a minute, then he said, "Areum, I have to leave in two days. I am stopping in Hong Kong for six months and then I have to go to Brunei for six months. That's a year."

"So soon?"

"That's why I wanted to speak with you. I want you to come with me."

"Woo Jin, how can I go with you now?" she asked.

"After this semester you can start your first year of residency any-where."

"I can't leave my mother and father. You see how sick my mom is."

"I know. You can fly back and forth. Money is not a problem. I think that I can afford to fly you at least once a month," said Woo Jin.

"Yes, Woo Jin. I know that money is not an problem to you. Why don't you come to see me here? That's a better idea."

"Okay. I can't do it right of way, but once I am settled, I will try to come. Why don't you stay in my apartment? It has a lot of security. And the security that I provided you will stay with you until you are no longer in danger."

"I am very grateful to you, but I will be too lonely here. The hotel is safer with lots of people going in and out of the hotel."

"What did Shin Kang-de say about how long you can stay at the hotel?" he asked. "He said that it's my home until I choose to leave."

Woo Jin looked at her with sadness in his eyes and he hugged her tightly. He didn't mention Sun-hee's pregnancy. He could not. He didn't want to lose the woman he loved.

"I am going to miss you so badly. I want us to get engaged before I left, but that's not possible now. Please stay with me until I leave. Please?"

"Okay. I will stay with you until you leave."

Areum called Kang-de to let him know what she was about to do. "Kang-de, I am staying the next two nights at Woo Jin's. He is leaving in two days. I wanted you to know so that you can keep the guards with you."

"Why are you telling me this, Areum? Do you want me to get upset? Go ahead and have fun. Bye," he said hanging up on her. Jealousy overpowered Kang-de and he threw the glass of wine, that he had in his hand, against the kitchen wall.

Woo Jin noticed that Areum was startled by what Kang-de had said. He gently took her hand and he told her that he wanted to be with her.

Areum replied, "When we get married, you can have all of me and more. I love you, Kim Woo Jin. You better be faithful to me. Okay?"

"I will. You better not sleep with that jerk Shin Kang-de."

They spend the two nights hugging and kissing each other, but they had no sex.

Areum packed Woo Jin's bags and took him to the airport. They walked hand in hand to security.

"Areum, I love you and I will see you soon. Okay? Hug me like you haven't seen me in years."

"You are so crazy. Safe travels. Call me when you get to Hong Kong," she said while hugging him.

"I will. Bye, baby," he said walking away from her.

Woo Jin went through security and Areum looked to her right and saw a familiar face. It was Yoomi standing at the check-in desk.

Who is she? And why is she following Woo Jin? she asked herself.

Areum turned and walked to the parking lot where her driver had parked Woo Jin's sports car. Woo Jin's security followed her car at a distance.

Woo Jin called Kang-de as he sat in the first-class lounge.

"Hey, it's me. She is mine. All mine. Don't think that because I am not in Seoul that you will ever have her. Make sure that she's protected. If anything happens to her because of you, then you will die with her."

"Kim Woo Jin, why don't you worry about your messed-up life? Areum is my concern and not yours. Did you tell her that Sun-hee is pregnant? I am sure that you have not. I won't tell her either. It's your responsibility to tell her."

"Don't concern yourself with my life. You make sure Areum stays safe."

"Goodbye, Woo Jin," Kang-de said hanging up his cell phone. "That bastard. One day I will make him pay for being so rude," murmured Woo Jin to himself.

A few minutes later, when Areum called Kang-de's room from the house phone, she got no answer. She called him on the cell phone and he answered in an upset tone, "Hello."

"Hi, Kang-de, may I come up to your suite?" she asked.

"No. I am in a meeting right now. Maybe later."

"Okay," she said in a disappointing tone.

Kang-de was busy speaking with Bob, Chul-Moo and a lot of security. "Bob, it's time to take care of unfinished business. First, Mr. Park. You know what has to be done. See my friend at the District Attorney's office. Make sure that you personally hand him all the documents in this envelope," he said handing Bob the envelope. "He's expecting you. Chul, I didn't see Mr. Chin coming at me until it was too late. He won't see you coming. Will he?"

Chul and Bob laughed simultaneously.

"Mr. Jong already lost something money can't buy, and that is his son's love. And I am not finished with him as yet. Okay, guys, that is all for now I will be downstairs in the boardroom on the fifth floor."

"Boss, how do you feel?" asked Bob.

"Fantastic. All my problems are going to be resolved today. My biggest problem is on a plane to Hong Kong. I feel great. Let's celebrate tonight."

"Okay, Boss. Chul, you bring the guys and I will bring the ladies," said Bob smiling at Chul.

"Sounds good to me. Now let's take care of what must be done."

Later that afternoon while Kang-de was in the boardroom with the managers of all his computer stores, Mr. Park was arrested for embezzlement, fraud and corporate espionage. Mr. Chin was arrested for murder and attempted murder. Mr. Jong's Board of Directors voted to replace him, thanks to Director 5.

Kang-de turned on the television to see Mr. Park and Mr. Chin in handcuffs. Mr. Jong was also escorted to police headquarters for questioning. Kang-de got a call from Chul.

"Hey, Chul. Is it all finished?"

"Yes, Boss. I could have easily deleted Mr. Chin from this world, but I did as you wish."

"If he gets off, then you will get your chance. But I have my associate waiting for Mr. Chin in jail," said Kang-de smiling.

Areum was in her mother's suite watching television when she saw Mr. Park and Mr. Jong with the police. She immediately called Bora to find out what was happening.

"What is happening to your dad? I just saw him on television being arrested."

"Areum, I can't speak with you right now. I will call you back."

Bora called Dave to find out what was happening. She had hoped that he would finally tell her what was really happening.

"Dave, what is going on? I see my dad and your dad in handcuffs. Tell me what is happening. I am about to become sick. Please tell me what is going on."

"I can't tell you much. I can only tell you that my dad has done bad things and he should pay for his sins. I am so sorry for any pain my family may have caused you."

"Dave, what are you talking about? What sins have your dad committed? Please talk to me. I don't know what to do, Dave. I can't face my mother. She must be so upset."

"Bora, I want you to focus on becoming a doctor. Concentrate on your career. Our parents have embarrassed us, but you need to keep going. Bora, I will always love you. I just can't be with you right now. May I call you later?"

"Yeah. We need to talk. Right now I have to go and see my mother."

Dave went to Mr. Jong's company headquarters. His dad's assistants greeted him and escorted him through the main lobby where members of the Board of Directors, including Director 5, had lined up to greet Dave. The lobby consisted of thousands of square feet of marble, and sculptures from Europe. Dave gazed at all the men waiting to greet him.

"I want to see all company employees in the boardroom now, please."

They all gathered in the boardroom to hear Dave speak. The room was quiet and the occupants stared at Dave's face, hoping to read his emotions.

"You all have heard that your CEO has been taken to the police station. I want you all to know that today the Board of Directors have removed CEO Jong as head of this company. Therefore, in order to save this vast conglomerate, the board of Directors have asked me to temporarily assume the responsibilities of Chief Executive Officer. I need all of you to help me save this company. We have always operated like a family and I would like to continue in that manner," he said. "Now I know that some of you might not be happy with the board's decision, but please don't let that impact your productivity. If I fail, then you will fail too. Let us get to work to keep this company strong and financially sound. Thank you for your attention."

Everyone queued to congratulate Dave, but he greeted them with sadness on his face.

Minutes later at the Parks' residence, Bora ran into her home looking for her mother. She saw her mother crying, as she entered the library.

"Mom, are you, you okay? What has Dad done? Why has he been arrested?"

"I don't know what is happening. Your dad never included me in the business. I need to make phone calls. I am so confused. I need to call that woman Sun-hee. I believe she is still his lawyer."

Mrs. Park called Sun-hee to come to her home. Reluctantly, Sun-hee went to see Mrs. Park. She nervously entered the Parks' home.

"I called you here because I want you to get my husband out of jail. Money is not a problem."

"I am sorry, Mrs. Park, but I am no longer your husband's lawyer. If you need a lawyer, then I will find one for you."

"I just hired you back. Please help Mr. Park. He helped you start your law firm, didn't he?"

Sun-hee was shocked that Mrs. Park knew about her affair with Mr. Park. "I will go to the police station to see him and I will post his bail."

"Thank you on behalf of my husband," said Mrs. Park.

Sun-hee left the Park's residence and stopped at her office. She called Kang-de to get his opinion on what she had just agreed to.

"Hello, Kang-de. How are you? You saw the news about Mr. Jong and Mr. Park, right?"

"Yes. Why?"

"I wanted you to know that Mrs. Park asked me to represent Mr. Park at his bail hearing."

"Sun-hee, are you out of your mind? You should not get entangled with those people again. Your safety is important. Don't be hasty. You have a baby to think about. Don't do it. Get someone else to represent him."

"You are right, Kang-de. Thanks. I am going to get Attorney Choi to represent him. I will let Mrs. Park know."

Sunhee called Mrs. Park and told her that Attorney Choi had agreed to represent Mr. Park. She told her that he was the best lawyer in Seoul.

"I am disappointed but I will accept your word that he is the best lawyer in Seoul. Tell him to contact me immediately," Mrs. Park replied.

Chapter Forty-three

Mr. Park, Bora, Bob, Areum, Woo Jin,
Kang-de, Chul, Dave, and Sun-hee

While Mr. Park sat in jail over the weekend, he contacted Minjae, who had not been charged with a crime. He told Minjae where to get the money to give to his lawyer. Minjae followed his instructions and handed Attorney Choi a black attaché case.

Mr. Park received bail after posting ten million won with the courts. He had successfully gotten his bail reduced from fifteen million won, thanks to the well-connected attorney Choi.

When Mr. Park arrived home he was furious with Kang-de because he found out that Kang-de had presented evidence against him and the evidence was strong. Bora was told that Kang-de was the person who had her father arrested. She called Areum to tell her to ask Kang-de to have the charges against her father dismissed.

Areum informed her that she couldn't do that. "I do not interfere in Kang-de's business. I don't have that kind of influence over him. I am so sorry about your dad. I am sure that it will work out."

There was silence at the other end of the cell phone. Bora had hung up the phone.

Areum called Kang-de to tell him what Bora had asked. "Kang-de. Bora wanted me to convince you to change your mind about sending Mr. Park to prison."

"What did you tell her?"

"I told her no. I could not do that. I told her that I do not interfere into your private affairs."

"Areum. You are truly my friend. Come upstairs. I want to tell you something."

She hung up her cell and went upstairs.

As she entered his suite, he was staring out the window with a glass of alcohol in his hand. He turned around and looked at her.

"Why do you want to see me?"

"Here, take this and drink all of it at one time."

"Why do I need to drink vodka?" she asked.

"Do you remember that I told you that I had something to tell you but it could wait?"

"Yeah," she replied slowly anticipating what he was about to say to her.

"Well, I don't know how to tell you this without hurting you," he said.

"You found a girlfriend?" Areum asked.

"No, no, no. Woo Jin is still sleeping with Sunhee. I am sorry, Areum."

"What? What did you just say? You must be mistaken. That cannot be true. When did he find time to see her? He told me that he had stopped seeing her?"

Areum felt her heart sink to her stomach. She ran to the bathroom to throw up. "Areum, you will be okay. I know that it's a shock now, but you will be fine."

"I have to go," she said while walking hastily out of Kang-de's suite.

"Go where? Do not go to see Sun-hee until you have calmed down."

"I have to go," she said firmly.

"Since you won't listen to me, please let the guards go with you."

"No, no, no," she said in an angry tone.

"Okay, Areum. Calm down and stay here until you feel better."

"I will be fine," she said in a low tone, and she walked out of his suite and headed to Sun-hee's office. It took her a few minutes to get to Sun-hee's office.

Sun-hee saw Areum and said, "I was expecting you to come and see me, but not so soon. Who told you?"

"Don't concern yourself about how I found out. Were you that desperate that you need to sleep with an engaged man?"

"To whom is he engaged?" asked Sun-hee in an arrogant tone.

"TO ME!"

"Woo Jin never mentioned anything about being engaged to you," she replied. "Sun-hee, the only reason that you are still standing upright is because I don't want to go to jail."

"Don't let that stop you. Do you think that I am afraid of you?"

"You should be. You don't want to be here when I get upset," said Areum walking toward Sun-hee.

Suddenly, there was a heavy knock on Sun-hee's office door. It was Bob Goo opening the door. Kang-de called him after Areum stormed out of his suite.

"Miss Areum, the Boss said that I should take you home."

"Yes, Bob. Get her out of my office. Bob, please wait outside while I show this woman who she is messing with."

Areum grabbed at Sun-hee's jacket but Sun-hee moved away quickly. Bob lifted Areum and took her to the elevator. He put her down when the elevator door closed.

"Bob, why did you do that? You should have let me at least slap the smirk off her face." "Boss says that you might be very angry and he didn't want you hurting anyone."

"She deserves to feel a little pain because I am in pain."

Bob drove Areum to the hotel and Areum arrive at Kang-de suite looking very upset with him.

"Did I save Sun-hee from your wrath?" he asked smiling.

"Kang-de, next time don't send anyone to get me. Let me handle my own affairs. Why is everyone protecting that woman? First it was Woo Jin, and now you? Who is protecting me?" said Areum with tears in her eyes.

Areum ran out of Kang-de suite and went down to her suite. She lay across her bed and wept. Kang-de followed behind her a few seconds later. He told her guard to step aside as he knocked on her door.

"Areum, open the door. Areum, open the door right now. Areum, don't let me destroy my property by kicking down this door. Lee Areum, open this door now. Guard, go and get me the keycard for this room."

The guard returned with the keycard. Kang-de opened her door. He walked into the bedroom and saw Areum lying across her bed and she was weeping quietly.

"Oh, my sweet. Don't cry. I am here. Come, let me hug you."

She remained on the bed. Kang-de grabbed both her hands, pulled her toward him and he hugged her tightly as she continued to sob.

"I thought that you were a strong lady. I would never have told you had I thought that you would be in such pain. Stop crying. Let's go out tonight. You don't have any clinic tomorrow," he said rocking her in his arms.

"You are still recuperating. People are looking for you. We can't go out and I don't want to go out."

"Yes, we can. I am feeling fine. My headache is gone. We are going out. And don't worry about who is looking for me. I am ready for anything and everything this time."

"I don't feel like socializing. I don't want to see anybody tonight," she said.

"Areum, we are going out. Get dressed. I will wait right here for you."

Areum went into the bathroom, took a shower and wore the same red dress she previously wore. Kang-de saw that she wore the same dress and he called housekeeping.

"Please have the boutique send up a few dresses for this room. No red ones. Tell them that's for the same lady who bought the red dress. They have her size."

An half-hour later, the doorbell rang and it was the lady from the boutique. She brought a variety of clothes for Areum to choose. Areum chose a royal blue Gucci pants suit with a silk scarf.

"Now this is my girl. You take my breath away. Come on, let's go out on the town. It's time for me to be seen as well."

"I am really not in the mood for this outing, but if it will make you happy then let's go."

"Yes, make me happy."

Bob, Areum, Kang-de and twelve of his security team went out on Kang-de's yacht. Chul and several ladies were waiting for them. The crew took the yacht away from the dock. Kang-de began to speak as they sailed. "Attention. Everyone except you ladies, please come upstairs on deck. Areum, you stay here with the ladies." Kang-de began to speak to the men. "Guys, you are my family. We have been through some rough times these past months, but we have prevailed. I want to give a special thank-you to Bob and Chul. You have shown me what true loyalty means. I have twelve envelopes here. One for each of you men. Inside you will see my appreciation for your hard work."

The men opened their envelopes and everyone yelled out, "Thank you, Boss. Wow."

Kang-de gave each one 100,000.00 won.

Chul got a new BMW car plus 1,000,000.00 won and Bob got a new house in one of the wealthiest communities in Seoul.

"This is too much. We are happy to work for you. You have always been kind to us. I can't accept this. You are like my brother," said Bob.

"Yes, Boss, this is just too much. I have a car," said Chul.

"Hey, guys. If I didn't think that you deserved these gifts, then I would never have given them to you. Now shut up and let's eat and party. Everyone, go downstairs. Bob, send Areum up, please."

Areum went and joined Kang-de on deck.

"Hey, my girl. Come and sit next to me. How do you feel now? Give me your hand. Let me keep it warm. Areum, I have had a crush on you for so long. I really didn't want to tell you such a terrible news, but I thought that you should know who you were dealing with. The day we recognized each other again was the best day of my life. I love you with all my heart. I want you to trust that I will never intentionally hurt you. I am in love with you, Areum."

"Kang-de, I don't know what to say. Thank you for loving me. You deserve to be loved by a good woman. I don't know if I qualify as a good woman anymore."

"Don't degrade yourself because you got your feelings hurt. You liked Woo Jin. You never loved Woo Jin. Areum, with love you're all the way into it, if it's real. There is no grey area. When I hug you, your body tells me that you want me. If you loved Woo Jin, you would never have those feelings for me."

"You might be right. But I can't pretend that I don't have feelings for him. I am hurt right now. I want to talk to Woo Jin and settle this for good."

"You can't have both of us. I can't share you. My heart and my body belongs to you. I can't, I won't share you," said Kang-de looking at her with passion in his eyes. "You have until the end of this year to choose. If it's Woo Jin then fine. But the feelings I have for you will never die. I love you, Lee Areum. Never forget that." Kang-de kissed her on the forehead and he went downstairs of the yacht and joined his guests.

Areum held her face in her hand while she thought about what she wanted to do. The phone rang and Woo Jin was on the other line. Areum watched it ring until it went into voicemail.

Woo Jin called Sun-hee to see how she was feeling.

"How do you think that I feel? Your fiancé came by to fight with me."

"Areum did that? Maybe she knows. I am sorry. I will speak with her. So what have you decided? I can't be a dad right now. I am too far away to help you with a baby."

"I have already told you that I am keeping this baby. You don't need to concern yourself. I can afford it."

"In two months' time I will get time off. We need to talk," he said. He disconnected from Sun-hee and he called Areum again. She answered the phone.

"Hello, Woo Jin. I have just one question for you. Have you slept with Sun-hee since you've been with me?"

"Yes. Once. I am sorry."

"So you lied to me when you said that you have not slept with her since we have been dating."

"Areum, I can explain."

"Explain why you broke my heart into pieces? I have to go now."

"Areum, Areum, Areum."

Areum hung up and joined the party. Kang-de looked at her face and saw the sadness in her eyes.

"Come with me."

"Where to? You can't just leave your guests alone."

"Why not? They're having fun without me. Lock the door."

"What do you want from me, Kang-de?"

"I just want to stay here for a while. Now all the guys will think that you and I had fun."

"Kang-de, what about my honor and respect? They will think that I am a loose woman."

"Oh, Areum. They already think that you are my woman. Don't worry so much."

"I did say that I would do anything for you. Didn't I?" she asked.

"Areum, I would never make love to you with a group of employees in the next room. I know exactly where I want to make love to you."

"Get me off this yacht now."

"Areum. Are you upset?" asked Kang-de.

"No, I want you to take me to that place now."

"What? Wait. I am not into rebounds. Think about what you are saying."

"Let's put it this way. If I choose Woo Jin, then you'll never know what you missed. Now at least you got to me first."

"I like your CRAZY reasoning. Okay. Let's go."

The helicopter took less than an hour to reach Kang-de's home in Ansan. The house was a two-story Tuscan home with a high gate that opened into a long driveway with beautiful gardens on both sides. A large stable with horses could be seen on the far right of the garden.

Kang-de's opened the large mahogany front door which was designed by Southeast Asian carpenters. He escorted Areum through the long hallway that ended into a circular foyer. He stepped down three stairs that separated the foyer from the living room which was designed in Mediterranean blue with teak wood trimming. An antique chandelier extended from the wood ceiling. He turned left through a door that opened into the dining room. In the center of the room there was a rectangle table made out of mahogany wood. A large chandelier brightened the table and a grand china cabinet covered one side of the wall.

Areum followed Kang-de into the rustic chef kitchen that had hanging copper pots extended over a large island. "Oh, my gosh, Kang-de, this house is beautiful. And the architecture is magnificent."

"Thank you. Are you hungry? I can cook something for you."

"No, we just had a big meal on the yacht."

"Well, let me show you the rest of the house," he said.

Kang-de took her to the library, the family room, the game room, and the pool.

"Wow, the parties here must be great."

"I don't entertain people at this house. This my sanctuary. Would you like to see where I meditate?" he asked her.

"Sure."

He took her to a room filled with white candles and a broad mat. She noticed an open door attached to the room.

"What's in there?" she asked, pointing to the room.

"Go and see for yourself."

It was the master bedroom which had a king-sized bed with a large iron filigree designed headboard. A red and white silk bedspread covered the red Egyptian cotton sheet that hung off the side of the bed. Areum noticed a Persian rug lying beside the bed. She looked up and noticed the vault ceiling with a chandelier made of gold and diamond shaped crystals. The floors were made of marble tiles imported from Spain.

"Kang-de, you really live here by yourself? Okay, Kang-de, how many women have slept on this bed? Oh, I am sorry. I shouldn't ask you such a personal question."

"None. I have never brought a woman to this house."

"Never?" asked Areum.

"I will say it one more time. Never have I brought a woman into this house, except for the housekeepers. This is my sanctuary."

Areum smiled when she heard what Kang-de said.

"What would you like to drink to calm your nerves? I can feel your energy across the room."

"A glass of wine, please."

"My pleasure. I'll get you a bottle of French wine from the cellar. Yes. There's a wine cellar too."

"Where is your bathroom? I'd like to take a shower if that's okay with you."

"Walk through that door. You can use any towel you see."

Areum entered the bathroom and she noticed gold faucets were hanging over the sink, over the shower and in the cultured marble bathtub. Spanish mosaic tiles covered the bathroom walls.

"This man is too much," Areum said to herself.

She took a shower and she wrapped herself in a beige bath towel that was large enough to wrap around her body twice. As she walked out of the bathroom, she noticed Kang-de kneeling at the fireplace. The log was catching when he got up and handed her a glass of wine.

"Make yourself comfortable. I am going to take a shower."

She drank the wine and she poured herself another glass of wine. She took two gulp and the glass was empty. Her heartbeat was erratic and her nerves on edge. Kang-de came out of the bathroom and saw Areum sitting on the lounge chair near the fireplace. He went and sat on the bed.

"Areum, come in the bed. I promise that I will be gentle with you."

"Kang-de, I am feeling very nice."

"Areum, do not get drunk. I want you to remember everything."

Areum lay on the bed and snuggled under Kang-de's arm. He bend his head and kissed her softly on the lips, and on her neck. She returned a kiss to his earlobe and neck. He let his tongue navigate her neck. Areum felt a warm sensations shooting through her body. Kang-de removed the towel that had covered her body. He looked at her body and he could feel the muscles in his body tingle. He proceeded to suck on her breast and he let his tongue glide in a straight line to her private parts. Kang-de let his tongue dance between her legs. She moaned out loud and she grabbed him by his hair and pulled him up before she climaxed.

She rolled on top of him and proceeded to kiss his entire body. Kang-de began to moan as Areum let her mouth engulf his private parts. She let her fingers glide between his thighs. He yelled out, pulled her up, and he rolled her over and gently entered her body after putting on a condom. She gasped in pain and then moaned as he slowly thrust his private parts into her.

"Areum, are you okay?" he whispered to her.

"Oh, yes," she whispered as she felt his private part moving deeper inside of her.

He turned her over and entered her from behind. She turned her head and he kissed her while grabbing her body tightly toward him.

"Am I hurting you?" he asked.

"No," she whispered as she moaned from the sweetness of his hard muscle that was slowly moving inside her.

Moments later Kang-de let her climb on top of him and ride him until he sat up and grabbed her in ecstasy. They climaxed together. He held her for a minute which seemed like an hour. The pounding of their heartbeats was the only sound that could be heard in the room. Kang-de smiled at her as she cuddle beside him. Areum was too embarrassed to say anything.

"Areum, are you sure that you are a virgin? You seem to know a lot. I must tell you that every second was worth the wait. Feel my heart. It's beating so rapidly."

Areum felt his heart racing.

"Oh, Kang-de, I am so embarrassed and my head hurts in ecstasy."

"Don't be embarrassed. We are adults and we have all night. I am going to make you give me a good body workout," he said smiling at her.

They made love on and off all night. Kang-de took her off the bed and made love to her on the rug. Then he held her against the wall and thust his private part into her. Later he pulled her onto the couch, lifted her legs and poured, what felt to Areum, like his entire body into her. He groaned as he climaxed inside of her. She held him tightly and she climaxed.

"Kang-de, I am so happy that you took me to another planet. I think that I am going to be addicted to you. Right now, I want you again."

"That's what I want to hear. I want every part of your body and I am going to take it over and over. Oh, I forgot that you have clinic this morning. Sorry."

"Kang-de, you are a dangerous man. I am not leaving this room today. I want to feel you inside me again," she said nibbling on his earlobe.

"Areum. Who is dangerous, you or me? I think it's you. I might have to call the police on you," he said laughing.

"Go ahead and call them. They will just see me making love with you. You feel so, so, so, so good inside of me. I want some more," she said as she climbed on top of him.

"Areum, I thought that you were shy and naive. What have I gotten myself into?"

Areum sat on him and rode him up and down until he screamed in ecstasy. He grabbed her and held her tightly. They climaxed together and fell asleep. Kang-de and Areum slept until one o'clock in the afternoon.

Areum cell phone rang and woke her. Woo Jin was calling. She looked at it and turned it down. Kang-de looked at her and laid his naked body halfway on her back.

"Areum, are you planning to leave me now?"

"What? Kang-de, I will only leave you if you stop making love to me," she said laughing.

"I am serious. Are you planning to leave me for him?"

"Kang-de, I am not going anywhere for a while. I have my medicine. I don't want anything to interfere with that. Well, at least almost nothing. Your body can interfere with me anytime."

"Areum, I should have never slept with you."

"Yeah, you woke up a sleeping lioness. Ha-ha. Love me, like you did last night and this morning."

"You sure are greedy, but I love this side of you," he said while thrusting himself inside her as hard as he could.

She screamed and he poured himself inside of her harder.

"Oh, Kang-de, I love you," she said as she moaned loudly.

"Areum!" he screamed as he withdrew quickly.

"Areum, I am sorry. I forgot to put on the condom this time. That's why I withdrew so quickly."

"It's okay. Don't forget it next time," she said as she went to take a shower. "Do you want to take a shower with me?" she asked.

"Yeah. I need you to wash my back for me," he said laughing.

"Maybe I will wash all of you. Can I get a repeat?" she asked.

"Oh, my gosh. I've got a sex addict with me."

"No, you just feel and taste sweet. Come on. One more time," she said urging him.

"Give me a minute. I am only a man."

Kang-de entered the shower with Areum. Before showering with her, he fell to his knees and he sucked hard on her private parts as if it were his first time. Areum grabbed his hair and yelled out as she climaxed. Kang-de turned on the shower and let the water run down her breast while he washed her breast. She turned him around and scrubbed his back gently in a circle.

Kang-de turned off the water, took a towel and gently dried her entire body. She did the same thing to him. He kissed her for several minutes which stimulated an arousal from both of them. He let her hand grab his private parts.

"Areum, no more. We have lots of time to enjoy each other. Greedy woman."

"My body is shivering, it wants you. Just a quickie," she said.

"You have me for a lifetime. You will have me whenever you want me. But, now we must go home."

Kang-de's housekeepers resided in an apartment on the side of the property. They were told to take three days off while Kang-de was there. Kang-de got dressed and prepared a meal for himself and Areum. He fed her throughout the meal. After eating, Kang-de and Areum were escorted by their security back to Seoul.

Upon arrival at the ITO Hotel, they entered the lobby separately. Kang-de went to his restaurant in the hotel and Areum went upstairs with her bodyguard. Kang-de called Bob to find out what was happening while he was away. Bob's cell phone went into voicemail.

Meanwhile, Areum thought about what she did with Kang-de and she told herself that she couldn't face Kang-de ever again.

Suddenly, Woo Jin called Areum to let her know that he was back at his apartment. Areum took a shower and went to see Woo Jin.

"Hi, Areum. You look good. How are you?"

"Not good."

"I am so sorry. I never meant for this to happen. It was an accident. I love you, Areum, and I want to marry you."

"You betrayed me, Woo Jin."

"I am sorry. I am really sorry. Areum, I don't want Sun-hee. I am going to take responsibility for the baby. But, I have no intention of marrying her. I told her that."

"Baby? What baby? Sun-hee is pregnant? Oh, no, no."

"I am sorry. I've always spoken the truth to you. It was an accident, Areum. I have no excuse. I did something out of my character. Please try to understand, Areum. It happened the night of the fight with Kang-de and…."

"Stop. I don't want an explanation."

"Please forgive me, Areum."

"I am not interested in your apology. I can't deal with you right now. I can't think of you and Sun-hee as parents. I have to go."

"Areum, did Kang-de tell you that Sun-hee was pregnant? Because Sun-hee told him before she told me."

"What?"

"Yes. He knew. Didn't he tell you?"

"Woo Jin, I don't care. He didn't make a baby with Sun-hee. You did."

"Areum, please, I can't leave you like this. I don't want to go knowing that you are so hurt."

"This can't be fixed right now. I am leaving."

"Areum! Areum!" he yelled. Woo Jin tried to prevent her from leaving his apartment.

"Woo Jin, let me go right now. I need to think."

"Please remember that I love you very much. I've loved you from the day we met and I will always love you."

Areum walked out crying and Woo Jin's eyes were filled with tears as he realized that he might have lost her. Areum's cell phone rang while her guard drove her back to the hotel.

"Where are you? I thought you were home studying. I am at your door."

"No. Woo Jin is back at his apartment and he wanted to speak with me."

"And you went to see him," Kang-de said in a disappointing tone.

"You knew Sun-hee was pregnant, didn't you?" she asked.

"Yes, but it was not my story to tell. I did tell you that he was still sleeping with her."

"That is not the same as telling me that she is pregnant. So, you pitied me. Is that why you made love to me?"

"Areum. I am a grown man. I don't play games. You know that."

"Yeah."

"If you know that, then why are you speaking to me like this?"

"Because I feel betrayed by the three of you," she said.

"Betrayed? Sun-hee told me that she was pregnant in confidence. If I had told you, then that's betrayal. Areum, I have a lot on my mind. We had a great time so far. Don't spoil my mood."

"Okay. I will speak with you tomorrow." Areum turned off her cell phone and went to her mother's suite.

Kang-de woke up early the next morning and he took two guards with him to Woo Jin's apartment. The security at Woo Jin's apartment let him through the gate and he rang Woo Jin's doorbell.

"Woo Jin, We need to talk."

"Come in. What do you want to talk about? Let me guess, Areum?"

"I am sure that you know that I own one-fifth of your company's stock."

"And? You still don't have enough to assume control. So what do you want? Are you here to exchange stocks for Areum?"

"I want you to cut ties with my Areum. You will only hurt her. You have done irreversible damage to her already. She is devastated by what you and Sun-hee have done. You think that you know her but you don't. She is a sensitive lady and her heart is fragile. Let her go now."

"Don't you think that I know what I have done to her? I fell in love with her the first day that I met her. I regret my actions so much. I can't let her go. I love her."

"You will have to let her go because she is going to let you go."

"Don't count on that. I'm going to fight for her. Oh, by the way. Does Areum know that you are a GANGSTER? Does she know that you have a dark side?" asked Woo Jin.

"Well, since you know that. You should be very careful how you speak to me."

"Oh, Shin Kang-de. You should be very scared of me. I don't fight fair. I always get what I want."

"Now I know for sure that you don't know the woman you claim to love. She will forgive you for hurting her, but she is done with you permanently."

"Go and marry Yoomi. Yes, I know everything about her too."

"You bastard. I should have killed you a long time ago."

"Stand in line, Woo Jin. Go and take care of your baby. Leave my Areum alone," he said walking out of Woo Jin's apartment and leaving the door open.

"I am not giving her up. Do you hear me?!" Woo Jin picked up his cell and called his dad. He had to make changes to his schedule.

"Hello, Dad. I have some bad news and I am coming to Hong Kong tomorrow to let you know what it is."

Late in the afternoon, Woo Jin arrived in Hong Kong and he took a hired car service to his parents' home. As he entered his home, his father noticed that he was troubled. Woo Jin ask him to have a seat in the library. His mother followed behind Woo Jin. The room was silent, so silent that you could hear a pin if it were to drop on the floor.

"Woo Jin, why are you back so quickly?" Mr. Kim asked.

"Mom, Dad, I have to delay my start time on the rig. I have unfinished business in Seoul and I won't be able to resolve it if I am away on a rig."

"Woo Jin, what business could you possibly have in Seoul that would make you delay your rightful position in this company? I thought that you were finished with graduate school," asked Mr. Kim.

Mrs. Kim asked, "Woo Jin, what could you possibly be talking about? Is it that girl Areum? Is she pregnant?"

"No, Mother. I can't discuss it with you right now. I just need to delay my start date for a few months. Please, Dad."

"There are a group of people waiting for you to assume control. They will not take no for an answer. Let's make a deal. You work two weeks on the rig and you get two off. How is that?"

"Dad, that will not work. I am willing to work in the Seoul office and do consultations by Skype. I really need to conclude my unfinished business. Please, Dad."

"Woo Jin. Something bad must have really happened. You will tell me soon? Right?" asked Mr. Kim as he looked at Woo Jin nodding his head. "Okay, Woo Jin. Stay in Seoul for now. You can work from the Seoul office. I will let the shareholders know."

"Thank you, Father. I won't disappoint you. I will speak with the men on the rig myself. I will go there myself."

"I am very disappointed that you are about to delay your destiny," said Mrs. Kim.

"Mother, please let me live my life the best way I know how. Dad, I will go to see the men on the rig tomorrow. Please contact the Seoul office and let them know that I will be working there for a while."

"Okay, son. I will do that."

Woo Jin kept his promise and the next day he flew to Brunei to speak with the men on the rig. The rig was four stories in height and at the center of the platform, was a large structure resembling the Eiffel Tower. Several metal pipes covered the third floor. The second floor sleeping quarters were designed to look like military barracks. The quarters contained all the amenities that an apartment would have. The one hundred men who worked there ate and slept there every other month. Woo Jin landed on the heliport landing strip that was located on the fourth floor.

The men greeted him and they escorted him throughout the off-shore rig. After two hours of orientation, Woo Jin advised the men that he would delay joining their team until the new year.

Everyone on the rig, looked disappointed but they accepted his decision. He shook their hands and returned to the helicopter that was waiting to take him to the mainland.

Meanwhile in Seoul, Kang-de tried to contact Areum but she did not answer. Kang-de went to her suite and it was empty.

"Guard, where is Miss Areum? Did she go to the clinic? Where are the rest of her security?"

"Sir, she took two men with her to the clinic. Would you like me to call them?"

"No, no. I will speak with her later."

Areum saw Bora during their time at the clinic and she apologized for not being able to convince Kang-de to drop the charges against Mr. Park. Bora accepted her apology.

"Bora, how is Dave? He seems so distraught the last time I saw him."

"I don't know. My mind is in so many places that I don't know where to start."

"Keep talking to him. He will tell you eventually."

"I am going to see him later. I must find out. I can't take the secrecy any longer. I am not a child."

"Bora, I am finished for the day and I want to go and see my dad tomorrow. I've finished seeing all my patients. I am off clinical duties for the next three days. Bora, only you and my mom know that I am going to the South."

"What about Woo Jin and Kang-de?"

"I am a little annoyed with both of them. I don't want to bother you with my problems. Go and take care of your problems first. I will see you in a few days."

After leaving Areum, Bora went to have an early dinner with Dave at the ITO Hotel. Bora sat across from Dave at a booth in the back of the restaurant. "Dave, I want to know what is going on with you. Why have you suddenly changed your behavior toward me. What have I done to offend you?"

"Bora, come and sit next to me."

Bora moved and sat next to him.

He held her hand and said, "My dad did the most unforgivable thing. I can't even bring myself to say what he did."

"Dave, just tell me please. I don't care what he did. Just tell me."

"I am not sure, but my dad may have been the one who tried to have you kidnapped."

"What? What did you just say? Why would he do that to me?"

"I don't know, Bora. I can only conclude that you were just a pawn in the rivalry between him and your dad. They own the same kind of business, so I can only conclude that it has to do with business."

"I am truly shocked. Dave, I am mad at your dad but why would you want to break up with me?"

"It is so humiliating and embarrassing. I can't ask you to forgive my dad. I feel just as guilty as my dad. I can't speak about it anymore. I am so, so, so, so sorry, Bora."

"Dave, I love you so much. Our parents are not us. We can elope if you're feeling embarrassed. I want to be your wife."

"Bora, give me a little time to get over this humiliation. I love you too. This is why it hurts so badly. Please forgive my dad, Bora. I am truly sorry for what he has done."

"Stop blaming yourself. Just stop it. My dad is guilty of a lot of things too. Do you see me blaming myself for his wrong deeds? Dave, please stop it."

Kang-de walked into the restaurant and saw Bora and Dave seated at a booth. He went over to greet them.

"Good evening, Bora and Dave. It is good to see you both. I know you both are probably very unhappy with me right now, but I did what I had to do to protect my company. Dave, I have nothing personal against you. In fact, I like you and Bora a lot, but I have to protect my company."

"Kang-de, I just wished that you had come to me first."

"This is too overwhelming for you both. And I am sure that your parents would not have liked me to discuss their business with you. I am sorry. By the way, Bora, have you seen Areum today?"

"Yeah, at the clinic. What's wrong?"

"Nothing is wrong. I just have not heard from her all day. Her security have not reported in as yet. Well, goodnight to the both of you."

Bora and Dave remained at the restaurant and Kang-de went upstairs to call Bob. "Goodnight, Bob. I am trying to reach Areum's security guards and they are not responding. What's going on?"

"Boss, Areum told them not to answer you. They are all fine. She went to see her dad and she told them not to tell you. Is she upset with you?"

"I am not sure. Are they still with her?"

"Yes, Boss. She can't get away from them."

"Good. Okay, Bob, go to sleep."

Kang-de spent the night awake thinking about Areum. In the meantime, Areum spent the night talking with her dad.

"Areum, why did you come to see me when you still have work to do? Did something else happen to your mother? Is Kang-de okay?"

"Yes, and Mother is feeling the same, but why do you ask about him? Dad, I have not seen you in such a long time. I was worried about you. I love you, Daddy."

"I love you too, my child. You look sad. What is wrong?"

"You always knew when I was sad. Oh, Daddy, my heart is sick. The two people that I trusted with my life have betrayed me. I feel sick to my stomach."

"Oh, Areum, what happened?"

" I can't bring myself to talk about it. I just wanted to come and see you, Dad. Your words have always made me feel better."

"Well, you must be talking about Kang-de and that man you met in school. I don't know him but I know Kang-de very well and I can tell you one thing. He loves you very much. He would never intentionally hurt you. I think that his protectiveness has been misunderstood by you, Areum. Think about it. I am sure that he felt that he was protecting you from whatever happened."

"Well...."

"Don't be upset with him, Areum. He is a good man. He is a loyal man. Give him a chance. Sometimes the heart wants what is not good for it. I am getting old and I want you to have someone who loves you until the end of time. I need you to stay with Kang-de."

Areum began to cry.

"Oh, my baby, don't cry, Areum. Everything is going to be just fine." He thought about the listening devices in his home and he said, "Let your guards sleep in the guest bedroom. You can have my room and I will sleep in the living room."

Areum and her security guards fell asleep quickly. They were tired from the long trip to the south. Mr. Lee lay awake on the couch thinking about his wife and daughter. He fell asleep after a while.

Three hours later, a black sedan filled with men pulled up at Mr. Lee's home. They quietly got out of the car and went to the Mr. Lee's back door. They tried to open it when the alarm sounded and they ran. The guards jumped up with guns drawn and they ran to Areum and grabbed her off the bed. Frightened from the alarm, she screamed for her father. Mr. Lee had already crawled toward Areum. He hugged her as she quivered in his arms.

"Guard, what is happening?"

"It's okay, Miss Areum, we won't let anything happen to you or your dad."

One of the guards, Yang, went out the back door to see if the men were still outside. He returned shortly and informed the other guard that they had left.

"Mr. Lee, we will be leaving shortly. I must take Miss Areum back to Seoul. Do you want to come with us?"

"Yeah, Dad, please come with us," said Areum.

"No, you hurry and take her back to Seoul. I will be there shortly," he whispered.

The next morning, Mr. Lee called Kang-de to speak with him.

"Hello, Kang-de. Areum was here with me. She should be home already. Did something happen between the two of you?"

"No, Sir. She misunderstood something that I told her."

"Please forgive her. She loves you."

"Can you come to see me tomorrow? It's about Areum."

"I am unable to come right now. I have a lot going on here. Can't you tell me over the phone?"

"I cannot. I need you to come and see me. I don't want Areum to know that I spoke with you," said Mr. Lee.

"Okay. I will be there tomorrow," Kang-de said with the thought that something was different about Mr. Lee's voice.

Kang-de heard a click after Mr. Lee hung up the phone. Immediately he realized that Mr. Lee's phone was bugged.

Chapter Forty-four

Kang-de, Mr. Lee, Chul, Woo Jin,
Bob, Roger Goo, Areum, and Maria

Early the next morning, Kang-de traveled to see Mr. Lee, and he took Chul, Bob and two guards with him. They arrived at the airport in Busan very late. Bad weather delayed their departure. The drive from the airport to Mr. Lee's home took twenty minutes.

"I am glad that you brought security with you. I am being watched," said Mr. Lee whispering to Kang-de.

"Watched? Why?"

Mr. Lee signaled that there was a bug in the house.

"Chul, Bob, be on the alert. I think we have company. Mr. Lee, I am taking you with me right now."

Mr. Lee was able to take the briefcase that was given to him by Ambassador Shin and an overnight bag with him.

Kang-de, Chul, Bob, Mr. Lee and the two guards pulled away quickly into an SUV and headed onto the highway. Each time Chul changed lanes, a black sedan followed closely behind them.

"Boss, it looks like we are being followed."

"Chul, get off at the next exit and stop the car," said Kang-de.

The black sedan exited and stop behind the SUV.

"Let's go find out why they are following us," said Kang-de. "Mr. Lee, stay in the car. Do not come out of the car, no matter what you see."

The two guards, Chul and Bob jumped out with knives and guns drawn. Kang-de opened the back door of his SUV and Mr. Lee grabbed his arms.

"Kang-de, you must survive. Your parents' death was not an accident."

"What? I will be right back."

Kang-de, Chul, Bob and the two guards beat one of the men into unconsciousness. Chul broke the second man's arm. Bob took a shovel from the trunk of the SUV and he used it to hit the third man in his back. The man fell to the ground. Kang-de used his right leg to kick the fourth man and he fell back onto the sedan and then to the ground. The two guards grabbed one of the men and brought him to Kang-de bleeding from the mouth. The guards had broken several of the man's teeth.

"Who sent you?" asked Kang-de.

"I don't know. We got instructions to watch him and report back," said the man mumbling from the pain inflicted by the guards.

"Bob, take their cell phones. Chul, you and your men get rid of them. Then meet me at the jet."

"With pleasure."

Chul and his men returned to the jet twenty-five minutes later and the it took off for Seoul. Kang-de sat facing Mr. Lee on the plane. The jet was a private luxury jet which could accommodate ten passengers. Some of its features included two leather sofas, chairs that could be converted into beds and state-of-the-art lighting. Persian carpet extended throughout the jet. The two men sat at a mahogany table and Bob brought them a bottle of whiskey with two glasses. Chul and Bob sat opposite Kang-de and Mr. Lee, while the guards sat on the couch.

"Mr. Lee, please tell me everything. What did you mean by my parents' death was not an accident? Uncle Roger never mentioned anything about my parents' death," Kang-de said. "They killed your parents and the train conductor which caused the train to crash."

"Who are THEY and why would anyone want to kill my parents?"

"Your dad was supposed to be a double agent for them."

"What? How is that possible?"

"Where do I start? Years ago, your father told me an incredible story about your grandparents and your twelve-year-old uncle. He said that they were murdered when your father was six years old. Three men entered their home and shot your grandparents. Your uncle heard the shots and hid your father under the bed, whose floor had a trap door. When the gunmen came into your uncle's room, they killed your uncle.

"They could not find your dad so they shot at the mattress and at the closet. One of the bullet struck your dad in the shoulder and he covered his mouth to prevent the killers from hearing him scream. He lay under the trap door for what he said was an eternity, but it was for several hours. After the killers searched the home they left.

"The neighbors, who were like family to your grandfather, found your dad hidden in the trap door under the bed. They took him to their home and they noticed that the bullet had gone through his shoulder. They cleaned his wounds and bandaged it.

"I asked him why didn't they take him to the hospital. He said that a gunshot wound had to be reported to the police and the poor neighbors were afraid that the killers would find out that your dad was alive and kill them all.

"Your dad was in shock for several days. He was unable to speak about what had happened. He stayed at the neighbor's home for six months. One day four men came to the neighbor's home and threatened them with bodily harm. The neighbor had already placed your father on a fishing boat that was headed to Busan. Young, tired and unable to speak, one of the fisherman took your dad to his home where he lived for thirteen years. He was given a new last name, Shin."

"Do you mean that Shin is not my last name?"

"No, it's not. Your dad never told me his real last name. Your dad worked hard at obtaining an education. He did odd jobs and he met many important people who liked him. He met and married your mother and she was instrumental in hiding his past. Your mother helped him obtain the Ambassador post in the United States."

"I can't believe what I am hearing. How is it possible? What was my grandfather involved in and why didn't my dad tell me this years ago? He didn't tell me anything on the plane. Uncle Roger never said anything even though we lived together in New York."

"The Shins gave your father a lots of documents that they found in a bag that was attached to him, on the fishing boat. They kept it for him until he turned twenty years old. I supposed they felt that he was mature enough to handle whatever he found in them."

"I need another drink. Was my grandfather a spy or a criminal?"

"I don't know. I didn't ask your dad. I know that he belonged to a secret organization that did bad things without being punished."

"Oh, my gosh. What else don't I know?"

"Several years ago a man met your dad in New York and he told your dad that he would expose his true citizenship unless he handed over files that your grandfather stole and he wanted your dad to gather information on certain diplomats who worked for the government."

"No. I don't believe what I am hearing," said Kang-de.

"Your dad agreed. At least he pretended to agree. He got all the information from the secret organization and he turned it over to the NIS. He also handed the secret organization the secret files after he made copies. Someone must have found out about his double crossing them and they assassinated both of your parents on the train. The train crash was to cover up the killings."

"Oh, no. All those people killed to cover up two murders. Who are we dealing with, Mr. Lee?"

"Kang-de, last night someone tried to break into my house. Thank goodness your guards were there. They grabbed Areum and protected her." Mr. Lee handed a brown envelope to Kang-de. "They were looking for this envelope which has the list of names of the organization members."

Kang-de fell back into his seat with a stunned look on his face. Bob brought him a glass of vodka.

"Is this why they killed my family?"

As he opened the envelope and looked at the list of names, Mr. Lee said, "Kang-de, there is more. That boy that Areum is with. What is his name?"

"Kim Woo Jin," said Bob.

"Yes. His dad is second in command of that secret organization."

Kang-de, Chul and Bob yelled out, "WHAT?"

"Bob! Why didn't you find this out when you investigated Kim Woo Jin?"

"They're called SECRET organization for a reason. I don't think Woo Jin is a member and I don't believe that he knows his dad is a member," said Mr. Lee.

"Boss. I would have heard if Woo Jin was a member."

"You don't know that for sure. I should have killed him a long time ago. I almost killed him in the garden at my hotel. Mr. Lee, why did you not tell me this before?"

"I am so sorry, but I got a phone call right before Areum arrived in Seoul. The voice on the phone said to shut my mouth forever, or they would kill Areum. They told me that they had travelled on the plane with her to Seoul.

"I was too scared and I didn't want to endanger you or my family. And you were too young and in shock when your parents died. I couldn't tell you something so shocking. Roger Goo knew about everything, but he told me not to tell you because you might do something irrational."

"So why are you telling me now? You should have told me earlier, Mr. Lee," said Kang-de in a disappointing tone. "Uncle Roger should have told me earlier."

"I am telling you this because they poisoned my wife. I believe they gave her poison to make it look like cancer. I knew that she was sick and it broke my heart. That's why I did not go to the hospital when she was admitted."

"What?" said Chul.

"Who the hell are these people? What is going on? How do you know that she was poisoned?"

"They told me that they could get to her. They told me that the doctor who saw her at her last checkup already injected her with poison. I couldn't tell her, but I think she knows that something was done to her. They sent me a message that Areum would be next."

"That's why you should have told me. I could have stopped this madness earlier."

"Sorry, but I just couldn't endanger the two of you. Your parents wanted me to protect you. How could I let you endanger your life?"

"Mr. Lee, someone tried to kill me. They ran me off the road."

"What? When? Are you okay?"

"I am fine. We have to get Mrs. Lee an antidote for the poison."

"It's too late. She is dying. When I found out that she was poisoned, I called some friends of your dad from the Embassy for help. They tried but they could not counteract the poison in her system."

"Did you call my father, Roger Goo?" asked Bob. "He called me."

"Why didn't Uncle Roger tell me about all of this?" asked Kang-de.

"He didn't want to endanger your life. Do you remember the gunshot in his leg? It was an attempt on his life. He didn't want to alarm you. He had you followed, but you've made it difficult for your father's people to keep up with you," said Mr. Lee.

"I thought that my dad really did retire the day we flew home to Seoul. I had no idea that we were fleeing from killers. I believed what Uncle Roger told me about his injured leg."

"Kang-de, you were young then. We couldn't tell you about such an horrific thing. I don't think Roger Goo told you either. Right, Bob?"

"No, Sir. I was raised by my mother here in Seoul. My dad didn't come home often. He once told me that he had a dangerous job and he had to protect the Ambassador from dangerous people. But that was all he said."

"I didn't know that he couldn't fly for a reason. Wow. Well, somebody is going to pay for killing my parents. Bob, as soon as we land find out where Woo Jin and his parents are right now."

The jet landed in Seoul and Kang-de immediately dialed a number in Hong Kong. He spoke with someone for about thirty minutes.

"Mr. Lee, when I am finished with this secret organization, they will regret that they killed my family. Thank you for this incredible information. You will be staying at the hotel. It's the safest place for you."

"I am sorry, Kang-de."

"No. I am sorry. If you hadn't been employed by my dad, then Mrs. Lee and Areum would never have been placed in danger."

Kang-de, Chul, Bob and Mr. Lee arrived at the ITO Hotel and took an underground elevator to their suite. Kang-de's guards escorted Mr. Lee to his room. Bob began to work on finding out the location of Woo Jin's family.

"Bob, find out who Mr. Kim met while he was here in Seoul. I think I already know, but let's verify. And I told you to find out about who Mrs. Hwang met before she came to see me."

"Boss, what are you thinking about?"

"I'm thinking about Mr. Chin and Woo Jin. When you and I were at Mr. Park's home, Woo Jin stared at Mr. Chin as if he knew him. I believe he does. I'm going to destroy them one by one."

Areum and her security were in her suite when the guard called Kang-de. "Boss, we are back. Sorry for not calling you. Ms. Areum insisted that we should not call anyone," said Bodyguard Yang.

"Is Miss Areum paying you?"

"No, Sir," said Yang.

"Well, the next time you do something like this, consider yourself fired. I make the decisions here. You got that?"

"Sorry, Boss. We are really sorry. We did call Manager Bob."

"Again. Who is paying you?" Yang replied.

"You are, Boss."

"Where is Ms. Areum now?"

"She is here in her suite, Sir."

"You may leave her and return to your duties downstairs."

Kang-de picked up the phone to call her and he hung up. In the meantime, Areum was at Kang-de's door ringing his bell.

"Hello, come in. Why did you make such a reckless decision? Do you know that you could have been kidnapped or killed? Do you think this is a joke? These bad men are serious. They are not just kidding with you. They can hurt you. Areum, I don't have time for your temper tantrums," said Kang-de in an angry tone. "If you want to stay mad with me fine. My conscience is clear. I did you no harm. So I am not apologizing to you."

"Are you finished talking? Yes, I was very upset with you because you and I became intimate enough that you should have told me everything. Instead you left out the most important information."

"Are you back to that betrayal thing again? I didn't want you to get hurt by my statement. I felt so bad telling you that he was still seeing her. How could I possibly tell you that she was pregnant? I could not."

"Okay. You have made your point. I am sorry for disappearing. I just needed to get away from it all."

"The next time you want to disappear, please let me know. Come here, let me hug you." Areum walked over to him and he hugged her tightly.

"Areum, you need to be careful. Okay?"

"Okay, I promise to be very careful and I won't do anything without telling you. My mind is occupied with Woo Jin and Sun-hee."

"Areum, clear your mind. Right now I want to feel your warmth," he said.

Kang-de led her by the hand into his bedroom. He grabbed her face and kissed her lips. Then he closed the door and locked it. Areum unbuttoned his shirt, pulled it off and threw it on the bed.

"Areum, what are you doing to me?"

"Be quiet and kiss me," she said.

"Okay, Miss Areum."

Kang-de turned down the lights and closed the curtains. They sat on the bed as Kang-de removed her blouse exposing her bra. She lay on the bed and he removed her skirt. Areum sat up and loosened his belt. She kissed him on his torso while he unbuttoned his pants. He pulled down his pants, put on a condom and he entered her as she moaned from the sweet feeling of his private parts moving inside her.

"Baby, I want you so much," he said as he dug deeper into her body.

"Oh, yes, Kang-de, I love to feel you inside me."

"Yes, baby," he said

"KANG-DE! Kang-de!" yelled Areum as she climaxed.

Kang-de grabbed her and he moaned as he climaxed.

"Areum, it is a pleasure to make love to you. I am hooked."

"It's confession time. I missed your body those few days that I was gone. I am addicted to it. What am I going to do?" she asked.

"About what? Are we talking about somebody else? Because if you are, then you will do nothing. Let me handle him."

"No, no, no, Kang-de. I will deal with him. I am talking about your sexy body and my addiction to it."

"Thank you, Areum, for making me feel loved."

He wrapped his legs around her naked body and they lay on his bed absorbing each other's energy.

Kang-de cell phone rang as he lay naked in bed with Areum.

"Hello. How are you, Nana?"

"Master Shin, how are you? I can't talk very long, but I heard Mr. Park and his employee talking about you. They mention about evidence disappearing," said Maria, Mr. Park's maid.

"Okay. Thanks for the information. Please be careful," said Kang-de hanging up.

"Is everything okay? Kang-de, I worry about you so much. I would be devastated if something happened to you again. Please be careful," said Areum.

"I can promise you that I am going to protect myself."

"Good. I want you around me and my family for a long time," said Areum.

"Areum. Speaking of family, your dad is staying in this hotel."

"Why is he here? I was just with him. Is he in danger?"

"No. He just needs to stay with us for a while. He wants to see your mother. He's resting now. See him later."

"Did he tell you that last night men tried to break into his home while I was there? Your men took care of the situation."

"Yes, he did mention something to me but Yang did not give me any report." Kang-de got up and put on his pants. He called Yang's cell phone. "Yang, I want to see you in my suite now."

Areum slowly got dressed and walked out to the living room.

"I think that I should go. You look angry."

"No, you are not leaving. Sit down," said Kang-de.

Yang arrived at Kang-de's suite promptly.

"Yang, why did you not tell me that men tried to break into Mr. Lee's home? Why did you not say anything while you were here earlier?"

"Boss, you were already furious with me. I didn't want to get you more upset. We took care of the situation and I brought Miss Areum home immediately. I even offered to take Mr. Lee with us but he refused."

"You are beginning to annoy me. Let this be the last time you make decisions for me. Do we understand each other? Yang, I like you. Don't let me have to part ways with you."

"I am very, very sorry, Boss. It will not happen again," Yang said walking out the door.

Areum watched Yang walk out the door. "Kang-de, what is going on? I want to know. Why would someone want to break into my parents' home?"

"Areum, it's nothing for you to worry about. Have you seen your mother? Go and tell her hello."

Kang-de waited for Areum to leave and he called Bob.

"Bob, we need to talk. Come over as soon as possible."

Bob arrived at the ITO Hotel within minutes after he was called by Kang-de.

"I've just received word that Mr. Park intends to have the evidence against him disappear."

"What do you want to do, Boss? Let me know."

"We won't do anything now. If we react then he will know that someone in his circle betrayed him. The person who told me was my nanny for many years and I will not put her in danger.

"Then should we let him get away with his crimes?"

"He won't. But information on this secret organization is more important right now."

Chul walked in while Kang-de and Bob spoke about the secret organization.

"Hey, Chul, how are you?"

"Boss, you won't believe this. Yejoon and CFO were found floating in the river with multiple stab wounds."

"Why am I not surprised? Mr. Park and Mr. Jong are getting rid of all the evidence. Paper and Human. I admire them. But I am not finished with them."

"Boss, do you want me to take care of them?"

"Not yet. Leave them alone. Switch the security team for Areum and Mrs. Lee. Sun-hee is now Woo Jin's responsibility."

"Chul, get me the best bodyguards that you can find. I want Boss to be well protected," said Bob.

"You got it."

327

"Bob, I can take care of myself. You know that."

"Yes, but until we find out about this secret organization, you need more protection."

"Yes, Boss, we will protect you," said Chul.

"Listen, guys, just make sure Ms. Areum is well protected. I am more cautious since the attempt on my life. And Chul, I want you to check out my bodyguard Yang. He has been acting very careless lately. Make sure that he is only working for me and not my enemy. Okay?"

"Consider it done. Boss, if he is working for our enemy, I will personally kill him after I torture him."

"That would be unfortunate for him, because I like him," said Kang-de.

Chapter Forty-five

Areum, Kang-de, Mr. and Mrs. Lee, Woo Jin, Chul, and Bob

Areum waited until the next morning to go to the hospital to see her mother. The nurse had just finished taking Mrs. Lee's temperature when Areum walked in.

"Hi, Mama. How are you today?"

"Not so good today. The chemotherapy is making me feel sick. "

"Sorry, Mom. I will ask the doctor to switch your medication. Bora's dad had suggested this medicine. I will have the doctor change it."

"I want to sleep for a while, if you don't mind."

"Okay, Mom. I will stay here until you wake up. I love you, Mama."

"I love you very much. And Kang-de too." Woo Jin called Areum while she sat at her mother's bedside.

"Hello, Woo Jin."

"Hi, Areum. How are you? You're always on my mind."

"I feel so disrespected," said Areum.

"I am so, so sorry. I can't begin to tell you how sorry I am that I hurt you. I love you, Areum, and I will never stop loving you."

"You know that I will tolerate anything except disrespect. There is no explaining what you did with Sun-hee. I need time to think."

"Please let me see you. I want to see you."

"Okay, meet me at the library."

"No. Where are you? I will come and get you."

"I am at the hospital with my mother."

"I will be there in twenty minutes."

Woo Jin arrived at the hospital and Areum met him at the door.

"Hi, Areum. How is your mother?"

"Not good today. She is feeling sick. I wanted to tell you not to come because I want to stay with her for a while."

"It's okay. I will stay with you. Could we go outside for a few minutes?"

"I don't have anything more to say about the situation."

"Well, I do. You are someone special to me. I don't deserve a girl like you. I love you. My inexcusable action occurred during the lowest night in my life," he said, indicating the fight with Kang-de. "I will never forgive myself for what I did to you. How can I redeem myself to you?"

"I don't think that we can resolve this quickly. I have something to tell you. And maybe you will feel differently about me after you hear what I have to say."

"What is it, Areum?"

"After I found out about you and Sun-hee, I was devastated. I felt so heartbroken and inadequate. Ah, I slept with Kang-de."

"You did what? What the hell did you just say?"

"Do you think that you have a right to be upset with me?" asked Areum.

"Yes. You are my woman! My woman! Why did you do that? Why? How could you do that with him?" Woo Jin screamed.

"He loves me and he didn't cheat on me."

He picked up a chair and threw it at the wall that divided the flower bed from the pavement.

"How could you do this to me? You know how Kang-de and I feel about each other. Why him? Oh, Areum, why did you do that?"

"Go and ask Sun-hee. You knew how I felt about her. Yet you chose to get her pregnant. How could you do that to me?"

"I have got to get out of here before I regret my actions."

Woo Jin headed to Kang-de's hotel looking for a fight. He stormed in the lobby yelling loudly. All the patrons looked at him as he yelled out Kang-de's name.

"Kang-de, where are you? Kang-de, I want you to come and face me right now, you bastard. Shin Kang-de, don't let me destroy this hotel. You son of a bitch. I am going to break everything in here if you don't come and face me now."

Bob looked at Kang-de's security cameras and saw Woo Jin pounding on the reservation desk. Patrons were walking away from him in fear. Security stood at a distance watching him as he yelled.

"Boss, take a look at this. He's making a scene, but security is watching him."

"Tell them to let him come up to my suite. If he wants a fight, this time he will die in this room."

"He won't get far. Boss, let me avenge your parents by killing him now," said Bob.

"Yeah, Boss. You are not a hundred percent better and his death will send a message to his father," said Chul.

"I'm fine. Let him come upstairs. Go ahead and let him upstairs," said Kang-de urging Bob.

Woo Jin arrived at Kang-de's suite in a rage. Bob and Chul walked in front of Kang-de as Woo Jin approached him.

"Do you want me to speak in front of your employees? Because I will."

"Woo Jin, would you like a beating or a drink? You choose."

"You slept with Areum. You knew that she is my woman. How could you disrespect her like that?"

Kang-de yelled out, "Disrespect Areum? I love her and I have never hid that from you or her. She was my girl first."

"She was your girl in your fantasy world. She was never your reality. Why did you do that to her? You knew that she was a virgin. I wanted her to remain that way until our wedding night. How could you?"

"Have a drink and let's talk man to man."

"I don't want to drink with you. Ever."

"Areum loves me. My body and soul belongs to her. Woo Jin, walk away from her. I told you before that she would walk away from you," Kang-de said.

"She had rebound sex with you. Don't be delusional, Kang-de. She was trying to punish me by sleeping with you. I will never leave her. I am going to forgive her and hopefully she will forgive me someday. You are not going to get the love of my life."

Bob walked to Kang-de's door and held it open for him to leave.

Kang-de looked bothered by what Woo Jin said to him. He replied, "Woo Jin, go back to Hong Kong. Tell your father that I said hello."

He looked at Kang-de, smiled and walked out of his suite. Chul escorted him downstairs into the lobby.

"Boss, are you okay?"

"Bob, Woo Jin's smile tells me that he is staying in Seoul. When Miss Areum comes home, bring her to me."

His phone rang within minutes of calling her name. She called Kang-de screaming.

"Kang-de, Mom is in a coma. She is not waking up. Oh, my gosh! What am I going to do?"

"Stay calm. I am on my way. Bob, get Mr. Lee. Please take us to the hospital. Areum's mother is in a coma."

Kang-de, Mr. Lee and Bob arrived at the hospital and entered Mrs. Lee's room. Areum saw Kang-de and her dad and she ran to them.

"Kang-de! Dad! The doctor says Mom is in a coma. Mom, wake up. Oh, no, no, no. Mommy!"

"Where is the doctor, Areum? Bob, go and find the doctor, please. Areum, you are a doctor. I want you to get into that mindset right now. I know she is your mother but you are her doctor too."

"Kang-de, I am scared. I am really scared."

"It's okay, honey. I am here now. We will get through this together."

"Yes. She is going to be fine, Areum," said Mr. Lee.

Kang-de and Mr. Lee looked at each other because they knew Mrs. Lee was poisoned.

The doctor entered the room and said, "You called for me?"

Kang-de replied, "Yes, Doctor. What happened to Mrs. Lee?"

"Yes. What happened to my wife?"

"She had an cerebral hemorrhage which is also known as a hemorrhagic stroke and there is bleeding on the brain."

"Why don't you perform surgery to relieve the bleeding on the brain?"

"We would have done that but it would be futile to do that now because of her elevated blood pressure and her weak heart rate."

"Doctor, please do something," said Areum.

"Please get the best neurosurgeon to take a look at her. Money is not a problem. You can give her medicine to lower her blood pressure. Can't you?" asked Kang-de.

With hesitation, the doctor called for a CT scan.

"Mrs. Lee received intravenous fluids which had blood pressure medicine in it. We are going to try to lower her blood pressure and then try to stop the bleeding on the brain. I can't promise you success but we will do our best," said the neurosurgeon as he helped wheel Mrs. Lee into surgery.

Hours later the neurosurgeon who operated on Mrs. Lee went to see Areum, Mr. Lee and Kang-de and he told them that he was sorry that the operation was not a success.

"What are you saying, Doctor? Be truthful with us," said Areum.

He replied, "She is not going to survive until the end of the week. I am sorry. We did everything we could."

"Oh, no, no, no, no. Please, Doctor. Please help my mother."

"No. No. No," said Mr. Lee.

"I am really sorry. Mr. Shin, Mr. Lee, Miss. Lee. We will make her comfortable. That's all we can do," said the doctor, as he walked to the nurses' station to fill out her chart.

Areum began to cry. Mr. Lee hugged her. Kang-de hugged them both. They remained with Mrs. Lee after she was brought into her room and they spent the night, hoping for a miracle.

Early the next morning, Woo Jin arrived at the hospital.

"Areum, what happened to your mom? Our family doctor called to tell me that your mom was in a coma. You should have called me," he said.

"I do not want to fight now."

Kang-de and Mr. Lee overheard Woo Jin's statement and they walked out of Mrs. Lee's room.

"Mr. Lee, I'm so sorry. I can't believe that someone would hurt such a lovely lady. Do you think that the neurosurgeon is part of the secret organization?" asked Kang-de. "I just can't trust anyone at this point."

Mr. Lee replied that he didn't know about the surgeon, but he knew that they couldn't save her.

"I'm going to make them pay," said Kang-de in anger.

"What are you doing here?" asked Woo Jin.

"You are not important right now. Mrs. Lee is fighting for her life. Let's act like gentlemen. Areum needs both of us," said Kang-de.

"No. She only needs me."

Areum walked up and overheard Woo Jin telling Kang-de to leave.

Kang-de turned around and saw Areum. "I will be in your mom's room," he said.

Furious about his wife, Mr. Lee walked out of her room and said, "Woo Jin, I don't want you here. Please leave."

"I'm sorry, Mr. Lee, I won't get in the way. I will be in the waiting room."

Mr. Lee returned to his wife's bedside and said, "Honey, please wake up. I am here with you. Kang-de is here too."

Kang-de moved close to her bedside and said, "Mom. Yes, I called you Mom. Please wake up."

Mr. Lee looked at Kang-de holding his wife's hand and he said, "Thank you, Kang-de, for everything. I feel like killing Woo Jin to send a message to his father."

"Mr. Lee. Do not worry. Leave the Kim family to me."

"Mr. Lee, it is good that you are here with her. I'm sure that she can hear you." Areum walked in and stood alongside her mother's bedside. "Mama. Oh, Mama. Please don't leave me."

A doctor walked into the room to check on her vitals.

"Doctor, are you sure that there is not another treatment that can help her?"

Before the doctor could respond, Woo Jin entered into the room and said, "Yes, Doctor. Why can't you try another treatment? Money is no object. Let me call my family doctor."

Suddenly, Mr. Lee yelled, "NO! Thank you, Woo Jin."

"I'm sorry, Mr. Lee, I feel so helpless," said Woo Jin walking away.

Kang-de, Areum and Mr. Lee said their personal goodbyes to Mrs. Lee in sequence. Woo Jin went back to the waiting area as each one said goodbye to her.

"Mrs. Lee, you have been a mother to me when I needed one. I promise you that I will take care of Areum. And I will get revenge for you. I'm so, so sorry. I wished that I had known about my father's past earlier. I LOVE YOU."

Kang-de began to cry as he thought about his parents' death and Mrs. Lee pending death. Then Areum spoke crying to her mother.

"Mama, you are the most beautiful woman that I have ever known. You are such a lady and I don't want you to leave me, Mommy. Please don't leave me, Mama. I'm sorry that I wasn't a better daughter to you, I don't know what I am going to do without you."

Next, Mr. Lee spoke softly and said, "Honey, we have had a wonderful life. You have been the best wife a man could ask for. Do you realize that we have had one disagreement during our entire marriage? How will I live without you? I don't know, but I don't want you to suffer." He whispered in her ear, "If you feel like you want to go, then leave me. Areum and I will be fine. Farewell, my love. We will meet again, my love. I love you more than life my beautiful wife. I'm so sorry that I didn't protect you. I am really sorry that I didn't protect you." Mr. Lee kissed her on the forehead and said, "I will get revenge for you, I promise."

Later that night, Mrs. Lee's heart rate slowly decreased and she died. Kang-de kissed her forehead and he left the room crying. Areum sobbed uncontrollably. Mr. Lee remained in shock. He had tried to prepare himself for the day that his wife would succumb to her illness, but he became overwhelmed. The doctor declared the time of death as one in the morning.

Woo Jin entered the room and saw that the heart monitor had been disconnected. He hugged Areum while she cried.

"Oh, Areum, I am so sorry. I am here for you. I am not leaving you."

"Oh, Woo Jin. I want my mommy."

"I know, honey. I am so sorry. Let me hug you for a while."

Kang-de walked into the room and saw Woo Jin hugging Areum. He turned and walked out of the room without saying anything. Mr. Lee saw Kang-de walking away from the room and he yelled out to Kang-de.

"We have work to do. We need to bury your mother-in-law." He wanted Woo Jin to hear what he said to Kang-de.

Woo Jin looked at Mr. Lee and Kang-de and he held Areum tightly. "Thank you, Mr. Lee. I needed to hear those words from you. Yes, we must prepare for her burial and revenge for her and my mom and dad."

"She told me that she left burial instructions with you," said Mr. Lee.

"Yes, she did. I have it in the hotel safe. Could you please call Areum? Tell her that I want to speak with her. I don't want a confrontation with the son of a murderer tonight because I might kill him."

"Kang-de, do not be afraid to take what you want. You go and tell Areum that you want to speak with her. We have given you our blessings. Areum belongs with you."

Kang-de slowly walked up to Areum and asked to speak with her.

"Kang-de, please give her a moment to grieve for her mother," said Woo Jin.

"This is about her mother," said Kang-de in an annoyed tone.

"Kang-de, please give me a minute. I will speak with you outside."

Minutes later Areum went out to speak with Kang-de and her dad.

"What did you need, Kang-de?" she asked.

"Your dad and I wanted to know if you want to make the arrangement for your mom's funeral, or did you want me to do it?"

"No. Woo Jin and I will do it."

Kang-de looked surprised and Mr. Lee looked at Kang-de in shock. "Okay. Let me know what date you plan to have it," said Kang-de walking slowly away from Areum.

He suddenly remembered Woo Jin's words to him, rebound sex, and a sudden pain shot through his head. He grabbed his head and walked toward the hospital front door.

Mr. Lee yelled out, "Lee Areum, your mom gave Kang-de instructions on her burial. Let Kang-de handle it. I am sorry, Woo Jin, but I do not want your participation in burying my wife. I think that your family has done enough. "

Kang-de turned and stared at Mr. Lee intensely and he stopped speaking.

Areum replied, "No, Dad. She is my mother and I want to handle her burial. Kang-de, if you want to give me her instructions, then Woo Jin and I will handle it."

"Yeah, sure. You can have it tonight. I am leaving," said Kang-de punching in Bob's number in his cell phone.

Bob arrived at the hospital to pick up Kang-de and he paid his respect to Mr. Lee and Areum.

While driving Kang-de, Bob said, "Boss, I'm sorry about your loss. I know that you loved Mrs. Lee. Boss, this is a bad time to tell you this, but Mr. Park's and Mr. Jong's cases were dismissed for lack of evidence. Mr. Chin is still in jail but he might get released. And Mrs. Hwang met with Woo Jin and Mr. Jong while she was here."

"Well, I expected to hear bad news as well. The evidence has vanished."

"What are you going to do about them?" asked Bob.

"Nothing right now. I have another problem that is going to be a bit difficult to resolve," said Kang-de as he turned and looked out the window.

Bob looked at Kang-de and said, "It's Woo Jin, right?"

"I feel like I am about to lose my one love."

"Did something happen between you and Areum?"

"No. But I just have a bad feeling that I cannot shake."

"Why don't you tell her that she is with the son of the man who killed her mother? She deserves to know."

"Not now. She won't believe it. She is in too much pain. After all, I can't believe what I heard either."

"Boss. You are a very nice person. If she can't see that you love her, then forget about her. Move on. Many women have been trying to date you and you have disregard them all. Why don't you start dating? And why are you preventing me and Chul from killing him now?"

"Okay, Bob. That's enough. Let's talk about something else."

Mr. Lee called Kang-de and said, "Kang-de. Thanks again for everything. You look sad when you left the hospital, don't be. Mrs. Lee would want you to celebrate her life. She loved you."

"I am fine, Mr. Lee. I'm sorry that I left so abruptly. I have a meeting at the hotel. Did you want the guards to take you to the hotel now?"

"No. I want to stay with Areum and my wife's body."

"I understand. I will be at the hotel. I will be working on exacting our revenge."

Two days later, Woo Jin and Areum arranged Mrs. Lee's burial. Kang-de and Bora attended. Dave Jong did not. After the burial, everyone, except Kang-de and Bob, went to have refreshments at the Enfield Hotel. Kang-de called Areum but she did not respond.

The next morning he knocked on her suite. He noticed that the guards were missing. No one answered. Her security teams called Kang-de and told him that Mr. Kim Woo Jin told them that Miss. Areum will no longer need them. He told them that he would take care of her security.

"What did Miss Areum say?"

"She didn't say anything. What do you want us to do?"

"I want you to do nothing. They are adults. They can make their own decisions. Tell the men to return to hotel duties." Bob, I am glad that you are here. I want you to call Chul. He and I are going on a trip tomorrow. We are going to New York for one month. I am also going to look for some of my friends in Hong Kong. And then I will be back in Korea. I will be spending a few months at my apartment on Jeju Island when I return. Look after Mr. Lee. Don't let him go out without security. And keep an eye on Areum."

"Boss, I am almost done getting all the information about Mr. Kim and his organization."

"Okay. Call me when you've gotten it. Chul knows that he is coming with me. As usual, you are in charge while I am gone."

"I am happy that you're taking Chul with you. It makes me feel better. Give my love to my father. Please let me know how he looks and feels," said Bob.

The next day, Areum woke early and she called Kang-de and got no answer. She went to see Bob at the nightclub. Woo Jin waited outside.

"Hi, Bob. Where is Kang-de? I have been trying to get in touch with him all day."

"He went to America."

"What? When did he leave?"

"After the burial. He tried to contact you but got no answer. Your security told him that they were no longer needed."

"Bob, I want to speak with Kang-de."

"Sorry, Miss Areum, he is not accepting calls."

"Bob, please tell him to call me. When is he returning?"

"In a few months."

"A few months?" Surprised by what she just heard, Areum called her dad. "Dad, how are you? Are you okay? You went to the hotel so quickly. Woo Jin wanted to speak with you."

Mr. Lee forced himself not to speak badly of Woo Jin while on the phone with Areum. Her cell phone could be bugged and she could be harmed. "I am fine. Kang-de went away. He did say that he would call me."

"Dad, did he leave a number where he can be reached?"

"No. He did not. Areum, do not hurt Kang-de's feelings. He loves you very much. I am warning you."

"Dad!"

Areum left the club and got in the car with Woo Jin. He noticed that she looked sad.

"Areum, is Kang-de okay?"

"Yes."

"Areum, I want to let you know that I am going to work out of our Seoul office until the end of this year. It will give us time to work on our relationship."

"That's great. You will be close to your baby."

"Can we not speak about that right now?"

She remained silent while he drove her to the clinic. Her thoughts were on how to end their relationship without hurting his feelings. She sensed that it was not going to end well for either of them.

That afternoon, Areum went to work at the clinic with her mind focused on Kang-de. She saw Bora and they spoke briefly. She had hoped that Bora would not ask about her relationship with Kang-de and Woo Jin. It would be too difficult to discuss.

"I'm sorry for your loss. By the way, Areum, my dad is free."

"He is? That's great, Bora. I'm happy for you. How is Dave's dad?"

"He is free too."

"Good for you. I wish you all the best."

Areum thought to herself that Kang-de knew about Mr. Park and Mr. Jong's release already.

"Could that announcement cause him to leave Seoul?" she asked herself walking into a patient's room.

One month and two weeks had passed and Kang-de and Chul returned from New York via Hong Kong. Bob met them at the ITO Hotel.

"Hi, Bob, how is business?"

"Fine, Boss. Everyone missed you. How was New York and how is my father?"

"Uncle Roger is fine. He told me a lot of things about my parents' death. He explained why he didn't tell me everything earlier. We had a good time. He is expecting you in New York this year. Bob, New York is still busy. I forgot that it opens twenty-four hours. Chul and I took care of a lot of things and we stopped in Hong Kong for two weeks to visit friends. There are a few events that are about to happen. Just watch the news," said Kang-de.

"Boss, Areum came to look for you. She was shocked that you left without speaking with her. I did tell her that you tried to reach her before you left. She wanted your number in New York but I didn't give it to her."

"Good. Well, I am off to Jeju Island tomorrow. Chul will stay here. I will take one of the hotel security guards with me. I will switch them every two weeks. Chul said that Bodyguard Yang is loyal to me, so he will spend the last week with me."

"Okay, Boss. How are you really feeling?"

"I am fine, Bob. I heard that the suite is empty."

"Yes. Areum has been staying with Woo Jin."

"Okay."

Bob looked at Kang-de when he turned to look out the window. "Oh, Boss, I can tell that you are hurting."

"I am okay, Bob. As a matter of fact, I feel great right now. Please get the jet ready for tomorrow."

Kang-de and his security flew to Jeju Island before sunrise the next morning. A car was waiting to take them to his condominium. His condo was decorated with porcelain busts of ancient roman emperors. Floor-to-ceiling bookshelves decorated one side of the living room and a large painting of his parents hung on the other wall.

In the living room a glass table divided the two beige couches that were accented by an Indian rug. A mahogany table sat in the center of the dining room and a beautiful chandelier hung over the dining table. The bedroom walls had large glass mirrors hanging on both sides of the bed.

The bedroom ceiling was decorated with the same brocade material that hung as drapes and bedspread. At a distance the bathroom walls were decorated with gold reflective materials. Once the light were switched off, the gold shined brightly in the bathroom. Kang-de spent his time on the island meditating and plotting the demise of the secret organization and its allies.

Chapter Forty-six

Areum, Woo Jin, Kang-de, Bob, Mr. Park,
Mr. Jong, Mr. Kim, Mrs. Kim, and Mr. Lee

Woo Jin and Areum lived together for forty-five days. He prepared all the meals and he took her out as often as he could. They did not speak about Kang-de. Woo Jin's office assistant told him that Kang-de was not in Seoul. At least he had not been seen at his hotel for many weeks.

"Areum. I prepared a meal for you."

"Thanks so much. I am hungry."

"Areum, I know that your mom just passed away recently, but I want to be intimate with you."

"Woo Jin. I'm not in the mood for anything right now."

"Don't let me beg you."

"Oh, Woo Jin. I am feeling pressured. Please don't do that."

"Okay, fine."

Areum tried to hug him and he moved away. She grabbed the back of his shirt. "Come here."

Areum hugged him from behind. He turned around and kissed her. She kissed him back. "Come with me. We are going for a weekend trip."

Woo Jin took Areum to Jeju Island and rented a suite. They arrived late at night. "Areum, I did not want you to feel uncomfortable at my home."

"You know me well."

"Let's go out to eat," he said.

Areum and Woo Jin dined at a restaurant in the town. Two hours later, they returned to their suite.

"Areum, I am going to take a shower."

Areum thought about the time she and Kang-de spent on Jeju Island. Ten minutes later, Woo Jin finished showering and Areum went in the bathroom. She thought about what Kang-de would think if he knew that she was on Jeju Island with Woo Jin.

"What am I doing? What am I doing?" she asked herself.

"Areum, are you okay in there? You've been in there for a while."

"I am coming out now."

Areum walked out in a white chiffon mini night dress. Woo Jin looked at her and noticed that he could see her breast and her underwear. He smiled and handed her a glass of wine. Woo Jin and Areum drank half of the bottle.

"Areum, from the first day I saw you, I liked you. I only slept with Sunhee after I met you because I couldn't have you. You know that I am right."

"If you say so then I believe you."

"Honey, I want you badly."

Woo Jin softly kissed Areum. He took her to the master bedroom and he slowly removed the chiffon nightgown and kissed her throughout her body. He ran his tongue along her side up under her armpit.

"Woo Jin, where is the condom?"

"In my pants pocket. I will get it."

Woo Jin made love to Areum and he climaxed and lay on her back. Her mind was on Kang-de while she was making love with him.

"I feel so good right now. Thank you for letting me be intimate with you. I have wanted you for a long time. It was worth the wait," he said. "We must do this again," said Woo Jin.

"Sure, " replied Areum in a pretentious manner.

Early Saturday morning, Kang-de and his security went to the gym at the hotel where Areum and Woo Jin were staying. The gym at Kang-de's condominium was closed for repairs.

Areum and Woo Jin walked into the gym and she looked to her right and saw Kang-de lifting weights. She immediately went to greet him. He did not noticed her until he turned to the door.

"Good morning. Kang-de, why did you leave to the USA so suddenly and why are you here on Jeju Island? What's the matter with you?"

"Areum, I am fine. Woo Jin is waiting for you. Why don't you go back to him before he creates a scene?"

"Listen, Kang-de. We need to talk. Maybe not now, but I want to speak with you. I need to explain what I am doing."

"Oh, I can see what you are doing here. Let's not speak to each other anymore."

"Kang-de! I am sorry if I offended you. I didn't mean to. There is a reason for my behavior. I can't explain it to you now."

Kang-de looked at her and continued to exercise with sadness on his face.

Areum slowly walked toward Woo Jin and he asked, "Areum, what is he doing here?"

"I don't know. He didn't say."

"Let's exercise. We have more workouts to do tonight."

Areum used the treadmill that faced Kang-de. She stared at him while she exercised. He glanced at her for a while then he left.

Areum watched him as he left the gym with Min-jun, his security guard.

Woo Jin noticed that she was staring at Kang-de and he said, "Areum, let's leave in the next twenty minutes. I want to go to the beach."

"Okay."

Thirty minutes later, Kang-de was looking out his window that faced the beach. He saw Woo Jin and Areum walking along the beach. He noticed that Areum was looking around while Woo Jin had his arms around her neck. He could see them but they could not see him.

Meanwhile the phone rang in Kang-de's apartment. Bob was on the other line.

"Hey, Bob, what's going on?"

"Boss, can you see the news? It's very interesting. The United States government have assumed control of Mr. Park's and Mr. Jong's assets in the States. And they have an arrest warrant issued for Mr. Jong. They have indicted him for fraud and corruption."

"I know. Bob, we need to talk. A lot of things happened in New York."

"Boss. Revenge is sweet."

"I don't call it revenge. I call it a teaching lesson for my enemies. Mr. Jong tried to kill me and Mr. Kim met with him on several occasions while he was in Seoul. I will leave him to his son, Dave. Mr. Jong is suffering greatly. The heir to his fortune wants nothing to do with him. He is suffering."

"You should let me and Chul hurt him a little."

"You will get your chance. Bye, Bob."

Kang-de continued looking at Woo Jin and Areum play on the beach.

"Areum, come here. I want to kiss you," said Woo Jin.

"Later," she said.

Woo Jin grabbed her and kissed her passionately. He knew that Kang-de was somewhere looking at them. He held her tightly as he kissed her passionately.

"That bastard knows that I am watching him. Min-jun, get me a pill for my headache, please."

Areum felt awkward by the kiss because she sensed that Kang-de was watching them. "Woo Jin, let's go back to the hotel."

"Yeah," he said smiling brightly.

Woo Jin made love with Areum and he climaxed and fell asleep. Early the next morning she asked Woo Jin if he would mind her going to speak with Kang-de.

"Yes, I do mind, but if you feel the need to speak with him then do it. And don't stay long. Otherwise I will have to come and get you."

Areum put on a skirt and blouse and she went downstairs in the lobby. She called Bob on her cell phone to get Kang-de's address on the island.

"Bob, I am on Jeju Island. I want to see Kang-de. Where can I find him? Please don't deny me the opportunity to speak with him before I leave. Bob, I know he is here because I saw him yesterday."

Bob hesitated for a moment and then he gave her Kang-de's address.

Areum walked to Kang-de's condominium and the doorman allowed her in after she told him that she was his girlfriend. She went upstairs and knocked on Kang-de's apartment. Security Man Min-jun answered the door.

"Hi. I am here to see Mr. Shin Kang-de. May I speak with him, please?" she asked, hoping that he would let her in.

"Please wait here."

"Who is it, Min?" asked Kang-de.

"It's Miss Areum. She wants to speak with you."

"Tell her that I will call her."

"Mr. Shin says that he will call you."

"Tell him that I will be standing right here until he speaks with me."

"Boss, she says that—"

"I heard her. Let her in. Give me two hours and then come back. Areum, how did you find me? And what do you want to talk about?"

"I am sorry if I hurt your feelings. Why are you acting like this? What did I do?"

"If you don't know, then I can't tell you."

"It's Woo Jin. Isn't it?"

"Well, you are not stupid!"

"Kang-de, you have done so much for me and my family. I just wanted to give you a break. I didn't want you to feel as if I were using you. I never wanted you to feel that way because I am not."

He shouted at her, "Stop treating me like a child. I am a grown man. I do whatever I want because I can. Why do you make assumptions about my feelings?! You insulted me in front of that jerk and I am hurt."

"I am so sorry. I didn't mean to do that."

"Well, you did. What else do you want to talk about?"

"Bora told me that Mr. Park and Mr. Jong are free. I want you to be careful."

"Don't worry about me. Worry about yourself."

"I will always worry about you. You are very important to me."

"When do you find time to worry about me? When you are sleeping with Woo Jin?"

"Yes," she said sarcastically.

"Lee Areum, stop it! I don't want to speak with you right now. Please leave and don't come back here."

"No. Not until you accept my apology."

"I said leave. Please don't torture me."

Areum tried to hug him. He grabbed her arms before she could reach his neck. Areum tried to kiss him. He moved his head. She grabbed his waist. He didn't stop her.

"I miss you terribly. I am so sorry if I hurt your feelings. I really am. Please let me make it up to you."

"You are with Woo Jin. I won't accept second place to him. You don't love me, so why are you bothering me? I am only your rebound man."

Areum began to cry. "Why are you saying this to me? I only have ONE LOVE."

"Areum, you are sleeping with two men. I can't accept that. I can't share you. I don't want to do that. It's too painful for me. Please leave."

Kang-de went to open his door. Areum placed her back against it and the door closed. Areum grabbed Kang-de and she kissed him. He gave in and kissed her roughly. Areum pulled up his shirt and kissed his chest. He lifted up her skirt and pulled down her underwear. He turned her around and he unzipped his pants and made passionate love to her against the door without a condom. They climaxed together.

"Areum, what do you want from me?"

"I want you. I've decided that this body belongs to you."

"What about your heart? Does it belong to me too?"

"Kang-de, when Mom died I realize that you were the one for me. I just wanted to give Woo Jin a chance before I say goodbye to him. Please understand, he has been very good to me. Just give me some time. I will not be with him again. I promise."

"Don't expect me to agree with your living and sleeping with Woo Jin. I can't accept that. Do you really think that I will tolerate this agreement? By the way are you two using a condom?"

"Yes, Kang-de. You are the one I don't use a condom with. Woo Jin is leaving at the end of the year. Please work with me, Kang-de."

"Areum, please get out. Let me know when you are free. Until then there will be no more physical contact between us. Don't come near me, okay? Goodbye."

Areum felt sad when she saw Kang-de opened the door and closed it behind her. Kang-de threw a pillow against the door and he pounded on the wall with his fist.

Later the phone rang in Kang-de's house. It was a private number. He let his finger touch the answer button.

"You had me arrested and I lost my son. How should I repay you for the destruction of my family? My son won't speak with me. I have lost my seat on my company's board. It's all thanks to you. Now the American government is after me. Watch your back, Shin Kang-de."

Kang-de replied, "Mr. Jong, I hate threats. Perhaps you should watch your back. You are wearing a grey suit and you are sitting in a café, right?"

Mr. Jong jumped up. "How did you...?"

"Stop threatening me. Go and take care of your son, Dave. I would hate to see anything happen to him. Maybe his car will fall off a cliff. Or maybe he will disappear. What do you think about that? If you ever threaten me again, then I will make you end up like my CFO and Yejoon. Didn't the police find them floating in the river? This is a promise, Mr. Jong. As for Mr. Chin, he is going to do time in prison, if he survives." Kang-de hung up on Mr. Jong.

Shaken by Kang-de's words, Mr. Jong called his hired assassins. "Hello. This is Mr. Jong. Cancel the contract on Shin Kang-de."

The voice at the other end said, "We cannot without Mr. Park's permission."

Immediately Mr. Jong called Mr. Park. "Hi, Mr. Park. We have to cancel the contract. You know what I mean?"

"Why? That bastard made the United States government indict me and they've frozen all my assets. He made them issue a warrant for me and one for you too. Why should we not kill him?"

"Because he has a lot of evidence on us and if we kill him, I am sure they will reappear. Besides, he's following me and maybe you too. So, will you let it go for now? Mr. Park, this man has powerful friends too. We can't continue to ask our inside man in the police department for help. Mr. Park, I believe Kang-de knows who he is. If he gets caught, then he will take us down with him."

"I will think about it. That bastard needs to be punished. I will find a way."

"Mr. Park, let it go for now. You and I have big problems in America that we have to address. I'm calling my friends in Hong Kong. They will tell me what to do about Kang-de."

Hong Kong
Woo Jin bought tickets for himself and Areum to go to Hong Kong. Areum called her dad to let him know that she was going out of town for a few days.

"Hi, Dad. How are you doing?"

"I am doing fine, my child. Kang-de called me yesterday. He told me where he was. Lee Areum, what is going on with you and Kang-de? He told me that everything was fine between the two of you. I don't believe him."

"Dad, everything is fine. I wanted to tell you that I am going to Hong Kong for the weekend."

"Hong Kong? Are you going with that young man? Why are you with him and not with Kang-de? What is the matter with you? Kang-de has been so good to this family and you are treating him badly. Areum, I insist that you stop this madness now. Do not go with him. He and his family are dangerous."

"Dad, I know what I am doing. I asked Kang-de to be patient with me for a few months and he refused."

"You are ungrateful. I raised you better. You are living with our enemy. That boy's family are dangerous people."

"What? Please understand? I love Kang-de but Woo Jin has been good to me and I want him to see that I appreciate him too. When Mom died, I felt a deeper connection to Kang-de. I realized that he is the man for me. But you taught me to be good to people, so I am trying to be good to Woo Jin. Please understand."

"I do not understand and neither does Kang-de. He is hurting. I can tell in his voice. Woo Jin and his family are very dangerous."

"I will work it out with Kang-de," said Areum.

"Do it before it's too late. Good men like Kang-de do not stay single forever. Don't be stupid. You might end up losing him."

"Dad, I have to go now. I will be back on Monday."

Woo Jin and Areum flew to Hong Kong in spite of her father's objections. The plane landed in Hong Kong and Woo Jin welcomed her to Hong Kong.

"It's a beautiful city. Woo Jin. Wow."

"Areum, look over there. That's our driver. Let's go."

"Woo Jin, did you book a hotel for me? It's not proper to stay at your home. Your parents would be very upset."

"Hey, Areum. I'm not crazy. We are not married as yet. I booked a hotel not far from my house. You won't be bored because I will be with you most of the time."

"Okay. But why are we here?"

"We are here to let my parents know that I plan to marry you and also to tell them about the baby."

"Woo Jin. You can't tell them everything all at once. They might get a heart attack. I haven't forgiven you for cheating on me. So don't tell them about marriage as of yet. If you want to tell them about the baby, fine."

"Areum, I have to be honest about everything. You know that the baby is due in a few months. I want them to find out from me."

"Okay. But please don't take me to your home when you tell them."

Woo Jin checked Areum into a hotel. He took her to lunch and then he went to his parents' home.

"Hello, Mom, Dad. How are you?"

"Woo Jin, what brings you here this weekend?"

"I have to tell you something."

"Did you get that Areum girl pregnant?" asked Mrs. Kim.

"No, Mother, but I am going to be a father."

"What? Woo Jin! How could you do this to us and to yourself? Where is this person? Who is she?"

"She's a lawyer I met while I was in school. She wants to take responsibility for the baby because she is financially stable."

"Oh, Woo Jin, how could you get a girl pregnant at this time in your life? What about the family business? What do you plan on doing?"

"I intend to continue working. I will accept responsibility for the baby but I am not marrying that girl."

"No, you are not marrying anybody except Yoomi."

"Mother. I don't want to marry Yoomi. I want to marry Areum."

"Absolutely not. Yoomi has been waiting on you for a long time. We are not going through this nonsense with that girl Areum again."

"She is not just that girl. I love her and she is here in Hong Kong with me."

"Do not bring her to my house. I don't want her here."

"I thought that this was my house too. If she can't come here, then I am going back to Seoul tonight."

"Kim Woo Jin, what is wrong with you? Why are you being so rude?"

"I came here to see you and you both are attacking me. Areum is a good lady. She is the woman I want."

"Has she accepted your proposal as yet? I am sure that she has not. And she will not either. You have another woman pregnant."

"Mother!"

"You have ruined your life. Yoomi might still accept you because her family is desperate to marry her off. Think, Woo Jin. Think hard and long. When are you going to accept your duties in Brunei?"

"I told you that I had to resolve my problems in Seoul. I am bringing Areum here for tea tomorrow. Please be nice to her."

"Don't worry, Woo Jin. We will be kind to her."

Mr. Kim went into his car and made a phone call. "Hello, I have the daughter of Mr. Lee, the Embassy worker. Should I eliminate her now? She is with my son."

The person on the other line said, "Not yet."

"Okay," said Mr. Kim as his driver exited the driveway and onto the street.

A few hours later, Woo Jin brought Areum to his home. She hesitated to enter the house.

"Woo Jin, why did you bring me here? You know that your mother doesn't like me."

"Areum, I like you and that is what is important."

Woo Jin rang the doorbell and the butler opened the door. "Hi, Leung."

"Welcome, Master. Miss, welcome."

"Where is everyone?"

"Madam is in the library and Mr. Kim is not here."

Chapter Forty-seven

Mr. and Mrs. Hwang, Woo Jin, Areum, and Mrs. Kim

On the way home, Mr. Kim's driver slowly drove down the steep mountain road that had no barrier. A truck driving down the mountain with great speed hit Mr. Kim's car with force. It pushed Mr. Kim's car over the mountain side causing it to roll several times. The truck sped away without being seen. A bus driver saw the wrecked car and called the police.

Six hours had passed and the phone rang at the Kim's residence.

"Hello, good evening," said the butler.

"Is this the Kims' residence?"

"Yes. Whom may I say is speaking?"

"It's the police."

"Leung, who is it?" asked Woo Jin.

"The police."

Woo Jin grabbed the telephone from Leung. "How may I help you?"

"There was an accident and the victims were taken to the hospital. The driver was killed and a Mr. Kim was badly injured."

"What? Which hospital is he in?"

"Woo Jin, what is going on?" asked Mrs. Kim.

"Mom, it's Dad. He was in an accident. Let's go. Areum...."

"I will come with you," she said. Mrs. Kim shouted, "No. You stay here!"

"It's okay, Areum. You stay here. The butler will see to your needs. We have to go now."

"Best wishes with your dad."

Mrs. Kim and Woo Jin arrived at the hospital.

"Nurse, where is Mr. Kim? He was brought in here today."

"He is in the emergency room. The doctors are seeing to him."

Mrs. Kim and Woo Jin tried to enter the emergency room and was stopped by hospital security.

"Sir, you cannot enter."

"I want to see my father."

"The doctors are trying to save his life. Please let them do their job."

"My husband is on the board of this hospital. I want to see him."

"It's okay, Mother. We will wait outside."

The news media arrived minutes after Woo Jin and his mother entered the hospital. They saw Mrs. Kim and they rushed to interview her. Then they saw Woo Jin and they cornered him by the emergency doors.

"Mr. Kim, what can you tell us about the accident? What happened to CEO Kim?"

"No comment."

Woo Jin took his mother and walked away while the media followed them. Hospital security escorted Woo Jin and his mother into a private lounge where they waited for news about Mr. Kim's surgery. The wait was long and silent. Woo Jin held his mother's hand while they waited. They were both in tears.

It was a cloudy morning over Jeju Island. Bob had arrived at Kang-de's apartment and he decided to watch the cable news while Kang-de went through documents Roger Goo gave him.

"Boss, take a look at this news. Woo Jin's father had a terrible car accident in Hong Kong. His driver is dead. Look. There is Woo Jin and his mother at a hospital."

"I am sorry to hear. Teaching lessons can be deadly."

"Boss. Is that your doing? Wow, Boss. I knew that they shouldn't have messed with you. YOU GOT THEM."

"Areum called me earlier to let me know that she was traveling to Hong Kong. I believe that she wanted you to know where she was."

"I am no longer responsible for her. I don't want to know."

"She told me to tell you that she loves you."

"I said that I did not want to hear about Areum and her boyfriend Woo Jin. Turn the channel."

Bob changed the channel. "Wow, it's on all the channels."

"Then turn off the damn television."

"Okay, but your behavior lets me know that you are still in love with her. Boss, why don't you go and get her or call her? Do something."

"Bob. Please stop it. If you must know I have someone watching her while she is in Hong Kong. Bob, remember Mrs. Hwang who came to see me? I bought out her company."

"Why?"

"Two reasons. My Hong Kong friends verified Mr. Hwang's name in the secret file given to me by Mr. Lee. They believe he is the head of the secret organization. I told them to be certain before I kill him. And I am using her company to acquire Kim Industries."

"Boss, you are a genius."

"I have the boys in Hong Kong looking into Kim Industries and as we speak, their stocks are getting weaker by the minute. Let's just say that they will be worthless by tomorrow. Hey, Bob, look for news about Mr. Hwang too. It's coming up."

Meanwhile, at a Hong Kong hospital, surgery had just concluded and the surgeons advised Woo Jin and his mother that Mr. Kim's right leg and right hand were broken. He was still in intensive care because his spinal cord had been injured. The doctor escorted Woo Jin and his mother into the Intensive Care Unit. They saw Mr. Kim lying with bandages on his face and head. He had a cast on his leg and arm and metal braces were attached to his back.

"Dad, can you hear me? Wake up, Dad."

"Honey, can you hear me? Wake up, please. I need to know what happened to you."

"Yeah, Dad. We need to know what happened."

Mr. Kim remained unconscious for the next two days. Several men in black suits visited Mr. Kim while he was unconscious. Two of the men remained in his room as security. When the Hwangs arrived at the hospital late in the night. They were greeted by Woo Jin and Mrs. Kim.

"Woo Jin, Mrs. Kim, we are so sorry to hear about Chairman Kim. How is he?"

"He was badly hurt but he will survive," said Woo Jin.

"I am so sorry, Woo Jin. If you need anything, please let me know."

"Thank you, Yoomi. Mr. and Mrs. Hwang, thank you for coming. I appreciate your kind thoughts. Yoomi, it is good to see you. Please excuse me. I want to speak with the doctor."

Woo Jin walked over to the doctor who was standing at the nurses' station.

"Doctor, how badly hurt is he?"

"Well, Mr. Kim. His leg is broken in two places; his arm is broken and his spine is damaged. It will take months of therapy before his body heals."

"Doctor, please do everything possible to help him."

"We will take good care of Chairman Kim. He is our VIP in this hospital."

While Woo Jin walked away to call Areum, Mr. Hwang secretly spoke to the men dressed in black.

Mr. Hwang was in his late seventies. He had married a very young woman whose father was also a member of the secret society. Mr. Hwang was still handsome in his old age, but he was evil in his thoughts.

According to the secret files, he and Mr. Kim served in the military together. He, Mr. Kim and Kang-de's grandfather formed the secret organization when they were in their early twenties. Its members originally performed covert operations on behalf of the government, until all but one of its members became mercenaries for hire by any country who paid the most money. Shin Kang-de's grandfather refused to participate and was killed because he exposed the members of the secret society. Mr. Kim and Mr. Hwang were sent to prison for a long time. They escaped and went underground. They reinstated their secret organization and vowed to eliminate Kang-de's entire family.

Woo Jin called his home. It had been two days since he had spoken to Areum.

"Hello, Kim residence."

"Hi, Leung. May I speak with Miss Areum, please?"

"Yes, Master. How is Chairman Kim?"

"Badly hurt. Please put Miss Areum on the phone."

"Hello, Woo Jin, how is your dad?"

"He has a lot of broken bones. They are still examining him."

"I am sorry. Why don't I go back to Seoul tomorrow? You are going to have to stay here with your dad."

"Thanks, Areum. You are so thoughtful. I will have the driver take you the airport in the morning."

"Okay. Best wishes to you and your family."

"Areum, go straight to my place."

"Okay. I will be fine, Woo Jin."

"I love you, Lee Areum."

"Bye," said Areum as she left for the airport.

The plane landed at two o'clock in the afternoon and Areum and two security guards that were assigned to her by Woo Jin went directly to the hospital clinic. The guards waited in their car until Areum was ready to return to his apartment.

Chapter Forty-eight

Woo Jin, Kang-de, Bob, and Areum

Kang-de and Bob remained at Jeju Island for the weekend. They spent the weekend playing tennis and soccer.

"Bob, I have a meeting in Gangnam tomorrow. I wished that I could Skype so that I don't have to go to Seoul. But it's not possible."

"Okay, Boss, I will have the jet ready tomorrow."

The next morning, Kang-de and Bob flew to Seoul and went to the ITO Hotel.

Areum was already at the hotel having breakfast with her father. Kang-de, Min and Bob entered the hotel lobby and walked to the elevator. Bob looked to his right and saw Areum and her father.

"Boss, look over there."

"Where?"

"In the restaurant. It's Areum. She's in the restaurant with her father."

"So, let her eat."

"Boss!"

"I am going upstairs to my suite. You can wait here if you choose."

361

Areum saw Kang-de enter the elevator. She ran to the elevator, but the door closed before she could speak with him. He looked at her and held his head down while the elevator door close.

"Miss Areum. How are you? I didn't expect to see you here," said Bob.

"I came back early from Hong Kong. How is he?"

"Go and find out. He is upstairs."

"He doesn't want to see me."

"Miss Areum. He is hurting. Please go and speak with him."

"I don't know...."

"Miss Areum, did you come all the way here to have breakfast with your father?"

"Bob. Yes, I did. I came to support Kang-de's business and see my father."

"Please go and see him. We are only here for two days."

Bob went to have breakfast with Mr. Lee and Areum went and rang Kang-de's doorbell.

"Bob, did you forget the key code?" asked Kang-de opening the door.

"Hi, Kang-de."

"What are you doing here? You're supposed to be in Hong Kong."

"Did Bob tell you what I said? May I come in?" she asked.

"No. What do you want?" he asked, standing with the door slightly ajar.

"Please, Kang-de."

"I told you that I didn't want to see you until you've ended your relationship with Woo Jin and I meant it."

"Shin Kang-de. Don't let me beg. It's not a relationship. It's a friendship. That's all it is."

"Do not use me. Please." Kang-de was about to shut the door but Areum blocked the door with her handbag. He looked at her and said, "Areum, please go away."

"Do you really want me to go?"

"Please leave me before...."

"Kang-de, please let me stay. I have no pride when I am with you. I want you so badly. Please let me stay for a while."

Kang-de walked away from the door leaving it open. Kang-de sat on the couch and looked out the window. Areum closed the door and latched it. She walked over to the couch and breathed on the back of Kang-de's neck.

"Please don't do that. I have work to do."

"You have work right here."

Areum stuck her tongue in his ear and she licked his earlobe. Kang-de pulled her onto the couch and passionately kissed her. Kang-de stuck his tongue into her mouth. She sucked on his tongue and she could feel the muscles between his leg getting hard. She pulled on his shirt. He grabbed her hand.

"Don't do that."

"Yes, Kang-de, please let me do that."

Areum unbuttoned his shirt and stared at his chest. She sucked on his breast like a ravenous animal who has not had a meal in months.

"Oh, Kang-de, you are so gorgeous."

"Areum, what are you doing?"

"I want you to make love to me right now."

Areum unbuttoned his pants zipper and rubbed her mouth on the front of his pants. Kang-de pulled her dress over her head. He unlatched her bra and sucked on her breast. He placed his hand between her legs and rubbed her private parts. Areum kissed his neck and his face. Kang-de laid her on the couch, put on a condom and slowly entered her. She moaned in ecstasy.

"Oh, baby, I want you so much," said Areum. "Show me how much you love me," she said.

"No. You show me how much you love me."

Areum turned him over and she rode him slowly. She bent her head and sucked on his neck. He pushed her up and sucked on her breast with force.

"I love you, Kang-de. Oh, gosh. Kang-de, I am coming."

Before she could climax, Kang-de lifted her off of him.

"Kang-de!"

"Stop. I am not going to climax with you. You can't have me and Woo Jin. If you want me to make love to you, then you need to get rid of Woo Jin. Until then, this body is off limits to you."

"You want me, don't you?" asked Areum.

"I am not going to lie. I want you so much that my heart feels like it's exploding. But I will not share you with that guy. NO WAY."

Kang-de zipped his pants and sat up on the coach. Areum remained naked hoping that Kang-de would change his mind.

"Why are you not in Hong Kong?"

"Woo Jin needs to be with his family and I missed you. Mr. Kim was in a car accident. It's really bad."

Kang-de didn't respond.

"I could have had breakfast anywhere, but I chose your hotel."

"Thanks for the support, but don't come here to eat anymore. You are teasing me."

"I have to come. The sexiest man owns this hotel, and I want him. Oh, God, I want him so much."

"I am serious, Areum. As long as you are with Woo Jin, I don't want you to come here or to any of my establishments. I cannot share you."

"Are you abandoning me?"

"YES, and I mean it. Don't come in front of me again."

"Okay, Kang-de. I will do my best to let Woo Jin down easily."

Kang-de yelled, "Is that what you think that you are doing? There is not an easy way to let someone down as you describe it. You need to break it off quickly before things gets worse. What do you know about relationships?"

"Obviously nothing," she replied.

"That's right. You know nothing. Woo Jin has a child coming. He has a woman in Hong Kong whom he's destined to marry. Where do you think you fit in that madness? Stop this twisted insanity before you get hurt," he said thinking about the secret organization who killed her mother and his family. He wanted to tell her about Woo Jin's family, but he told himself that he could endanger her life if she knew. "I am not going to put myself in your mess. You go and sort it out right now," said Kang-de. "Goodbye."

"Okay, I will speak with him when he gets back," she said.

"Fine. In the meantime, I don't want to see you."

"Please, Kang-de. I cannot live without seeing you. Don't do that to me."

"You are doing it to yourself. You are an adult. Deal with this mess like an adult. And don't let me wait too long."

"My heart belongs to you right now. Do you want it?"

"Yes, yes, yes."

Areum tried to kiss Kang-de goodbye. He pulled away.

"AREUM! No, no, no. Go away."

"I didn't know that you could be this cold."

"I am not cold. You are the cold one. You are using me."

"Don't ever say that to me again," she said. "I would rather break off our relationship right now than use you."

"Please don't think like that. You still don't understand. When someone has been very kind to you, you should show kindness in return. That's what I am trying to do with him. It is not about the sex, because you are the master in that area."

Kang-de smiled upon hearing Areum admit that she thought that he was a better lover than Woo Jin.

"It's just about kindness. Please understand," she said.

"Well, I feel sick when I think about him touching you."

"I slept with him two times only. That's it."

"I don't want to hear that. I don't want anyone touching your body."

"Kang-de, this body belongs to you. How many times must I tell you that?"

"Then why is it that you are sleeping with another man?"

"I haven't since Jeju Island. It was the first time that he had touched me since I stayed with him and I think he did it because he knew you were on the island."

"Areum, please go and take care of your life," he said as he walked to the door to let her out.

Areum slowly walked out his door and he closed it behind her. She went to stay at Woo Jin's home until he returned from Hong Kong. Areum and Kang-de did not speak with each other for one month.

Each time she visited the hotel, he looked at her on the security camera desperately wanting to see her. But he told himself that he had to stay away from her although his heart and body ached for her.

His mind was consumed by thoughts of their sexual encounters and the ecstasy he felt when he made love with her. Bob's calls to him forced him to focus on his business. He had to concentrate on his company and his vengeance against Mr. Kim and Mr. Hwang. He waited for news that Mr. Kim died. And he wanted the death of Mr. Hwang to be imminent. He realized that killing Mr. Hwang wasn't going to be easy but it was going to happen eventually.

A call from Mr. Lee which said that Areum was graduating made him focus on her again. He wanted to do something for her because he loved her so much. She was his ONE LOVE.

Whatever he would do for her, he would do it anonymously. He couldn't let her know that he missed her and wanted her desperately. He and Mr. Lee planned her graduation party and he paid for it.

Chapter Forty-nine

Graduation day had arrived for Areum and Bora. Woo Jin returned from Hong Kong to see Areum graduate. He arrived fifteen minutes before graduation began. Areum and her security arrived early to the University auditorium where the graduation was being held. Bora's parents, Dave and Mr. Lee attended the graduation. Kang-de and Bob sat in the back of the auditorium, in order to avoid a scene with Woo Jin and Mr. Park.

Areum had hoped to see Kang-de and she let her eyes glanced around the auditorium. She looked to her right and saw Woo Jin with flowers in his hand. She looked to her left and she recognized her father waving a white handkerchief.

The ceremony took three and a half-hours. When it concluded, Woo Jin ran to her and hugged her before giving her flowers.

"Congratulations, Doctor Lee Areum. I am very proud of you."

"Thank you for coming, Woo Jin. How is your dad?"

"He is still in rehabilitation, but I would not miss this day."

Woo Jin's phone rang and he went outside to answer the phone. Areum saw Bob walking to her.

"Congratulations, Miss Areum. Best of luck in the future."

Areum looked around the auditorium for Kang-de but there were too many people. Bob looked at her and said, "Yes, he is here, Miss Areum. He sent these flowers for you."

Kang-de sent five dozen roses in assorted colors for Areum.

Woo Jin gave her one dozen orchids and one dozen chrysanthemums.

"Tell Mr. Shin Kang-de I said thanks and I am working it out. He knows what I mean." Bob walked down the aisle to sit with Kang-de. And Mr. Lee walked over to Areum and hugged her.

"Areum, I am having a graduation party at a reception hall for you tonight and I want you to invite your classmates."

"Dad, that's so nice of you, but I think Woo Jin wanted to take me out."

"Let Woo Jin take you to lunch now. And we will have a party tonight."

"Okay, Dad. I will tell him."

Areum told Woo Jin what her father said and he took her to lunch at the Enfield Hotel.

"Areum, I am so happy for you. Doctor! That sounds nice."

"Thanks, Woo Jin."

"Are you going to escort me to the party tonight?"

"Of course. I wouldn't want to disappoint you or your dad."

Areum invited Bora and Dave. She did not invite Mi-hi, who had disappeared from Bern Dormitory in the middle of the semester. Areum's classmates arrived early at the hall. It was decorated beautifully. Each table was designed with large flower centerpieces in the shape of a standing stethoscopes. The napkins, cups, plates and utensils were designed with the logo Dr. A. Lee and the cake was designed in the shape of a doctor's bag. Large bottles of crystal champagne were placed at each table. Each table had its own waiter and various assortments of foods.

Areum entered the hall wearing a green mini dress and black pumps. Everyone applauded. Woo Jin tried to hold her hand but she declined. He pulled out her chair and she sat with him.

"Dad, this is beautiful. When did you plan this?" she asked.

Mr. Lee smiled and walked to the microphone to thank everyone for coming to his daughter's graduation party.

"My wife would have loved to see Areum graduate, but she is here in spirit. Please raise your glasses to toast my daughter, Doctor Lee Areum."

Woo Jin walked up to the microphone after Mr. Lee walked away. "I would like to also make a toast to Doctor Lee, the heart surgeon. Best of luck to you and may your future always be bright. Cheers."

Woo Jin walked to Areum and kissed her on the forehead.

Mr. Lee took the mic from Woo Jin and said, "There is one more person who should make a toast to Doctor Lee. He has been very instrumental in keeping our family together and he organized this party tonight."

Areum looked around the hall when Mr. Lee said that Kang-de organized the party.

"Ladies and gentlemen, he is one of the kindest persons on this planet. Mr. Shin Kang-de, come to the microphone, please."

Woo Jin looked surprised and Areum was surprised to see Kang-de walking slowly to the microphone. Her heart began to beat fast.

Kang-de took the microphone, looked at Areum and said, "Areum, Mr. Lee, thank you for making me a part of your family. I am truly fortunate to have such a great family that I can depend on." He looked at Areum and said, "You know that I wish for you all that is good in this world. May your future be better than your dreams. Always reach for the stars and have faith in yourself. Don't ever lose your beautiful spirit. Congratulations."

Kang-de walked over to her table and shook her hands. Then he turned and walked away.

"Kang-de, please come back. I want to say something to you. Woo Jin, come to the microphone as well, please."

Woo Jin and Kang-de walked toward Areum.

"Ladies and gentlemen, I would like to publicly thank these two wonderful men who helped me achieve my goals. They made all my dreams come true. They were there when I was weak. They stood by me when I doubted myself. They gave me unconditional love. I am truly grateful to you both. I am so happy that you were both in my life when I needed you most. Thank you, Woo Jin. Thank you, Kang-de."

The people applauded Woo Jin and Kang-de. Kang-de nodded to Bob and he walked to the door. Areum watched Kang-de walk away. She felt her heart skip a beat as he turned, looked at her and smiled before going through the door.

"Thank you, Areum; it was my pleasure to have been able to help you. Those were kind words."

"Woo Jin, tomorrow I want to talk about us."

"Good. I want to talk about us too. Now let's dance."

The party ended at two in the morning. Mr. Lee was escorted home by the security guards Kang-de provided to him. Bora and Dave said their goodbyes an hour before the party ended. Woo Jin and Areum went home together. Woo Jin lifted her off her feet and he took her to his bedroom. He slowly placed Areum on his bed and he kissed her tenderly. He slowly removed his jacket and then his shirt. Areum could not help but look at his well-conditioned body. Before she could say anything to him, he started to kiss her neck.

"Woo Jin, don't you think that we should take a shower after partying so long?"

"No, I want to smell your beautiful scent. I want to see you in the raw."

Before she could say another word he kissed her with his tongue touching her tongue. He went deep into her mouth while slowly unzipping her beautiful green dress. He threw it to the floor and his hand went into her underwear. He slowly caress her private parts which made her forget about the shower. He unlatched her bra and she helped him remove it. His head went from her mouth to her breast. He sucked on them hard. Woo Jin paused for a moment and took out the condom from his pants pocket and he laid it on the bed. He proceeded to kiss her unwashed body while peeling the condom wrap open. He parted her thighs, caressed her private parts then thrust his hard muscle into her. She moaned as he pushed deeper and deeper into her.

"Areum, I missed you so much and I have been dreaming about this moment."

Areum was speechless as her mind went to Kang-de. She thought about him as she turned Woo Jin over and rode him relentlessly. He held her and turned her over and thrust himself into her from behind. He continued until he grabbed her by the shoulders, pulled her up and climaxed while holding her around the waist tightly.

Areum couldn't help but feel the rippling sensation from his body against hers, she climaxed. He lay on her naked back and went to sleep. Areum thought of Kang-de again. She felt guilty and she went to sleep.

Areum woke early to prepare breakfast for Woo Jin. He smiled as he looked at her nude body through the transparent gown that she was wearing.

"Areum, you are the nicest girl that I have ever met. You have a beautiful soul. You are strong, yet you are sensitive and you make good love to me. You pretend to be independent but you want the warmth of a man. Any man would gladly want you as a wife. I want you as my wife. Will you marry me? I don't have a ring as yet, but I know that you don't care about a ring at this moment."

"Woo Jin, you have brought joy to my life and I am so grateful for each day that I have spent with you. And yes, you are really sexy. But, you have great responsibilities that cannot be overlooked or discarded. You have a baby on the way and you will be CEO of Kim Industries which will demand 100 percent of your time. I have my career and marrying you will require that I put it on hold. I cannot do that. I love you but I can't marry you."

"Well, I can wait for you. We don't have to get married right now."

"Woo Jin, I can't marry you, ever. I don't want to marry anybody until I have completed my residency," she said.

"Not even Kang-de?"

"Not even Kang-de. But, I am going to live with him because he needs me. You don't."

Woo Jin yelled out, "Lee Areum, I need you too."

"No, you don't. I needed you, but you never needed me. I will always be thankful to you. You have been so good to me and I hope that you will find someone who will be good to you because you deserve it. You are a great man, Kim Woo Jin."

"Listen to me, Areum, I am going back to Hong Kong to look after my father. But our story is far from over. This is not the last word between us. Do you understand me?"

"Woo Jin!"

"No, this is not the end of us. It cannot be. I won't discuss this with you until I return," he said firmly. "Right now I have to pack documents to take to Hong Kong."

"I will pack for you," said Areum.

"No. I want to do it," he said with tears in his eyes.

"Okay, I will leave you alone. I am going to work. Do you want me to drive you to the airport?"

"No. This is not goodbye. I will be back soon. After last night, I cannot say goodbye. I won't. You are mine and I will be back to take what's mine."

"Please call to let me know that you have arrived safely. Goodbye, Woo Jin. When you get back, I won't be here."

Areum hugged Woo Jin and she went to the hospital residence dormitory, taking her suitcase with her. Woo Jin left for the airport in disbelief of what Areum just told him. He told himself that he can't process his relationship with Areum because he has to think about helping his father to recover.

Woo Jin called Kang-de while at the airport. "You think that you have won my woman, don't you? I am going to kill you slowly."

"Not if I kill you first. Watch your back, Woo Jin," said Kang-de.

"I will be seeing you soon," said Woo Jin.

A week after Woo Jin left for Hong Kong, Areum went to see Kang-de. She rang the bell at his suite. Kang-de was on the phone with Bob.

"Who is it?" he asked.

"It's me, Areum."

"I am on the phone. Please wait."

Kang-de did not open the door, but Areum waited outside until he had finished his phone conversation. "Bob, what did you just say?"

"Mr. Kim and Mr. Hwang had your parents killed. Mr. Chin was stabbed to death in prison and Mr. Hwang and his security guards were found dead in his car last night."

"Well, Mr. Chin didn't see death coming at him. Mr. Hwang didn't see death coming at him. That's too bad," said Kang-de. "I am sure they were told that I said hello before they died. Bob, when I went to Hong Kong I found out that Mr. Kim and his Boss Mr. Hwang had my family killed. That's why Mr. Kim will be in a wheelchair for the rest of his life. He should have died, that bastard. I'm not finished with him and his son. Woo Jin will feel my wrath if he interferes with me. I am sure that he and I will meet again. Mr. Hwang is dead and that's great but I want to destroy the secret organization and I am working on it." Kang-de hung up the phone and opened the door for Areum.

"Hi. Why did you leave my party so quickly?"

"Is that what you are here to talk to me about?"

"No. I am here to let you know that I am no longer with Woo Jin. I told him that it's over and that I was moving in with you."

"But you don't have to do that. It's your decision." Kang-de looked at her and asked, "When are you moving in with me?"

"Whenever you want me to."

"Then let's stay in the hotel for a while. I am looking for a new home to purchase. Since you and your dad are going to be living with me, we will need to go house hunting together."

"Okay. By the way, please allow me to contribute something to the new home and thank you for giving me that lavish party."

"You are welcome, Miss Independent Doctor. You are the boss. Do you have regrets about Woo Jin?"

"No. He doesn't need me. He will be fine."

Kang-de whispered to himself, "After I am finished with him and his family he won't be fine."

"Areum. Now that we are going to live together, will you accept an engagement ring? We don't have to get married right of way. I just want to preserve your honor."

"Thank you for protecting my honor. Yes, I will accept an engagement ring."

"I want to give it to you in a proper manner. Let's go out."

"No. This is the most intimate place to give me a ring."

Kang-de took the ring from his safe and he kneeled in front of Areum.

"Oh, Kang-de. How long have you had this ring?"

"I purchased it the day after we arrived from my house in Ansan. Lee Areum, you are my ONE LOVE. You have brought lots of happiness to my life. I love you very much. I need you. Are you willing to spend the rest of your life with me?"

Without hesitating Areum said, "Yes, Kang-de. I want to spend my life with you. I need you. I'm in love with you."

Kang-de placed the ring on Areum's finger. They hugged and kissed each other.

"Thank you, Areum, for choosing me. I have waited a long time for this moment. I love you more than I love my life."

"I love you too. Let's call my dad."

"Can we call your dad later?"

She saw that he had desire in his eyes and she took his hand and led him to the large couch that was in his library. He kissed her with passion and she kissed his entire face.

"I have missed you so much," he said as he removed her dress and laid it on the couch.

She unbuttoned his shirt and paused to look at his sensual and firm body. She wanted him badly.

He pulled down her underwear and he unzipped his pants before she could do it for him. He quickly put on the condom and he parted her legs and he entered her body as she moaned from the sweetness of his hard muscle trusting inside her body. The ecstasy that they both felt, brought them to a great climax. They lay on the couch in a locked position as they rubbed their naked bodies against each other.

"I love you, Areum."

"I love you too, Kang-de," said Areum as she kissed his soft lips.

Half-hour later, they showered together and got dressed.

Kang-de called Mr. Lee to his suite to tell him that Areum was willing to marry him.

"Oh, how wonderful. Where are you? May I come up?" he asked.

"Yes. Please."

Mr. Lee arrived at Kang-de's suite in a hurry. "My daughter, I wished that your mother were here to see this. Kang-de is a good man, Areum. I know that he will take good care of you."

"Yes, Dad, I know that and I will take very good care of him," she said looking at him with a smile on her face.

"Congratulations, Kang-de. I am very happy for you both."

"Thank you, Father. I will protect her with my life."

"I am confident that you will take care of my daughter."

Mr. Lee shook Kang-de's hand and Kang-de poured three glasses of champagne. They toasted to each other.

"To my woman. The beautiful Lee Areum."

"To my man the handsome and gorgeous Shin Kang-de."

"To justice for everyone," Kang-de whispered to Mr. Lee. "Areum, please excuse us for a minute."

Areum looked at Kang-de and smiled as she walked out of the living room. Kang-de and Mr. Lee openly spoke at the dining table.

"Mr. Lee, I got revenge on everybody who killed my family and your wife. And I am not finished as yet. I have almost completed acquiring Kim Industries and AZAXCO Pharmaceuticals. Mr. Jong is bankrupt as of yesterday. Dave had to step down as CEO. Mr. Jong's overseas assets are frozen or confiscated by the United States government. And the man who tried to steal my company, Mr. Park, he is heading to trial. This time he has no allies to help him hide the evidence. Mr. Chin died in jail. Mr. Hwang died in his car. Only Woo Jin and the secret organization are left for me to personally deal with. I am going to bankrupt them before I erase them. Mr. Kim is bound to a wheelchair but I am not done with him. He will die soon."

"My son, thank you so much. My wife's death and your parents' death are not in vain. Again, thank you."

Areum walked out into the living room with an empty glass in her hand.

Kang-de looked at her and said, "Areum, my ONE LOVE, come here. Let's toast to justice."

Chapter Fifty

Woo Jin, Mr. Kim, Mr. Lau,
and Members of the Secret Organization

Meanwhile in Hong Kong, Mr. Kim was hospitalized four months and he spent another six months in a rehabilitation facility. When he returned home he called a meeting with the secret organization at his residence. Mr. Kim, who was unable to walk, was wheeled into the meeting by Woo Jin.

"Gentlemen, thank you for coming. The reason I called you here is to inform you that due to health reasons, I have decided to relinquish my position in this organization and I am nominating my son, Kim Woo Jin, to be the next chairman of our organization. If there are no objections, then let us cast our votes now."

Everyone except Mr. Lau, a longtime member of the organization, voted to accept Woo Jin as the next chairman. He was the member who told the group that Kang-de had powerful friends in Hong Kong and they needed to be careful in their dealings with him.

Woo Jin pledged his loyalty to the organization and to the members. They greeted him fondly but he was skeptical about their mission as an organization. It was not clear in his mind what the organization's mission was, but he was about to find out.

A week later, Woo Jin sat at his father's desk sorting through his company's financial reports, when the private line that Mr. Kim used to communicate with members of the secret organization rang. He looked at the phone for a few seconds. Then he answered it slowly.

"Hello."

"Mr. Lau is dead."

"When? How? Was it a suicide?" asked Woo Jin.

"I am not sure, Sir. He was found dead in his bed," said the voice. "Sir, we have sterilized his home."

"Sterilized? What do you mean sterilized?" asked Woo Jin.

"We have cleaned it so that there is no evidence of him ever living there."

The voice disconnected, but Woo Jin held the disconnected phone for a moment. He was in shock. His heart beat rapidly while walking to see his father who was entertaining guests in the living room. He wanted to ask Mr. Kim what kind of organization sterilizes the homes of its members when they die, but he dare not question his father in front of guests.

"Woo Jin, join us," said Mr. Kim. "We have a big problem. I was just informed by our Chief Financial Officer, here, that Shin Kang-de has acquired fifty-one percent of our shares and he is now majority shareholder in our company."

"What? I knew that he had shares in Kim Industries but I was not informed that he had successfully acquired up to fifty-one percent of our shares."

"Chairman Kim, what are you going to do with this information?"

"He must be stopped," said Woo Jin. "And how do you plan on doing that?" asked one of the guests.

"I have not thought about it. I am just hearing this news and I am busy reviewing all our financial reports," Woo Jin said staring in the face of the Chief Financial Officer.

"Chairman Kim, there is more news. Shin Kang-de has begun selling off subsidiary companies of Kim Industries. Yesterday he sold two of our best companies to our enemies."

"What? What did you just say? I want the names of the everyone who had the guts to buy a piece of this company and I want it tonight," said Woo Jin in a very frantic tone..

Mr. Kim had a slight grin on his face because he realized that his son was about to become more treacherous that he was.

"My son, there is one last thing that I want you to know. Shin Kang-de is the man who attempted to kill me. He put me in this wheelchair. And, he killed Mr. Hwang."

"Father, are you sure Kang-de did this to you?"

"I am certain, my son," Mr. Kim said, handing Woo Jin a document that showed Mr. Lau had contacted Kang-de hours before the accident. "As you can see on this paper, he gave Shin Kang-de my schedule so that he could ambush me."

"Okay, Father. I will handle Shin Kang-de and all of our enemies. If you will excuse me, I have to make a few phone calls. Goodnight, everyone. Father, I will be back to put you to bed."

"Chairman Kim, you do not have to do that. The male nurse can do it by himself. You have been a good son, but you have more important things to take care of."

After hearing that Kang-de had tried to kill his father and was attempting to destroy his company, Woo Jin had become extremely angry. He was no longer the kind hearted man who loved Areum. He was now Chairman of a secret organization that kill and intimidate people for its existence.

A week had passed since Woo Jin heard several shocking news about the organization and his father's accident. He sat in his father's office waiting for the private phone to ring. It rang at 10 A.M. sharp. The voice said that the organization had eliminated two of the CEOs who had acquired subsidiaries of Kim Industries. And several others were physically intimidated.

"Good," Woo Jin said. "Did you devaluate the stocks in Hwang Industries? Shin Kang-de owns that too. The stocks should be of no value to him by next week."

"Yes, Sir. We have our best hacker on the case."

"Great. Good job. Keep at it. I want back my company by any means necessary. Do you understand?"

"Yes, Sir. The enforcers are on their way."

"Okay. Stay in touch."

Chapter Fifty-one

Woo Jin, the Secret Organization,
Kang-de, Bob, Sun-hee, and Areum

At the end of the year, Woo Jin had recovered 50 percent of his company's stocks because he had intimidated his enemies to return their shares in his company. Eventually, no one wanted to buy his company stocks because they feared being killed or beaten by members of the organization.

The hackers had successfully devaluated Hwang's Industries which sent the stocks tumbling. Woo Jin immediately bought controlling interest in the company. He and Kang-de were now owners of Hwang Industries.

Woo Jin called Kang-de to let him know that he was the person who was going to ruin him financially.

"Hello, who is this?" asked Kang-de.

"I once told you that I don't fight fair and I always get what I want. You didn't take me seriously. Did you? Well, you are about to have your worst nightmare come true. Take a look at your news tonight."

"Woo Jin, I thought that you were dead. How did I miss killing you?"

"You should have killed me that night in the garden. Now you will never get another chance. Watch your back. How do you want to die?"

"So. Have you become the new chairman of the secret organization?"

Woo Jin became quiet. He had no idea that Kang-de knew everything about his organization.

"Now that you have time to talk to me. Let me fill you in on a few things that you should know. Your father, the traitor and murderer, had my grandparents and parents killed. He killed Areum's mother and he tried to kill me. What should I have done with this information, Woo Jin? You tell me. What should I have done? Should I have forgiven your wicked father for all the sins that he committed? Should I have forgiven him for making me into an orphan? I am sure he didn't tell you what he did to my family and to Areum's family, the woman that you claim to love?"

Woo Jin remained silent.

"Did you kill Mr. Lau or was it your evil father? Woo Jin, you can expect a fight that will only end if one of us dies. I am coming to kill your father. Count on it."

"And you will die trying," he said hanging up on Kang-de.

Kang-de immediately called his friends in Hong Kong to tell them to get ready for a war.

"Hey, it looks like Kim Woo Jin is now chairman of the secret organization and he has a contract out for my death. You have my permission to kill him if you get a chance."

"Okay, Boss," said the person at the other end of the phone. "Be careful. He would only get that position if he were very dangerous. I hope that he comes to Seoul so that I can send him to his father in a crate."

Two weeks had passed and no one related to Shin Kang-de was killed.

Late Sunday evening, Chul and two of his men sat watching soccer in their office when two gun men opened fire on them killing two of his employees and injuring him. Chul, who always had his gun with him, returned fire killing one of the assassin. The other assassin escaped.

Chul called Kang-de to tell him that he was shot and two of his men were dead.

"Do you need to go to the hospital? Did you call an ambulance?"

"No. No hospital. Remember, the police will be involved. Boss, be careful."

"Okay, stay where you are. Bob and I will be right there," said Kang-de.

Bob went with a security team to Chul's office and Kang-de rode with Eddie his best driver and two bodyguards. They ran from the SUV and into Chul's office. Blood was everywhere. Kang-de and Bob took Chul to the hospital. They had created a false story to tell the police if necessary. Chul was in surgery for two hours. The bullet had exited his shoulder, and, he was expected to heal quickly.

"Bob, two good men are dead because of me. Woo Jin has started something that he has no idea how to finish, but I am going to finish it for him."

"How will Areum feel about you killing the man she once loved?"

"I will tell her everything once he is dead. I want him dead now," said Kang-de angrily. "I should have listened to you and Chul when you told me to kill him last year. I can only assume that he knows a lot about my operation and he is going to try and eliminate everyone around me before trying to kill me. That is what I would do if I were him. Bob, let's get ready for them."

"Okay, Boss. They have just turned you into their worst nightmare."

While Kang-de and Bob waited at the hospital for news about Chul, his friends in Hong Kong grabbed one of Mr. Kim's housekeeper while he was shopping for groceries. They bribed him for information on Woo Jin and Mr. Kim's schedule. The next day he took an emergency leave from the Kim's household which made Woo Jin suspicious.

That same night Kang-de's friends crashed into the Kim's residence, but it was empty. They called Kang-de to let him know that the Kim's had fled the home.

"Burn it down," said Kang-de. "Find them. Do not let them escape."

While the house burned, Woo Jin could see the flames from where he and his family were staying. He knew that his house was destroyed and he knew that it was Kang-de who did it.

Early the next morning six men arrived at Incheon airport. Four got into a cab that took them to the ITO Hotel. When they got to the front desk, they were told that there was no occupancy. The men walked out the door and into the awaiting cab. Kang-de and Bob watched the men from his communications room. He had them followed to a building that was formally owned by Mr. Jong. His men waited for them to come out, but they stayed there throughout the night.

Kang-de had Bob and his personal bodyguards move into the ITO Hotel. He wanted to protect them from any surprises Woo Jin had planned. The hotel staff were put on the alert. Everyone and everything were to be searched. Housekeepers were told to report anything and anyone that looked suspicious.

Woo Jin, the fifth man, went to his apartment and he called Sun-hee.

"Hi. How is the baby?"

"She is fine. Where are you? When are you coming to see the baby?" Sun-hee said excited that Woo Jin called.

"I am in town. I want you to bring the baby to my apartment this afternoon. Don't tell anyone that I am here. I am serious about that."

"I won't."

Within half an hour she and the baby were on their way to see Woo Jin.

Woo Jin's doorbell rang and he saw Sun-hee holding the baby in her arms. He quickly opened the door and took the baby from her.

"She's really beautiful," he said.

"She looks like you, Woo Jin."

"Yeah," he said smiling at the baby. "Sun-hee, this might be the only time that I will get to see my little girl. Some bad things are about to happen and I want you and her to go to my home in London for a while. I don't want to hear any excuses. There is no time to argue or to explain. I want my child safe. And you too."

"Woo Jin, what is happening? I need to know what is happening."

"There is no time to explain. You can work from home, right?"

"Yes. I don't have any court appointments this month."

"Well, your temporary home will be in London. It's just for a while."

"Okay, Woo Jin," she said with a smile on her face. She felt good that Woo Jin was still concerned about her.

"Good. You will be leaving tomorrow."

"Woo Jin!" said Sun-hee screaming.

"Sun-hee, I have already decided. You and this pretty baby are traveling tomorrow. Everything has been arranged for you and the baby. She has a nanny and her nursery has been prepared already. You really don't need to take anything with you."

Woo Jin spent the rest of the day feeding and playing with the baby while Sun-hee noticed that he had changed. His demeanor had changed. He wasn't the Woo Jin she knew. What could have made him so aloof? she wondered. Was it Kang-de? she asked herself. She secretly called him when she went home to pack her clothes.

Meanwhile at a hospital in Seoul, Areum spent the day seeing patients and consulting with other doctors. She took the elevator that stopped by the nurses' station and she glanced to her right and saw Kang-de and Bob.

"Hello, handsome husband-to-be. What brings you here? Were you waiting for me?" she asked.

"No. Chul is in the emergency room," said Kang-de looking at Bob.

"What happened?"

"He had an accident," Bob said.

"A car accident?"

"No, Areum. He was shot and now that you know, please go and find out how he's doing," said Kang-de.

"Kang-de. What is going on? Don't you think that it's time that you tell me everything? I am not a child. I am going to be your wife. I want to know what is going on with your life and I want to know after I find out about Chul," she said walking toward the emergency room.

"Boss, I think that it's time to tell her all the things that she needs to know."

"Yeah. Things have gotten out of hand with that crazy guy Woo Jin. I should let her know that his father killed her mother."

"Yeah, and a few other things as well," said Bob.

Areum entered the long hallway that had cubicles with patients on each side. Suddenly, her pager beeped and she pulled out her cellphone and dialed the number in the pager. "Hello, this is Doctor Lee."

"Hello, Doctor Lee. This is Kim Woo Jin."

"Hi, Woo Jin, how are you? Where are you calling me from?"

"I'm in a car outside the emergency door of the hospital. Areum, I want to see you. Can you come out for a minute?"

"I am a little busy. Can you wait for a few minutes?" she asked.

Woo Jin replied, "No, I am on my way to the airport. Can I please see you for a minute?"

"Okay, but just for a minute. I have a patient that I have to visit."

Areum walked out the front entrance to the emergency room. She called Kang-de when she stepped outside and saw Woo Jin.

"Kang-de, I am outside with Woo Jin."

"No, don't go into his car. Areum, it's a trap," he said running through the emergency room door.

The alarm went off and security tried to stop Kang-de and Bob while they sprint down the hall filled with patients. Bob pushed two of the security men aside clearing the way for Kang-de to run. When they got outside a black BMW sped off.

"Areum," screamed Kang-de on the phone.

The signal was gone. Kang-de called his bodyguards to bring the car to the side of the hospital.

"Bob, you and your men stay with Chul and be on the alert," he said hopping into the back seat of the SUV. There were four security guards in the SUV and three other guards were in the car that drove behind them. He tried to call Areum's cellphone, but it went into voicemail.

"Guys, I want the car behind us to go to Woo Jin's house. I don't think that he is stupid to take Areum to his home, but check it out anyway. Eddie, do you see the car anywhere?"

"No, Boss."

"Then go on the highway."

Eddie was one of Kang-de's friend from the States and he was also a former race car driver. Whenever Kang-de wanted to get somewhere quickly, he called Eddie because he knew where all the short cuts were in the city. Kang-de often used him as a bodyguard and driver.

While Kang-de drove down the highway looking for a black BMW, Areum and Woo Jin were in a white Mercedes Benz. He had parked it in the hospital underground garage.

"Areum, I am not going to harm you. I would never knowingly hurt you, so don't be afraid. I can see fear in your eyes."

"Why did you pull me into the car? What is happening, Woo Jin?"

"Kang-de has not told you?"

"Told me what? Are you two still fighting?" she asked in an annoyed tone.

"Fighting? I am not fighting with him, but he is fighting with me."

Areum looked at him with suspicion.

"Areum, he has done bad thing and there are people who want to hurt him."

"Are you one of those people who want to hurt him?"

He looked at her and nodded his head.

"Woo Jin! Why? Is it because of me?"

"It was, but not anymore. It is much bigger than you. I came to see you because I wanted to let you know that you need to leave Kang-de's side. I have no control over the people who want to harm him. It is out of my hands now."

"What are you saying, Woo Jin?"

"I am telling you that you are in danger if you stay with him."

"Woo Jin, would you really allow someone to hurt me?"

"Oh, Areum, are you not listening? I cannot stop them from hurting you. This is why I jeopardized my safety to come and tell you, in person, to take your father and leave Seoul for a while. Once everything is sorted out then you can return."

"I cannot leave him."

"Areum, because I still love you, I came here to tell you to leave Kang-de. Why are you being so stubborn? I could have forced you right now to leave him, but I love you too much to do that to you. Areum, I have to go now. Please leave the country. I am begging you."

She became frightened after listening to him and she pretended to agree with him. "Woo Jin, you look and sound different. What has happened to you since you went to Hong Kong? Where is that gorgeous, kind, sweet man that I once loved?"

"I am still here, but I have a great deal of responsibilities given to me and some of them are a matter of life or death. Anyway, I have to go before Kang-de figures out that we are still here. I will always love you, Doctor Lee. Don't ever forget that. Maybe one day we can get together and see each other without any problems. Get going," he said touching her face.

"Stay safe," she said smiling at him.

He looked at her for a long time before telling his driver to go.

Areum called Kang-de once Woo Jin car turned onto the main road.

"Kang-de, come back. Woo Jin never left the garage. He had me sitting in a white Mercedes Benz."

"Did he hurt you?"

"No. No. He came to warn me. Hurry back. We need to talk."

"Eddie, turn around. That bastard was at the hospital," he said punching in Bob's number into the phone.

Eddie Wai had arrived in Seoul one year earlier. He had given up his desire to race cars at events around the world. Instead, he left his glamorous life abroad to work for Kang-de. Eddie Wai became a driver and a bodyguard for Kang-de. He could catch up to anyone on the road. He was an extremely fast driver.

"Bob, Woo Jin was in the garage the entire time."

"I am on my way."

Bob hung up. He started down the sidewalk to the garage when he saw Areum coming up the ramp."

Ten minutes later Kang-de came running into the hospital. Areum saw him and ran to hug him.

"Oh, I was so scared that Woo Jin took you away from me."

"Kang-de, what is going on? Please tell me. Why does Woo Jin want to kill you?"

"Let's talk about it tomorrow. Right now I need you to find out about Chul."

Areum met the surgeon coming toward her and he informed her that Chul was in the recovery room and the bullet didn't damage his shoulder.

"When can he go home?" asked Areum.

"By the weekend," said the doctor.

Kang-de left Bob and several of Chul's men at the hospital. He took Areum to the ITO Hotel where they were still residing.

"Kang-de, please tell me everything."

"Where do I begin?"

Chapter Fifty-two

Woo Jin, Kang-de, and the Secret Organization

Woo Jin made it to the airport without any incident. He boarded his private jet without the five passengers. They remained in Seoul, awaiting their order to execute Kang-de.

He landed in Hong Kong late that evening and a van filled with five men drove him to an abandoned shack located under the freeway. The shack was covered by tall wild grass and it could only be seen by someone who knew of its existence.

There were seven men inside the shack when Woo Jin arrived. Three of them were blind-folded and tied to chairs. Woo Jin walked in and smiled at the four stocky men who took turn slapping the head and faces of the three hostages.

"You burned my house. You will tell me who ordered you to do that. Was it Shin Kang-de? Speak fast because I have no patience for people who refuses to confess."

"Sir, we don't know who ordered your home burn. We got a phone call to go to your home and extract a Mr. Kim. When he wasn't there we dialed a number and the voice told us to burn the house."

"Give me the number."

One of the men bowed his head and said that the cellphone was in his pocket. Woo Jin's security pulled it out, removed the blind-fold and had the man identified the number. Woo Jin made the man call the phone, but it went to voicemail.

Woo Jin kept the phone, nodded to the men and they untied the hostages, took them on the freeway and threw them off. He watched the men yell as they glided down to their deaths. Then he and his men left the scene and disappeared into the night fog.

The next morning Woo Jin called the number and someone answered.

"Your men are dead and you are next. I won't kill you if you tell me who ordered my home burned."

The phone disconnected and Woo Jin smiled.

"Take this phone to our friends in the telecommunication company. Find the owner of this phone. Quickly. I am going to eliminate all of Kang-de's friends one at a time," said Woo Jin with a cold tone in his voice.

Chapter Fifty-three

Kang-de, Areum, Bob, Eddie, the Voice, Woo Jin, and His Men

Areum sat on the couch facing the window with a mug in her hand. Kang-de pulled up a chair in front of her, looked into her eyes and said,

"Areum, I am going to tell you a story that will scare you, but I need you to be brave right now and listen. Many years ago my grandparents were assassinated while they slept in their beds. My uncle was also killed and my father was shot in the shoulder. He was the only survivor of our family. My father suffered many hardships while growing up. He had no real family. He was given the name Shin by the people who rescued him. The person responsible for that hardship is Mr. Kim, Woo Jin's father. He caused your parents and my parents to leave America and go into hiding. He killed my parents by staging a train derailment and he poisoned your mother."

"My mother? What does my mother have to do with any of this?"

"He killed her to keep your father quiet because your dad knows that he is a murderer. And he tried to kill you many times, but my men were watching you, even when you were at their home in Hong Kong. Areum, he sent Mr. Jong to kill me. I won't tell you anymore because I can see that you are frightened right now. I am sorry, Areum."

"Sorry for what?"

"I am sorry that my father got your family mixed up into this mess. Do you remember your father's objection to you going to Hong Kong? That's because they wanted to kill you there. I tried to stop Mr. Kim, but he survived, unfortunately."

"Oh, Kang-de. I am so sorry that I gave you and my dad so much trouble. But you should have told me earlier. I would never have gotten so close to Woo Jin."

"It's behind you now."

"Kang-de, be careful. Woo Jin wants to hurt you and he begged me to stay away from you."

"Maybe you should stay away. I don't want you in the middle of this war. And it has become a war."

"I told him and I am telling you. I am not leaving you."

Kang-de moved to the couch and he hugged her for a long time. "Areum, I would be devastated if something happened to you. I don't want to lose you. Maybe you should transfer to a hospital in America."

"No. I won't."

"Areum, I don't want to have to worry about you. They shot Chul and they are going to try to kill everyone close to me. Please think about it. Woo Jin now belongs to a secret organization that kills people without any penalty. He cannot be trusted. Don't ever go near him again."

"Okay," said Areum tightening her fingers around the mug. She thought about the nice Woo Jin who took care of her in the past. "How could he change like this?" she asked.

"I don't know, honey. He is surrounded by bad people. He might not have any control over them."

The weekend was uneventful and Chul was released from hospital with two male nurses assigned to him. Kang-de insisted that Chul stay at the ITO Hotel to recuperate from his wound. Chul agreed.

Early Monday morning, Kang-de's cellphone rang. It was a member of the fire department in Gangnam. His new store was burning and the blaze could be seen a mile away. The heat and the toxic air from the fire prevented the firemen from getting close to the store to contain the fire until it was too late.

"Where are my employees? Are there any of them trapped in the store?" he asked calmly.

"Sir, no one was inside the store," said the fire chief.

"I will be there soon."

Thinking that it could be a trap, Kang-de took five of his best bodyguards, including Eddie and Bob and they drove to Gangnam.

"Bob, you know that this is Woo Jin's doing, right?"

"Yeah, Boss. I was just thinking the same thing."

"Okay...."

Kang-de's telephone rang before he could finish his response to Bob. It was a familiar voice from Hong Kong.

"Boss, last night some of your men were killed by Mr. Kim's men. I think that they are looking for the rest of us."

"You know what to do. And when you are finished lose this phone and get a new number. Call me as soon as you get a new phone and be careful."

The SUV slowed down when it arrived near the scene. Fire trucks had blocked the street, preventing access to the fire. Kang-de looked at his burned store through the car window and said:

"Bob, I am going to Hong Kong. It's time to take this fight to the enemy."

Kang-de, Bob and Eddie walked down the blocked street and stared at the charred building.

"How many men should we take with us?" asked Bob, looking around.

"Only five of our best men. My friends in Hong Kong are many."

"When do we leave?" asked Bob.

"Friday. I want to get everything organized before we leave. I want security in all my hotels to be on high alert. Areum needs at least one female bodyguard. I will let her know who she is. Mr. Lee has enough security with him. All the clubs and the other computer stores must now have security on high alert. Woo Jin must not succeed in destroying my father's dream."

"Consider it taken care of, Boss."

Kang-de glanced across the street to look at the other buildings. Suddenly he noticed two men hurrying into a black sedan.

"Eddie, Bob, come with me."

The men ran across the road, but the car sped off through the crowd that stood looking at the destruction.

"Eddie, can you catch that car?" asked Kang-de running to the SUV that was parked a block away.

"Yeah," Eddie said feeling offended.

Kang-de had forgotten that he was once a professional race car driver who won many races.

Eddie sped down the road, turning left onto the adjacent street. He glided between cars until he spotted the black sedan. He pulled up beside it and turned the SUV into the driver's side, hitting the sedan with force. The sedan turned over onto its side. The two men tried to escape, limping with their damage legs. Bob and Eddie jumped out of the SUV and grabbed them by their necks. They tried to fight, but they were no match for Kang-de's men.

"Come here, you two. My boss wants to see you," said Bob.

The men were taken to Kang-de who was sitting quietly in the SUV.

"You have exactly three minutes to tell me where your boss is located. If you make me wait more than three minutes, then I will dump you in that river over there," said Kang-de in a very serious tone.

Bob and Eddie took turn punching on the men who were already in pain.

"I am waiting," said Kang-de looking at his watch.

Two minutes had passed and Kang-de told Eddie to drive the SUV under the bridge that stood above the river. The SUV pulled up near a marsh area and Bob and Eddie pulled the two men from the van. Kang-de walked up to them took out a long knife and raised his hand to stab one of the man.

Suddenly, the man shouted, "We got the order from the chairman. He travelled with us to Seoul. We don't know his name. We just know him as chairman."

Bob looked at Kang-de and said, "It has to be Woo Jin."

Kang-de looked at the two men and asked, "What were your instructions?"

"The chairman told four of us to go to ITO Hotel and pretend to check in. Then he told the two of us to burn all your computer stores. We started with the newest one and we were heading to another when you caught us."

"Tell me, what are the four men's orders?"

"They were instructed to take hostages in your hotels. In return, the hostages would be exchanged for you."

Kang-de looked at Eddie and Bob, then he dialed a number in his cellphone. "Mr. Moon, tell all your security team to get ready for a possible hostage incident. Tell the security at the other hotel to do the same."

Kang-de called his security team to be on the lookout for suspicious men walking into the lobby.

"And be on the lookout for four men who may enter the hotel together. Have some of the men walk around the lobby in plain clothes. I need to know what's going on inside my building. If anyone tries to invade the hotel, then hurt them before they get to the elevators."

"Got it, Boss."

"Where is your chairman? Is he waiting for you to return with him to Hong Kong?"

"Yes. We are supposed to meet him by the shipping yard, but he didn't tell us when. He said that he would contact us."

"Bob, take these two and lock them in the warehouse until this war is over. It will be over soon and I will come back to deal with the two of you," Kang-de said staring at the two men.

Kang-de stopped at the hospital to see Areum. He wanted to say goodbye to her. She saw him walking down the hospital hallway and she walked quickly toward him.

"Hi, what are you doing here? Did something happen?" she asked.

"No, not yet. Areum, I am going away for a few days. Should something happen to me, I want you to open the safe and read the instructions that I left inside. The combination is the year of your birth combined with mine," he said looking at her.

"Kang-de, please come back to me alive. You are going to kill Woo Jin, aren't you? Kang-de, please don't kill him."

"Areum, if he tries to kill me, then I will kill him. His father must die. That is not negotiable," said Kang-de looking at her.

"Be careful, honey. Do you really have to go away? Can't you just forget about Mr. Kim and Woo Jin?"

"No. Did you not hear me say that he killed my entire family and they poisoned your mother? What don't you understand? I am getting revenge on those bastards who have no conscience or remorse."

"Revenge only brings pain. Yes, they killed my mother and that is unforgivable, and I can't bring my mother back. But, I do not want to lose you. I cannot lose you, Kang-de. We do not have anyone but you. Please don't put yourself in harm's way. I am begging you."

"I promise that I won't put myself in harm's way."

Areum hugged him, kissed him for a few minutes and then watched him walk away until he disappeared out the hospital door.

Chapter Fifty-four

The Confrontation

Early in the morning, a private jet landed on a remote air strip in Hong Kong. Kang-de, Bob, Eddie and five assassins exited the small plane with black backpacks over their shoulders. Three black SUVs were waiting to take them to a secret location.

"Hello, my friend," said Kang-de to his driver. "Do you have everything ready for me?"

"Yes, Sir," said the driver walking to the trunk of the first SUV.

He opened the trunk and he unzipped four duffle bags that were filled with knives, rope darts, explosives and night vision goggles. He walked to the next SUV and opened that trunk which had two suitcases filled with guns. Kang-de tapped the driver on the shoulder, looked at him and smiled.

"Good job. It looks like we are ready for the unexpected. Do you have the map of Mr. Kim's secret location?"

"Yes, Sir," he said handing the map to Kang-de.

Bob moved in closer to Kang-de so that he could look at the map. "How do we get inside the compound?" asked Bob.

"We blast our way in," replied the driver smiling at Bob.

"No, no. This is a war and I like to surprise the enemy. I want to corner that bastard in his wheelchair. I don't want him to escape. He's a slippery little bastard."

"Okay, Sir. We will hit them tonight, but we must go now."

"By now the authorities are aware that a jetliner landed here," said Bob. "Let's go and get ourselves prepared. I expect Woo Jin to be there setting a trap for us, but we will be ready for him."

The night came quickly and it was dark and gloomy. The clouds covered the moon and the location had limited lights. Five vehicles and a garbage truck parked at the bottom of the hill. Two of the vehicles blocked the road to prevent anyone coming up or down the hill. Seventeen men walked up the hill until they reached a large mansion with a black iron gate.

"Are you sure that this is the place?" asked Kang-de whispering.

"Yes, I am sure," said his driver.

"There are no guards. I think that they are expecting us."

Kang-de signaled to five of his men to scale the wall. The men had no problem scaling the wall with their backpack filled with weapons. They noticed, through their night vision goggles, that the entrance to the house was accessible by walking up ten circular stairs that were attached to a veranda. The veranda had white walls, supported by marble columns and several men with weapons paced back and forth with guns in their hands.

Kang-de's men, who were all dressed in black, ran toward the stairs. Suddenly, dogs began to bark and flood lights were switched on around the house. A massive gunfire erupted from the veranda and Kang-de's men returned fire. Two of his men shot out the flood lights, which allowed Kang-de's men the ability to advance to the veranda without being seen. Four more men scaled the wall and they threw knives toward the direction where the gunfire were coming from. Three of Woo Jin's men were hit by knives, but gunfire continued to flow from the veranda.

Meanwhile, the garbage truck sped up the hill, turned and crashed through the gate. It absorbed lots of bullets, before coming to a stopat the circular stairs. The driver escaped before the truck crashed into the stairs. Six of Kang-de's men, who rode on the back of the truck, jumped off and ran to the side of the veranda wall. They crawled up the wall without being noticed by Woo Jin's men.

They threw knives to disarm the rest of Woo Jin's men who were on the Veranda. An SUV, filled with three men, drove through the gate. They got out of the SUV and ran up the stairs with automatic weapons in their hands.

They entered Woo Jin's home returning fire at anyone who shoot at them. Kang-de, Bob, Eddie and his five assassins walked slowly behind his men, armed with grenades and assault rifles.

They moved deliberately through each room, looking for Mr. Kim. They approached a room that was locked. Bob blasted the door lock, kicked it opened and quickly moved away. Immediately, gunfire came from the room. Kang-de, Bob, Eddie and three of his men opened fire into the room. The gun battle lasted for a few minutes. Kang-de signaled Eddie to throw a grenade into the room and they all dropped to the ground before it exploded. The blast blew a hole in the back wall exposing a small tunnel.

Bob waited for a few minutes then he crawled into the room. "Boss, come and look at this."

Kang-de walked into the room and saw a familiar face. It was the dead body of his security guard Yang. Kang-de had suspected him to be a traitor, but Chul had cleared him from suspicion.

"I knew that this bastard was working for Mr. Kim. Where is Mr. Kim?" asked Kang-de. Eddie pointed to the opening in the wall. "Boss, look at that. I think someone has escaped though there."

"Boys, some of you go outside and surround the house. I think Mr. Kim is trying to escape. Be careful, he has company with him," yelled Kang-de running into the exposed tunnel.

Bob, Eddie and his assassins ran in behind Kang-de with guns drawn.

The faint sound of a wheelchair could be heard when they got farther into the tunnel. Eddie ran ahead of Kang-de, Bob, and the assassins with a gun in his hand.

Bob ran to catch him and he heard a single gunshot that echoed through the passageway. He stopped and yelled, "Eddie, are you okay?"

He got no answer.

Kang-de yelled, "Edward, are you okay?"

He ran ahead of Bob when he saw the silhouette of a body lying on the concrete. It was Eddie. He had been shot in the chest and he was dead.

"Eddie," yelled Kang-de, grabbing his head from the concrete floor.

"Eddie," said Bob looking down at him.

"Open your eyes, Eddie," said Kang-de shaking him. "Oh, Eddie, Eddie, Eddie, I am so sorry."

"Boss, he is dead," said Bob.

"Stay here with him. Don't leave him alone. I will be back."

Kang-de grabbed his gun and walked rapidly down the tunnel. He listened for the sound of the wheelchair and he could hear it on his right. Kang-de slowly leaned his head around the bend and he saw Mr. Kim with three men. They were trying to gain access to an iron gate that was blocked on the other side by Kang-de's men.

One of the men saw Kang-de and fired at him. Kang-de returned fire killing one and wounding another. He walked up to Mr. Kim and his bodyguard, not realizing that Woo Jin was watching him from a large dark opening in the rock.

"Drop your gun and run away from this bastard, unless you want to die with him. Nobody should die for this bastard," said Kang-de.

The bodyguard quickly dropped his gun and hurriedly disappeared into the dark.

"Well, well, well, you son of a bitch, I have been waiting to meet you ever since I found out that you killed my family. I regret that the accident didn't kill you. You should have died, you evil bastard. Why did you kill them? Why did you kill my innocent parents and grandparents?" yelled Kang-de.

Mr. Kim smiled then said, "Your grandfather was a traitor. He was my best friend and we started this organization together. He took an oath to defend and protect the organization at all cost and he violated that oath by betraying me. He had me arrested and sent to prison. I had to sell my soul to escape and I vowed to kill everyone who betrayed me."

"You evil bastard. Why did you kill my father and mother? They had nothing to do with you."

"It was nothing personal. Your father found out what his father did to me and he promised to provide important information to the organization, but he too betrayed me. He exposed the organization and they agreed to killed him."

"No, you killed him. You bastard," said Kang-de slapping Mr. Kim across the face. "It is and was personal. You took my family away from me because of a stupid organization. How can you say it's not personal? You killed my mother and Areum's mother. Why?"

"They were casualties," said Mr. Kim reaching under the blanket that covered his legs.

Kang-de glanced at his hand going under his blanket and he shot Mr. Kim in his legs. His scream echoed throughout the tunnel.

"If you try any more tricks, then I will shoot you right now," he said, pulling out a gun from under Mr. Kim's blanket.

Bob heard the shots and ran toward the sound.

"You came to kill me so get on with it."

Kang-de raised his gun to shoot Mr. Kim, when suddenly a voice said, "Drop your gun, Kang-de, or I will shoot you right now." He dropped his hand to his side, but he continued to hold the gun. Kang-de turned around and looked at him smiling.

"Woo Jin, I have been expecting you. I am sure that you heard your father confess to murdering my family, so do you want to become a killer like him? Oh, I forgot, you've already become a killer and an arsonist."

"Kang-de," yelled Woo Jin. "I will kill you. I should have killed you a long time ago. Drop the damn gun. Now!"

Kang-de used his left hand to throw the gun to the side, but neither Mr. Kim, Kang-de or Woo Jin noticed that Bob had hid himself against the dark stones. He thought about which Kim he would kill first and he decided that Mr. Kim had to die first.

"You fool, you walked into my trap. How is your migraine headache? It should be getting worse," said Mr. Kim with a smile on his face. "You came to kill me, but you will be dead soon," he said laughing at Kang-de. "Kill him, Woo Jin. Kill him," said Mr. Kim whimpering and holding his bleeding leg. "This little shit shot me."

Woo Jin raised his hand to shoot Kang-de and Bob fired a shot into Mr. Kim's chest killing him instantly. Before Woo Jin could process what had happened to his father, Bob shot him in the back. Woo Jin fell forward in front of his father's wheelchair. Bob looked at Woo Jin and noticed that he was still breathing.

"Boss, he's still breathing," said Bob aiming his gun to finish off Woo Jin.

"Leave him. We have to get out of here."

They ran to the locked gate and banged on it. The gate opened and the men rushed in, looking at Mr. Kim and Woo Jin.

"Boys, go and get Eddie's body. It's around the corner."

Four of them ran to retrieve Eddie's body. They took him outside and placed him in the SUV slowly as if to show their respect to a fallen comrade.

"Bob, I promised Areum that I would not kill him, unless he tried to kill me first."

One of Kang-de's Hong Kong bodyguards dialed the police and told them that there were sounds of gunfire at a residence. He gave them the address and he hung up the phone, while running to one of the SUV that was parked in front of the house.

The SUVs sped away from the Kims' home in a hurry. They stopped about two miles away at the private airstrip where the jetliner was waiting for them. The engine was running as Kang-de said goodbye to his Hong Kong friends.

"My friends, I am sorry for getting you into this dilemma. I am sorry that you lost some of your men. I owe you my life. I am deeply grateful to you all. Thank you."

"Shin Kang-de, you are our family. Family help each other. Take care of yourself."

He shook hands with the men while watching Eddie's body being taken into the plane.

"Boss, let's go," said Bob smiling and waving at the Hong Kong security team.

Kang-de, and his five assassins, entered the jet. The jetliner took off with speed. Forty-five minutes later they were in international air space and Bob sighed a sign of relief.

The journey was solemn because Eddie had died and others lost their lives in the battle with Mr. Kim. Kang-de was in deep thought while Bob and the men poured champagne and passed it between them.

It was past midnight when the jetliner landed and the security took Eddie's body to an awaiting SUV. Kang-de stepped off the jet behind them and he heard a voice yelling out his name. Chul was there to greet him and his security team who had gone with Kang-de.

"Chul, are you okay?" asked Kang-de in a sad tone.

"Yes, Boss. Are you okay?"

"No, I am not okay. Eddie and some of my men from Hong Kong are dead. Eddie followed me to Seoul. Now, I wished that he had not done that. He should have stayed in New York," said Kang-de with tears in his eyes.

"Boss, any one of us would gladly die for you. You are more than a boss to us. You are our brother. I am sure that he had no regrets about working for you," said Chul tapping Kang-de on his shoulder.

Kang-de nodded and walked with him to the car that was waiting to take him to the ITO Hotel. Bob ran to join them. He got into the front seat and the car sped away onto the main airport road.

"Chul, Mr. Kim is dead and I shot Woo Jin in the back. He might not survive, but Boss gave him a chance by calling an ambulance," said Bob. "Boss, I think that you should have let me kill him."

Kang-de looked at him and shrugged his shoulder. "Areum would never forgive me if I had killed him."

It took two hours to get to the ITO Hotel, Kang-de entered his suite with a depressing look on his face. Suddenly, Areum ran out of the bedroom and greeted him with a kiss on the cheek.

"How did it go? Did you do what I think you did?" she asked.

"Let's not talk about my trip. I want to rest. My head hurts badly."

"Did you see Woo Jin? Is he still alive?"

"Areum, I am tired. Please leave me for a while. And yes, the last time I saw Woo Jin he was still alive," he said walking slowly into his bedroom.

She looked at him and sighed. She knew that he was feeling remorse for whatever he had done.

Kang-de slept until the next afternoon. He woke up with a migraine headache and the medicine he took were ineffective. He called Bob to come and see him. It took Bob a few seconds to get upstairs.

"Boss, what is wrong?"

"Bob, my headache is back and it's so bad that it hurts my eyes. Mr. Kim asked me how was my migraine. Do you think that he had someone like Yang poison me? Take me to a hospital, but don't call Areum. I don't want to worry her unnecessarily."

Bob nodded and escorted Kang-de downstairs to an awaiting car. They arrived at the hospital and a doctor admitted him to a private room. A nurse gave him medicine for his headache. He lay on the bed thinking about what Mr. Kim said to him. He thought about Yang and his betrayal.

Suddenly, Bob walked into his room. "Boss, Areum is working on the third floor today."

"Good. I don't want to alert her until I get a CT scan," he said staring at Bob. His phone rang and he handed it to Bob.

"Hello. Yes. Yes. Are you absolutely sure?" asked Bob with a shocking look on his face.

"Bob, what is wrong?"

"That was your friend in Hong Kong. He said that his source in the police department told him that when they arrived in the tunnel, they saw Mr. Kim, but Woo Jin's body was not there. There was a little amount of blood, but they didn't find him in the house or the tunnel."

"That son of a bitch must have worn a bulletproof vest." Kang-de shrugged and replied, "Bob, don't worry. I am glad that he is alive. We will meet him in Seoul next time. He will come to see me and if I am not dead, as is father predicts, then I will be happy to greet him with a bullet."

The wait to get a CT scan was long because it was very early in the morning and the hospital staff were busy attending to many patients. An hour after being admitted to the hospital, Kang-de went in for the CT scan. A doctor returned two hours later to advise him that his migraine is a result of his previous brain injury and he will always get a migraine headache when he exerts himself.

"So are you saying that I don't have a tumor on my brain?"

"No, you do not, but if you continue to stress yourself you will get a stroke. Please live a stress-free life, Mr. Shin," replied the doctor.

"Oh, it will be difficult, but I will do my best, Doctor."

"Boss, this is the best news we have heard in a long time. Let's celebrate with a bottle of water and some of your pills," said Bob laughing.

Chapter Fifty-five

Woo Jin, Kang-de, Bob, Chul, and Areum

A year and two months had passed since the incident in Hong Kong and Areum and Kang-de planned to marry next Saturday. His life with Areum was calm and uneventful. His computer businesses thrived and his clubs made lots of money. He opened a third hotel and he placed Areum and Mr. Lee's names on the deed with his. It was a happy time for them.

Bob had permanently moved into the ITO Hotel. He occupied one of the suites on the twenty-second floor and he had been dating one of Areum's female bodyguards for a year.

Chul recovered and moved his office to a secured building that could only be accessible after passing through three security check points. Roger Goo had retired and he moved to a retirement community under an assumed name in Florida.

The wedding ceremony was scheduled to begin at 12 noon on a sunny Saturday afternoon at the Golf Club. Kang-de, Chul and Bob arrived at the church early in the morning to perform security checks, before the two hundred guests arrived. The Club was built on one acres of land. It was surrounded by a beautiful green golf course. Guards were posted at each entrance of the Club and security drove around in golf carts. The Club was closed for the day as a favor to Kang-de by the owner. Identifications were checked at the entrance and each guests was given a bracelet that would reflect once the lights were turned off.

Kang-de's security teams were dressed in black tuxedo with green ties and white shirts. He wanted them to be identifiable should something happen.

Meanwhile at the Seoul airport five men arrived from Hong Kong and they exited the airport quickly. There were two SUV's parked in front of the arrival level with their engine running. Woo Jin got into the first SUV and it drove away with speed.

"Where is the venue and how many security do you estimate will be there?"

"Sir, about a hundred men in total and they are at a Golf Club in Gangnam," the security replied.

"Did anyone notice you?"

"No, Sir. They were too busy searching everything."

"Good. Let them keep searching. We are not going near there. Are you prepared to grab the target?"

"Yes, Sir. We are ready."

"Well, then, let's go and get what I came for and get back on the plane."

The minister arrived and Kang-de greeted him dressed in a white raw silk trimmed tuxedo suit with white shirt and white tie. Bob and Chul, his best men, were dressed in dark grey suits with white shirt and silver ties. All the guests were instructed, by Kang-de, to wear something white to symbolize the purity of his love for Areum.

As the guests began to arrive Kang-de became concerned that Areum had not called him to let him know that she was on her way. He pulled out his phone and he called her. "Where are you? Are you ready to become Mrs. Shin Kang-de?"

"Yes, I have been ready for a long time to become your wife. I love you and I promise to take good care of you. I cannot wait for our wedding night. Are you ready to be tied down?"

"Areum, you are my ONE LOVE. You are not tying me down. You are taking me on a journey of happiness. Living with you this past year has been a joy. I don't know what I would do without you. I love you, Lee Areum. Always remember that my heart belongs to you and only you."

"I love you, Shin Kang-de, and I am sending kisses through the phone. I will be there soon. I will see you later, honey."

"I am waiting for you. Hurry up."

Areum walked out of the elevator dressed in a white satin, formed-fitted wedding dress. She wore a pair of teardrop earrings and an elegant diamond bracelet decorated her right hand.

Mr. Lee, who was dressed in a black tuxedo with white shirt and black tie, escorted Areum to the awaiting limousine that was parked in front of the ITO Hotel. Mr. Lee and Areum sat together in the rear of the limousine and two of Areum's guards sat opposite them.

The limousine driver and a stranger were dressed as part of Kang-de's security team. The limousine drove a mile away from ITO Hotel when the stranger pulled out a gun and pointed it at Areum's two security guards.

"Remove your guns slowly and throw them out the window."

Surprised by the unexpected gunman's appearance, the guards threw their guns out the window and pondered what their next action should be.

Mr. Lee grabbed Areum's hand and yelled, "Who are you? Why are you doing this?"

The stranger removed his glasses, mustache and hat.

Areum's eyes open widely and Mr. Lee yelled, "Kim Woo Jin, what are you doing here and why are you pointing a gun at us?"

"Stop the car," Woo Jin said. "Everyone except Areum get out, and you two don't make any funny moves, if you want to live."

"I am not leaving my daughter in this car with you. I am staying here."

"Sir, I have no desire to harm you and I am certainly not going to harm Areum. I love her."

"Love! Did you say love? How can you say that you love me while you are pointing a gun at me and my father? Who are you? You are not the kind, gentle Woo Jin that I know."

"Areum, I have no desire to hurt you or your father. Please believe me. But if your father stays with you then my men might hurt him without my permission. Please, Mr. Lee, I promise not to hurt her. I just want to speak with her somewhere without any external interference."

Areum looked at Mr. Lee and nodded to her father to leave.

"No, no, no. I am not leaving you. Woo Jin, I will take my chance with your men. I am not leaving my daughter. If you wanted to speak with her, then you could have called her."

"Okay, this is your decision. I did warn you that I cannot control what might happen to you."

The limousine drove away with Areum and Mr. Lee holding hands. Her eyes had tears in them and Mr. Lee held her close to him. Woo Jin noticed that she was crying and he turned his head away.

"Areum, are you afraid of me? I am not like my father. I never wanted to harm anyone, but Kang-de killed my father and he has to pay for his sins."

"Yes, you are like your father," Mr. Lee said.

Woo Jin ignored his comment.

"Areum, you're Kang-de's weakness and I am very sorry, but he won't come to me unless you are with me."

"What are you talking about, Woo Jin? Your father murdered many people. He murdered Kang-de's entire family. He killed my wife, Areum's mother, and you sit there and tell me that you want to revenge your father's death. What planet do you live on? He should have died in a prison cell many years ago. Do you think that your father would not have killed you if it meant saving his precious secret organization?" asked Mr. Lee.

"Mr. Lee, I don't want to discuss my father's past. Kang-de didn't have to kill him. And he didn't have to put a bullet in my back."

Areum looked at him with disbelief.

"Oh, yes, Areum. He shot me in the back and left me to die."

"That's a lie. Bob shot you because you were pointing a gun at Kang-de. You tried to kill him and Bob defended him."

"I don't care who shot me. Kang-de's employee shot me. Therefore, he indirectly shot me in the back."

After driving for an hour, the limousine pulled into an abandoned warehouse that was located a mile from the airport. The driver, Seung-jae, stepped out of the limousine, opened the back door and forcefully dragged Mr. Lee out and threw him on the ground.

"No!" screamed Areum while watching her father falling to the ground. "Woo Jin, tell him not to hurt him, please, please."

Woo Jin looked at Seung-jae and nodded. Suddenly, he stepped away from Mr. Lee and closed the door, leaving Areum alone in the back seat.

The limousine sped away from the warehouse and onto an unpaved airport road, leaving a trail of dust behind it. Areum looked out the back window and saw her father running after the car, but he couldn't keep up with the speeding limousine.

"Woo Jin, stop the car and let me out now," she said yelling at him.

He looked at her and smiled. She tried to open the doors, but they were locked. "Why are you doing this to me?" she cried out loudly.

"I said that I wanted to speak with you without external interference and I meant it. I told you when I left Seoul that it was not the end of us. I meant that too."

Tears flowed down Areum's face and she screamed out, "Woo Jin, stop the car."

The driver continued driving until he pulled up to a jet liner.

"Don't worry, Areum, I am not going to fly away with you. It's just easier to talk to you on my plane."

The driver, Seung-jae, pulled her out of the limousine while she kicked at him.

"Behave yourself. Don't let me hurt you," he said looking at Woo Jin's facial expression.

Woo Jin was unaware that Seung-jae was an assassin hired by his father to kill Kang-de and Areum at any cost.

Areum pulled away from him and walked up the stairs into the jet. Woo Jin followed behind her. Seung-jae and two stocky men, who were waiting by the jet, entered the plane and closed the door.

Areum stood up in the jet and Woo Jin went into a closet, pulled out a bag and handed it to her. She refused to accept the bag from him.

"Let me out now. I want to go home."

"Areum, I told you that I wanted to talk to you. Please take the bag and go and get changed into something more comfortable."

"So you had this planned for a while now? You have clothes for me to change. Why are you doing this? Why are you doing this to me and my family? You said that you loved me. You made love to me. How can you love me and treat me like this?" she asked.

"Please go and change and I will explain everything to you. Please," he said, handing her the bag.

She grabbed it from him and went into the bathroom to change into jeans and sweater.

Areum was too frightened and angry to notice the beauty of Woo Jin's jetliner. She sat on one of the four beige leather chairs that was located at the front of the plane. A bar and two long couches were located in the rear of the plane. A Persian carpet covered the floor of the jet liner and an oak wood closet stood next to one of the couches. Antique lamps were attached to windows wherever tables were located.

Areum sat down in the chair and Woo Jin sat across from her, staring at her with sadness on his face.

"Okay, what did you want to speak with me about?" she asked.

"Do you remember my fight with Kang-de on the night of Bora's engagement party? That fight was because of you. And you did not let me explain why Sun-hee came to my apartment and how she ended up being pregnant."

"I am not interested in hearing about that now."

"Well, I want you to understand what really happened. If you had listened to me when I tried to explain to you the circumstances, then we would not have ended up in this tragedy. After the fight, I felt so humiliated and ashamed because you watched Kang-de beat me up. I had never lost a fight before. And I rarely get into fights with anyone. I wanted to hide myself from everyone, especially you. I couldn't accept your help that night. It was a humiliating scene for me. Sun-hee came over that night and she attended to my wounds. I really didn't want to see her again because I had told her that we were finished as friends."

"Woo Jin, I don't need to hear this. It's in the past."

"Yes, you do need to hear it," he said yelling. "She seduced me during the weakest moment in my life. Had it been the day before the fight, I would have thrown her out of my apartment. But it happened. I believe that she deliberately got pregnant that night."

"I know that already," Areum said.

"What! You knew and you said nothing to me? Why? And why did you sleep with Kang-de? You hurt me so badly by doing that. I am still hurt by your actions."

"You want to know why everything went crazy? It was your disrespectful behavior toward me. You humiliated me in front of others. You looked down upon me."

"No, I did not."

"Yes, you did. And you never needed me, Woo Jin. Kang-de did and still does because your murdering father destroyed his life."

"Areum, please don't say that about my father. I don't know that person who you are talking about. I only know my loving dad. I had no idea about this secret organization until he made me chairman," he said in a sincere tone.

"You should have said no thanks."

"How could I, when I found out, that same day, that my company is controlled by the secret organization? I am sorry about everything. I am deeply sorry about your mother. I still can't believe that my father was involved in the death of your mother and Kang-de's family. I am sorry, Areum, but it is Kang-de who has made me into this monster that you feel that I have become. He took my life from me. You were and still are my ONE LOVE."

"Well, your actions today tell me differently."

"Oh, Areum, don't you understand? A choice was made for me the day I went for the interview in Brunei. I had no choice about how I would live, but, I was allowed to ask for one favor from my father. That favor was to marry you," Woo Jin said with tears in his eyes. "He agreed, at least that is what he told me."

Before Areum could respond, Seung Jae interrupted and said, "Mr. Chairman, a phone call for you."

Woo Jin took the phone, looked at Areum and walked to the back of the plane. Meanwhile, Seung Jae stood by Areum's chair with his arms folded and his face staring at Woo Jin.

Chapter Fifty-six

Kang-de, Woo Jin, Areum, Bob, Eddie, and Chul

Kang-de's cell phone rang while he stood outside the church waiting for Areum.

"Hello, where are you? What?" he shouted signaling to Bob and Chul."Guys, Woo Jin is definitely alive and he is on his way here."

"What?" said Bob and Chul simultaneously.

"One of my Hong Kong friends said that he got information that Woo Jin boarded a plane headed to Seoul."

"Boss, I told you that I should have shot him again," Bob said in frustration.

Chul's phone rang and his security guards informed him that Areum and Mr. Lee were kidnapped.

"What? How could you let that happen? Don't you know how to protect a client? That's the boss's wife-to-be. How could you let that crazy man take her away?" he shouted, while running to his Mercedes Benz.

"Chul, what is happening? Is it about Areum?"

"Yes, Boss. Woo Jin kidnapped her."

Kang-de's cell rang simultaneously and Mr. Lee shouted, "That Woo Jin character has my daughter! Come and get me, please! His driver threw me out of the car and they took off with her. Oh, no, no, no, please come and get me," said Mr. Lee agitated.

"I am on my way, Mr. Lee. Where are you?" he asked walking calmly into the church to tell the minister that he had to delay the service because the bride was not feeling well.

The minister nodded his head and he announced to the crowd that the wedding was postponed until further notice.

Areum's bodyguards were picked up by four of Chul's men and they met Mr. Lee at a warehouse located outside of the Airport. Ten minutes later, Kang-de, Chul and Bob pulled into the warehouse and they ran to Mr. Lee.

"Are you okay, Mr. Lee?" asked Kang-de using his eyes to observe him.

"Which way did they go, Mr. Lee, and did you get the license plate's number?" asked Bob.

"I am sorry, Bob. I did not. The dust from the limousine made it difficult for me to see anything."

"I saw the license plate," said Areum's female bodyguard looking down at the ground. "I am sorry, Boss," she said dropping to the ground in front of Kang-de. "Get up. We have work to do."

"Give me the license plate's number," said Chul writing it down as she recited it to him. Immediately, he called someone to trace the limousine plates.

"Chul, I don't think that the license plate will come back legitimate. Woo Jin wants to play cat and mouse. I think that he wants me to chase him for a while. Then he will call me to let me know where he is. Let's go home and wait for his call."

"Please, Kang-de, I don't want to wait for him to call me. I want to find my daughter now," said Mr. Lee.

"It is okay, Sir. He will call me. We have no idea where he could be. He knows that I know the address of all his real estate properties, so he won't take her to any of them. Let's go home and wait for him to call. We are not going to chase after him. I do not think that he will harm Areum. He loves her."

"That's what he kept saying to me and Areum. He insisted that he would not harm her," said Mr. Lee in a worried tone.

"He would not harm her, but I don't know about the people who surround him," said Kang-de. "They concern me."

The next three hours in Kang-de's suite were solemn. Kang-de paced back and forth looking at his cell. Mr. Lee stared at him, hoping that Kang-de's phone would ring. He waited and waited.

Bob and Chul sat on the couch staring at each other and glancing at Kang-de's movements.

An hour later, Chul got a phone call. "Hello, what information do you have for me?" he asked. "You found it where? Okay, we are on our way. Boss, we found the limousine and it's parked on a service road by an airport hangar."

"Okay, gather the men. Let's go and find Areum."

Kang-de entered Bob's car without noticing that Bob's car trunk was partially opened. Chul rode with Mr. Lee and one of his security members. Two cars and four SUVs filled with men followed behind Bob's car as it entered the highway that took them toward the airport.

"Bob, I am feeling very uneasy. I have felt this way since yesterday. I knew that something bad was going to happen. And it has. What if they kill Areum?" Kang-de asked.

"Boss, don't worry. We will bring her home safely."

Kang-de nodded in silent agreement.

A few minutes later, the phone in his pocket rang and he pulled it out and answered. "Hello, this is Shin Kang-de. Where is Areum?"

Woo Jin, who was alarmed by his statement, said, "How did you know that it was me? I called you from a private line."

"Cut out the bullshit, Woo Jin. Where are you and where is Areum? She has nothing to do with this fight between you and me. Let her go home to her father."

"Shut up. You don't get to dictate to me. You killed my father and you have to accept the consequences."

"Fine. Let Areum go and I will stay with you. You want me to pay with my life? No problem, but I am asking you not to get her involved in this matter. You love her? Don't you?" Kang-de asked.

"I am on a jet plane at the end of west cargo road and I want you to come alone. If my men sees you with anyone, then I am flying out of here with Areum. And you will never see her again."

"Okay," said Kang-de looking at Bob.

The phone disconnected once he agreed to Woo Jin's terms.

"Boss, he wants you to come alone, right? His men are going to kill you. I can't let that happen. My father told me to protect you at all cost. I cannot let you go alone. Where is he hiding?"

"Bob, pull over. It's okay. I have four knives on me. I intend to defend myself. Tell the guards to remain with you and Chul at the end of the road. He is on a jet plane about three kilometers from here. I am going up there alone."

"Boss. Please."

"Bob. If I don't come out of there alive, look into the office safe and follow the instructions that I left in there. The combination is in an envelope taped underneath the table." Kang-de tapped Bob on his shoulder and Bob bowed and said, "If you die tonight, then so will Woo Jin and his entire security team. That's a promise."

Chul and Mr. Lee ran up to Bob's car when they saw that it had pulled over and Kang-de was walking to the driver's side.

"Boss, what are you doing?" asked Chul.

"I am going to see Woo Jin alone."

"You cannot go to meet Woo Jin and his men by yourself."

"Chul, I have to. He wants to exchange Areum for me. That's his plan and if he sees any of you, then he will fly away with Areum."

"My son, it's a trap and you are walking into it. Be careful. Please," said Mr. Lee hugging Kang-de.

Unknown to Kang-de one of Chul's best shooters had hidden in Bob's car trunk before it left the hotel. Kang-de smiled at the three men and he entered the car and drove north on the cargo road toward the jet.

"Chul, have your men get a heavy transport truck. Steal one if you have to. We have to stop that plane from taking off."

"Sure, Bob," he said walking quickly to the cars to instruct his men. "Mr. Lee, don't worry, I have every intention of stopping that plane and I want to kill that son of a bitch Woo Jin so badly, but the Boss keeps letting him live. I know that he's concerned about Areum's feelings, but I feel that there must be a reason why he hasn't killed him. The Kang-de of old days would have killed him a long time ago."

"I think that he feels compassion for Woo Jin. He realizes that Woo Jin has a soft side to him and he doesn't want to take his life," said Mr. Lee.

"He is not the same Woo Jin who lived in Seoul. He has totally changed and I am going to kill him if he harms Kang-de or your daughter."

Mr. Lee nodded and went to sit in Chul's SUV.

Chapter Fifty-seven

Kang-de, Woo Jin, Areum, Bob, and Chul and His Men

It took Kang-de a few minutes to arrive at the jetliner that was parked adjacent to a hangar. He pulled up and parked behind the tail of the jet. He noticed that it's engine was running and the fumes that were expelled from the engine were suffocating his nostrils. Kang-de got out of the car and walked, up the steps, to the plane door. He knocked on it and stepped back. The door slowly opened and two stocky men dressed in black T-shirts and black pants came down the four steps and pulled Kang-de into the jet with a single lift.

Meanwhile, Chul's lone security man slowly opened the car trunk. He placed a mini-UZI across his shoulder and he took a hand held drill with him. He ran toward the back tires and drilled multiple holes in them. Then he walked in a direct line under the jet and he drilled holes in the front tire. The noise from the engine made it impossible for the men on the plane to hear what was happening outside.

Kang-de took a blow to his head, from one of Woo Jin's men, which caused him to fall onto the carpet. Areum, who was sitting in one of the beige leather chairs, screamed and got up to help Kang-de. Immediately,

Seung-jae pushed her back into her chair. He said nothing, as he stared at her with his cold black eyes.

Kang-de held his bleeding head and said, "I am here. Now let Areum go home to her father."

"Shut up," said one of Woo Jin's men.

Woo Jin looked at Kang-de and smiled. "Areum, Kang-de must really love you because he came in here knowing that he will not be leaving."

"Woo Jin, I am begging you to stop this madness. Please don't kill him. Why have you changed so much? Where is the man that I fell in love with? Where is my kind, sweet, loving Woo Jin?"

"Were you not listening to what I told you?" he yelled.

"Kang-de has never done anything to you," she said looking at him lying on the carpet.

"Are you serious? He killed my father and shot me. He even burned down my two homes. Areum. What are you saying? He is not innocent."

"Neither are you. You burned down his store. Your father killed his entire family. He even killed my mother. The mother who you claim to love. I don't blame you for mother's death since you apologized to me earlier. I have accepted your explanation about everything. So why are you doing this now? Let him go, Woo Jin."

"He shot me and he left me to die. How can I not kill him?"

Immediately Seung-jae pointed a gun at Kang-de and fired at him hitting him in the shoulder. Areum screamed and scratched Seung-jae on his arm. He slapped her in the face. Woo Jin pushed him causing him to collapse against the window. When he attempted to get up, several bullets tore through his back killing him instantly.

Woo Jin pulled Areum to the carpet and he lay on top of her to absorb the shattering glass falling from the window. Kang-de pulled a pillow off the couch and put it over his head to shield it from the broken glass that was falling at a rapid pace. He settled his body on the carpet between two couch while the shooting continued for several minutes.

While the bullets destroyed the interior of the jet liner, Kang-de looked at Areum on the floor and he winked to let her know that he was fine.

When the shooting ended, Woo Jin yelled out to his pilot to take off, but he had no idea that his pilot was the first person to be killed.

"Captain Chu, what are you waiting for?" Woo Jin asked.

After he realized that the jet was not moving, his security man crawled into the cockpit, pulled out the dead captain from his seat and started to move the plane. The signals in the plane indicated that the tires were flat.

"Sir, the lights are on indicating that the tires are flat."

"What?" he said looking at Kang-de. "Tell your men outside to stop shooting, otherwise I am going to shoot you now. Do it now."

"I have to open the door to speak with them. I don't know who is out there," said Kang-de slowly pulling himself up onto the couch.

"Yeah, right. I told you to come alone, but you want to play games with me. Okay, let's play games," Woo Jin said pointing the gun at Kang-de's head. He pulled Kang-de up by his bloody shirt and pushed him to the door. "Open it. Open it right now."

"You better do as my boss says, otherwise I will shoot her now," said Woo Jin's security guard pointing his gun at Areum's neck.

Kang-de slowly opened the door and Areum yelled out, "Don't shoot!"

The guard knocked her unconscious with his gun.

"Hey out there, I have a gun at your boss's head. Do you want to see him die? If you want him to live come out and drop your weapons. I don't have time to play with any of you. Come out now," yelled Woo Jin.

The lone gun man slowly walked out with his hands over his head. Within seconds he began to run away from the plane. Woo Jin shot at him and suddenly the jetliner made a massive jerk causing Kang-de and Woo Jin to fall from the plane.

Chul had borrowed a food truck to ram the jetliner from its right side. Bob, Chul and five of his men jumped out of the truck. Three of the security men ran into the plane with guns drawn, but all the occupants were unconscious. They grabbed Areum and removed her from the jet. Chul and one of his men grabbed Kang-de and pulled him to an arriving SUV that took him to the hospital.

Bob remained with the bleeding Woo Jin until he became conscious.

"You have cheated death over and over again. Every time I tell the Boss to let me kill you, he would say no. I should have put a bullet in your head in that tunnel. I wanted to do that so badly, but Boss Kang-de told me to let you live. Why do you think that he has let you live for so long? Answer me, you evil bastard. I believe that you are just as evil as your father. You burned down his store. You kidnapped his woman and you just shot him. Give me a good reason why I should not put a bullet in your head today. You and your organization have become a real nuisance."

"How is Areum?" asked Woo Jin in a slurred voice.

"You have the nerve to ask how she is? This is all your family's fault. But, guess what. I am not going to kill you today," said Bob using his gun to mildly tap against Woo Jin's head. "I am going to turn you over to the police. Oh, look, here they come!"

About ten police cars surrounded the jetliner and Woo Jin was taken into custody. "Let's not meet again. The next time any of us see you, you will die," whispered Bob to Woo Jin as he is handcuffed and escorted to the police car.

Six months later, Kang-de and Areum had fully recovered from their injuries. They got married at a courthouse with Bob, Chul and Mr. Lee as witnesses.

"Oh, Areum, finally we can breathe easily. The past months have been very difficult for both of us. I am sorry. Are you happy, honey?"

"Yes, honey. I am so happy to be Mrs. Shin Kang-de. I hope that this feeling of happiness continues for a long time. I love you so much."

"Let's start a family right away," he said.

"Yes, let start tonight," she said smiling at his face.

He kissed her passionately in front of her father.

"Okay, you two, do that in private," said Mr. Lee laughing.

Bob and Chul laughed at Kang-de's embarrassed facial expression.

Kang-de, Areum, Chul, Bob and Mr. Lee enjoyed a quiet dinner in his suite, when Bob's phone rang.

"Hello. What?" he said quietly listening to the person at the other end of the phone. "Okay, I will let him know."

"Who is it, Bob, and what's happening?" Kang-de asked looking at Areum.

Bob hesitated to speak in front of Areum.

"It's okay, Bob, she is my wife and my partner now. Tell me what you have to say in front of her."

"Well, did you know that Woo Jin was born in London and not South Korea?"

"No. I never checked into his birthplace."

"I did," Areum said. "He told me when we first met."

"Well, he was deported to England last night. He is never allowed back in South Korea."

"Good," said Areum.

"Yes, good for everyone," said Kang-de.

"Boss, may I have a word with you in the kitchen?"

"Sure, Bob," he said walking into the kitchen.

"Boss, did you organize this deportation? Yes or no?"

"Yes, I did. Having him in jail here is just too close to my family. I had my friends arrange to deport him as quickly as possible. Besides, Woo Jin sent Sun-hee and her baby to London so that's the best place for him. But if he ever sets his foot in this country again, you have the green light to kill him."

"Why were you always saving his life?"

"Because his death will keep the good memory of him alive in Areum's heart. I want my wife to only think of me as her ONE LOVE.

And Sun-hee called to beg me not to kill him before she went to England. In fact, her friends in the justice system are the ones who helped to get him deported."

"Best wishes to you, Boss."

"Thanks, Bob. Thanks, Chul. Thanks for everything," Kang-de said, walking Bob, Chul and Mr. Lee to his front door. He closed the door and he went and sat next to his wife on the couch.

CPSIA information can be obtained
at www.ICGtesting.com
Printed in the USA
BVHW04s1037050818
523595BV00024B/394/P